Born Audrey Cooper just before the Second World War, Audrey Reimann lived in Macclesfield in Cheshire, where she was educated at Beech Lane School and the Macclesfield Grammar School for Girls.

She has lived in Southport in Lancashire and, for the last seventeen years, in the countryside outside Edinburgh but her heart is still in the market-and-mill-town she writes about.

'My dreams are all set in Macclesfield,' she says, 'and though now they are peopled with just as many Lancastrians and Scots as Maxonians, I still feel that Macclesfield is where I belong.'

Audrey Reimann's first novel *The Moses Child* is also available in Corgi paperback. She is married, has three children of her own, and has been foster-mother to many more.

Also by Audrey Reimann

THE MOSES CHILD

and published by Corgi Books

PRAISE FOR THE MORNING

Audrey Reimann

CORGI BOOKS

PRAISE FOR THE MORNING
A CORGI BOOK 0 552 14196 8

First publication in Great Britain

PRINTING HISTORY
Corgi edition published 1991

This book is set in 10/11 pt Plantin
by County Typesetters, Margate, Kent

Corgi Books are published by Transworld Publishers Ltd.,
61–63 Uxbridge Road, Ealing, London W5 5SA, in Australia
by Transworld Publishers (Australia) Pty. Ltd., 15–23 Helles
Avenue, Moorebank, NSW 2170, and in New Zealand by
Transworld Publishers (N.Z.) Ltd., Cnr. Moselle and
Waipareira Avenues, Henderson, Auckland.

Printed and bound in Great Britain by
Cox & Wyman Ltd., Reading

AUTHOR'S NOTE

For the purpose of story-telling I have altered the name
of the town from Macclesfield to Middlefield, changed
the names and even the direction of some of the main
streets, missed out Jordangate completely and taken far
too many liberties with a lovely, medieval town. But
Macclesfield was in my mind when I wrote *The Moses
Child* and *Praise for the Morning*. This much will be
evident to anyone brought up in that dear place of mills
and markets and steep cobbled streets down which a barrel
of treacle once rolled; where once there dwelt a court jester
called Maggoty Johnson and a Saxon named Macca tilled
his field.

The estate and village of Suttonford and all the
characters in my story are imaginary.

Perhaps it was not too high-handed of me to do this to
Macclesfield, as during research I discovered that, though
the Domesday book names Macclesfield, in thirteenth
century records reference was made to Mydelfield.

Audrey Reimann

PART ONE

CHAPTER ONE

1919

Caroline Aurora Shrigley, known to everyone in Middlefield as Miss Shrigley and, to her young sister only, as Carrie, sat in her attic bedroom watching everything that went on in the market square. Had anyone asked, she would have described herself as being 25 years old, unlovely and unloved and the owner and sole proprietor of the Temperance Hotel in the ancient Cheshire town.

It was five o'clock on a Sunday afternoon in July and the sun was beating down, heating the smooth brown cobblestones under her window where ragged children from the Wallgate, the steep hill that joined the top market to the cattle market below, were chalking pictures. At the other end of the square two courting couples were walking. They were circumspect, knowing full well that twenty or so pairs of eyes were following their progress, watching for anything, as Carrie was.

If Walter Stubbs hadn't been killed at the battle of the Dardanelles, Carrie thought, she might have been walking out herself. Not that he'd said anything, but he always used to keep a nice bit of beef for her lodgers and on his last leave he'd sat beside her in chapel.

Young Brenda Baker and Philip Gallimore had come into the square up the hundred and eight steps from the cattle market and bold as brass were linking arms and laughing.

Mrs Gallimore would have trouble on her hands with that pair, in Carrie's opinion. But it was Sunday and she should not harbour uncharitable thoughts. In another hour she'd be in chapel again, but she could not stop thinking about yesterday. Jane, her 13-year-old sister, whom she'd brought up single-handed since their father had died, had made a proper exhibition of herself.

The Sunday School's anniversary treat had been the occasion. The chapel members always went to Jack Cooper's farm at Rainow, in the foothills of the Pennines for their annual picnic. The picnic was followed, in the evening, with a concert in the chapel's meeting hall.

What had got into Jane, Carrie didn't know. Normally, Jane hardly passed an opinion of her own that didn't accord with Carrie's, though Jane could be stubborn.

Jane's pretty, heart-shaped face had a determined look about it. 'Carrie,' she'd said, on the charabanc, 'I'm not going to recite at the concert.'

Carrie looked down at her sister. 'You are,' she said with quiet firmness. 'You always recite.' Then she quietly added, after looking round to see no-one was listening. 'I've spent good money on elocution lessons for you. You'll do a poem. Like you always do.'

'I won't.'

'Don't answer back!' Carrie ordered in a whisper. 'There's half the chapel here, watching.'

Jane had said no more until they had climbed down and were seated by a dry-stone wall at Rainow, in a small hay meadow. The food was being carried from the charabanc by the chapel elders and their wives and there was a lot of merriment as the old wives, the bossy ones, tried to control the little children who were bouncing around and squealing with excitement. Other women were spreading white cloths over the trestle tables, bustling; trying to pretend that they were in charge when all of them knew that Mrs Gregson, the opinionated wife of a solicitor, was. You could hear Mrs Gregson barking out her orders five miles away, Carrie thought.

Carrie let them get on with it. She didn't believe in

joining in and Mrs Gregson knew better than to ask her. She kept herself to herself; always had. She turned to Jane.

'What were you thinking of doing?' she asked, brushing a fly from the navy skirt of her summer suit. 'If you aren't doing the recitation? Play the piano? You're not as good on the piano as you are at reciting.'

'I'm not doing anything,' Jane said. 'Not this year.'

'Why? What's up? Has someone been disp— dis— whatever it is about you?'

'No, Carrie. No-one's been disparaging about me.' Jane took off her straw hat and laid it on the grass beside her. 'But the others . . . the others of my age don't have to do it any more – reciting and playing the piano,' she said in a resolute voice.

Carrie's voice went high when she was annoyed. 'What do you mean? The others of your age don't do it? What others?' she asked. 'Have they been callin' you? They want a good tellin' off. That's what they want.'

'I've told you, Carrie, that you don't say "callin' you" when you mean people are talking about you behind your back. It's not proper grammar. That's what they teach us at the elocution lessons,' Jane had answered, firmly.

'All right. All right,' Carrie cut in. The elocution lessons were worth paying for. Jane knew a lot. But she knew that Jane was trying not to answer her question. 'What do they say then? What do they do to upset you?'

'They laugh at me,' Jane answered. 'The boys – they tease me.'

'Well, they've no right to. And you must take no notice. Have no truck with them.'

'Yes, but . . .' Jane had started to say, but Carrie was losing patience with her.

'I sing,' Carrie told her firmly. 'I sing at every concert. Father used to give the address and the epilogue. They expect it.'

'Why should they expect it?'

11

'We're looked up to, Jane. We are what's called pillars. Pillars of the chapel. It was our great-grandfather Josiah Shrigley as built the chapel.'

'That doesn't make any difference. I'm not reciting.'

There had been no shade in the field and with her red hair and pale skin Carrie felt the heat more than most. She stood up and rummaged in her handbag for her glasses. She hated wearing them in public but she needed to see if the grass had stained her cream kid shoes. And she wanted to see Jane's expression. She put them on carefully; the wire arms, though she'd wrapped lambswool around them, were inclined to rub the skin behind her ears, irritating and reddening it.

Jane was looking almost defiant. 'You can't force me to recite, Carrie,' she said.

Carrie made a great effort to control herself. There had been times lately when she felt she could strike Jane. She'd only done it once, years ago, and been sorry afterwards. Now she drew in her breath sharply. 'We'll see,' she said. 'Later. Come on. Let's get our tea.'

Jane had been perfectly well behaved at the picnic and on the 'chara' going back, though Carrie would not have noticed if Jane had been peeved. Carrie did not profess to have what some women claimed to have; a sixth sense or any such rubbish. She was a sensible, down-to-earth woman and didn't go in for any of that. No; she kept herself to herself, kept Jane right, they were held in esteem by the Middlefield people, as their father had been. It was simply a matter of putting your duty first. Father had always told her so. If you wanted to rise in the world, be respected, be an important person in the town – and she did – you never gave any cause for gossip, especially in a town that was rife with it.

It had been too hot in the field. She'd been glad when they'd been driven back to town when the sun went down. She'd been glad when the concert had started.

The chapel meeting hall was cool and she and Jane sat at

the back at the end of a row of rush-seated chairs. The door behind them was open on to the street and a light draught of air played across her shoulders and ankles, like a caress, she thought. Jane had fidgeted a lot.

'Keep still, Jane,' she whispered. 'You'll make me miss my turn.'

'What are you singing, Carrie?' Jane asked in a loud whisper.

'*The Last Rose of Summer*,' she replied, putting her finger to her lips. 'In the first half, then *Behold Me Standing at the Door*. What are you reciting? *The Charge of the Light Brigade*?'

To Carrie's embarrassment and annoyance and in defiance of all she'd been taught, Jane pushed back her chair and ran from the hall. Everyone had looked at them. What could she have said? She'd never know how she'd kept her composure or how she'd lied to the chapel elders, saying Jane had been overcome with the heat. She'd never know how she'd got through her own songs, apologized for Jane and left the concert hall. Only to find her sister, all smiles and contrition, waiting up for her with a peace offering of a nice pot of Mazawattee tea and some Osborne biscuits.

She'd said no more about it at the time. Maybe it *had* been the heat. Anyway it was quite uncharacteristic of Jane.

But that was yesterday. It was just as hot today, here at her window overlooking the square.

Carrie let her eyes go over the heads of Brenda Baker and Philip Gallimore to the town hall, a fine sandstone building with Palladian columns.

Walter's name was on the big roll of honour in there. Two polished oak roll-of-honour boards nearly filled one wall of the assembly room, bearing the names of those who fell; all in gold letters, all in alphabetical order; so many names. Nearly all the young men in the town had gone.

Those who had returned were changed by the horrors

they'd lived through. A lot had been gassed; they could only walk a few steps before they had to stop, cough and spit. There were men with arms and legs gone and most of these men, with no jobs to go to, were bitter. One or two had been shell-shocked and they were, in a way, the worst, carrying their wounds inside their heads.

Carrie understood that. She felt for the shell-shocked. She had seen nothing of life outside the narrow world she inhabited but she'd seen first her mother and then her father die; she'd been left to bring up her young sister and to struggle to make a living for them from the lodging house. She was already an old maid. There'd be plenty of old maids too, after a war, she knew. But there were times when she wondered if she too was becoming bitter; for, inside, she felt herself to be young; with moods that swung from the wild and fanciful to the hopeless.

But she had to conceal these moods; she had to pretend to a control she knew she lacked. Her father had said, many times, that she lacked moderation. She wished with all her heart to be a worthy successor to him; wished that she could be like the few who had returned from the war unscathed.

But even they, the ones who had come through it without any outward sign, seemed to be determined to forget; filling every spare minute with activity, wanting it all; wanting it now, like her two Irish lodgers.

All at once she heard a commotion and turned her head to see the Kennedy brothers crossing over from the Swan, carrying cases.

'When Irish eyes are smiling,' the big one was singing.

Carrie, and probably everyone in the square, could hear them as they came to a noisy halt, looking up at her window. 'All the world seems bright and gay . . .' He was out of tune an' all and his brother was holding on to his arm, encouraging him.

What sort of hotel would the neighbours think she ran? Carrie put her head out of the open window. 'If you two

14

have been drinking. If Douglas McGregor's been giving you drink, you can take your bags right back,' she called.

'Oh, we've not been drinking. Indeed we've not!' Patrick Kennedy was looking up at her with eyes full of laughter as he flourished his cap in the air. 'We've been collecting our luggage. Haven't we, Danny me lad?'

Danny, smaller and younger, was tugging at his brother's sleeve in warning but she saw that he was on the brink of laughter as well.

'You've been here for two weeks. Why have you still got stuff over at the Swan?' she snapped. 'Don't stand there with everyone listening. Come in quietly. It's Sunday.'

She returned to her seat. Sunday didn't matter to them; they were Roman Catholics. They went to mass on Sunday mornings and that was it. They might have been drinking, round the back at the Swan. She wouldn't put it past them. Roman Catholics could get away with anything as long as they went and confessed. Then they could start all over again, sinning afresh.

Douglas McGregor, who kept the Swan, was a Catholic an' all. He and his wife had come to Middlefield last December, just after the Armistice. He'd been followed, soon after, by the Kennedy brothers. He'd been in the navy with the older one, Patrick Kennedy.

Apart from the McGregors being Roman Catholics she had nothing against them. And her father used to say, 'There's good and bad in everyone. Even Roman Catholics.' The McGregors were respectable like herself and Douglas McGregor had joined the Middlefield Choral Society. He was a serious singer. And the best tenor they'd got. It was a pity he'd sent the Irishmen over to her, that was all.

She should be getting ready for chapel but she stayed a little longer at the window. She liked to sit in her attic bedroom; it was the nicest room in the house and she had the best view of the square from here, on the short side.

The Temperance Hotel was almost at the corner where the Wallgate dropped steeply down round the church wall, behind the ancient church of St Michael and All Angels, to the cattle market below. The main roads of Middlefield all began in the market square. Rivergate, the steep hill at the other corner of the block from the Temperance Hotel, sloped downwards towards the river Hollin. Cotton and silk mills lined the river banks all the way along to the cattle market and beyond.

The other main street, Churchgate, came into the square past the Swan. She couldn't see the Pennine hills from here, the church tower was in the way.

Sunday afternoon was the only time the square was quiet. She wondered if Jane was home yet. She hadn't seen her come in. Her sister's bedroom was along the top landing from hers and Jane generally popped her head round the door when she came upstairs.

At chapel this morning the text had been, 'The pomp and vanities of this wicked world and all the sinful lusts of the flesh.' Pride and vanity were sins. Everyone knew that. The minister said that drinking was a sinful lust. And it was, or why should her father have opened the Temperance Hotel? Her father had taught her all about sin.

Did enjoying food count as a lust of the flesh? She was fussy about food and could only eat what she had cooked or had supervised in its preparation. She had a good appetite but it had dropped off lately, since the Kennedy brothers had come. She'd never have taken them in only business was bad.

Douglas McGregor had said they were fine men. He'd told her they were looking for cheaper rooms than they had at the Swan. But they never seemed to stick to their own rooms – they were always under her feet when they came in from their work – always around her, especially the older one who kept coming into the kitchen when she was cooking – putting her off her food.

It didn't matter. She'd been putting a bit of weight on before and was glad it had gone. It was the first time she'd been able to feel her ribs.

Carrie put her hand under her blouse, feeling the dampness where it gathered beneath her full breasts. Oh, it was hot. She wore nothing under the blouse and she took hold of the edge and flapped it gently to cool herself. She liked the feel of silk next to her skin. She wouldn't change her things for chapel and it was far too hot to wear stays. Nobody would see the outline of her when she had her coat on.

She could hear them downstairs, laughing and joking on Sundays. Roman Catholics.

She didn't think much of Church of England folk either; the folk who went to St Michael's. They were nearly as bad as Roman Catholics with their pomp and show. At the chapel they didn't go in for all that; all that parading, bobbing up and down, cross bearing and white-gowned choirboys.

She was in the chapel choir. Nobody bent the knee at chapel. Everyone was as good as everyone else. God didn't expect people to bow. There were no graven images to bow to in chapel.

And the church bells were always going. It was all right for them on the far side of the square but she had to shut her windows on Sunday mornings they were so loud.

Mind, she was always having to shut her windows for one thing or another, flanked as she was by the shops. On her left as you looked at it from the front was the drysalter and chandlery run by the Cartledge family, and on the right was Potts Brothers, high-class grocer.

Between the two, Carrie thought, as she regarded the square, it was hard to say which was the worse neighbour. Not that she went in for neighbouring.

On Mondays and Tuesdays the kitchen window had to be kept shut when Frank Cartledge took delivery of paraffin and molasses and used his backyard to tip them into jars and bottles. She couldn't abide the smell of that place.

Still it pleased her to think how Frank Cartledge wanted

17

to buy the Temperance Hotel. He'd told her he was thinking of opening a chemist's and pharmacy as well. He'd started making up his own medicines and was doing a good trade, but he could look elsewhere for more space. She wasn't selling.

Wednesdays were noisy and smelly with the market-stalls right up to her front door, as were Saturdays. On Thursdays and Fridays she had to keep the front windows closed when the Potts' set their coffee roaster going. They had a big, red-painted iron furnace in the room next to her house and didn't seem to mind folks looking in – for there was nothing up at the window. People stopped and watched Herbert Potts, red faced and half dressed, shovelling hot coals and roasted beans all day long, filling the square with throat-catching fumes. They had a big grinder in there – a noisy object – and always one of the assistants turning the handle.

The Potts brothers wanted to buy her hotel as well. They wanted a bigger shop. They kept hinting that if ever she wanted to sell . . . They'd have to come down to earth; they'd been charging too much for everything when the war was on. And they hadn't put their prices down since.

Some people – people here in Middlefield, people like the Potts and Cartledges – hadn't done too badly out of the war if they'd money to offer for her hotel. She hadn't done well. Lodgings before the war were fourteen shillings a week, now she could charge eighteen and six but she couldn't always get the lodgers. It hadn't been easy. But she'd managed. And she wouldn't sell. Her father had opened the Temperance Hotel. It had been a declaration of faith to her father; a Haven of Temperance and Sobriety he'd called it. He'd had a way with words.

The square was deserted now. All the windows in the Temperance were open to let in the cooling, heather-scented breeze that was blowing off the hills and moor, billowing the net curtains gently into the rooms.

Carrie left the window and crossed to her washstand. It had brass inlays on the legs. She liked nice furniture and had the best bits here in her room, where she could keep her eyes on them. By the other window, the one that looked over the yard, was her kidney-shaped dressing table. She'd had it done out in white cotton lawn with blue satin ribbons. She always kept something scented on it. Today a bowl of cabbage roses filled the attic with their sweet perfume.

She unpinned and combed back her thick, red hair, pulling it hard, away from her face, twisting and turning it until the unruly, abundant mass was pulled into a severe, heavy knot at the back of her neck. She looked at herself in the oval mirror above the washstand as she fastened her mother-of-pearl side-combs against her temples. She was tall and full-figured; had high cheekbones in a long face, too large a mouth, good white teeth and large, round, short-sighted eyes of deep sapphire blue.

Sometimes, when she looked at herself, she was startled out of her wits by the expression and luminosity of those eyes. Then she would remember her father and the way he used to tell her that vanity was the deadliest sin of them all. 'Pride and vanity,' he used to say, 'go before a fall.' So she had grown up wondering where pride ended and vanity began and not being sure if pride and self-respect weren't two sides of the same coin.

Anyway, it was safer to regard herself as plain; not to give herself airs; not to feel pride in hair that was blazing with colour and life; not to notice the milky whiteness of her unblemished skin. It was safer to put such vanities out of mind as unworthy of the god-fearing, purposeful woman her father had intended her to be. It was better that she thought of herself as exceptionally plain.

She did nothing on a Sunday but attend chapel, morning and evening, and teach Sunday School once, in the afternoon. For the other six days she laboured, running the lodging-house. But six days shalt thou labour, the Bible said. It was the word of the Lord and she kept to it as her parents had done; the Ways of Righteousness, her father would have said.

Her father hadn't allowed them to even speak of anything but religious matters on Sundays. She had been taught to speak only of pure and simple things on Sundays. But, no matter how hard she tried, she could not control her thoughts, which were forever straying from the pure and simple.

But she could never do as some did. She was upright. She had strong principles.

And it was a constant reminder, living so near to the Wallgate, of how low folks could sink. Just below her hotel, only a few yards from the respectability of the square, lived some of the poorest families in the town in filthy conditions with filthy smells that made your stomach heave to walk by. They weren't all like that. But it was hard for people like Mrs Gallimore who lived halfway down, on Churchwall Street. Mrs Gallimore was proud and clean. It was hard for her, trying to keep her house and family right when there were so many dirty folk around her.

Carrie opened her bedroom door and looked down the landing. Where was Jane? After Sunday School she'd gone for a walk in the park and Carrie hadn't heard her come back. She was probably downstairs talking to Mrs Bettley who came on Sundays to help the girl who did the bedrooms. Mrs Bettley put out a cold supper for the lodgers on Sundays. There was no cooking done on the Day of Rest. It didn't cost much extra for Mrs Bettley to come on Sundays. Mrs Bettley wasn't Chapel.

'I'm getting slack with our Jane,' Carrie said to herself as she went back into the room for her hat and coat. 'I should make her come to chapel with me. I think she only goes to Sunday School so she can go sauntering round West Park afterwards. She's 13. It's time she started to act like a young woman instead of going round with that crowd, parading round the bandstand in their Sunday best and leaving their elders' sides to go wandering in the cemetery.'

Yes, she'd best find out what Jane was up to. Jane ought to do nothing but Bible study on Sundays, as she herself had. Recently Jane had taken up drawing and painting, Danny Kennedy's hobby. Drawing and painting was all right if you had a minute or two to spare on a weekday but Carrie was sure her father wouldn't have approved of it on a Sunday. Father would never have allowed it and Mother would have agreed. Mother had been a saint.

She pinned on a green straw hat that went with her summer coat. The coat was cut in a restrained style with black collar and lapels. It was long, down to her ankles. She didn't like the new short skirts the younger ones were wearing. Her gloves were in the hallstand drawer, downstairs. Carrie closed her door and went down.

Maggie Bettley was in the hall. 'The older one,' Maggie jerked her head towards the parlour door, 'the big Irishman. He wants to see you.'

'Is Jane back?' Carrie asked sharply. She'd be late for chapel if she didn't watch out.

'Yes, Miss Shrigley. She's having her tea in the dining room, with the lodgers.'

'With the lodgers?' Carrie's voice went high.

The sound of it had brought the older Kennedy to the parlour door. 'Can I speak to you, Miss Shrigley?' he asked in his deep, lilting voice.

'I can spare you a minute,' Carrie answered. She turned to Mrs Bettley. 'Tell our Jane to get her Bible study done after tea. I'll not have her sitting around with the lodgers.'

Maggie scuttled back up the corridor to the kitchen. The hall was dark and Carrie caught her sleeve against an umbrella handle that one of the lodgers had left turned outwards She'd need to start wearing her glasses all the time.

In the parlour, Patrick Kennedy stood by the fireplace

21

in front of the painted firescreen, his bold eyes trying to hold her gaze.

'What is it?' she asked. She'd not say any more about him singing in the square. It was himself he made look foolish. But his manner always made her feel uncomfortable, aware of herself. Her heartbeat seemed to step up whenever he came near. 'Can't it wait till tomorrow? It's Sunday.'

'It can. It can,' he answered with a smile. He was a handsome man with dancing blue eyes; tall with brown, curling hair that was a bit too long; four years older than herself, she knew, and about six years older than his brother, Danny.

At this moment he had struck a devil-may-care pose, resting one large hand on the polished mantel. 'I need some advice from a woman,' he said. 'It's about the houses I'm building. I thought,' – it sounded like 'taut' the way he said it – 'I thought that I'd design the kitchens to suit the ladies.'

'All right. I'll see you after chapel,' she said quickly, leaving the room. 'I'm late.'

As she hastened down Churchgate towards the chapel, Carrie found she was thinking continuously about Patrick Kennedy. He had an air, an aura, about him she'd never known on any man before and she wondered if she were a little afraid of him. It was probably because he was Roman Catholic, she decided. You never knew what went on in those places where they prayed to saints, fiddled with beads and lit candles. It was horrible thinking about it.

She went as fast as she could. She could not go in late to the choir stalls. They'd all be whispering, all the women, and wanting to know what had kept her.

That time Walter had sat next to her all the tongues had started wagging. She knew they had. And there hadn't been an understanding or anything. Even if he'd spoken, she wasn't sure that marriage was what she'd wanted.

22

Father had never wanted her to get married; he'd told her so.

She'd read all about marriage in those books – some she'd sent for and some the minister's wife had lent her soon after Walter Stubbs had shown an interest in her. It had been a real eye-opener. She still couldn't get over it. The minister's wife having books like that, with coloured pictures of insides and men's parts. You'd never think it. The minister's wife was that prim and proper.

Marriages, true marriages, one man and one woman joined for life in the sight of God, were made in heaven any road, so she'd missed her chance when Walter had died. All the same, she couldn't help but wonder what it would be like – a man doing those things – loving you.

And what was she doing anyway, thinking about marriage and understandings when all he wanted, all Patrick Kennedy wanted, was to talk about back kitchens! As if she knew or cared about kitchens. They were just rooms with a tap, a sink and a cooking stove. Perhaps he was going to put gas stoves in the posh houses they were building. That'd be it. He'd want to see how her gas stove worked.

She got there in time and filed in to the choir stalls after the others. She was the tallest so she stood at the back. But the service was slow. Everything seemed to be dragging along tonight. Alderman Cecil Ratcliffe – he had a big shoe shop on Rivergate – lay preacher, a bit of a know-all, had given the sermon. It had been on a text from Proverbs, 'Boast not thyself of tomorrow; for thou knowest not what a day may bring forth.'

Someone else could have made more of that, an' all. Someone with a bit of fire. Someone like her father had been. She liked good, rousing sermons with the preacher looking into your eyes, pointing his finger and thundering in a deep voice.

Cecil Ratcliffe had a weak voice. He was tall and thin and stood with his back to the choir so that all she could

23

see of him was the back of his narrow neck and his hands, white-knuckled, tense, on the edge of the pulpit.

Anyway, she knew what tomorrow would bring forth for her, just the same as every Monday and nothing to boast about.

She was glad they didn't go in for pomp and show at chapel, no processions or anything. As soon as the last hymn was over she'd slip out by the side door. She didn't want to stand around outside, gossiping.

At last. 'Hymn number four hundred and twenty-two,' Cecil Ratcliffe was saying in those considered, light tones. '*Blessed Assurance*.'

Good. It was a short hymn and she liked the ones with a refrain. The organ wheezed for the introduction and they all stood.

'BLESSED ASSURANCE, JESUS IS MINE: O WHAT A FORETASTE . . .'

Her mind went back to the afternoon 'Design the kitchens to suit the ladies!' he'd said. Design them indeed!

'OF GLORY DIVINE . . .'

She wondered if he'd be in the parlour still. He and Danny generally went for a walk after supper.

'HEIR OF SALVATION, PURCHASE OF GOD . . .'

He'd asked once or twice if she'd like a walk an' all.

'BORN OF THE SPIRIT, WASHED IN HIS BLOOD . . .'

Being Irish he'd not understand what that would mean to the folk who sat in their upstairs windows watching all that went on – if she went for a walk with a man.

'THIS IS MY STOR-EE . . .' she sang.

Courting couples went walking, down Rivergate and along the canal banks to the aqueduct – 'Th'Accadoc', the locals called it.

'THIS IS MY SONG . . .'

But she'd never been.

'PRAISING MY SAVIOUR ALL THE DAY LONG.'

CHAPTER TWO

It was light outside and only half past eight. Carrie went quickly back to the square.

He opened the front door to her. Patrick Kennedy did. Her own front door. She'd tell him about that. She wouldn't have her lodgers taking liberties. She was sick of it, the way he disconcerted her. He had a funny smell as well. People did; everyone had their own smell only his was more noticeable. Now her heart was going nineteen to the dozen again, making her choke for breath. He made her angry.

She gave him a stern look. 'Where's Jane?' she asked when the door was closed behind her.

'In the parlour,' he told her, as bold as you like. 'She's copying a chapter of the Bible, like you said. Me brother's in there too, reading.'

Carrie opened the parlour door and saw Jane, little and childish where she sat at the window table, push a sheet of drawing paper inside her Bible hurriedly. 'I'm copying out, Carrie,' she said. 'Do you want me to make you a cup of tea?'

'No. Sit down. I'll do it meself,' Carrie told her. 'But you should be in the living room or the kitchen. You know I keep this room for the lodgers.' She glanced over at Danny Kennedy who promptly put down his book and leapt to his feet.

'I'll leave,' he said.

Carrie saw Jane blush with embarrassment. 'Stay where you are,' she said. 'It's not important. Don't make a habit of it, that's all.'

She thought she'd hang her coat up and put a cardigan on – she'd gone chilly – before she made the tea but, when she turned back into the hall, Patrick Kennedy was standing at the foot of the stairs, blocking her way. She'd have to brush against him if she wanted to get past – so she'd not go up.

'Would you like to take a turn around the square with me, Miss Shrigley?' he asked.

Carrie looked sharply at him. 'I can't do that,' she said, then all at once, not wanting him to see that she had put a different interpretation on his invitation from that which he'd meant, she reddened and turned away, making for the corridor and kitchen in her best coat.

At the end of the corridor was a small living room that held a deal table, two upholstered armchairs and a cooking range which she only lit in the winter. She took off her hat and coat and placed them over an armchair.

Beyond the living room was the wide and shallow kitchen, a tacked-on addition to the house. She filled the iron kettle at the sink which was set at one end and crossed the stone-flagged floor to put it on the gas stove at the other side. It was a dark and cold room, the walls hadn't been whitewashed for as long as she could remember. She'd never been able to do it or had enough money to pay anyone to do it for her. Above the gas stove, next to the matches was a square tea-caddy and a large earthenware teapot.

As soon as the kettle boiled, Carrie reached for the wooden tray which was kept beside the stove, placed the filled teapot on it and carried it to the living room where she set it on the table.

Patrick Kennedy was there, in her living room. There was a dining room for the lodgers next to the parlour. She drew in her breath sharply. 'I've told you before. This part of the house is private,' she said, all snippy, to show him.

'I wanted to talk to you,' he said. 'Don't be angry with

me. Oh, Caroline Aurora! You're too young to be acting like an old maid.'

'How dare you!' Carrie felt colour flood into her face. Anger and embarrassment joined to inflame her. 'You . . . you've been following me about. Haven't you?' she demanded.

He'd closed the door behind him and was smiling widely, unconcerned at her outrage. 'Carrie,' he said in the low, musical way he had. 'Have you no feelings?'

Then his hands were on her shoulders, pressing her arms down against her sides. She had no idea what to do. He was in earnest. She saw in his eyes that he was full of desire and suddenly she twisted under his hands, stepped back and struck him, hard across the side of the head.

'Don't touch me,' she was shouting. 'You can leave my house. Go! Go!' Her left hand came up and caught him over the mouth, catching him off-balance, making him fall backwards, knocking the teapot as he stumbled.

To Carrie's horror the brown pot turned on its side, the lid clattered to the floor and boiling liquid poured down on to Patrick's neck as he dropped to his knees.

'Holy Mother of God!' he yelled, leaping to his feet, pushing her aside, running, steaming into the kitchen.

What had she done? Perhaps he hadn't been going to . . . Oh, heavens. 'Patrick!' she cried, running now behind him to where he stood at the sink, panicking as she always did at the sight of injury or sickness.

Her hands were shaking as she turned the tap and cupped cold water in them, tipping it over his neck. His head was down, low over the sink and he was groaning as she doused a dishcloth under the tap and placed it on the scalded skin.

'Take your coat off,' she said, her voice catching in her throat with fear. 'Here. I'll do it.' With trembling fingers she unbuttoned his tweed jacket and tried to ease his poor burnt arm through the sleeve.

And it was off and he'd stopped moaning, and he'd

slipped his good arm around her waist, and his fingers were sliding under her blouse upwards until they reached her breast. And it was as if his hand was electric or something, and he was holding her hard up against himself. He smelt of coal-tar soap and leather and her head was reeling with the scent of him. His face was wet and his wet mouth was on hers, and the banging of her heart was not from fear but from a sudden leaping response that was coming to her as if she'd known all along that this was the way it would be. That she'd gladly leave the paths of righteousness, when she found a man to love.

At half-past eleven on Christmas Eve that same year, a 24-year-old Scotsman, Douglas McGregor, stood at an upstairs window of the Swan, one of the oldest coaching inns in Cheshire. The Swan, left to him by a childless aunt, faced the town hall across the cobbled market square. Next to the town hall was the church of St Michael and All Angels whose muffled bell was tolling slowly, calling worshippers to the late service.

The moon was high, the night was brilliant with stars and the church's bell-tower made a sharp outline against the distant mountains. People crossed the gaslit square in twos and threes and, from where he stood, Douglas McGregor could have seen, through the open church door, a line of ornate gilded chandeliers hanging from the high reaches of the vaulted roof on long brass chains. Each one held aloft a hundred or more small flames, lit to celebrate a birth so long ago.

Douglas saw none of it. His brown eyes were blurred with tears. His newborn son's lusty cries coming from the next room could not compensate for the loss of Jeannie, who had slipped so quietly and quickly into death minutes after the baby was delivered.

The priest had left. He had baptized the baby in case it did not survive, naming him Alan, with Patrick Kennedy as the child's only godparent. By now the priest would be preparing to celebrate mass at St Alban's and in a minute Dr Walker would leave childbed and deathbed and find him waiting here. The doctor would have no comfort to offer.

McGregor knew this, but 'Why?' he wanted to ask, 'Why Jeannie? Why so young? She was nineteen. I survived four years of war; two torpedo attacks. I came home to Jeannie and a future as a fisherman. I believed that risk and peril were things of the past.'

The image of his dead wife, white and expressionless, swam before his eyes. Then he remembered Jeannie's face as it had been, when, little more than a year ago, they had first set eyes on the Swan.

It had taken them two days to travel from their Scottish village to Middlefield, an ancient town built on an escarpment at the foot of the Pennine hills. It was night when the train halted at the station in Middlefield's cattle market. Facing them was the steep rise of the Wallgate, which, with the nearby ancient steps, linked the two markets. The Swan, they knew, was in the market place at the town's highest point.

Their instructions were to walk up the Wallgate, which rose steeply around and under the towering church. They set off, tired and weary, past squalid rows of dismal cottages whose inhabitants filled the narrow side streets with their cries. Their hearts sank as they glanced down dark alleyways and saw noisy taverns and slime-filled gutters.

At last they reached the top and halted, breathing deeply after the climb. They stood and they stared. They stood at the high iron gates of St Michael and All Angels and looked across at the Swan, a white-washed, three-storey inn which took up almost half of one side of the square.

'Is that ours, Douglas? Really ours?' she'd whispered, holding tightly on to his hand as if she'd been afraid of falling.

Between the inn and the shops an arched entrance led to

29

stables and coachyards and the inn's oak-framed windows and dark timbering stood out clearly even on a half lit night such as last December's. The colourful sign above double oak doors was attractive but unnecessary since 'The Swan Inn' was painted in large black letters between the first and second storeys.

Now Douglas lifted the sash and felt the frosty air catch the back of his tight throat. He closed his eyes for a second, trying once more to shut out the image of Jeannie's lifeless face, afraid that this picture would for ever be superimposed in his memory on the face he loved.

He thought back to early summer when she'd told him, blushing like a young maid, that their child was expected before the turn of the year. He remembered feeling pride swelling in his chest.

'We'll find a house,' he told her as he hugged her to him. 'The Swan's respectable – a fine living – but it's no a place to bring up children.'

His few months as owner had shown him that they could afford to rent one of the houses on the edge of town, where the narrow, medieval streets broadened out into straight roads and, wandering randomly from these, the lanes and widely-spaced houses of the well to do. Patrick and Danny Kennedy were building houses for rent up there.

'I wouldn't want my bairns to live near the rough end of town,' Jeannie had said. 'I don't like to see children dirty and hungry, like the poor wee beggars down the Wallgate and Churchwall Street. I'd love a house, Douggie. A big one, with a garden. Can we afford it?'

He remembered the excitement in her face as she'd added, echoing his own thoughts, 'Patrick and Danny Kennedy are building houses on Lincoln Drive. There's two'll be ready come spring and we'll have a big family, God willin'.'

Their house would be ready in early summer and only himself and the child to fill it. Now the baby's plaintive cries were filling the dark space behind him. Would he be able to bring up their son alone? Should he send the wee one up to Scotland to be brought up by its aunts and uncles? No, he wanted to keep the child by him.

Douglas leaned out over the sill, feeling cold air sharp against his face, chilling the dampness under his eyes. The bells of St Michael's were pealing out now, the joyful sound ringing out over the rooftops of the ancient mill town, over the apex of the town hall roof and out across the empty Pennine hills, whose higher slopes were already shining white, making them appear nearer, reminding Douglas of the Grampian mountains of home.

The Wallgate and its network of smaller streets was well served with rough taverns and the sounds of drunken revelry reached Douglas's ears; an ugly cacophony that even the bells could not drown.

He pulled the window down at the sound, behind him, of Dr Walker entering the room.

'I'm sorry, McGregor.' The young doctor stood beside him. 'We could have done nothing even if we'd been expecting it.'

'Did she suffer?' Douglas asked and his voice was strained to his ears. He swallowed hard to gain control, not wanting the doctor to see how deep his grief went or guess that once he was alone he would give himself over, in privacy, to the tears that were welling up in his throat.

'No. She'd know nothing. She'd just feel tired. She lay back and closed her eyes. You saw the rest.'

Jeannie had sunk against the pillows and closed her eyes after Douglas had held her. It was a few minutes before the nurse noticed her pallor and the light, sighing breathing that told of the haemorrhage that was taking her so quickly from them and would prove impossible to halt.

'There's a woman on Rivergate who lost her baby yesterday. Shall I ask her to nurse your son for you for the first few weeks?' the doctor asked.

'If that's the best thing. Do what ye have to.' Douglas

drew the curtains across the window and switched on the light. 'I'll keep the bairn with me here. I'll no send him oot. Ask the woman to come here to feed him, will ye?'

'I will. And I'll ask Jack Cooper, the farmer, to come to see you. His wife delivers the country babies. She keeps a special cow and a goat for the ones whose mothers can't feed them.' Dr Walker put a hand on the big Scotsman's shoulder in a gesture of friendship, paused for a moment and added, 'He's a fine boy. Strong and healthy.'

Douglas looked at the doctor and saw in his face a sadness that mirrored his own. The man had done his best to save Jeannie and he'd feel the death of a patient deeply. Douglas was not alone in his loss.

'Thank ye,' he said. 'I'll be a good father to him.'

It had been going on for six months and her need of him was growing. It was mid-February, midnight, and bitter cold outside. Inside the Temperance Hotel the windows were hoary with frost.

Carrie always waited until the house was asleep before she could go to his room on silent, slippered feet; downstairs to the room beneath her own where he waited for her. Under the sheets she was naked. She would put her silk chemise on, under her dressing gown as soon as the house was still. He liked to have something to take off her, he said. It excited him.

She did not allow him to come to her. Nobody would think it odd that she, the owner, should be the last to retire she had told him. But if she had permitted him to come to her then she would not have been able to refuse him. As it was, she could deny herself the sinful lusts of the flesh and wonder, on the chosen lonely nights, at her hypocrisy. For she was more than ever pious, at chapel, and she knew that she was as a whited sepulchre.

Since the very first time, she'd tried not to ask herself what her father would have said. For she'd become a different woman from the one her father had meant her to be. She was truly sinful now. She had come to delight in her voluptuous feelings, finding that she was living in a state of heightened awareness, letting her imagination have control of her. All the things her father had warned her against.

Odours were stronger, colours were brighter, words and music could move her to tears. Even the bells, which before had seemed to be tolling her life away, now matched the strong heartbeat that always preceeded Patrick's arrival. She knew when he was approaching the house for her heart set up its thumping seconds before her ears caught the sound of his footfall outside in the street.

And she was softer, her clumsy stiffness gone, she moved easily, gracefully, in time to the music in her head and the strong thud of her pulses. And it was all the things her father had warned her against.

At the start she had felt that it was written on her face for all to see. Her hands used to shake when she handed him his letters at breakfast. She had avoided his eye, afraid that in front of other lodgers the leaping passion they aroused in one another with no more than a quick glance would give the lie to their formality of manner. Yet nobody had seen it.

Now she allowed him to take her to her bed, in her own room, on the two afternoons each week when Mrs Bettley and the bedroom girl weren't there.

Tonight she lay, waiting. There was no sound but that of her own heart hammering in her throat and her ears. She would go to him tonight and in the morning, at dawn, she would return to her cold bed in her scented room.

She looked at the shaft of moonlight, palely lighting the window, and remembered. Last night, after their loving, they had talked for a while. She had a habit of reliving it, remembering every word, every look, and dwelling on them when he wasn't there.

They had been in his bed, until an hour before dawn

when he'd lit the gas light above the bed and leaned, looking down at her.

'Caroline Aurora,' he'd said in the deep baritone voice that made her insides curl up. 'What beautiful names.' A great wide smile had come over his face then and he'd asked her, 'Do you know who Aurora was?'

'Is it something to do with Aberdeen?'

'No. Aurora was the goddess of dawn.'

'Huh,' she'd said. He knew a lot. He and Danny had had a lot of schooling in Ireland. They'd gone to a Catholic college, he'd told her. It was funny really. You'd think that people who'd had a lot of schooling wouldn't have to work as they did. 'So what did she do?'

'She rose from the bed of her husband at the end of each night to open, with her rosy fingers, the Gates of Day. Then Apollo drove the sun chariot from the eastern palace.'

She smiled back at him, relaxed. 'That's what I do, isn't it?' she said. 'I spend my nights with you. Rise at dawn.'

He was laughing softly at her, placing a finger over her lips to hush her as he told her the rest of the story. 'After Aurora had flung back the pearly gates she'd flash across the darkness before the Sun God drove his fiery steeds across the heavens.'

Carrie always seemed to be two paces behind him in his flights of fancy. She was still dwelling on the first part of the story. 'Well, you're not my husband,' she said.

'Aurora turned her husband into a grasshopper when he became old and ugly,' Patrick went on, smiling, teasing her, 'for she'd gifted him with eternal life, but not eternal youth and she knew he would never die.'

'What happened next?'

He was laughing as he told her, 'She fell in love with a young hunter and schemed to have him kill her rival.'

'She wasn't very virtuous then, was she?' Carrie said. 'They were pagans. As bad as those in Shakespeare's stories if you ask me. All that stabbing and killing!'

34

'The gods were immortal,' he explained. 'They didn't have to think about mortal sin.' Then he looked serious for once. 'But you don't open the gates, Carrie, like your namesake. You won't go out into the day, into the daylight, with me.'

'What do you mean?'

'I mean,' he started to say, then touched her face and held it so that she had to look into his eyes. 'If I asked you to follow me, Carrie, when I leave . . .'

'Leave?' she asked quickly. 'You're not leaving, are you?'

'I'm staying until Danny's settled. He's a settling man.'

'What are you, then?' she interrupted, fear of losing him making her voice go high and sharp.

'A wanderer, Caroline Aurora. I'm not done with it. I was a sailor when the war came, a wandering, free-roaming merchant sailor.'

He lay back and took her hand in his. 'Would you come with me?' he said, without looking at her. 'Would you open your gates?'

'Don't talk daft,' she answered.

'Carrie, my love,' he said, holding her fingers in a tight grip that seemed to be telling her something at odds with the gentle tone of his voice. 'I've something to tell you. Something to ask you. You must try to understand. I want you to come away with me.'

She felt fearful for what he was about to say. She snatched her hand from his and sat up, her loose hair falling across her face and shoulders, hiding her.

'I don't understand you at all,' she replied, puzzled and edgy now. 'What are you asking? You want me to leave all this.' She waved her bare arm around. 'All this. All me and me Dad have worked for? Our Jane? The chapel? This is my life, Patrick. It's everything to me.'

'And yet you love me,' he said softly. 'When you are at your most needful, when I make love to you, you tell me that you love me.'

35

She was silent for a moment. She had said it. But it wasn't true. For that was one of the worst things. She didn't love him – she only wanted him. It was lust she felt, wicked, sinful lust of the flesh.

'I don't love you.'

'You do, Caroline Aurora,' he answered in the knowing, quiet way he had. 'You do. Oh, you do.'

'I don't. I feel ashamed of myself for doing what we do. That's not love.'

'It's love, Carrie,' he said with quiet emphasis.

'It's not the sort I could change my life for,' she told him before lying down beside him again.

'It's the only kind that matters. Between a man and a woman,' he'd continued, ignoring her worries.

'Don't you feel shame?' she said. 'Guilt?'

'I do. I go in mortal sin, Carrie.'

'Yes,' she answered. 'But you're a Roman Catholic. You can go and confess.' She sat up again quickly and looked at him. 'You don't . . . you haven't . . . you've not confessed, have you?'

'Sure. I've confessed.'

Now she was becoming worried. She fought to keep her voice down as she said, 'You've told that priest? That young priest at St Alban's?'

'Yes.'

'You've not said who you've sinned with. Not mentioned my name, have you?'

'I have.' He was smiling at her, for all the world like a man with no cares.

'So that priest knows? That young priest? I'll never dare look him in the eye.'

'He's bound to secrecy, Carrie,' he said, but his eyes were laughing at her.

'But he knows!' She felt a flush of anger rising in her, in the face of his amusement. 'What did he say?'

His face was serious again. 'He said that I should want to be married to the woman I love.'

'And what did you tell him? That I'd never betray my father's memory? That I'd never leave the chapel?'

'Oh, Carrie,' he'd said, pulling her down on to himself, 'Come here.' And then they'd been aroused again and they had been in such need that thoughts of sin and such things had been of no account until afterwards when she had risen to dress and return to her room.

He'd looked at her tenderly then and said, 'There is a big, beautiful world out there, Caroline Aurora. It's yours for the taking. You should go out of your night. Open the Gates of Day.'

'What are you talking about?' she'd asked him.

'Why do you keep Jane on at school?' he'd asked her. 'She's fourteen. She could leave and help you.'

Carrie pulled the belt tight around her waist and looked at him. 'I promised my father, before he died. Jane was to have a better chance than I had,' she said. 'I had to leave school – to help Mother. Help her run this place. But I can manage it by myself. I had to, after Dad died.'

He reached for her hand. 'You could have time to enjoy life, Carrie, if you let Jane do her share.'

'Enjoy life? What do you mean? Don't I enjoy it now?' she demanded, her voice again going high, defensive. 'My father taught me to put her and my Christian duty first.'

'You still obey him, don't you? Your father. He's been gone all these years.'

'I wouldn't want to live any other way,' she told him, 'and it keeps coming to me. What he'd think of this.'

'Oh, Carrie girl, don't put too much into this,' he said, pulling her towards him again. 'Don't make this – this that we do – your only pleasure.'

'It's not! Not my only pleasure.' She pushed him away and drew back. 'I like other things you know.'

'What other things?'

'I enjoy singing,' she answered, 'at chapel. I used to do a bit of tapestry. Until my eyes got bad.'

'What about dancin'? D'ye never go to the dancin'

parlour, Carrie? Never do the two-step? There's young women dancing every afternoon. There's tea-dances . . .'

He was grinning as he said it, knowing it would annoy her, knowing that she didn't hold with dancing and cavorting, with worldly pleasures, displaying yourself. And why should he want her to go out, dancing, meeting men?

'You say all these things on purpose, don't you?' she said. 'You like to see me gettin' mad?'

'Sure and ye're lovely when ye're mad, Carrie,' he answered. He took hold of her wrists, playfully, pulling her back on to his bed, pretending to have to hold her down. 'You always strike out, don't you, girl? You struck me before you'd kiss me.'

Now he was leaning over her, pulling the dressing gown away, his mouth moving towards her breast. If she let him carry on, he'd start it all again, and she'd let him. Even now, when she was annoyed with him for teasing her, her body was obeying the touch of his hands, of his mouth; her insides were turning to water as his face buried down on to her. And she wanted to. Again she wanted to . . .

She fought down her need this time and pushed him, quickly, away from her. 'I have to fight meself; fight off the guilt every time I let you near me,' she said, meaning it and yet knowing that he would laugh at her.

He was smiling and shaking his head at the same time; looking at her with an expression in his eyes of . . . Of what? Was it love? Or pity?

'What gave you pleasure before?' he asked. 'Before me?'

It upset her when he spoke that way and she turned her face away from him, looked at the curtains as she answered. 'We're not put here for our own pleasure, Patrick Kennedy. We are here to please the Lord. It's the way I was brought up. That's what my father taught me.' She stood and tightened the cord of her dressing-gown, feeling with her toes on the cold linoleum for her slippers.

'Is that why you've denied yourself all the things a girl would want? Is that why you've given them to Jane?'

'What are you talking about? Given 'em to Jane?' She faced him again, her questioning eyes fixed on his handsome face.

'It's Jane that's had the schooling, Carrie. It's your sister you've sent for the lessons in music, the talking lessons. What d'ye call them?'

'Elocution. I wanted her to talk nice. Better than I do.'

'And she does. She does, me girl. It's a bit pedantic, but it's nice. She's a credit to you. But what about yourself? What about you, Carrie?'

'What about me?'

'Oh, ye're a fine woman, Carrie. But ye see it all wrong. Ye're denying the truth to yourself.'

'What truth?'

'That ye're a woman driven by your senses. You've strong, powerful senses, Carrie.'

He wasn't laughing at her now. He was beside her, his blue eyes holding hers, wanting her to admit to all the things he had in his own head. She was not one for talking about such things.

'When your eyesight's going, your hearing gets sharper,' she answered.

'It's not just your hearing, woman. It's all the rest. You think you've a sensitive skin, you think you're easily upset by smells. But it's these . . . These are instincts in you and ye're denying them. You're denying that they drive you.'

'And what drives you then? You seem to know a lot about me . . .'

He had a funny look in his eyes, as if he were apologizing for something. 'I'm a weak man,' he said softly. 'And you're beautiful, Carrie. A beautiful, passionate woman who leads weak men astray.'

'Don't talk like that. I'm not beautiful. I'm plain.' She knew what he was after. He was trying to make it look as if it were all her fault. 'You can't make me feel better about it by flattering me, Patrick Kennedy. You don't know me at all.'

He had taken her in his arms then and held her fiercely and said in a tight, strangled kind of voice. 'Don't trust me, Carrie girl. I'm a wandering man. I'm no good for ye.'

That book about marriage had never mentioned how you felt, how your body could leap into life when your lover touched you, how you'd let him do whatever he wanted to do, even when you knew you were bringing down the wrath of God on your head. And how you were as bad as him, wanting more all the time, like a ravenous creature, so that you could think of nothing else.

Was that a sound?

He told her that Danny didn't know, that Danny hadn't guessed. She couldn't bear to think that Danny might know. What did Danny think when his brother left the building site on Wednesday and Friday afternoons? Did Danny believe that Patrick was seeing his friend, Douglas McGregor? Or did he guess that Patrick spent the afternoons in her bedroom, making her take her clothes off and walk around the room for him, making her say things she didn't mean, about her loving him and wanting him? And him saying that it was love, telling her, like the devil himself, that it was the only kind of love that mattered.

It wasn't true. True love was different. Married love was all about respect. If she'd ever married it would have been to a man she'd have respected – a man like Walter Stubbs, decent, hard-working and respectable. A good man, like her father, a man who wouldn't have known lust if he'd tripped over it.

She always asked for forgiveness for the lust, at chapel, silently and when she said her prayers. But she'd never gone up to the front to give a testimony and declare herself a sinner. If she did she'd have to stop. She'd have to send him away. Or marry him.

She couldn't marry him. He was a Roman Catholic and she'd have nothing to do with that. And he hadn't asked her. But that was because he was a Roman Catholic. He'd know she'd have to refuse.

Wouldn't she?

She went down to his room. Her heart was going like a sledgehammer. She turned the door handle.

He was in the room, standing there in the moonlight, broad and hard, tanned and strong, pulling her towards him, smiling down at her, knowing by the look in her eyes, by the breath that was coming fast that she wanted his loving.

'And is me lovely girl ready for me then?'

He had his left arm around her waist and with his right hand he unbuttoned the silk chemise, exposing her firm, full breasts to the touch of his roughened, workman's hands, now kissing them, feeling them firming against his mouth, making her head light, her body liquid with longing.

'By all the saints, ye're a beautiful woman, Carrie Shrigley,' he said as he drew her hard against his own eager body. 'Ye've the figure of Venus and a fire inside you.'

He shouldn't talk like that. It was wrong. But she was making those soft sounds that came into her throat unbidden, betraying her own urgent need of him.

'And you are aching for me, are you not?' he asked, breathing the words hoarsely whilst his scratchy face raked against her neck and his hands slid down, over her thighs.

'Yes,' she moaned, dropping on to the bed, pulling him down on top of herself, needing the weight of his body on hers.

He was making her wait, he liked to do that, make her wait, until she could bear it no longer, until she reached for him and gave a little gasp as he went into her and she heard him say, 'You can't stop yourself, now, can you Carrie?'

But his need, she knew, was as great as hers and he could pretend all he liked but he could no more stop than she could. And his mouth was on hers and she had her hands on his back, holding him into her, her ankles locked

41

together around him and, as her insides quickened in time with his, she heard her own voice, catching, repeating over and over, faster and faster, 'I love you, love you, love you, Patrick Kennedy,' until at last her abandoned cry came and he grasped her hips tight against his own in his last forcing push into her, groaning yet laughing at the same time.

And their bodies were stilled, and with his weight heavy on her and him still inside her she looked up and smiled into his lovely face in the moonlight.

He was stroking her face now, and planting little kisses all over her and in another minute they would be aroused again yet able to take their pleasures slowly until dawn and the sounds of a waking town would drive her back to her room.

'We'll have to do something about this, Carrie,' he said at last, easing himself off her. 'I try to stop meself in time. But it's getting harder. And tonight . . . I'm sorry, girl.'

It was the devil and all his works, talking about their sin together as if it were something to be proud of – his not being able to stop in time. 'What do you mean?' she asked.

'I mean, girl, that ye'll find yourself with a child on the way.'

'Oh, that. I can't have children,' she told him, pulling up the sheet to her chin, cold now, wishing herself gone, not wanting to explain.

'What's wrong with you? Why can't you?' he asked with a sharp edge of questioning in his voice.

'I'm not made like other women,' she answered quietly.

It always upset her when she thought about how nature had deceived her. Women were supposed to bleed every month, all the books said so. But she didn't. She hated the very word – the proper word. She couldn't bring herself to say menstruate out loud. She'd never even told the doctor.

'Oh, but you are, me girl. You're made exactly like the rest. Only fuller, riper,' he was saying. He was smiling now and trying to tease her, trying to pull the sheet down and look at her again. 'What makes you think you're different?'

She let go of the sheet and watched his face as desire flamed in his eyes again. 'I only have my courses now and again,' she told him.

'Like, how often?' he asked, playing with her again, making her respond again under the probing of his hand.

'Once a year,' she said. 'I had one about last August. I'll not have another until summer.'

'Oh, Carrie. My beautiful goddess! I love you girl,' he said as he lay back and, laughing softly, pulled her across to lie on top of himself.

CHAPTER THREE

The house was ready in June; the baby was weaned and in need of a nanny and Douglas was faced with a short, sturdy woman of indeterminate age. He had not asked her age when she'd applied for the job, though since she'd brought up three sons of her own he guessed it to be between 40 and 50. She seemed energetic and kind and would be easy to live with, he decided, choosing her over the droves of younger women who had come in answer to his advertisement.

Mrs Tansley had white hair, a broad, happy face and an almost square body. She scurried rather than walked, and this she did in a purposeful manner, making an impression on Douglas of a woman who knew what she was about.

She smiled at Douglas as he held out his hand to her but her eyes had already fixed upon the black pram where it stood in the back parlour of the Swan and her face broke into a wide smile as she went towards it. She lifted the baby gently but firmly, seated herself on a low chair, placed the child on her ample lap and began to talk to him as only motherly women can, bringing a chuckle from the delighted infant.

'Ee! He's a proper little darling.' She beamed at Douglas but returned her attention immediately to the baby. 'Who's Nanny Tansley's little bit o' sunshine then?' she said. Alan laughed his first real laugh and began to kick his legs with the excitement of it all. Douglas made up his mind to look no further.

Nanny Tansley supervised the move. They would only

need a live-in housemaid, she told Douglas. If he liked plain food, she'd cook for them.

It was going to be a costly business, but he was building up a firm reputation for a well-run inn with a good bar trade. If he worked even harder, opened up the four top-floor bedrooms for letting to travellers, and asked his cook's husband to help out when they were busy, giving him a few nights a week at home with his son, he could do it.

There was plenty to do and he did not want to give himself too much time for reflection.

He had no wish to remarry. He was a devout Catholic; not narrow in outlook or disdainful of those with different needs, but for him there would never be another wife. He'd not expect the kind of love he'd shared with Jeannie without wedlock so he'd devote his life to bringing up his son and to the business that would provide for them.

He made friends with Jack Cooper, the farmer who Dr Walker had introduced him to, finding him to be a man of quiet manner and great understanding. He visited Jack and his wife, Martha, at Rainow Farm whenever he could.

Douglas was energetic and practical. He loved the farm. It was good to be able to swing your arms without smacking anyone in the face and the wide-open spaces gave him the same feeling of freedom that the sea had done.

He had thought that the little fire of love had died within him. But gradually, as the days passed and his son grew, Douglas found delight in his child's company and his hopes once more were turned to the future.

As soon as Alan was old enough they'd go up to the farm together. The Coopers had a son, Nathaniel, 7 years old, born to them late in life. Alan would like it out there when he grew up, Douglas was sure. He laughed at himself for making plans so early – the baby was only nine months old. He'd teach his son to sail, too, on their summer holidays in Scotland.

And, despite the losses some were suffering in the post-war slump, the Swan was prospering and the town of Middlefield growing. Lincoln Drive no longer had open country at its back. Patrick, his old friend from the navy, and his brother Danny were building a row of semi-detached houses behind the high walls of Douglas's halfacre. The row was to be named Wells Road and the houses were small but respectable with long, narrow gardens. They'd not even be seen when his fruit trees matured and formed an orchard.

But he wished that his own house was paid for. He wished they would sell to him for he could borrow from a building society. And he worried sometimes about the Kennedy brothers for, good builders though they were, they seemed not to have much head for money. They were building houses and putting them out for rent. It would take them many a year to reap their rewards.

When Patrick and Danny came to see him, and they seldom visited nowadays, he'd try to advise them, tell them to sell a few houses off. They were always short of capital.

September came in with strong winds that stripped her lilac tree of leaves. Carrie swept them up in the mornings and put them in the compost-bin that Patrick had made for her out of cedar wood. Next spring she'd get someone to dig the little patch of earth that was not really a garden, just a strip under the wall that separated her yard from the Potts's. She'd grow wallflowers and roses; flowers that scented the yard.

She was going to give the lodgers stew for their supper now it was autumn, and rice pudding to follow. She liked rice pudding. She'd had Maggie Bettley light the range in the living room so there were two ovens to make use of, one hot and a cooler one. She'd ask Mrs Bettley to bake some bread in the hot oven this afternoon. She'd taught Maggie Bettley to bake.

She couldn't stand peeling onions though she liked the

46

taste, and here she was, head averted, eyes streaming when Patrick came into the kitchen.

'What are you here for?' she asked, a bit sharpish. It was Tuesday. He knew she wasn't free on Tuesday afternoons. The bedroom girl did the ironing on Tuesday afternoons and Mrs Bettley came in. They'd think something was up if they came in and found one of the lodgers in here.

'Not what you think, Carrie,' he answered. 'I want to talk to you.'

'Well, you'll have to wait. Till I've done this.' She pointed to the heap of vegetables. 'I can't waste time in talking until the stew's in the oven,' she replied, giving him a watery-eyed, cross look.

He was looking a bit dejected, standing there saying nothing. He usually had plenty of backchat. She'd become used to it lately, laughing at his talk sometimes. But only in private. She kept up the appearance of cool indifference in front of everyone.

'Are you sickening for something?' she said, concern coming into her voice. 'You look a bit pale.'

She had not a great deal of sympathy with illness; she was never ill. Her father had been the same. Only he had been ill. He'd known he was dying but never said a word until right at the last. Her father, though, would have had nothing to fear. He'd have been ready to meet his maker. She doubted if Patrick would dare face his. But then, he'd told her, Catholics either went to purgatory first or straight to hell. She'd probably finish up there too, if she didn't marry him and make it all above-board.

'I'm a worried man, not a sick one,' he said. He turned away and went down the hall towards the parlour.

Carrie went on peeling the onions. He'd have to wait until she was ready. When she'd done and cleaned round the sink and emptied the peelings on to the rubbish heap, she put glycerine jelly on to her hands and went to the parlour.

47

He was sitting in the leather chair, by the fire, his head in his hands, elbows resting on his knees. He didn't even look up when she closed the door.

'Well?' she said. He didn't move for a moment then, just before she lost patience with him he lifted his face and she saw that he was on the point of tears. 'What's up?'

'I'm ruined,' he said in a dead, dry voice. 'The money's all gone. I can't finish the houses.'

What was he telling her for? What could she do about it? 'You should have sold some then, shouldn't you?' she answered. 'You'll have to stop building and get some sold off.'

'I can't sell them before they're finished. There's no more money, Carrie.' He'd put his head back in his hands again.

'If you're worrying about paying your board and lodgings,' she said quickly, 'you can leave it over. I can wait till your money comes in.'

'It's not just me lodgings, Carrie. I'll have to go home to Ireland.'

He sounded worn out, beaten. It seemed to her that he was making more of it than was necessary and it made her reply in exasperation. 'And leave everything? Why?'

'It was borrowed money, Carrie. Unless I can sell them, or borrow more, I'm finished.'

It was a shock, hearing him say that. Borrowing, owing money, was as bad as a crime. 'You mean to tell me that you've been doing all those houses on borrowed money?' She snapped the words out.

'Yes.'

She could hear her father's voice now, 'Neither a borrower nor a lender be,' he used to say. He'd had a way with words, and not just words. He had a horror, a loathing of debt, had her father. And he'd passed it on to her. She had never owed a penny in her life. Debt was the ultimate degradation.

'Then you'll have to sell them. And get people paid back.'

48

He didn't seem to be listening. He just sat there with his shoulders slumped forward.

'D'you hear me?' she asked, a bit louder, though not loud enough for anyone outside the door to hear.

'You don't understand. I need money. I need it now. Or I'll go to jail.'

Carrie sat down at the table, her back to him, fingers drumming on the table, her thoughts a turmoil. What should she do? Was it Christian to lend him money? Was it Christian to let him go to jail? What would her father have done? Her father had despised moneylenders. He'd seen too much of it, he'd told her. Her father had sworn to himself that in his own life he and his family would hold their heads high. And they had . . . until now.

'Oh, God save us,' she breathed. 'How much do you need?' She turned to look at him.

'Eight hundred pounds,' he answered in a despairing voice.

'I haven't got eight hundred pounds,' she snapped back.

She turned her back on him again. Eight hundred pounds was a fortune but the Temperance Hotel was worth more than that. Frank Cartledge had asked her to sell it to him for a thousand and the Potts had offered her eleven hundred.

'I wouldn't take it if you had, Carrie,' he said. 'I'll go home to Dublin.'

She ought to let him go home to Dublin. Once he'd left her life would go back to what it had been. She'd soon forget him. She'd be able to hold her head up in chapel again, not be afraid everyone could see it written all over her face, her shame. Nobody had guessed up to now. Not Jane nor Danny – she'd soon know if they had found out about her and Patrick. The bedroom maid didn't know. Maggie Bettley didn't know. She could put it behind her. Never see him again. Never be tempted again. Never want him again. Never.

But she couldn't do it. She couldn't let him go. If this

was love . . . and the Bible said, 'faith, hope, charity . . . but the greatest of these is charity.' And Charity meant Love. She must do what had to be done. She stood up and went to stand before him. She took hold of his hands and looked into his poor, frightened face.

'I'll marry you, Patrick,' she said. 'I'll sell the hotel to the Potts. We'll pay off the creditors and live in one of your houses.'

'Carrie girl,' he said, pulling her towards him and burying his face in her chest. 'I don't deserve ye. But I'll not fail ye. I swear it.'

'Then go to your creditors and tell 'em they'll have their money,' she said gently, pushing him away. 'It's the beginning of September. I'll have the money for you by the middle of the month. We'll get married as soon as we can.'

He didn't even kiss her, just sat there, looking bewildered. She went to the door, leaving him to think. 'Don't tell my sister or Danny,' she said quietly. 'I'll tell Jane when the time's right.'

Later, when she went to his room, he seemed to have recovered some of his spirit. Yet strangely they neither of them were moved to lovemaking. They sat there, holding hands in the dark whilst he told her how much he loved her, really loved her, not just lust, he said. He loved her like a man should love a wife but that they must not marry yet, until the creditors were paid. For if he married her and the creditors made trouble then she, being his wife, would be held as responsible as himself.

No, he said, she must have a loan drawn up, with herself as creditor and the unfinished houses as her security. They would marry later on, when it was all settled, privately, between themselves.

It sounded a sensible arrangement. Though what the minister would say about the pillar of the chapel marrying a Roman Catholic she could only surmise.

'Will we move into one of the houses right off?' she

asked. That would set the tongues wagging if they did.

'No. You just rent a house – any house – somewhere cheap, for the time being. Danny and I will go back to the Swan. Douglas McGregor will let us have a room. We'll move into Wells Road once we're married,' he said.

Douglas drew the curtains in the back parlour. The bar was quiet on a Tuesday night; the barman would manage without his help. It was the night he normally went to choir practice but the choir could manage without him for once. He placed a tray with three glasses and the whisky bottle on the unpolished table and raked the fire to a blaze before putting a few more lumps of coal into the flames. It was chilly for September.

Hearing them coming in the back way he went to the door of the parlour and called out, 'Patrick! Danny! Come in and have a dram. I want to talk to ye.'

'Down in a minute,' Patrick called back. 'We'll have a wash and be with you.'

Douglas stood with his back to the fire when they came into the room. He was taller than Patrick and, for once, felt it to be an advantage. He had to talk seriously to them tonight. For he was fond of both Kennedy brothers and owed his life to Patrick.

They had served in the navy together during the war. Had it not been for Able Seaman Patrick Kennedy's bravery in keeping him, the Chief, afloat after the second torpedo attack, Douglas knew he would not be here tonight.

And Patrick Kennedy would never have him speak of the hours they had spent in the water, with himself holding Douglas, until the rescue boat had picked them up at dawn. All he would ever say was that they were lucky they had been torpedoed in the English Channel and not the deep cold water of the North Sea. He'd made light of it and had refused to allow Douglas to ask the captain to recommend him for a medal, though Douglas himself had been awarded a DSO for his part in a later sea battle.

'Begorrah, Danny! Would ye look at this?' Patrick was saying, turning on the Irish brogue to make them easy and full of laughter. 'And from a Scotsman, too. Drink up me lad.'

Douglas smiled and waved a hand to indicate that they were to help themselves. Then he pushed back his dark hair and turned a serious look on them. 'What's this I hear,' he asked. 'About you selling your business to Miss Shrigley?'

'Would ye listen to the man, Danny?' Patrick was saying, flippant, but not smiling, not looking at Douglas. 'Where in the name of God did ye hear such talk?'

'It's true then?' Douglas asked. 'I was told by that, that slimy alderman. By Cecil Ratcliffe.'

'Cecil Ratcliffe? How does he know?' Patrick looked him in the eye now, worried.

'These things, these rumours go through the council chambers like, like a dose of salts,' Douglas answered. 'And there's men on the council who talk. If ye've anything to hide in this town ye keep your mouth tight shut.'

'Aye. It's true. But we're going to sell the houses. We're going to finish them off, aren't we Danny lad?' Patrick turned to his brother, as if, Douglas thought, he was looking for reassurance. 'We'll have 'em done in no time. And the good woman'll have her money back, with interest.'

'I ken ye've no head for business, Patrick,' Douglas said gravely, 'but ye could have said, man. I can arrange a mortgage to pay for my house. Ye could have come to me.'

'Sure and I've no wish to trade on your generosity, friend.' Patrick slapped his hand on Douglas's shoulder but again it seemed to Douglas, without real conviction behind his words or actions. 'You can talk business. Buy your house from the good woman yourself. Let's say no more about it.'

'But yon woman – Miss Shrigley? She's sold her house. She's sold everything to buy. She's livin' in the back streets.' Douglas looked hard at Patrick, trying to see what might lie behind such foolishness. 'I did nae think she was an incautious woman. And it's folly. She should not have done it, Patrick. Not when ye look at it from her side.'

Patrick had paled but Douglas saw that he was still trying to look confident. 'She's got control, Douglas,' he said evenly. 'She's got a business head on her shoulders. I've only borrowed from her. She's prepared to wait. She'll get her money back and more besides, once the houses are finished and sold.'

'And ye've had it all drawn up by lawyers, have ye?' Douglas interrupted him. 'Is it legal, Patrick? Ye've to be so very careful.'

'I don't want to say more,' Patrick said. 'It will all be right when the houses are sold.'

Douglas knew that Patrick was not a practical man. It was for his brother's sake that Patrick was setting up as a builder. Danny's lungs had been damaged by mustard gas and he had to have outdoor work. As soon as Danny was established, settled down, Patrick would leave Middlefield and the building trade, Douglas was sure.

Tonight though, it was plain that there was no more to be said. Douglas poured whisky for them all and pulled up the leather armchairs to the fireside. He would have to withhold his fears. They would have a pleasant evening, sharing yarns and whisky, here by the fire. He would keep to himself the disquiet that this whole business was making him feel. But if ever Patrick Kennedy needed his help, he would give it unsparingly.

Carrie placed the tea-cups on the table that was cramped under the window of the tiny room. The cottage had only one room and a scullery downstairs and two small bedrooms upstairs. It wasn't too bad, really, and only temporary, so why Jane was being so miserable she had no

53

idea. She let Jane paint and draw to her heart's content since she'd left school but it didn't seem to be enough for her. She could not help but worry about her sister as she sat waiting for her, upstairs changing her clothes, to come down.

Her sister had been looking pale for a while. Carrie had paid little attention to Jane over the months – the year and a bit it would be, she supposed – that she and Patrick and been carrying on. Now she was filled with guilt, remembering the promises she'd made to her father about bringing Jane up 'in the fear of the Lord.'

She had time to think, to dwell on her guilt, now that she no longer spent her nights in flagrant disobedience of her father's code of conduct. But, she told herself, she'd have no need to feel either guilt or remorse once the houses were sold and they could come out into the open with it, man and wife. It would shock some folks, especially the ones at the chapel; the chapel founder's granddaughter marrying a Roman Catholic, but with Patrick beside her she'd look them in the eye and brazen it out.

And how she wanted that day to come. How she longed for the feel of his arms again. He'd been right about her – she was all senses. And now she missed the smell of him, she even missed the palpitations. She was sick, sick without him. Every day that passed she felt it, a cold empty sickness that overcame and swamped her as she longed for him.

It was hard now. It was hard not to see him, not to want him, to pretend that she was still the plain Miss Shrigley the whole town and the chapel still knew her to be, when in her heart and body, in every but the legal sense, she was his. In the eyes of the Lord they were married, she was sure.

She'd only seen him once in the fortnight they'd lived here. It had been a glowing mid-September evening, warm and still. He'd met her after choir practice, waited for her round the corner where no-one would see them. They had walked up towards the hills, into the forest that bordered the new reservoir.

Patrick had been in a romantic mood. She'd never seen him behave like that before, holding her hand, putting an arm around her waist, every now and again stopping to kiss her. Then, by the water, in a sunset that was blazing gold and red across the western edge of the lake, he had made love to her. And such sweet love he'd made, tender and lingering.

Afterwards he'd knelt beside her, unpinned her hair and begun to comb it where it lay across her shoulders, while he sang to her. And she hadn't known he could sing. He had a warm deep voice, rich and lilting and he'd sung Scottish songs of love.

'Oh, my love is like a red, red rose, that's newly sprung in June,' he'd sung. Tears had come to her eyes then, and she'd never been one for tears.

He'd turned her round, still singing to her, touched her face gently to wipe her tears, and sung,

'Ye banks and braes o' bonny Doon, how can ye bloom sae fresh and fair,' and she hadn't heard it before, not right to the end. She'd asked him to repeat the second verse for her, as she couldn't understand the broad Scots and he'd sung it again. Beautiful, and sad it had been.

'Oft have I roved by bonny Doon,' he'd begun, holding her hands and looking deep into her eyes.

'To see the rose and woodbine twine;
And many a bird sang o' it's love, and fondly so did I o' mine;
Wi' lightsome heart I pulled a rose, full sweet upon its thorny tree!
And my false lover stole my rose, but ah! he left the thorn wi' me.'

The tears had rolled unchecked down her cheeks when he finished and held her gently in his arms.

'I love you, my darling girl,' he said. 'I want you with me.'

'I love you, too, Patrick,' she'd answered in a wave of feeling for him, for herself, for this night. 'I love you so much.'

It was true. She loved him. Without him, living apart from him, her life was unreal. She only came to life in his presence. She knew now what he'd meant about opening the Gates of Day. She wanted to do it, wanted to go out into the honest open daylight. She was ready.

He had pulled a red rose for her, too, on the way back, from a garden full of them. She'd pressed it inside her Bible.

Since that night he had been working hard, building until there was no light left, getting the houses done. And Patrick had said he'd better not come to the house at night, for it would be impossible to keep their love affair secret, if he came to see her here.

Carrie brought her thoughts back to the present as she heard Jane's footfall on the stairs.

Jane came into the room and sat by the fire, rubbing her hands together as if she were frozen, with, Carrie thought, a face like a wet weekend.

'What's matter?' she asked. 'What's up, Jane? You've had a face like a, like a . . .'

Jane turned a worried face on to her and Carrie felt her annoyance dissolve. The poor girl didn't like living here, she knew that. She looked at her sister who seemed so child-like, so tiny and pretty and . . . so . . . so lost.

'It won't be for long, love,' she said. 'As soon as they've sold the first two houses we'll have our money back and we can move into the next one. We'll be living in a nice place, Jane.'

'Oh, Carrie,' Jane said in a small voice. 'I'm so unhappy.' She put her hands over her face. 'I want to tell you something. And I can't . . .'

'You don't like it here, do you love?' Carrie asked. 'Is it the neighbours, or what? One or two are all right. You like Brenda Gallimore. You must ignore the others. I never have truck with neighbours, love.'

'It's not here, Carrie. It's not here that's making me sad.' She was trying not to cry, looking at Carrie as if pleading with her to understand. As if she wanted Carrie to see what it was that was troubling her. 'It's, oh, it's . . . everything's different. I wish we were back in the square.'

Carrie touched Jane on the shoulder tenderly. 'Come on, love. Dry your eyes.'

She passed a white linen napkin to her sister. She'd brought all the good stuff with her. She couldn't abide nasty things; thick cups, cheap cloth. She poured the tea from her silver teapot into the fine china cups and put the milk and sugar in for Jane, a lot of sugar for Jane. 'Here. Drink this. You'll feel better.'

Jane took the cup and began to sip. She had lovely manners, had Jane, Carrie thought indulgently. Carrie liked to see Jane acting like a lady. She had better start taking more care of her sister.

'Have you finished your elocution lessons, love?' she said. 'Is it the end of term? I thought you always went, regular, on Wednesdays. It's two o'clock.'

'I'm going, Carrie. I'll drink my tea and put my things on,' Jane said, a pale smile breaking through at last. She looked so pretty when she smiled. 'I'll be late back. I've to rehearse for the speech-giving tonight.' Jane handed the half-empty cup back to her. 'What are you doing this afternoon?'

'I'm going to wash my hair,' Carrie said. 'I'll boil the water on the gas and shut the back door. Then I'll sit by the fire till it's dry.'

Outside, in the yard she shared with the other six houses on her side of the entry, Carrie kept a waterbutt. She liked to use rainwater for her hair and green, soft soap. She didn't like the feel of tapwater. It made the hair feel sticky, wouldn't rinse the soap off properly.

She saw Jane off to elocution; watched her walk along the street, a heavy bagful of books or something on her arm; head held high, not even seeing the women who

57

stopped their gossiping to look at her as she passed. She wasn't a bit stuck-up, not Jane. She just didn't seem to notice her surroundings; she always seemed to have her head in the clouds. It was out of character, Jane's little outburst.

Carrie watched her turn the corner on to the steps that led up to the market place. Jane looked well in the blue coat and matching hat that Carrie had bought for her. She liked the shorter skirts on Jane. Jane had been to a barber's and had her hair cropped. Carrie smiled, remembering how she'd been outraged at first, then come grudgingly to admit that the new style suited her sister even though it made her look more grown-up.

She waved to Brenda Gallimore who was six months gone with her first baby, went back inside and tidied away Jane's tea-cup. She hadn't wanted tea herself. Since she'd come here she couldn't abide tea. Maybe the water was different in Churchwall Street. She'd drink milk for the time being.

She opened the back door and saw that the yard was empty. The women of Churchwall Street, the decent ones, spent more time at their front steps than they did in the yard. It was as if, she thought, they were afraid of missing anything. They scrubbed their front steps, whitened them with the donkey-stones they got from the rag-and-bone-man, whitened the strip of flagstones in front of their houses, then stood, apron-wrapped and bare-armed, passing judgement on all that came their way.

Under the sink she kept a white enamelled pail and tall, matching water-pitcher. She took them outside, to get her water.

In the walled yard were two w.c.s to the six houses and they were set at the far end of the yard, where the old water tap was. Nowadays they had water in the kitchens and the tap was used for yard-swilling and filling dolly-tubs on washdays. Someone had left it on and Carrie put down her pail and went towards it to turn it off.

Just as she was bending down to pick up her jug she felt someone tapping on her shoulder and nearly jumped out of her skin with alarm. It had happened again. She hadn't seen anyone come into the yard. She'd have to get new glasses. She straightened with a little cry and turned to look at the woman who stood before her.

'Well?' she said. 'Are you looking for someone?'

The woman was short, thin, shapeless and poor-looking. She wore a fringed shawl around her shoulders and the face above it was lined and had a peevish turn at the mouth. She had a new travelling bag in her right hand and in her left, a walking stick.

'Sure an' I'm looking for Patrick Kennedy,' the woman said. 'I went to the Temperance Hotel. It was closed. The man in the next-door shop told me to come here. He said Miss Shrigley who used to keep the hotel would know where he had gone to.'

'That's right,' Carrie cut in. The woman had hardly stopped for breath. What a babbling, gabbling creature she was.

'So I'm looking for Miss Shrigley.'

'I am Miss Shrigley,' Carrie said in a quieter voice. 'And what are you wanting with Patrick Kennedy?'

The woman gave her a sharp look. 'I'm wanting to find me husband,' she said. 'Me fugitive, wandering, bankrupt husband.'

Carrie felt as if she had been struck. The colour drained from her face. Her tongue stuck to the roof of her mouth and her voice, when she answered, had taken on the high note that came when she was angry, only this time it was fear making it strange to her ears as she said, 'Mrs Kennedy?'

'Mrs Kennedy indeed. That I am. Then you'll be the good woman he wrote about. The one who's lent him the money?'

Her legs were weak. Nausea washed over her. The blood drained from her head.

'You'd better come in,' she said. She did not know how she got into the cottage; how she found herself sitting across the hearth from this old woman; from Patrick Kennedy's wife.

When Bridget Kennedy left the house Carrie sank into the armchair by the fireside. She felt faint, sick and deathly cold.

She would dwell on the story the woman had told to her. She must believe it. So patently true was it, so clearly had that little woman been speaking the truth that Carrie knew she had been cruelly deceived.

Her hands were like ice but she did nothing about them. She let them lie, limp in her lap, as she thought.

She had sat here in this very chair for an hour, listening, nodding, pretending to quiet indignation when all the time she'd wanted to scream and rage. She'd wanted to run from the house, to run to the building site, to beg him to tell her that they were lies, all lies; that he wasn't an undischarged bankrupt and under threat of imprisonment; that he wasn't a smooth-talking rogue who had charmed her out of her inheritance; that, most of all he was not, could not be, married to the worried little Irish woman who was facing her.

She rose to her feet, went into the scullery and was violently, painfully sick into the little, brown, slopstone sink. Tears followed her sickness, then trembling and quaking made her hold on to the edge of the sink until her hands felt as if they were blocks of stone. As the shaking subsided, as the sensation of spinning like a top went from her, Carrie felt numbness, blessed numbness descend upon her.

If she allowed, even once, she thought, her senses take charge of her she was lost. She knew what she must do. She must salvage her inheritance. She would tidy herself, put on the face the town had always seen, become again the firm and upright Miss Shrigley.

Half an hour after Bridget Kennedy had left the cottage, Carrie, dispassionate and resolved, entered the offices of a firm of Middlefield solicitors, Messrs Gregson, Tatton and Henshaw.

She was shown into the inner office and greeted by Joseph Gregson, the senior partner, who said, 'Sit down, Miss Shrigley and tell me why you are here.'

'You know that I have sold the Temperance Hotel?' Carrie said. She saw him nod gravely. 'And no doubt you and all the chapel thought I had taken leave of my senses.'

'Er . . . we . . . I made no judgment about your affairs, Miss Shrigley,' the old man said. 'Though you will remember that at the time I cautioned you.'

'You did. You told me that I woud be better advised to continue running the lodging-house.'

'Yes.'

'And I would not hear of it?'

'We can all make mistakes.'

Carrie interrupted him. 'I should have taken your advice, Mr Gregson. The man who sold me the building company is an undischarged bankrupt. It wasn't his to sell.'

'Oh, dear.'

'I want to have him arrested. For fraud. Can you help me or do I go to the police?'

'I think, Miss Shrigley, that this is a clear case of fraud and false pretences. The man . . . Your relationship with him was purely a business arrangement?'

She saw that he was asking what was merely an obligatory question.

'There was no other reason for my action than a wish to secure a future for myself and my sister, Mr Gregson.'

'Quite so, quite so, Miss Shrigley,' he said. 'Then, since there is no question of collusion, I shall do my best to save what I can of this – this business for you.'

'Thank you. And please, please make haste.'

Once the door of the office had closed behind her Carrie went back to Churchwall Street to wait for Jane. And

61

where was Jane? Jane should have been home hours ago. She would have to tell Jane everything. She did not want to see Patrick Kennedy again. If she had to appear as a witness, of course, she would do it but from that moment on, she told herself, an episode in her life was over. A gate had closed.

CHAPTER FOUR

Eight months later, in Wells Road, on the 10th of May 1921 Carrie waited at the gate of number 23.

It was six o'clock in the morning, just light and with the cool freshness that speaks of a warm day ahead. The house behind her was the last in a row of new semidetached houses most of whose small front gardens had not been cleared of builders' tools and rubble.

She wore a loose dress of brown cotton that drooped to her ankles, a long shapeless cardigan of lighter brown and, on her feet, expensive lizardskin shoes with turned Louis heels and buttoned straps.

She appeared impatient; she peered short-sightedly, right and left, up and down the quiet road until she saw Jack Cooper's painted milk trap turn the corner. She pressed her lips tight and waited for him to cover the few yards to her gate.

Jack Cooper was surprised to see Miss Shrigley here for she'd not been seen at her house in Churchwall Street for almost two months. When he'd asked, her neighbours there told him she'd gone to Ireland to find her young sister and bring her home.

He thought of her as a stony-faced woman who rebuffed all attempts at friendship; not the sort to pass the time of day in the kind of exchange some of his customers enjoyed. He pulled the horse up in front of her and waited for her to speak.

'Ask your missus to come. I want her to see my sister. Tell her to bring her medicine bag,' she said in a hushed, anxious voice though there was nobody to hear her.

Jack Cooper pushed his grey hair from his forehead, climbed down the wooden step at the back of the trap and looked directly at her.

'What's up?' he asked.

'My sister and her husband have come home.' She spoke in an urgent way, inclining her head towards him, as if afraid she'd be overheard. 'Jane had her baby last night and she wants to get rid of her milk. Your Martha's to come down and give her some herbs.'

Jack knew his customers. He'd been delivering milk in the town for thirty years. Carrie Shrigley seemed ill at ease for the first time since he'd known her.

'Get rid of her milk?' He tucked his red hands into the pocket of his linen coat and replied in a voice at once abrupt and disdainful. 'I've never heard such talk. Why would she want to do that?'

'She does. It's rubbish. She's teeming with it. And it's rubbish.' Her face was becoming red and angry now and she took a step nearer to him, as if to let him know who was the authority on the subject. 'She wants to get shot of it and you're to bring a quart every morning. From your best cow.'

Carrie Shrigley evidently did not like being spoken to as if she were a numbskull. Her diffidence had been short-lived for she glared at him.

'And see it's fresh, Jack Cooper. From a cow that's got new milk.' She handed him an earthenware jug. 'We'll have a quart now, an' all.'

Jack lifted the lid of a tinned churn and began to stir the milk with a long-handled ladle. 'She married Danny Kennedy, then, your Jane? She got married in Ireland, did she?'

'Yes. And I want no more talk about it.' Carrie Shrigley took the jug and looked at him in the eye. 'So get your Martha here today and we'll have done with it.' She opened the wooden gate and began to walk with deliberate steps to the front door then, turning, she added. 'You can start leaving me a pint a day in Churchwall Street from next week. I'm only stopping here until tomorrow.'

'Is it a boy or a girl?'

'A girl. We're calling her Rose.'

'Hup, hup.' Jack moved the horse along to the next pair of houses. So, Carrie Shrigley had come out all right in the end. After that big court case Patrick Kennedy was doing time in Strangeways and she'd got what was left of his business. She'd taken a job in a mill and had borrowed money to have the houses finished. One or two were occupied, the others were being done. Nobody knew for sure if Carrie Shrigley had sold or rented them out but she'd kept number 23 Wells Road for herself. She'd a good, sharp head for business.

But she'd not been so sharp at seeing what was right under her nose. It had been no surprise to anyone in the town but Miss Shrigley when her little sister had run away to wed Danny Kennedy in Dublin. The sharp-minded business woman had not seen that the younger Irishman and her little sister had fallen in love.

And it had been no surprise to anyone in Middlefield when Miss Shrigley went to Ireland to find them and order them to return.

Jack Cooper filled the jugs and bowls that were set out on the front porches of the houses. It was going to be a warm day; a good day for a newborn baby.

'Hup, hup,' he said to horse. 'We'll be back again later, old lad. We'll have to get Martha down here with her herbs and potions.'

Carrie closed the front door quietly behind her. She did not want to wake the baby in its first sleep. She took the jug of milk to the kitchen and set it in a shallow pan of cold water before placing a saucer and linen teatowel over the top, wetting the ends of the cloth to keep the milk cool as the water evaporated.

She went back into the living room after she had done

this and sank into the wooden-armed easy chair by the fireplace.

Well, she'd done it. A weak smile crossed her face.

She'd disguised her pregnant state under tight corsets and loose clothes until the seventh month when she'd gone to Ireland to look for Jane and Danny. Even they had not guessed how far gone she was, but it was not only for her sake they had returned. She'd found them, half-starved, in lodgings they couldn't pay for. They had lied about Jane's age to get married and were afraid to return to England in case Danny had committed a crime in marrying her.

Carrie had given them money for another four weeks' residence, extracted promises from them that they would come home and caught the boat to Liverpool.

When she came back she'd kept out of sight in this house for the last month, only going outdoors into the garden; having her groceries delivered to the back door. She had carried it well, her pregnancy. Being tall and wide hipped she had 'carried it all round' and though she'd looked as if she'd put on a lot of weight it had been easy to conceal her state until the last month. From the eighth month she had stayed indoors; just sitting, filling her days with knitting and stitching.

Then finally, last night, only hours after Jane and Danny had come back she'd delivered her own baby in silence, here on the floor whilst her young sister slept upstairs with her feckless husband.

Between her pains she'd spread a clean sheet over the linoleum and brought out of the cupboard the binder strips of white flannel and the baby garments in white wool and winceyette she'd prepared and hidden months ago. She'd kept the fire in so there'd be hot water for washing afterwards.

In Churchwall Street the women helped one another in childbirth. They couldn't afford doctors and midwives and even if you kept yourself to yourself, as Carrie did, someone would come to the door when a neighbour's labour started. Since she'd gone to live there she had been present at four births; the last one Brenda Gallimore's. The one before Brenda's she'd delivered herself, so she'd known what to expect.

She had never cried out once.

When her pains were at their height she'd ground her teeth and forced herself to be quiet, telling herself that the worse they were, the nearer it was. She'd propped herself against the armchair and braced her feet against the steel fender, her hands gripping the chair arms above her head.

She'd not been able to stop the grunting and panting noises she'd made at the last, when she thought the final efforts were beyond her, but she'd known what to do when, after the last, most sustained and prolonged one, the body was out.

She'd not even had to slap its bottom. It had gasped for air and given a great cry as it came. And she'd tied and cut her own cord and laid the baby aside, wrapped in an old sheet, until she'd expelled the afterbirth, all in a piece.

She'd only rested ten minutes before she'd risen, cleaned herself up and dressed. Then she'd carried the baby to the kitchen and laid it on the wooden draining board whilst she filled the deep sink with warm water. She'd washed the peaceful infant and dressed it, checking carefully to see that it's limbs moved properly.

She'd slid her little finger inside the child's mouth to check that it didn't have a cleft palate before placing it in the cradle she'd earlier brought from the attic. Then she'd gone outside to wait for Jack Cooper.

There wasn't a lot to it really, she thought. She didn't know why some women made such a fuss, screaming and shouting. And she would not come over all daft like some she'd seen – slopping all over their babies. She couldn't, anyway. Jane would bring it up for her while she went to work.

Carrie ran a hand through her hair, her long fingers raking through the damp ginger waves as she felt in her cardigan pocket for a hairclip. She fastened it and leaned back again, her head on the thinly-padded chairback. She felt nothing yet. No surge of emotion. No rush of maternal affection. And she was glad. The child must never know she was its mother.

Only Jane and Danny Kennedy would know, besides herself and, soon, Martha Cooper. But the farmer's wife was a good woman who'd keep her own counsel. Martha had delivered dozens of babies in her time, and people knew that not a word of their business would ever go past the door on Martha Cooper's lips. She'd do for Carrie what she did for the women whose babies were stillborn – get rid of what was there and bind her tight.

The baby stirred and Carrie turned her head to look. As she watched, a tiny fist came up to its mouth and the little jaws began to work, sucking at clenched fingers so small and perfect.

Most of the babies Carrie had seen were ugly little things, like wrinkled monkeys. But she, who must be unsentimental, could see that her own was different. To tell the truth she had never seen such a beautiful baby. The face and head were round, not squashed or squeezed like some she'd seen. She wasn't even red-faced but had a pale, translucent skin and a head covered with fair, downy hair.

The baby was snuffling, her fists were open and her tiny fingers clawed feebly at her smooth, round cheeks. Carrie pulled herself together, reminded herself of her intention. She mustn't suckle the child.

In the cupboard were two boat-shaped, glass feeding bottles with red rubber teats and valves. There was milk in the larder and everyone knew that babies didn't need feeding for hours after birth. Once Jane got up she'd go to bed and sleep. She was tired.

The sucking sounds were getting stronger and the infant was beginning to whimper – and now what was happening? Her breasts began to prickle and sting in response to

68

the cries and she could feel the milk begin to run, inside her dress. Dark patches were appearing on the front of her loose bodice.

Should she wake Jane and tell her to come downstairs? No, she'd do what had to be done, this once, though she'd sworn not to.

Carrie lifted her daughter on to her lap and laid her across, flat on her back as she slowly unbuttoned the bodice of her brown cotton dress, leaning forward as she did so, lifting the baby's head until the little searching mouth fastened on to her large, comforting nipple and the tiny hands reached up to the big, warm breast.

Her features softened as she felt the strong little jaws pressing, heard the loud gulping sounds of the baby and felt, deep inside herself, a tightening as if invisible laces were being drawn together, binding the little creature to her as surely a if she'd never left her body.

And now, as Rose's sucking settled into a steady pulling Carrie felt the other side dripping, losing its milk in an unstoppable stream. She gently lifted her baby, drew the nipple away from the eager little mouth and turned her around to face the other breast.

Then the tiny eyelids opened and a gleam of intense blue gazed into Carrie's own. And, as she looked into the eyes of her baby, wave after wave of feeling overwhelmed her; primitive, protective feelings for her child; so strong they brought rolling tears which she had to wipe away with the sleeve of her cardigan whilst Rose drank her fill.

At length the baby let the nipple go and lay, her soft pink mouth open, head lolling against her mother's breast in an attitude of such sweet contentment that Carrie had to avert her head before her tears fell on to the angelic face. It felt so wonderful, her baby's skin against her own, her body relaxed and warm, her arm encircling the miraculous being whose tiny head now nuzzled into the hollow space beneath her chin.

She forced herself to move. 'I'll not do this again, Rose,'

she whispered as she laid the baby in the cradle. She buttoned her bodice and gazed longingly at her sleeping daughter.

'Jane's going to be your mother. Not me,' she said. 'But I'll not let you want for anything. I'll work for you. I'll get another lodging house; save my money. I'll keep it all for you, love.'

The baby was sound asleep, breathing deeply as she tucked the coverlet around the child and gazed at the perfection that she had brought into being.

'I'll watch you better than I did with our Jane. This must never happen to you,' Carrie continued. 'At last, I've got something to live for.'

She pulled herself upright and left the room. Her weary feet on the stairs made them creak and she wondered at her young sister who could sleep through the night's activity. Jane was only fifteen. But she'd have to grow up quickly, now.

Carrie pushed open the bedroom door. There they were, wrapped around each other like a couple of daft kids and him a man of 25. She heard her feet, noisy on the boards as the couple slept on.

'Wake up!' Carrie shook her sister's shoulder. 'Come on. Don't wake Danny.'

Jane's eyes opened. 'What?' she began, sitting up sleepily, pushing the dishevelled hair from her face.

'Get up. Come downstairs. I've somethin' to show you,' Carrie ordered. She held out Jane's check dressing gown as Jane slid her feet to the floor and obeyed her, stumbling, only half-awake, after Carrie as they made their way down the stairs and into the living room.

'Look! There!' Carrie demanded. 'Go on. Look in the cradle.'

Jane padded across the floor and stared, incredulous, at the baby. Then she turned to face up to her sister.

'Oh, Carrie,' she cried, her voice thrilled yet anguished. 'Did you do it all on your own? I thought you'd have sent

for someone. You said you weren't due for a month yet.'
Jane's hands stretched out towards the child but she
looked to her sister for permission before touching her.

Carrie nodded her assent, her expression soft as she saw
the delight on Jane's. 'Pick her up,' she said gruffly. 'Have
a good look. She's yours now. I'm going to bed.'

She turned quickly and left the room to climb the stairs
again, slower now but determined not to let her sister see
the suffering in her eyes as she listened to Jane's cries of
joy as she held her new-born niece.

Her room, at the opposite end of the narrow landing
from her sister's room was cold, the bed rumpled where
she had lain earlier. Carrie closed the door carefully
behind her before she crossed the almost empty room and
sank facedown on to her bed, pushing her face into the
pillow to muffle the terrible cries that now she was alone
she could give way to.

When she awoke it was late in the afternoon. She had one
more obstacle to surmount. She washed and attended to
herself in the bathroom before going downstairs.

Danny Kennedy stood with his back to the fire. He was
of medium height, brown haired and blue-eyed with a
good-humoured face and a jauntiness which Carrie
believed displayed lack of character. Like his brother
before him, he had deceived her. He had run away with
Jane on the very day that she had found out the truth
about Patrick. She wasn't going to have him make any of
the decisions.

'Well now,' he said in the Irish brogue that was so like
his brother's it sent quick, painful recognition through
Carrie every time she heard him speak. 'So you've had me
brother's baby then? And a fine-looking child she is. Are
you going to write to Patrick?'

Carrie knew he was trying to assert himself.

'He's not to know about it,' she said, moving forward,
her mouth set in a firm line. 'A criminal? Do you think I'd

71

let him have anything to do with the child?' Her voice was high and red spots burned on her cheeks.

'If Paddy's a criminal then he's one of your making,' Danny said quickly, cutting, defending his brother. 'It was you who prosecuted. You called the charges: fraud and false pretences.'

'Yes. And he deserved it. I sold all we had; the hotel and everything to help you two when you got beyond yourselves, building, building, going on building before the first ones were sold.'

'You know nothing of the building trade.'

'No. And I knew nothing of Catholics. I knew nothing of the Irish. I knew nothing of seducers and liars. But I know now!'

'Me brother didn't know you were with child, Carrie,' Danny was saying, trying to calm her she supposed. 'If he'd known he'd have . . .'

'He'd have what? What would he have done?' Carrie flung the question at him. 'Made a bigamist of himself? Would he have said "I'll send for Bridget." Eh? Was he waiting until I'd given him every penny I had?'

'Lent him, Carrie. You know he'd have paid you back when the houses were sold.'

'Oh! And he'd have settled himself and Bridget in one of them and left me living in the worst street in the town, the laughing stock of Middlefield.'

'He didn't know, Carrie. You never told him. Do you not see, woman? Patrick would have looked after you. He'd have wanted to. His wife, Bridget . . . It was all over years ago. She's a lot older than him. They have no children.' He began to cough as he did after a long speech.

'So he married her for her money an' all, did he?' Carrie replied contemptuously.

'You don't understand,' Danny said, but there was weariness in his expression.

'And I don't want to. I don't understand you either. But I know that we've had all this out,' she continued, 'in Dublin.'

She made her voice harsh as she went on, 'Our Jane's only fifteen. She needs permission from me to wed. And you knew it when you married her.'

He did not answer her.

'You're going out this afternoon, Danny Kennedy,' she said with what she hoped was finality, 'to register that baby as the legitimate child of your marriage. I'll keep my part of the bargain. I'll keep you both, and your children if needs be. But you'll do as I say. You'll bring that child up as if she were yours. You'll go to work too. I've got you a job in the insurance offices.'

'You're not in a position to make all the rules, Carrie,' Danny protested.

It was a poor show of strength. Carrie saw it in his eyes. He'd do as he was told. He wanted to live here with Jane. He said nothing when she continued.

'And if you don't like the arrangement, Danny Kennedy, you can take yourself back to Ireland and wait for your brother to be released. But I don't think you'll do that, will you?' she finished.

He made no reply. Jane's footsteps were heard on the stairs and she came into the room, her face a picture of happiness.

'I've put her in the bedroom, Carrie,' she said. 'She's lovely.' She went to Danny's side and he slipped an arm across her slight shoulders as she spoke. 'Can you bear to leave her?' she said. 'I couldn't if I'd had her. You could stay at home and be a proper mother to her.' She looked up at her husband for confirmation. 'We could all live here together. Danny'll be earning, won't you love?'

'Yes.'

'And he said, before you came down, Carrie, that he'd be happy to look after us all. And when Patrick's done his five years, he could,' her voice began to trail away as she looked at Carrie's face, 'live here as well,' she added in a fearful tone.

'You know what I said. The child's yours. I can't keep

her.' Carrie's voice was slow and resolute. 'And I never want to see her father.'

Tears had sprung to Jane's eyes. 'Don't you feel anything for her, Carrie?'

There was a silence before Carrie answered. 'I'll tell you this, Jane.' She paused, all at once fearing that she would break down before them. There was a hard, painful knot in her throat. She took a deep breath and continued. 'I'll never feel for another human being what I feel for that child. But I'll not let my feelings ruin her life.'

'Oh, Carrie,' Jane pleaded. 'You're making a big mistake. She'll grow up loving me and Danny – and you'll find yourself getting jealous and bitter.'

'No. I'll not,' Carrie replied.

'You own this house. You could live here. You could bring your child up – be a mother to her.'

'And have them all pointing a finger at her? Have them whispering about us? No!'

'Why do you care so much about what people say, Carrie?' Jane pleaded. 'People forget. In a few years' time . . .'

'Of course they don't forget.' She was recovering her composure now. It was vital that she did not go to pieces. 'They still talk about what folks' grandparents did. And I want my daughter looked up to. That's all that matters. That she can hold her head up.'

'If she's to be brought up as our child then she'll be brought up Roman Catholic. Have you thought of that?' Danny added, emboldened by his wife's show of courage. 'You'll not be able to prevent it.'

'Then you must make sure she knows what's right, mustn't you, Danny Kennedy? You must see she doesn't grow up believing she can do wrong and have it all forgiven over a few prayers,' Carrie answered bitterly.

'There's more to it than that,' Jane began.

'Tell that to Patrick then,' Carrie interrupted, 'when he comes out.'

Danny placed an arm protectively around Jane. 'We'll not argue on the day me brother's child's born,' he said. 'We'll bring her up as our own.' Jane was crying freely now, pressing her face into his chest.

'Then get yourself down to the registry office before it closes,' Carrie said. 'I'm expecting Martha Cooper soon and I'll want a bit of privacy.'

CHAPTER FIVE

Rose Kennedy was a healthy baby. She had hair the colour of copper, like her mother's and her aunt's, eyes of deep sapphire blue and a pale skin that freckled on her nose and chubby forearms. And as she grew she was quick; as quick to learn as any child ever had been.

Rose had been aware of Aunt Carrie from her earliest days. Her aunt did not live with them but came to the house every evening after she finished work at the mill. She came on Saturdays for her dinner which they ate at one o'clock and she came on Sunday afternoons.

Aunt Carrie went to chapel on Sunday mornings and again at night. She sang in the chapel and with the Middlefield Choral Society choir in a clear soprano voice that was nothing like her speaking voice. Her speaking voice was high-pitched when she was annoyed and lower, with a strong local accent when she wasn't.

And Aunt Carrie wanted people to look up to her but she didn't seem really to like other people very much. She didn't want anyone to know their business. She didn't like friends coming to the house. She advised them to 'keep themselves to themselves,' and said they should 'have no truck with folks.'

Rose loved her but she knew the tempers and moods of Aunt Carrie and tried hard to please her.

Wells Road joined Chester Road at the top end and there it was that Rose's church and school were set. Chester Road was busy with cars and horses and carts but there was no need for her to cross the road because both church and school were on the side that adjoined Wells

Road and Rose had, from the start, walked to school alone. She would have liked Mum to meet her out, as some of the other mothers did, but she was a big girl now – 5. Her sister, Mary, was 2. The baby, Vivienne was 1 year old.

Today, careless of the autumn rain, she ran with a headlong eagerness home to Mum and her sisters as soon as school was out. Mum had taught her to read before she went to school and Sister Theresa let her take a book home every day; she could never wait to read a new chapter to Mum or show her the page of sums with blue ticks against her answers.

'Look what I've done today, Mum,' she shrieked as she flew into the living room and threw herself on to Mum's lap. Mum was laughing with her and trying to get her to simmer down.

'Rose, darling. Be patient.'

Mum always said that, but she said it in such a kindly way that Rose gave her a huge hug and a great hard kiss and tried to push down the love and excitement that constantly bubbled up inside her.

As soon as the little ones were in their cots, she and Mum had their tea together, sitting at the table that was laid for Dad's supper. Mum cut thick slices of bread and spread them quickly with yellow margarine before placing big spoonfuls of plum jam in the centres and folding the pieces across so that Rose had to open her mouth as wide as it would go.

When she had eaten, Mum said, 'Go upstairs and take your school dress off, darling. Fold it nicely. I'll get Dad's supper ready.'

Rose went upstairs and changed out of her school dress and pinafore. She put on her nightdress and untied the hair ribbon which she then wound tight round the back rail of her bedroom chair, pinning it carefully so it wouldn't fray, making it flat again to tie back her tangly red hair next morning. Then she went downstairs again and helped Mum before Dad came home.

When Dad had eaten his supper and Aunt Carrie had arrived, they all sat at the big table; and these were the times Rose loved best, when they were all together and content. Rose brought her wooden pencil box and placed it on the cleared, unpolished table and watched Aunt Carrie reach into her deep brown bag, bring out the exercise book and carefully write the date at the top of a new page. Then Rose, in her best lettering, had to write down all she'd learned and finish off with a crayonned picture. The picture, she understood, must never be of Our Lord or Our Lady.

Rose liked to see the look of satisfaction, that was nearly a smile, on Aunt Carrie's face when the work was done.

Afterwards she went upstairs and climbed into bed and made a nest for herself in the deep flock mattress that Mum shook every day. She could hear the tinkle of tea-cups and, although she could not make out the words, she could hear the comforting mumble of voices from downstairs which were punctuated every few minutes with the high-pitched tones of Aunt Carrie.

Downstairs, Carrie faced Danny across the room. He'd been getting a bit cocky lately, had Danny, since he'd been promoted. She asked him to repeat the announcement he'd just made.

'What are you going on about?' she demanded. 'You only went to see your brother last week. You said you've spoken to Douglas McGregor about it. About what?'

'I'm talking about me brother's release. He comes out next month. The prison governor's written to Douglas at the Swan, to see if Douglas will take him,' Danny said. 'Patrick's wanting to see you.'

'He wants to see me?' Her voice had gone high. Alarm was rising quickly in her, making her face flush. 'You've told him! You've told him about the child, haven't you?'

'Of course I haven't.' Danny answered quickly, then, in

a slower voice added. 'He's known all along, Carrie. He knew, right at the start, when I told him that Jane and I had had a baby.'

'Knew what?' she interrupted. 'Knew what?'

'He said he knew I was doing it to save you, knew you'd have to save your reputation, knew that it was you, that you'd had his baby.'

'You didn't tell him it was true, did you?' she asked.

'No,' Danny answered. 'I denied it. It hurt me to do it to him, but I told him the child was ours.'

'And Douglas McGregor? What's he interfering for?' She took a step backwards. She didn't want Danny getting thick with Douglas McGregor again. If she thought they talked about her and her business behind her back . . . 'Why has he said he'll take him in?'

Danny looked troubled, he didn't have the strutting look he'd been putting on recently. 'Douglas knows nothing,' he answered. 'We lived at the Swan when we first came to Middlefield. He and Patrick were in the navy together. We built his house. He was a good friend to us. That's all.'

'I expect it's the priests. They've put him up to it, have they?' Carrie blazed.

'Oh, Carrie. Don't you think you'd better tell him? Let him see her?' Jane burst out.

'No!' she answered sharply.

It was a shock to her. She should have expected it and she hadn't. 'He'll never see her. She's mine. Not his.'

Carrie turned on Jane. 'And she's not yours either. So don't tell me what I should do.' She didn't normally lose her temper with Jane and she saw the quick leap of angry retaliation come to Danny's face.

She sat down at the table. 'Give me a minute to think,' she said.

'You should have thought before.' Danny thumped the side of his hand on the table, making the cups and saucers jump and rattle. 'You've had five years to think about it.

Patrick wants to live with you. You could come clean with it – stop pretending. Rose is only five. She'll settle down.'

The baby began to cry. Jane leapt to her feet and ran from the room. The light was going but Carrie saw Jane's agitated expression, saw her sister's troubled face as she left the room to comfort the child.

Danny had opened the door for Jane and now he closed it and came quickly back to stand over her, his face distorted with anger.

'And I'll not have you speak to my wife like that ever again,' he said. 'How do you think we feel? We don't want to lose Rose.' His face was inches from hers, his mouth drawn into a tight line. 'But I have to help my brother. It's my bounden duty to do so.'

She was not going to be able to ride roughshod over him. He was holding himself back from striking her. He was revealing his true feeling for her. It was written all over his face. He hated her.

'But I owe you nothing, Carrie Shrigley,' he was saying. 'I've nothing to thank you for. If it were not for Jane I'd see you in hell before I'd lift a finger for you.'

His voice went quieter now, distaste in every word as he added, 'He's forgiven you, you know. He thinks he got what he deserved. He thinks that going to prison, pleading guilty, was the only way to see that you got the money. He'll not hear a word against you.'

'He did get what he deserved!'

'But if the court had known you were a loose woman. If they'd known the full story. That you were expecting his child.' He broke off, his face distorted with bitterness.

'And just what did you think I'd do Danny? Did you think for a minute I'd go around in sackcloth and ashes?' she said in as calm a tone as she could manage. 'Did you think I'd take myself and Jane off to the workhouse? Go on the parish? Ask for charity? Me? Me that's never asked anything from anyone in my life? Oh, no. You underestimated me, both you and Patrick.'

Danny was running out of steam now, she could tell. When he spoke again his expression was changed, it was as if he despaired of making her understand.

'He wants to come back,' he said. 'He has a right to see his child.'

Carrie fought down the temper that was near to surfacing again. She always wanted to strike out when she was angry, it was something she had always done. To calm herself she took off her glasses and began to clean the thick lenses with a corner of her apron. She put them on slowly and returned her gaze to her brother-in-law.

'He'll never have sight of the child. I want nothing to do with him,' she said.

She saw a look cross Danny's face. Was it disappointment? Or relief? She neither knew nor cared. 'Go to Manchester. Meet him out and take him to Dublin. When you're there you can go to the Irish Linen Bank. I'll have money – two hundred pounds – transferred to an account there, dependent on a signed pledge that Patrick Kennedy will never set foot in England again. There'll be no money without the pledge. He'll make no protest. He'll take the money and sign if I know Patrick Kennedy. It will set him up in business. Him and Bridget. We'll be shot of him for ever.'

There was a moment's silence whilst he considered it.

'Oh, but you're a hard woman,' he said at last.

But the fight had gone out of him. His eyes were no longer challenging. He loved Rose as if she were his own; she saw that he didn't want to lose her. Danny was relieved. He was glad she was taking the initiative. He'd been unable to stand up to his brother.

'I have to try to be a hard woman, Danny,' she said slowly. 'If we were all as soft as you and Jane we'd have mud thrown in our faces. The whole world would know. It's me who keeps everybody right.' She got up from the table and gave him a cold look. 'And it's me that's telling you to send your brother back where he belongs.'

'You'll tell me nothing. Don't think for a minute that I'm backing down. You've shown your hand. I've taken note,' he answered in a tone coldly furious with exasperation. 'But if it should ever come to a clash of wills and I don't have to consider anyone else, you'll have met your match.'

She took it to be a fine show of bravado. She walked past him and reached for her hat, which she'd placed on top of the alcove cupboard, and pulled it down firmly over her ears, not bothering to check in the mirror how it looked. At this moment she didn't care about her looks.

'Now I'll go and see Douglas McGregor. I'll tell him to cancel that room at the Swan,' she said as she left the room.

Jane was pacing the hall, the baby clutched to her.

'It's all right, Jane. I'm not changing anything,' Carrie said as she pushed her arms into the sleeves of her cloth coat. 'Danny's going to give his brother money to set up in Ireland. We'll carry on as before.'

The rain hadn't let up. Her glasses made it look as if there were haloes round the gaslamps. The clock on the new factory in Chester Road said nine o'clock. Douglas McGregor would be behind the bar of the Swan at this time. She'd never been into a bar. Drunkenness was the devil and all his works made manifest. But she'd seen plenty of drunken men. She wasn't afraid. Tomorrow wouldn't do.

Some of the shops were lit up but Carrie didn't stop to look. As far as she was concerned, those who left the lights on at night were putting it on their prices. Her footsteps made a hollow ringing sound on the flagstones as she hastened to the Swan. She had to know if Patrick had told Douglas McGregor that he was Rose's father. Douglas McGregor had been visiting him in prison. Why waste time and sympathy on a criminal? 'They're all Roman Catholics,' she told herself. 'They can forgive each other

82

anything: lying, stealing and – that horrible sin – adultery.'

The greengrocer's had had electric light put in she noticed as she passed the shop. Lights blazing away and nothing to look at; just a few empty baskets and some 'everlasting' flowers.

She told Jane and Danny not to waste electricity. 'Leave it off if you're not doing anything. You can talk just as well in the dark,' she always said. In Churchwall Street they only had gas and that only in the kitchens.

Had she been rash – saying she'd give Patrick Kennedy £200? Would he have gone for £50? No. He wouldn't. And she would not be surprised if Danny Kennedy stayed in Dublin with him for he'd never have a chance of that much money again.

They would think it was all she had. They would think it was all she'd made from the sale of the houses. For there wasn't a soul who knew just how well she'd done, getting the houses finished off cheaply and selling them at a good price. When the court had awarded her the property, she'd gone, cap in hand, to Douglas McGregor and asked him to arrange a loan for her. It had proved impossible to borrow money on her own account as a woman with no real assets. She had needed to borrow to finish the houses. And Douglas had done it. He had taken a risk for her and gone guarantor.

Perhaps he had felt guilty for sending them to her in the first place. Perhaps it was because they were all Roman Catholics – they looked after their own. But she had sold the two houses in Lincoln Drive; Douglas and the other tenant had bought theirs. She had finished building the others in Wells Road, sold four of them and paid the loan back in less than twelve months. And she still had the rent money coming in from the other houses in Wells Road.

Two hundred pounds was a lot of money but it wasn't a quarter of what she'd made. Carrie smiled grimly to herself as she turned into the market square.

There were a lot of men about, loafing around the door of the Swan and leaning against the pillars of the town hall opposite. One or two were drunk already. A tall fellow, about 20 years old, one of the Baker lads, was in her way.

Carrie stopped in front of him and lifted her umbrella. 'Get off the step!' she ordered in her loudest voice. She knew he'd obey, if only from surprise. He moved aside quickly.

Douglas saw Carrie Shrigley pushing her way through the crowded bar, elbowing old men aside without apology. She had a determined look about her. The men seemed to fall back as she advanced, such was her battling air.

'Miss Shrigley? What will ye be wanting?' he said, a smile breaking across his face as she stood facing him over the wide, wet counter. 'Ye'll no be after a dram, I take it?'

'Don't try to make a fool of me, Douglas McGregor,' she answered sharply. 'I want to talk to you. In the back. Where it's private.'

A few of the men sniggered and Carrie Shrigley rounded on them.

'All right,' Douglas said quickly, before she could start an argument. 'I didn't mean to make fun of you, Miss Shrigley. Follow me.' He lifted the flap to allow her through and went ahead into the back parlour. The young barman could manage without his help for a while.

'Well now,' he said when the door was closed behind them and she stood facing him; a formidable woman. Her coat reached to just above her surprisingly fine ankles, flaming red hair escaped from under the close-fitting hat of brown felt, her hands clutched a large shopping bag and an umbrella and she peered at him through distorting, thick lenses in a steel spectacle frame.

'What is it?' he asked.

'You're giving a room to Patrick Kennedy?'

'Aye. I've had a letter . . .'

'From prison? From Strangeways?'

Her tone was high-pitched, irate, nothing like the pure, clear soprano of her singing voice. This edginess grated on Douglas but he tried not to let her see that it rattled him. 'He'll be a free man, Miss Shrigley. He's done his punishment,' he told her in a reasonable tone.

She was pink-faced now and evidently very angry. 'And you'll let him come back? A man that's thieved and robbed in the town? A gaolbird?'

Douglas could see that she would not listen to reason. 'As I recall he was sentenced for fraud and false pretences. Not theft,' he answered.

'What's fraud? What's false pretences if it's not robbing? He talked me out of my house; he robbed me of my good name; promised anything to get his hands on my money.' She was gripping her bag, white-knuckled with anger.

Douglas interrupted her swiftly. 'He's been tried. He's paid his penalty and now he must be forgiven. And helped,' he told her. 'I know ye're still bitter but ye've suffered nae worse than wounded pride,' he said.

He was starting to lose patience with her. 'Och! Men have been known to behave worse than Patrick Kennedy has,' he added. 'He could have played you false, tried to seduce you. He might even have pretended he wanted to marry you . . .'

It was a cruel thing to say to a woman, especially a woman with whom, Douglas believed, no man would ever want to dally. Most men, like himself he believed, preferred soft little clinging women. He went on, to make her see the truth, 'If yon fellow had been a villain, he'd have gone to any lengths without a thought.' He hoped it would make her think a little harder about showing a spot of charity to one who had only wronged her over money.

He saw a look pass over Carrie Shrigley's face at his words, almost a look of relief, though he hadn't thought his preaching tolerance and forgiveness was having effect. It made him go on. 'But the truth of the matter, Miss

Shrigley, is that the Swan is a tavern – I've legal obligations. I cannae refuse lodging to a traveller. So there you have it.'

'Yes,' she countered, 'and your faith would make you take him if the law didn't, wouldn't it? You'd not turn away a Catholic who'd had absolution.'

Douglas would not put up with her any longer though he'd never been a man to gossip or take sides in another's argument. 'If you want my opinion, I'll give it ye,' he said coldly. 'Patrick Kennedy need never have gone to prison if you'd shown a mite o' compassion. He swore to repay you if you'd give him a chance.'

'I can't afford to give chances.' She had turned her back on him and was going towards the door when she turned, her hand on the doorknob.

'I'm grateful to you, Douglas, for guaranteeing the loan, for arranging the mortgages,' she said quietly. 'But I've paid it back. It was the only time in my life that I was beholden to anyone and it's not in my nature to eat humble pie.'

'Och,' Douglas began. 'You need never mention that again.'

'I'll see to it that he cancels his booking,' she said. 'I will visit Strangeways myself and tell him so. People have forgotten it now. It's five years since. I'm looked up to. Everyone at chapel thinks he got what he deserved. Patrick Kennedy will not set foot in this town even if you and all your priests beg him to come.'

It was raining again, the steady, drenching rain that would not let up all day. The tops of the tall buildings in Manchester's Piccadilly seemed to merge in greyness with the low sky. The pavements outside the London Road station were black and slippery under Carrie's shoes.

She'd have to take a taxi. She wasn't going to ask anyone for directions to Strangeways. If she noted the way the taxi went she could return to the station by tram. She did not have long to wait and soon was leaning back against the leather upholstery.

'Strangeways Prison,' she said sharply to the driver. 'And don't take the long road round.' He could think what he liked. She peered through the side window that was all but opaque. 'How d'you get this down?' she called out.

'Wind the handle, missus. The one in the middle,' the man answered through the glass window.

Carrie lowered the window and tried to memorize the names of the roads as the driver slowed down at each turn, signalling through his open window with his right hand. But her eyes weren't up to it – her sight must be getting worse. It was a long way too. She would have to ask him to meet her out.

'You can see the prison from 'ere,' the driver said over his shoulder. 'On yer right.'

She could only just make it out, though it was big enough. Dominating it was a windowless column of a tower that appeared to be topped with a galleried lookout.

'Will you come for me?' she asked after she'd wound the window back up. 'I'll be no more than an hour.'

Carrie's mouth tightened at the prospect of the coming meeting. It was nearly ten to three. 'Come for me at four o'clock,' she said.

The sprawling red-brick prison looked menacing. It had a high wall, right up to the top floor of the buildings. There was open space all around the gaol and it was set on a slight rise. She could see almost the whole extent of it. High above, over the unbroken wall that surrounded it, yet close to it, were the tiny barred windows of the cells.

Carrie shivered and looked straight ahead at the lodge entrance with bow-fronted turrets from whose windows the guards would be able to scan the city for miles around. Between these conical-roofed turrets to the height of the second storey was a massive arched sandstone gateway with heavy wooden doors, the right one having a smaller, inset door with a square peep-hole, for opening to visitors.

There were several women outside, standing under a notice board, waiting. Carrie stood at the end of the bedraggled line. Nobody spoke to her.

When the small door opened they were shown in by a warder who ordered them to follow him. As if they were criminals too, Carrie thought. Through a paved courtyard they went, under a clock and into the building; doors were closed and locked behind them. She felt cheap, degraded, like those other women must feel. She could hear the prisoners now, men with rough voices, a growling background to the echoing noise of many heavy feet.

Her heart was going fast again. The smell was awful, even here in the corridor. She'd be dead within a month, in a place like this.

A warder showed her into the cell where they'd bring him. It was cold and oppressive. Across the room was a wooden counter and above it an iron grille. There was a bench running round the wall and nothing at all on the other side. They'd have to stand. There was a foul stench, even in here.

She heard footsteps approaching, hollow and distant, then louder as they reached the door and she jumped when the key turned in the lock on the other side of the room and he came in, behind a warder.

She almost fainted with the smell and the unbearable horror of it all. She would have to force herself to look into his face; force herself to ignore the palpitations, the violent heartbeating that always came in his presence.

How could it be? After all he'd done? After five years? When she had made herself forget everything but his treachery, how could her body be telling her that her outward appearance of calm was assumed? But it had always been so. They had never communicated on a normal level, never talked lightly. They had always raised violent feelings in one another; their contact had always been instant and emotional. Now she would have to be other than she was.

She set her face and looked at him, the man she had once loved to distraction. He was wearing prison clothes. He was thinner but clean-shaven. She'd expected to see him bearded and broken-looking. The confident air had gone.

She made a tremendous effort. She ignored the banging in her chest, put from herself all but her determination to see this through, her determination to prevent him from trying to come back into her life.

'Well, Carrie. This is a pleasure,' he was saying. His deep voice was weaker.

Carrie turned to the warder; a different one from the one she'd seen earlier. 'Do you have to stand there, listening?' she demanded sharply.

He seemed startled by the suddenness of her attack. 'I am required to be present,' he told her.

'You can say what you like, Carrie.' Patrick was smiling at her now but she saw the strain behind his eyes.

She wouldn't weaken. She would carry it through. 'You're not coming back to Middlefield,' she began, avoiding his eyes, looking at the grille. 'You'd have to have work to go to. I've read all the laws about it and I'm going to see you keep them.'

'I wanted to see you. I wanted to talk to you. I've been thinking a lot,' Patrick was saying, whispering the words, trying not to let the warder hear. 'I want to come back to you, Carrie.'

'You are coming out under licence,' she went on, ingoring his plea. 'It's called ticket of leave. You have to have a job to go to or you'll be sent back inside.'

'I'll get work. Douglas McGregor is going to take me on,' he said. 'Believe me, Carrie. Douglas feels he is partly responsible. He says it should never have happened. He says if he'd sent us to lodge somewhere else . . .'

'You'll go home to your wife. Your wife!' Carrie's voice was shrill now and tears were springing to her eyes. 'That's where you belong!' she cried.

'Me marriage is over. I wanted to tell you.'

'You can't get out of it though, can you?' She flung the taunt at him, violently.

'Bridget doesn't want me back. It was a mistake in the first place,' he said.

'You are married to her! Married! Married!' she heard herself shout as the tears ran down her face.

He had put his face right up to the grille, as if he didn't care now, what the warder thought. 'You had no alternative, Carrie. I know that,' he said in a loud whisper. 'But now you have a choice. Come with me, love. Follow your instincts. You're a woman made for love. We had something beautiful. It isn't given to everyone, Carrie.'

She saw gleaming hope and desire in his eyes and felt every nerve in her body stretching out to him. She must not let him see that his words were like physical pain to her. She forced her voice down, choked it into its normal pitch and said with the greatest effort she had ever made,

'You are married, Patrick Kennedy. Your wife is waiting for you, in Dublin.'

'She doesn't want me,' he said.

'And I wouldn't look at you again if your church canonized you,' she made herself say. 'So you'll have to go back to her. Won't you?'

'And there's the matter of me child.' Patrick spoke with quiet desperation.

All at once the heat of passion left her. Carrie felt a cold anger against him, at his daring to talk about 'his' child; she saw the warder look sharply at him.

'You haven't a child,' she said evenly.

'Danny says they had a baby, but I know it was you, Carrie. Our baby. Rose Kennedy.'

'Not me. Oh no, Patrick. It was our Jane who had the babies. She and Danny have had three. It's him and Jane as have had babies. I've got nothing,' she said with slow deliberation.

He had gone white. The expression of hope had gone

from his eyes. 'What do you want, Carrie? What do you want of me? You've got the houses. You've got me brother and your sister under control. What in God's name do you want?' he said.

'Your brother's coming to see you. I'll give him two tickets to Dublin. There'll be money in the Irish Linen Bank; two hundred pounds. It's what I feel is owing. To you and Danny.'

'You want Danny to go back with me, do you?' Patrick asked. 'He'll not do that. He loves his wife and children.'

'I can look after our Jane and the children,' Carrie told him. 'It makes no difference to me if he goes or stays. He might stay. But there again, he might be tempted by the money, for he only earns twenty-five shillings a week. And I charge them eight and six for the rent.'

'Is that all you care for now? Money?' He was shouting at her. 'You were a fine woman, Carrie Shrigley. What's become of you?'

'Quiet!' The warder had gone for his arm and was twisting it, making him wince, pulling him away from the counter towards the door behind him.

He was still protesting as they dragged him out of her sight. She could hear him. She heard a gate slam in the distance, then there was silence.

CHAPTER SIX

When the door clanged behind the warder, Patrick slumped on to the hard bench-bed and tried to collect his thoughts. He fought down the anger that was still in him; he had learned over these years that silent fury made incarceration harder to bear and that the best way to control the feeling was to come to a decision.

He looked down at his hands, tightly clenched in his lap, and deliberately loosened them. He had known; he'd known all along, even when he was telling her that she was a woman driven, that there was more to Carrie Shrigley than sensuality. He'd known since the first time he'd seen her, crossing the market square on a Saturday morning, taller than the women around her, straight and proud, her flaming hair pulled tightly back into a severe knot, that he could not take his eyes off her and had to get to know her. If love at first sight existed, and he'd have laughed at the idea before he first saw her, then he had come as near to it as anyone ever had. And he'd sensed, before he had even spoken to her, from her face, her walk, from her dress, that she was a strong woman of strong purpose and strong passions.

The noise of the other prisoners returning from work was growing louder; whistles were being blown, bells were clanging, but the shouts and tramping boots outside his cell were no longer a menace. He had a cell to himself at last. They were feeding him better, letting his hair grow, all so that he'd be in good shape when he was released. He put up a hand and felt the hair. It was good not to feel the shaven stubble, though he had not got the good head of hair he'd arrived with five years ago. It was greying, and thinner – but so was he. He stood and flexed the muscles on his legs. In a week or so he'd be done with it all.

And he'd be done with Carrie, by the look of it. He had been drawn to her as he had never been drawn to a woman in his life before. The restlessness, the wanderlust that had been a part of him until he met her, he had believed, at the start of their love affair, would leave him if he had Carrie Shrigley at his side. Yet she had been so fierce, so inflexibly religious, so frightened by her own passions that he dared not reveal to her his own careless, improvident past.

Carrie would never have understood, having only known her strict father, that young men could grow wild living without fear of authority; that he had gone from one town to another, one occupation to another, joining the merchant navy to see the world, playing the fool on his leaves, even marrying when he and his drinking partner, old Bridget, had thought to settle.

It had been the war that had freed him. Joining the Royal Navy – the great adventure, the terrible fear, the active service and the realization that if he survived then his life would take on meaning – had changed him. War had made him want to forget the past. His old Chief Petty Officer McGregor had told him to keep in touch and he found that McGregor had gone to a little town in Cheshire. Danny had gone with him; Danny, invalided out of the fusiliers, his lungs damaged from the poison gas. They had both wanted to start anew.

He heard a whistle blowing. He didn't want to eat. Tonight he would refuse the thin soup, stale bread and strong, stewed tea. The warder outside his cell would not put him on punishment. Patrick went to the door and listened. Yes, it was the easy-going warder who was on duty tonight.

Sitting on the bench again, his thoughts went back. Carrie never forgave herself for revelling in the wonderful, glorious passion he had for her – or her own eagerness to share it. It would have been impossible to confess to her that he was a married man and a bankrupt Irish builder. He'd tried to tell her but fear of losing her had stopped him.

Suddenly, in one of those flashes of memory that came without warning, he could smell the clean fresh air off the hills and the scent of her room, taste the light saltiness on her skin, feel the silken warmth of her, hear her sighing when they were sated – and he wanted to weep.

He got up again and restlessly strode up and down the small narrow cell, forcing his mind from sweet recollection. Carrie loved him still, he knew that. He'd seen it in her face today. A man couldn't know a woman as he'd known her – love a woman as he had loved her – and not know it. It was she who knew nothing of love. Carrie, who had never looked up to anyone in her life, except perhaps her father, and him only in death, believed that what she called respect was love. She would never find that kind of love – she never saw herself as anyone's subordinate.

And the child? She'd called their child Rose. Whether she knew it or not it had been the memory of that night, the evening by the lake when the child was conceived, that had prompted her to call the child – his child – Rose.

But she'd have nothing to do with him now. And he could not blame her. From what he knew about her, she'd not have known she was with child at the time of the trial. But he had known. He had known the moment it happened. And he'd known for sure when she'd stood up in the witness box, avoiding his eyes, pale and hollow eyed. Her denial hadn't fooled him.

He'd not go back to Middlefield. He'd not embarrass her or Danny and Jane with his own wants. He'd never been the settling sort; not like Danny. Jane and Danny would give his child a proper upbringing – they'd be better parents than he or even Carrie would. He had wanted her – Carrie – with or without a child. He'd never craved fatherhood for its own sake. And she was the same, though she couldn't see it. She believed, he could tell, that she had handed the baby over because it was the best thing for the child. He was sure she thought it an unselfish act – maybe she saw it as her own punishment – but she had not seen what she was doing, what she had done every time there was a choice to be made. She had refused to open the gates of her being; refused to go out, truthful, into the day.

Together, with or without a child, with or without the blessing of a church, they could have shared a lifetime of loving.

Now his anger was returning. He had no interest in any other woman. One day she would know it too; she would be his. But he'd paid the price for his weakness; he'd taken the rap for his folly. He'd have no more of it. There were to be no more recriminations.

Carrie could keep her money. He'd have none of it. He'd take what Douglas McGregor had already offered to him, the fare to Australia, an introduction to Douglas's cousin there and a job on a sheep station. He'd make good and one day, he'd see his daughter. He had always been a wandering man.

Rose liked to think about ages and dates. Mum had just had a big birthday. Dad said she'd been coming of age and had bought her a lovely gold wristwatch. Aunt Carrie, she had discovered, was 33 and she, Rose, on the summer day when she fell off the garden wall, was 6 years old.

Mum was busy indoors with Mary and Vivienne and she had sent Rose out into the garden to play on the swing Dad had built for her. The swing had a narrow wooden seat and thick ropes which went right through the top bar where they were knotted together. If she swung very high the ropes made a lovely groaning sound and she felt as if she could sail off into the sky, so far above the grass was she.

It was August and very hot and the breeze she made, swishing through the air, ruffled her hair. But through her ruffled hair, when she rose to the top of each upward swing, she could see a boy in the garden over the wall from hers.

When at last she stopped, gouging the grass with the soles of her sandals to drag the swing to a halt, she went towards the wall and tried to climb it. There was a garden roller right against the wall and she pulled herself on to it, holding tight with plump little hands. She had lost one of her front teeth and made sipping noises as she poked her head over the top of the high brick wall. The mop of red hair was escaping from the big white bow on top of her head and a heavy strand fell forward across her eyes.

Now she couldn't see for the hair. She raised a sandalled foot until she had it over the coping stones, her face creased in concentration as she lifted herself slowly upwards. When both legs were up she found that she had her back to the other garden and would have to stand.

She balanced herself for a second, half-standing, and opened her blue eyes wide in astonishment as she looked for the first time into the leafy orchard of the house in Lincoln Drive.

A boy was cycling round the trees at a furious pace, his thin legs going so fast they appeared circular. He had black hair, silky on top and very short to his ears. His head was held close to the handlebars whilst his eyes were narrow slits under a furrowed forehead. He made a noise like the cars she'd seen on the roads and he leaned this way and that, wheeling and turning. Rose's eyes followed him as he drove ever faster, circling first one tree then another, never letting up the growling, throaty noise.

She stood right up and managed to get both feet pointing the same way. Then her untidy hair fell forward again and as she lifted her hand to push it back she found herself tipping over, hands outstretched to save herself and nothing to reach for, arms and legs hitting the wall as she fell; landing with a painful shock in the long grass at Alan McGregor's wheels.

Rose began to cry. Already her knees had little red beads of blood popping through the dirt where they'd scraped against the wall. Her hands too, were prickling and long purple scratches marked her arms.

'I fell,' Rose wailed, holding out her hands to the boy who stood before her, red-faced from his exertions, yet solemn.

'Stop crying,' the boy demanded.

Rose managed to stifle her tears. The boy appeared to her to be very bossy. He might become rough like the boys in the boys' playground at school were. The boys at school were only noisy and scary when they were all together though. This boy was by himself. She stuffed her fists into her wet eyes to clear the tears and sniffed loudly.

She looked up to see that the boy had propped his bicycle against an apple tree and was standing before her, a hand outstretched to help her to her feet.

'Come inside,' he said. 'I'll wash your knees.'

The grass was shorter near the trees. It no longer brushed against her legs and Rose held on to the boy's hand as he led her across a vast lawn strewn with toys, to the open French window.

A fat lady with white hair was sleeping in an armchair, her short legs supported on a little stool. The boy put a finger to his lips.

'Nanny Tansley,' he whispered. 'We'll go to the kitchen.'

Rose padded over the deep pile of Indian carpet and followed the boy along a wide hall, keeping to the carpet runner so as not to make a sound until they reached a big square kitchen, tiled in white to a height above their heads.

Alan placed a folded towel on the wooden draining-board and held out his hands to the little girl. She raised her arms and, as he tried to lift her, wound them around his neck and held tight.

'No,' he said. 'You're to sit on the towel.' This was

going to be the hard part. He knew what to do once she was seated. He put her down again and watched in fascination as her eyes filled with tears, her mouth crumpled and dirty little fists flew up to her face.

'Don't cry,' he said firmly. 'I'll bring a chair. You can climb up.'

Alan had only played with boys up to now. There were no girls at his school. Some of his friends had sisters but they didn't join in with the boys' games. He knew they were silly because his friends said so. They cry a lot, his best friend, Gerald, had told him.

When she was finally settled on the towel and her tears had subsided he asked, 'What's your name?'

'Rose Kennedy. What's your name?'

'Alan McGregor,' he told her. 'How old are you?'

'Six.'

'I'm nearly eight. Well, seven and a half,' he added truthfully.

She held her hands out to him and he washed them thoroughly with the flannel Nan kept in a white china dish under the sink. He'd also brought out cotton wool, bandages and iodine but he wondered whether or not to use the iodine, in case she cried again. She had screwed up her eyes and pushed her face towards him. Alan rinsed the cloth and wiped her face.

'Don't cry when I wash your knees,' he ordered in his most grown-up voice.

Her eyes never left his as he wiped and doused the angry red patches. She drew her breath in sharply when he pressed the towel, none too gently, to dry them.

'You have to have iodine on when they're clean.' Alan watched her face intently for signs of another 'waterfall' as Nan called it. 'Are you brave? Like boys are?'

She nodded her head vigorously, compressed her lips and held tightly to the edge of the towel, silent as he pressed the iodine-drenched cotton to her raw knees.

Dad had taught him not to cry when he hurt himself.

His Dad was brave. His Dad was the bravest and strongest man in the world.

This little girl didn't cry. She must be very brave, for a girl, he decided.

Her lively hair bounced as she shook her head and the sun, streaming through the window behind her, lit the bronze curls with sudden brilliance. He'd have a go at tying her hair ribbon when her knees were clean.

'I'm going to be a doctor when I grow up,' he said solemnly. 'I can bandage legs.'

'I'm going to be a mummy,' she told him. 'Where's your mummy?'

'I haven't got one,' he answered.

'You have to have a mummy. Everyone has a mummy,' she said.

'Mine's dead.'

'Oh.'

He wondered what it would be like; having a mother. Nan Tansley was nice, but she wasn't young and pretty like a lot of real mothers were. But real mothers didn't let you get dirty, Gerald said. He and Dad went to Nat Cooper's farm and rode on carts; they got dirty and wet whenever they could and nobody told them not to.

He rolled bandages around her knees until the sore parts were covered completely and he finished off with very large knots in front of her shins before helping her to climb down, straight-legged, on to the mat.

He caught sight of Nan as he lowered Rose. She must have woken up at last.

'Well, young man! Where did you find your little patient, eh?' Nan said.

'She fell in. Over the wall,' Alan told her.

'From Wells Road? We'd better take her back then, before her mother gets a fright like I did,' Nanny Tansley said. 'Get a little treat for her, Alan. She's a brave girl.'

Alan chose the biggest banana in the fruit bowl and handed it to Rose. 'Can't she stay here for a while,

Nan?' he said. 'She can play with my toys.'

He didn't want to let her go now he'd found her. She was as good as a boy, not crying when she had iodine put on a cut. His Dad wouldn't be home until tea-time and he had nobody at all to play with.

'Come on then. We'll go and ask her mother. Follow Nanny Tansley. Eeh, you are a one, Alan. Poor Nan looked high and low for you. Poor Nan just took a peep at the paper and the next thing she knew, you were bandaging up your little friend's knees. What's your name, love?'

She led them out into Lincoln Drive and round the corner to Rose's house. Alan walked beside Rose as they followed Nan's broad figure.

'Will you come and play?' he asked her. 'I've got jigsaws and a toy farm in the playroom.'

'Can I ride your bicycle?' She had stopped for a minute to tuck up the end of bandage that had loosened and her eyes were bright blue and full of laughter.

'I've got a fairy-cycle that's too small for me. You can ride that, if you like,' he promised and wondered what else he might offer, to tempt her. 'You can be my best friend,' he added.

'Can we play Mums and Dads?'

Alan thought for a few seconds. He wasn't sure how you played that game. 'I'll be the Dad,' he said at last.

'I can come when Aunt Carrie's at her house,' Rose said. 'I've never had a friend.'

Rose ran ahead of Alan and Nan Tansley into the house. 'Mum,' she yelled. 'Come and see my friend.' She was gasping for breath, saying, 'Sorry I fell off the wall, Mum,' at the same time as she pulled Alan into the room that must have seemed small and crowded after the big house over the wall.

Then Mum and Nanny Tansley shook hands and laughed and chatted and sent her and Alan into the garden to play whilst they held the little ones.

Rose pointed out the little patch of flowers that Dad grew and the row of lettuces but Alan wanted to see if he could climb the wall she'd fallen from. She watched him, lost in admiration as he found cracks between the bricks, pulled himself easily on to the rounded top and walked the length of the narrow garden without falling off.

'Show me how,' she pleaded. Alan had long thin legs with large, lumpy knees that seemed wider than his thighs or shins, enormous feet and ankles and a wiry body. He stretched out his arms as he reached the end and turned carefully for the run back.

'Girls can't climb, silly!' he called, without taking his eyes off the wall.

'They can!'

'Can't!' He'd reached the other end and was placing his feet, heel to heel for the return, but Rose was scrambling up, fitting her small feet into the cracks he'd used, loosening the bandages on her knees until at last, straining and panting, she straddled the top and her blue eyes were triumphant as she laughed at him.

'See! Silly!'

Churchwall Street, where Carrie had lived for the last six years, was halfway between the market square and the cattle market in Waters Green. One end of Churchwall Street opened on to the Wallgate, the other end on to the Hundred and eight steps. Her own backyard had, ten feet below it, the backyard of one of the big houses of Waters Green.

Waters Green comprised the cattle market and the open space in front of the railway station. The Wallgate rose out of Waters Green to the market square. There was a bakery, a smithy and soon there was to be an omnibus station. The cattle market was only used for selling cattle on Tuesdays. On Wednesdays, Fridays and Saturdays, Waters Green and the steep Wallgate were filled with marketstalls.

The river Hollin flowed, swift and stained with dye, between the railway line and the mills. It must have been the river, Carrie thought, that had given the lower market its name of Waters Green, for there wasn't a blade of grass to be seen.

But it would be a champion place to open a Temperance Hotel. There'd be business coming in, from the railway, and farmers wanting breakfasts and dinners on market days. It should do better than the old place in the market square. And it would redeem her in her father's eyes, if he was watching, knowing that she was keeping her promise to him, making a new haven of sobriety or whatever it was he'd called it.

The Waters Green house that backed up against her cottage was a lodging-house and the old couple wanted to sell. They'd told her they were getting too old for it, but Carrie knew better. They couldn't make money, that was their trouble.

It was getting dark. Here in Churchwall Street the light went early, though the morning sun beamed directly into her rooms. It was November and cold. Outside, in the yard, leaves from the sycamores in the churchyard lay in damp profusion. She'd sweep them in the morning. Right now she concentrated on the figures in front of her, her eyes inches from the sheet of paper as she made her calculations.

She sat straight and let out a big sigh. A smile crossed her face. She had enough; enough to buy the place in the bottom market. Wells Management, as she was called on paper, had £1,900 in balance in the District Bank in Manchester where prying Middlefield eyes wouldn't know about it. The money was from rents, interest on rents and the two houses she'd sold. There was £50 in £5 notes, under the bread-crock on the cellar steps waiting to be put into the account and a good £200 worth of jewellery if she had to sell it.

There was enough coming in for her never to have to

work again if that was what she wanted. She could live here in the tiny cottage and still be able to give help to those who needed it; Jane and Danny and, here in Churchwall Street, Brenda Gallimore and her ever-growing family. But she wouldn't do that. She would make more money. She did not want to sell any of her property though. She liked buying property. It gave her a fine feeling of proud ownership, knowing that some of the houses in Middlefield belonged to her. She had a good legal man in Manchester too who would buy for her under the name of Wells Management, whenever she was ready.

She was full of energy; always had been. She needed to work and she wanted the standing that another Temperance Hotel would give to her.

She opened her cupboard and set a cup, saucer and plate on the table. Then she reached down into the hearth and took hold of the red cotton kettle-holder that Rose had knitted. She used it to place the filled kettle over the coals on the iron swinging-trivet. Then she scooped tea into her silver teapot and sat back to wait for the kettle to boil.

It was lovely, remembering Rose's little face when she'd given her the kettle-holder; her first piece of knitting. Yet she, herself, was afraid of responding too warmly to the child, afraid that her feelings would overwhelm her. So she had to fight back the impulse to hold the little one to her; had to signal to Jane to distract the child's attention; had to stand by and watch Rose give to Jane what Carrie knew should be hers, the love and trust of her own daughter. And she had to fight back her jealousy.

The tea was ready and, as she drank, Carrie turned her thoughts from Rose and smiled with satisfaction to think that the Potts wanted to sell her old property back to her. But she wouldn't take it. Not even for what they'd offered it to her for; £200 less than they'd paid. She wouldn't want to live there again, remembering all the time.

Anyway, Carrie thought, the marketplace wasn't what it had been. There was a labour exchange now, in the market square, and always a queue of men outside.

It was awful to see them, and see the mills closing down or going on short-time. A lot of the men had been in the war; many were on crutches, others still coughing up from the gassings. And some of them reduced now to begging. There was one who was propped against the side of an entry; he had no legs. His wife wheeled him in every morning and left him sitting all day with his old cap on the flagstones in front of him. And there was the blind man who begged near the station.

Well, there'd be a job for someone when she left the mill. She'd be glad to go. She'd never taken to millwork, though Cecil Ratcliffe from the chapel had kindly found her a good job; supervising in his brother-in-law's factory. Her eyes weren't really up to much close work. If her sight went she'd be able to manage a lodging-house.

And when Rose was a big girl she'd come and live with her; help her.

Alan was happy to have Rose come round to see him in Lincoln Drive but never felt as comfortable at her house. It seemed to him that, unlike his own home, where he never heard voices raised, the Wells Road household rang with chatter, laughter and argument. Rose's house was usually filled with joyful sound, though he felt a quick drop in spirits whenever their Aunt Carrie came in.

When the aunt arrived unexpectedly he could feel her eyes chilling him, making him feel that he had done wrong and he would depart quickly before she asked, 'Isn't it time the McGregor lad went home for his tea?'

He'd see the blush come to Rose's cheeks, for shame at her aunt's words, if he didn't leave before she uttered them, and he felt sorry for Rose who seemed to feel the weight of her aunt's attention.

He spoke to his father about it but his father merely smiled and said, 'Aye. She's a crabbit old hen. Let the wee lassie come round here then.'

104

But today they were far away from Middlefield, Rose and Aunt Carrie.

Dad put his arm around Alan's shoulder as they sat on the harbour wall in the long Scottish twilight. Together they watched the sun sink in a sheet of flame behind the mountains and the sky above turn from gold to crimson and purple, listening as the inky water at the back of the wall slapped gently against the painted sides of the boats.

The holiday was over. Tomorrow they'd come down to the shore before the sun was up for a last look at the pewter sea and silver sky and Alan would push his bare feet into pale shaking sand where fast waves foamed against the wide beach.

Dad was a sailor in his bones. He'd told Alan that in his heart he always would be. He loved the sea and the people of the village; the men who spoke a tongue Alan could not understand and the strong women who walked barefoot at dawn to the nearby town, carrying heavy creels of fish and calling their wares in harsh, plaintive voices. Alan wondered if his mother had looked like them, for she'd been a fisherman's wife.

'Back to Middlefield tomorrow, Son.' Dad stood up and felt in the pocket of his old jacket for his pipe and tobacco pouch. 'Will you be sorry?'

'I like it here, Dad, but I want to get back home. To see Nan and Rose and go up to the farm, maybe.' Alan was tall for 9 years of age; a skinny lad of enormous energy and quick intelligence. His brown eyes were alive with anticipation and, try as he might, he could not conceal his excitement at the prospect of the long train journey ahead.

'Will we stay overnight in Edinburgh?' he asked and saw with relief that his father grinned between tamping the tobacco and drawing the flame slowly over the round bowl of his pipe.

'Aye. We'll bide a night in Auld Reekie.'

'And climb Arthur's Seat and look for aeroplanes?' Alan added.

'Och aye,' his father replied. 'What a laddie! Is the sea no enough for you that you want to fly now?' But he was still smiling as Alan followed behind the big broad back of his father to the cluster of whitewashed cottages beyond the high-water mark.

Dad opened the latch on the backyard gate of Aunt Isa's house and waited for him to pass under his arm.

'Ye'll need to get an early night, son. We'll be off at the crack o' dawn,' he said. 'Get yourself up the stairs when ye've had your supper.'

'Will you come up for a talk, Dad?' Alan asked. 'And read the letter from my godfather, again?'

'Aye. Of course I will.'

Dad would sometimes sit on the end of his bed and listen to him and now and then tell of times gone by, before Alan was born. This evening Dad would tell the familiar story again, the way Alan liked to hear it, as if he were reading from a book. Then he would read the letter Patrick had sent from Canada where he and Uncle John McGregor had sailed to.

Alan waited until Dad had smoked his pipe, out on the 'little green' as Aunt Isa called the tiny patch of grass at the back of the cottage.

He heard Dad's feet on the narrow wooden stair and watched him duck his head through the low doorway. He pulled himself up against the pillows and wrapped his arms around his knees as the tale unfolded. Alan always felt unaccountably angry when Dad got to the part where his mother died. He wanted to know how it was she had died. Had he killed her? How could a healthy young woman die in childbirth when he'd seen sheep and cows give birth safely?

Then he always wanted to laugh when Dad told him about finding Nan Tansley. He was so relieved that they had found her.

'Well, Alan. Is that enough?'

Douglas had come to the end of the story. 'You don't

want all the bits you can remember, do you?'

'No,' Alan answered. 'Read Patrick's letter now, will you?'

Douglas took a fat, crumpled envelope from his jacket pocket and lay the pages on the counterpane, grinned at Alan and began.

'Dear Douglas and Godson,' he read. 'John McGregor and I have decided to seek our fortune in Canada. We sailed across the Tasman Sea from Sydney to Auckland, New Zealand. There we booked two berths on an iron-floored mailboat to Vancouver.

'Three days out from Auckland we arrived in Suva, Fiji. Hot, like steaming soup was Suva. We were thirsty all the time and were given wooden bowlfuls of a drink that tastes like soapy water. It was their national drink, Kaava; made from fermented coconut.

'The Pacific is vast, yet centuries ago the Polynesians crossed it, paddling canoes laden with women and children. It took us a week to sail from Fiji to the pretty Hawaiian Islands in a heaving, pitching sea. But when we arrived the weather was hot and calm and the dusky young maidens of Honolulu waded out to us through a turquoise sea to bring leis – garlands of paper flowers – to hang around our necks.

'We hired a taxi and saw the island; sugar cane and pineapple plantations; two thousand foot cliffs – so tall that their tops were lost in a greenish mist – that dropped sheer into the deep blue sea.

'Now we are here, just docked in the sparkling waters of Vancouver Sound, looking across to tall skyscrapers with steep, blue, wooded mountains beyond them. We shall stay here for a few days before we go on the Canadian Pacific Railway to Winnipeg where John wants to look up the Canadian McGregor clan.'

'It makes you want to see it all, doesn't it, Dad?' Alan said when his father had reached the end.

'Aye. He makes places seem real, the way he describes

107

them,' Douglas answered. 'Will ye be wanting to sail, or to fly when ye're a man, laddie?'

'I'm going to be a doctor when I grow up,' Alan said eagerly. 'I'm going to save mothers like Nat and his father do with cows and sheep. I've watched them being born, Dad, and I've never seen one die.'

'You don't owe your life to anyone, Alan,' Douglas assured him. 'You've a long way to go before you make your mind up, son.' He ruffled Alan's hair affectionately. 'Get some sleep now. Good night.'

Alan did not understand what Dad meant about not owing his life to anyone. He'd always wanted to be a doctor, ever since he'd held a bleating new-born lamb for Nat and watched Nat bring the ewe back from the edge of death. After Nat had pulled the other, dead lamb out of the ewe he'd heaved the mother on to her feet again and they'd given her the lamb Alan had held. Alan had felt tears of relief running down his face when the mother sheep began to lick the lamb and nudge the poor fumbling creature until it was in the right place to drink from her.

He didn't want to be a vet in case he had to destroy animals. A doctor was what he'd be – or a pilot.

He knelt on his bed and watched the sky which would lighten into dawn in a few hours. He couldn't sleep for thinking about the coming day when they'd cross the three long spans and great steel trusses of the Forth Rail Bridge. He and Dad would leave their bags, walk down the Royal Mile into Holyrood park and climb the big mountain right to the top.

From the summit they'd be able to see the city spread out around their feet and he'd take Dad's field glasses and look for the Tiger Moths and Sopwiths he'd seen flying from the airfield the last time they were there and he'd beg Dad to let him go up for a pleasure flight.

CHAPTER SEVEN

Aunt Carrie didn't like any of them to have friends outside
the family, especially Rose, who just wished that Aunt
Carrie liked her best friend, Alan. Rose told her aunt that
Mary and Vivienne had one another and didn't need
friends but that she had nobody to play with, only Alan.
But Aunt Carrie still went into one of her moods when she
saw him.

It was nearly time for Rose's first communion and Mum
was making a beautiful white dress for her. The material
was cotton lawn, Mum said. When it was finished she was
going to show it to Alan.

Every day at one o'clock Mum placed a Windsor chair
near the big cupboard that reached from the floor to the
ceiling of the living room. The oak-stained cupboard fitted
in beside the fireplace and its top had doors while below
were four deep drawers. They called the top shelf the
Secret Shelf because nobody was tall enough to reach it
and they didn't own stepladders. Mum had to pull out the
drawers to form steps or climb from the chair into the top
drawer. Today she climbed up from the chair and fished
with the mat-beater until the parcel flew out into the room
to be caught by Rose.

'Got it, Mum!' Rose called as the pillowcase containing
her dress landed in her open hands.

Mum was slight and very thin and Rose held her breath
as her mother felt gingerly behind herself for the seat of
the chair. 'You're there,' she said, laughing as Mum
hopped down on to the rag mat.

'Take your blouse off, darling,' Mum said. 'I want to fit

the bodice before you go back to school.'

Rose unbuttoned her winceyette blouse and stood, arms outstretched, keeping still so as not to feel the little cold pins touching her skin as Mum tugged and frowned over the task of fitting the pieces.

'Why do you have to hide it, Mum?' she asked. 'Doesn't Aunt Carrie know you're making my dress?'

'No,' Mum mumbled behind the spokes of pins that were firmly clamped between her lips.

'Why would she be angry? Is it because she hates Roman Catholics?' Rose asked.

Mum unpinned the bodice and laid the pieces carefully on the clean pillowcase, over the top of the treadle sewing machine that was her pride and joy. She took Rose by the shoulders and turned her round to face her.

'Don't talk like that, Rose,' she said. 'Your aunt and I were brought up Chapel. I wanted to be a Catholic when I got married, to be like your Dad, but Aunt Carrie thinks the Church made me change . . . that I had to join them.'

Rose loved Aunt Carrie and it seemed to her that if only Aunt Carrie went to St Albans and listened to the sisters, she would be happy all the time. Rose felt the hot tears welling up behind her eyes. She put her arms around Mum's neck.

'I wish Aunt Carrie was a Catholic too, Mum. I wish she came to our church.'

They did not see the kitchen door open. They had forgotten that Aunt Carrie was coming to the house after she'd been tested for new glasses and it was Mum who first lifted her head from Rose's tight hold and flinched at the sight of her sister who stood, white-faced, watching them.

'So this is what goes on when I'm out, is it?' Aunt Carrie spoke in the ominous voice they knew sometimes foretold a burst of bitter rage. 'You talk about me behind my back, do you?'

'Carrie – we're only . . .' Mum straightened up but she was guarded, Rose sensed.

110

'Mum's making my communion dress, Aunt Carrie,' Rose said with a boldness that was mostly pretence, for a firm rule of her aunt's was that she was never to answer back. 'We're just fitting it before I go back to school.'

'Is that so, my fine girl?' Aunt Carrie pushed the door to behind her and came to where they were standing. She snatched the cut-out pieces, pins and pillowcase and threw them into the fire, pushing the bodice into the red coals with the poker. 'We'll see about that.'

Aunt Carrie was fiery, not pretty like Mum, and now, when her cheeks were going red and the blue eyes behind the thick lenses flashed, Rose's confidence left her and she began to cry. She was afraid that Aunt Carrie would strike them. Sometimes her aunt lifted her hand as if she was going to hit out. She wished Dad were here. Aunt Carrie was never like this when Dad was at home.

'And what's this I hear about you playing with the McGregor lad?' She bent down, pulled Rose's hands away from her face and looked into her eyes. 'Who said you could go playing with strangers?'

'He's not a stranger. He's my friend,' Rose protested through her tears. 'He's my best friend.'

This seemed to infuriate Aunt Carrie even more but she turned from her to Mum.

'Put your things on. Get yourself back to school,' she said to Rose, over her shoulder. 'Your Mum and I have some talking to do.'

Rose buttoned her blouse with shaking fingers, left the house and ran back to school, lurching sobs making her chest painful as she turned the corner of Wells Road and nearly knocked Dad off his feet

'What's the matter with me darling?' Dad lifted her high in the air, his merry eyes clouding when he saw her tear-streaked face.

'It's Aunt Carrie,' Rose sobbed. 'Burning my communion dress and shouting at Mum.'

Dad's face set into firm lines. 'Is she?' he said harshly.

He put her down gently on the pavement and tapped her bottom. 'Don't you worry your sweet head about Aunt Carrie,' he added to comfort her but his tone was angry. 'She knew you were going to take your first communion. I'll put a stop to her nonsense.'

Carrie turned on Jane as soon as Rose had gone. 'What's all this?' she said. 'Who says she's going to . . . to take your communion? All that heathen nonsense? I won't have it.'

Jane had a determined look on her face. 'Sit down, Carrie,' she said softly. 'You must understand. She has to make her first confession. Take her first communion. You can't let her belong to the faith and not be a member.'

'I said . . . I said all along, that she'd be brought up with yours,' Carrie answered quickly. 'But I never said you could do what you wanted.' Indignation filled her. How could they do this? She wanted to strike out. 'I won't have it. I won't have the child decked out like . . . like a sacrifice. In white with flowers on her head. I've seen it, seen 'em parading up the street.'

Jane was standing her ground, her back to the mantel-shelf, the look of fright on her face giving the lie to her words. 'You'll have to stop it, Carrie,' she was saying in an appealing voice when Danny came bursting into the house.

He seemed to take it all in, Carrie noticed. He turned on her, one arm around Jane, white faced and furious. 'You've done it again, haven't you?' he said. 'You've come in here, telling us how to run our family, bullying your sister.'

'I've just found out what you're up to, Danny Kennedy,' Carrie blazed. 'You'll not take my child and do what you want with her.'

Danny took Jane by the arm and led her to the uncleared table where he made her sit. Then he turned on Carrie.

112

'You will let Rose grow up a good Catholic girl,' he said, as if every word was carefully thought out. As if he'd been rehearsing it. 'There is nothing you can do about it. Stop resenting our love for her.'

How dare he speak to her like that? A wave of anger swept through Carrie. She went towards him, her hand raised to hit him but he forestalled her. He came swiftly forward, caught her wrist in a grip of iron and twisted her arm until she cried out.

'If you did your job properly,' she said when he'd let her hand go, 'You'd . . .'

Now his voice was icy as he interrupted her. 'Our job?'

'Yes.' She flung the words at him. 'Your job! I pay you! I employ you. Both of you. You are bringing her up for me!'

As soon as she heard Jane's incredulous gasp she knew that she had gone too far. She knew it as soon as she saw the cold horror in Danny Kennedy's eyes.

'Do you really believe that?' he asked slowly.

She couldn't stop now. 'Of course. It's my house. I buy the food. I pay the bills. And she's my daughter!'

There was a pause when Danny looked into her face, dislike for her in every line of him.

'Prove it!' His tone was one of contempt.

'What? What do you mean?'

'You can't prove it, Carrie.' Danny went back to Jane's side and placed an arm around her shoulder. 'There's proof, proof incontrovertible, that she's our child. Ours!'

Jane was clutching on to his hand with both of hers. Tears were bright in her eyes. 'Don't, Danny. Don't,' she whispered. 'Don't do that to her.'

But Danny went on, in a voice of authority, as if he'd been wanting to say it for years. 'You have no claim to her. Forget you ever had her. And leave us in peace.'

Carrie felt as if the floor were giving way under her. It wasn't true. Were they turning against her? Were they going to turn her own child against her? Surely there was someone who knew that Rose was hers.

She took a deep breath and hesitated for a moment.

'There's your brother,' she said at last. 'Patrick knows. He knows she's mine.'

'So!' Danny said. 'At last. You've spoken his name. You said you never wanted to hear it. You'd wiped him from your mind, you said.'

He almost looked triumphant now, to Carrie.

'Then, when it suits you to remember, his name trips off your tongue.'

It was true, she knew. She had never spoken about him. But never had a single day gone by when she had not had to struggle to forget.

'We all lied to Patrick,' Danny was saying. 'He accepts that Rose is ours.'

Carrie pulled herself together. 'You write to him. You read his letters out to the children. You act as if he's some kind of conquering hero,' she flared. 'You hold him up as an example to the children. You can't tell me he thinks she's yours.'

'Patrick does not make special reference to Rose,' Danny said, in a controlled tone that Carrie had never heard him use before. 'And, let me tell you, from the day Jane and I held that baby – from the moment we stood in church and had her baptized – she was ours in the sight of the Lord. She became our child. Ours!'

'You can't do that,' Carrie said. Her anger had gone. Now it was her turn to be frightened.

'I think Patrick has forgotten his first doubts,' Danny said. He looked at her coldly. 'Do the same,' he ordered. 'Forget. From now on, we will pay our rent money into an account at the bank where it will be recorded in the proper manner. I'll feed and clothe my own family. We don't want your money. Or your interference.'

Jane had wiped her eyes on a corner of the tablecloth and was trying to stop him now. 'Don't be hard on her, Danny,' she said.

'How can you?' Carrie began.

But he would not be stopped. He raised his hand as if calling for silence from Jane who sat there, letting him say it. 'Oh, I can! I warned you. You've gone too far.'

Carrie knew now that she really had pushed Danny too far. She had better appeal to his decency. She let her shoulders slacken, she dropped her eyes from his and went to the chair at the fireside.

'I didn't mean it,' she said at last, looking at Jane as she spoke. She had not meant to upset Jane. It was Danny and this whole religious business that maddened her. 'I'm sorry, Jane. I'm sorry I made you cry. But you must know. You must know how I feel. You weren't brought up to believe all this.'

It seemed that Danny was not content with an apology. His lip was curling in a sneer as he added, rubbing salt into her wound, 'So, if you want to see Rose – our daughter – you'll have to behave yourself.'

'Danny, Danny! Don't!' Jane said. 'She's my sister. I love her. Don't hurt her, please!'

He turned back to Jane and kissed her on her forehead. 'It's all right, sweetheart. I'll not be dictated to, that's all.'

Then he turned back to Carrie and, tight lipped said, 'You are a tyrant. You've used us all for your own ends. You used Patrick to give you the child you wanted. You didn't want him afterwards.'

'That's a lie! A lie, Danny Kennedy! May you be struck down!' Carrie managed to say, breathless now with indignation, and still he went on.

'You've used Jane and me, to bring up Rose for you, thinking us soft and eager. You didn't want to lose face in the town. Oh, no. You must be looked up to. Be seen as the upright Miss Shrigley.'

'Jane!' Carrie appealed, 'Tell him it's not true.'

Danny was standing over her now, fury in his eyes. 'I expect you've some grand idea that one day you'll tell her, as if you were bestowing a favour, that you are the woman

115

who gave birth to her. Well, let me tell you – you'll do her more of a favour by keeping it to yourself. I'll not let my family go in fear of you. You've made an enemy of me brother. Don't make any more.'

Carrie didn't know what he was talking about. Enemies? She hadn't an enemy in the world. All she tried to do was her Christian duty.

But the strangest part of all, for Rose, was that on the following day Aunt Carrie came to the house after tea carrying a cardboard box as well as her brown shopping bag. She placed the box on the table and told Rose to look inside.

Rose untied the knots in the string as she'd been taught to do. Her hands were shaking: she knew it would be something nice for Aunt Carrie had the look on her face that came when she was particularly pleased. Rose felt Aunt Carrie's eyes on her as her small hands lifted the lid and moved aside the layers of tissue paper.

'Oh! Oh, look!' she whispered.

It was the most beautiful dress Rose had ever seen, made of white satin, with tiny pearls around the edge of the little scalloped collar and more around the front of the waist. It had a wide sash attached at the sides and tied in a big bow at the back where satin-covered buttons were placed, close together in a long line nearly to the hem. The skirt was full, gathered into folds and at the hem was a band of satin-stitch embroidery. It wasn't meant to be worn again and again because it would be impossible to let down such a hem. And underneath the satin skirt was a rustling taffeta petticoat.

Rose was overcome. 'For me?' She looked at Aunt Carrie and saw the look on her aunt's face.

'Take it out of the box then. Try it on,' Aunt Carrie said and Rose heard the eagerness, sensed the apology, in her aunt's voice.

Rose had a tight lump in her throat. She wanted to kiss

116

and hug and thank Aunt Carrie yet she knew that Aunt Carrie hated to see people showing their feelings. Aunt Carrie used to clench her teeth and stiffen, holding herself back, pushing Rose gently away, when she was little.

Now Rose dared not make a move towards her. There was a long silence before she flew upstairs and cried and cried. Then Mum came up and held her tight until she was calm and could put on the dress and show Aunt Carrie how lovely it looked.

And after Aunt Carrie had gone Mum let her go round to Alan's house, in the dress, with a coat over the top so that nobody else would see it.

Nan Tansley let her in. 'You've got something to show us, haven't you, Miss?' she said, her happy face splitting into a smile. 'I can see something pretty peeping out from under your coat.'

Rose peeled off the coat carefully and watched Nan's face as she opened her eyes wide and held her at arm's length to admire the dress.

'Eeh! I've never seen a prettier one,' she said. 'Go into the sitting room and show it to Alan and his Dad.'

Rose went as quietly as she could, holding her breath to give them a real surprise. At the door she stood for a moment, twisting her head to see that the bow was straight. She tried to hide her delight but, as she turned the handle of the sitting-room door, a huge smile flashed over her face and she could not help but keep it there.

Alan's Dad got to his feet. 'My word,' he said. 'You look like a . . . a little fairy.'

'I think I look like a bride,' she said. 'If I had a bunch of flowers I would. Wouldn't I Alan?'

Alan stood beside his Dad. 'Is it a wedding dress?' he asked.

'No, silly. It's my first-communion dress.'

'Will you wear one like that when you get married, then?'

It seemed that Alan was more concerned with the use of

the lovely dress, than noticing how pretty she looked. Rose found it exasperating, having to explain everything to a boy who clearly didn't know the difference between a wedding dress and a communion dress.

'I've told you before,' she said, shaking a finger at him, 'that I'm going to marry YOU when I grow up. And wear A LONG DRESS.'

Now Alan's Dad's laughter was booming out. But Alan was being silly, he deserved to be laughed at.

'So you'll be Mrs McGregor when you're a big girl, will you?' Alan's Dad asked.

'No. I won't,' Rose said. 'Alan will be called Mr Kennedy.'

'But,' Alan's Dad explained, 'the girl always takes the name of the boy when she marries.'

'No, she doesn't,' Rose told him firmly. 'The one who asks first is the one who chooses the name.'

And they were all laughing and admiring the dress and promising to come to church on the day she'd wear it and Rose had never felt so important in her whole life.

Mum must have said something to Aunt Carrie, too, for there was no more mention of Alan. They must have told Aunt Carrie to stop being so possessive for Rose was allowed to see her friend as often as she liked.

Danny's outburst had been a shock, there was no denying it. How could he say that she had made an enemy of Patrick? She had no enemies. And she never, never spoke about Patrick.

Carrie sat at her sitting-room window. It was the best and biggest room in the house. It was the room that would have been the main parlour. She didn't have a parlour in this Temperance Hotel. It only led to the lodgers taking liberties. They had a dining room and that was enough. She never spent time with the lodgers. Maggie Bettley and the girl saw to them.

Her room had a good view, overlooking Waters Green.

Outside, under her window and right up the Wallgate, the May Fair was in full swing. The fair came twice a year, in May and at the October Wakes. The noise of the crowds almost drowned the hurdy-gurdy music that came, scratchy-twanging mechanical music, from under the coloured canvas roofs towards her. Over the other side, around the iron stalls of the cattle market, she could see the crowds jostling around the coconut shy and the rifle-shooting bays.

It was years since she'd gone to the fair. She'd go down for an hour when she'd finished her cup of tea and decided what to do about Rose.

Now she remembered the rest of the row she'd had with Danny and Jane. Danny had been laying down the law, telling her how it would be from now on, telling her that Rose was to take her first communion, make her first confession – all that.

'And you'll come and watch it, if you've any soul, Carrie,' he'd said. 'She'll expect her aunt to be there.'

Oh, God! Could she do it? She remembered, with sickening clarity, the day Patrick told her that he'd confessed to that same priest all about himself and her. For all she knew that very priest would know that Patrick Kennedy was Rose's father. No. She couldn't. She'd feel she was betraying all she'd stood by, if she went into that place.

'And another thing,' he'd said. 'You'll allow her to have friends. What is it you dislike so much about her playing with young Alan McGregor?'

'You know very well,' she had answered. 'Douglas McGregor keeps in touch with your brother. Your brother is Alan McGregor's godfather. For all I know, your brother could have told him.'

'Nonsense. Patrick knows that Rose is ours. He'll abide by my wishes,' he'd answered her, full of importance. 'And so will you.'

It had been the right decision, she was sure it had,

119

letting Jane bring Rose up. She had kept her respectability. Nobody had questioned it. Rose was happy. And she would not have been happy, living here in Waters Green, the illegitimate daughter of a lodging-house keeper. But it wasn't right for Danny to deny her, for him not to acknowledge her own right to her own child. She felt the quickening pulse of anger against him. What had he said? That she was a tyrant? She tried to do her best for them, for Jane and Danny. They'd have a shock if she didn't. If they had to manage on what Danny earned there'd be a few changes. Danny didn't know that she gave money to Jane every week. She gave Jane £2 a week, to buy food and clothe the children.

She did her Christian duty to others as well. She helped the Gallimores – the decent, respectable poor. She helped them quietly as well, without any show, like you were supposed to do. 'To give and not to count the cost,' her father used to say when he put a guinea in the poor box.

It had been a shock when Danny had said that she couldn't prove she was Rose's mother. There were at least two people outside the family who knew: Patrick himself and Martha Cooper. Martha had attended to her on the day the child was born. Martha Cooper had taken off her milk and bound her. Martha Cooper had given her the stuff to take, the herbs and salts that she'd said would 'send her milk back'. Martha Cooper wouldn't have forgotten.

And Martha would be in Churchwall Street any day now, to deliver Brenda Gallimore's seventh baby. Brenda Gallimore, who was only a year or two younger than herself, would have her seventh baby in that little house in Churchwall Street. Flo, Brenda Gallimore's eldest, was a few months older than Rose.

But Martha had never even hinted. She'd never so much as mentioned Rose, never asked about the child.

On the day she'd had Rose, Carrie remembered, she'd spoken sharply to Martha, saying that she never expected to hear mention of what had taken place. And good cheerful Martha had turned on her, snapped out that she never betrayed a confidence and given her a look of grim disapproval. Martha had never said a word about it since that day. But surely she hadn't forgotten?

Carrie sipped her tea. She would make reference to it, discreetly, when she saw Martha at the birth. They still came for her, for Carrie, when there was a birth. She didn't get excited and she didn't panic at childbirth – not like she did for illness. No, they liked Carrie Shrigley there at a birthing. And she always took something with her; a fruit cake or a meat and potato pie for the family and a florin to put in the new-born's hand.

Carrie stood up. She would not need a coat. She put her cup and saucer on a tray, went to the door and, before locking it, looked around the room. There were some valuable miniatures over the fireplace. In the corner farthest from the window was a cabinet filled with Sèvres and Meissen, Rockingham and a few Chinese pieces. Her inlaid sideboard was covered with good silver and, in its bow-fronted drawers, there was enough Georgian cutlery to cater for a banquet. It was all good too. None of this modern deco rubbish. Rose's future would be provided for, if anything happened to her. And she wasn't going to make any announcements one day, like Danny said. She'd just keep it all for her, put it in her will.

She went down the stairs and out into the crowd. She'd have to get Danny to admit it. He couldn't deny for ever that Rose was hers. He must make a will, too and put her down as legal guardian of those girls, if anything happened to him and Jane.

Then, outside, she was caught up in the atmosphere of the fair and forgot her brush with Danny. Waves of music came to her over the noise of the crowds. It was funny how she didn't like merry-making yet she could never resist the May Fair, the smell of roasting meat on the spit, the tunes coming from all directions, the laughter of children.

Standing in front of the skittle alley, the swing boats riding high with their shrieking occupants behind her, a boxing booth next door with a crowd of young lads daring each other, she was all at once overcome with a longing to be carefree. Sometimes it hit her like this, like a weakness, and she let her desires have control of her imagination. She wanted all at once to have her own child by the hand, have her own man beside her, swing into the air, waste money on side-shows and rides, kick away all the traces of her conforming, non-conformist life.

'Miss Shrigley!'

The spell was broken. Old Mrs Gallimore was waving to her, trying to reach her through the crush. Carrie went towards her.

'Can yer come? Our Brenda's time's come,' Mrs Gallimore jabbered anxiously.

'Have you sent for Martha?' Carrie asked calmly.

'Haven't you heard?'

'Heard what?'

'Martha Cooper was widdered this afternoon,' Mrs Gallimore went on. 'It's all over the town. Her husband had a seizure and dropped dead on't spot. There's nobody else can deliver a baby proper-like. Will yer come?'

'Yes.' Carrie gave Mrs Gallimore a gentle push in the direction of the Hundred and eight steps. 'Get back to your Brenda. Tell her I'm on my way. I'll fetch my things.'

While Brenda was labouring, old Mrs Gallimore told Carrie all she knew about the death of Jack Cooper. Young Nat, who had been injured and was lame, would have to run the farm with the help of his mother. The boy was only about 14 years of age. Things would be hard for Martha for the next few years. The expectant mothers would not see much of Martha for a while.

It was two o'clock in the morning before Brenda Gallimore had been delivered of twin girls.

Later, when she returned to the Temperance Hotel in

the early hours of the morning, Carrie had come to a decision.

He'd not deny it like his brother was doing. Not him. Not Patrick Kennedy. In the sideboard cupboard, was an ebony box inlaid with ivory. In it were her writing things. She could take his address from the last letter he'd sent to Danny. They always left them on the mantelshelf at Wells Road.

He would have to say it, in writing. She must have it recognized for her own satisfaction. He was the only person in the world, beside herself, to whom the facts of Rose's birth mattered.

She went to her desk, spread a piece of deckle-edged note-paper out on her blotting pad, dipped the J-nibbed pen into the little china inkwell and, in the large sprawling hand which she had never been able to reduce to a neat copperplate, she wrote.

'Dear Patrick,' she began, 'You will be surprised to hear from me after all these years. Here are a few snapshots of me and our daughter, Rose.'

CHAPTER EIGHT

Alan's old playroom had been converted into a study and Rose, now an 11-year-old schoolgirl, sat on the cushioned window seat that ran round the square bay. Her hair had been tortured into plaits and she fiddled with the green satin ribbon where it lay on her shoulder. The rain drove relentlessly against the leaded window panes and the April garden was sodden and dreary.

'When do you sit the scholarship?' Alan asked.

Rose wanted to laugh at his bony wrists sticking out from his new school jacket. She wondered when he was going to stop growing. He was nearly as tall as his father and he wasn't 14 yet.

She threw the pigtail back and smiled. 'Next week. I'm dreading it,' she told him. 'I'm sure I'll never pass the thing and Aunt Carrie'll be mortified.'

Alan placed his armchair in front of her and stretched out his long legs. 'If you don't get to Middlefield High will you be very disappointed?'

'Yes. I think I'll die. I want to go. Though it was Aunt Carrie's idea that I try for there. Mum and Dad wouldn't mind if I went to the Catholic secondary.' Rose looked down at her wrinkled black stockings and began to hitch them up, pinching and pulling at the thick black cotton. 'It's the Latin I'm weak on,' she said. 'Please, Alan. Test me on the accusative, will you?'

'You're all right on it. We went through it again yesterday,' he said. 'You'll pass the Latin. Easily.'

She glared at him. 'It's all right for you. You did it at school. Aunt Carrie had to pay for a tutor for me.'

He gave her his oh-dear-me face, the one he made to tease her. Rose stuck her tongue out at him quickly before starting to giggle as she always did.

'Your Aunt Carrie'll want her money's worth,' he said. 'Is she just as bossy with Mary and Vivienne?'

'No.' Rose thought it a funny idea that Mary and Vivienne might be made to do anything. 'They're a bit slow. I don't think they'll ever learn much. Vivienne can only just read and she's been at school for three years.'

'Just because you're a little brain-box it doesn't mean that they're daft,' Alan said. 'You could help them.'

'Oh, I didn't mean that they're backward,' she replied hastily. 'It's just that, me being the eldest, my aunt seems to expect me to do everything.'

'Does she still boss your mother and father about?' Alan asked.

'I once asked why they let her do it,' Rose said.

'What did they say?'

'Mum said, "She can't help it, she's had a hard life," and Dad just laughed and said, "Don't let her worry you, my darling. Hell hath no fury like a woman scorned."' Rose threw her arms outwards in a dramatic gesture as she spoke, making him smile with her.

'Maybe she was jilted or something,' Alan suggested, then laughed as soon as he'd said it. 'I don't think anyone would dare jilt your aunt, do you?'

'No,' Rose began to giggle again. 'I can't imagine anyone daring to ask her for anything, never mind refuse her.' Her face went serious for a second before she added. 'Dad shouldn't say things like that. It's not kind. Aunt Carrie really loves us all.'

'She's keen for you to pass the scholarship, isn't she?' Alan said.

'Yes. That's the funny thing. Because if I get to the High School I'll be making a lot of new friends. And poor Aunt Carrie hates it if I talk about people she doesn't know. She always says "Why do you bother with them?"'

She grimaced as she tried to imitate her aunt's voice. 'And why it's always me she tries to keep near her, I don't know. It's really odd, Alan. She never asks where Mary and Viv are; she never takes them out with her. It's always me who goes out with her, every Sunday afternoon. She comes for me after her Sunday School.'

There were some bullseyes on the table. Alan reached over and threw one to Rose. Her hand shot out and she caught it whilst hardly stopping for breath. 'Where does she take you?' he asked.

She was trying to articulate her words with the handicap of a mouthful of bullseye. 'We go trailing through the cemetery so she can see who's put fresh flowers on the graves.' She was trying not to laugh; trying to keep the striped mint from popping out as she spoke.

'Then we walk round the swings. And they're padlocked on Sundays! Then when we get to her hotel, she just sits there and stares at me for a whole hour before she takes me home.'

She didn't bother to tell Alan about Aunt Carrie's sitting room, crammed with old furniture. That was a bit creepy. But Aunt Carrie's bedroom was lovely, and sometimes she'd beg her aunt to allow her to play in there and use all the things on her dressing table: the Yardley's lavender, the Oatine cleansing cream, the Grossmith face powder and the talcum powder in a box with painted ostrich feathers all round the rim. Rose loved the smell of Aunt Carrie's bedroom and the feel of Aunt Carrie's silky soft hand in her own as they walked home again. Aunt Carrie was a very strange woman.

'Perhaps she wishes she'd got children of her own,' Alan said.

'Perhaps,' she agreed noisily. 'But I don't want to talk any more about Aunt Carrie. It's wrong to talk about people behind their backs. Help me with the Latin, Alan. Please!'

*

The Kennedys' house was sparsely furnished. The floors were covered in linoleum with a pattern of orange and brown squares against a dun-coloured background. The living room had a thick rag mat in front of the fire, two armchairs with railed sides, an unpolished table with a matching bench and four Windsor chairs.

There was a front room, where Aunt Carrie kept a piano and a grandfather clock, both securely locked. In this room stood two leatherette armchairs and a whatnot. The front room had a carpet, grey and brown with a patterned border, and a framed photograph of a white building in Canberra, sent by Uncle Patrick, over the fireplace.

The room was opened at Christmas and on special occasions, as on the day the results were announced. That morning Rose had found two letters on the mat. One was a buff, official envelope addressed to herself, the other, with the Canadian stamp, was from Uncle Patrick.

Rose tore open the buff envelope and read; 'You have been awarded the Open Scholarship to Middlefield High School. Please indicate, by letter, if you intend to accept the place, which entitles you to free tuition for a maximum of seven years.'

There was more but Rose's eyes kept returning to those first few magic words.

'Mum! Dad! I've won it,' she almost screamed. 'I'll go round and tell Alan.'

She would never forget that day. Alan's father shook her hand and congratulated her.

'Ye've done well, lass,' he said. 'Ye'll go on now, to great things. I've no doubt.'

Nan Tansley beamed, blew her nose and dabbed at her eyes with a large blue handkerchief. 'Eeh, Rose. You're a right clever girl,' she said, over and over.

Alan, for the first time in his life, lifted her off her feet and hugged her. 'I knew you'd get it,' he said, looking as pleased as if he'd done it himself. 'Just think, Rose. There

127

are only three scholarship places for the whole town and you've won one. I'm proud of you.'

But it was Aunt Carrie's face that was, in a way, the best part. After she had told Alan, Rose went down to Waters Green to break the news. She almost ran, so eager was she to see Aunt Carrie's eyes light up with pleasure, for Aunt Carrie and she had always been close in a funny, arm's length kind of way. She knew how much it meant to her aunt, that she was a clever girl.

Aunt Carrie was in the market, buying fruit from one of the stalls, when Rose spotted her. She slipped in, between her aunt and a young woman who was buying, and pulled at the sleeve of Aunt Carrie's tweed costume. Aunt Carrie wouldn't want to be told here, 'in front of folks' as she'd likely say, so Rose said eagerly, 'I've something to tell you, Aunt Carrie. Something really big, really wonderful. Have you finished shopping?'

'Rose, love! You gave me a start,' Aunt Carrie said in the voice that was meant to sound stern, but Rose knew was hiding fondness and indulgence for her favourite niece. 'What ever's up?'

Rose tugged eagerly at her aunt, carried her shopping basket and urged her steps towards the Temperance Hotel.

As soon as they had put the basket down on the kitchen table Rose took her aunt's hands in hers and impulsively, though she knew Aunt Carrie liked to keep her distance, planted a great smacking kiss on the soft skin of her aunt's cheek.

'I've passed it!' she said, excitement making her gabble. 'The scholarship, Aunt Carrie! I've passed it.'

She stepped back and watched, in amazement and wonder, two great tears roll down Aunt Carrie's cheeks. Then she saw her aunt fumble in her costume pocket for a handkerchief, remove her glasses and rub furiously. She watched the mighty nose-blowing that followed and, finally, laughed eagerly as a smile spread across Aunt

Carrie's face; a smile as proud as if she had passed the scholarship herself.

Aunt Carrie took her into town and opened a savings account for her, with three guineas in it. Then, as if that were not enough, bought her a leather satchel and took her to the cycle shop in Rivergate and bought her a bicycle – a lovely black-painted bicycle with a basket on the front and a flat metal carrier on the back.

'You'll be able to ride home for your dinner, on that,' Aunt Carrie said. 'You'll never be able to stomach school meals.'

There was a shiny new bell on the handlebars and it rang true and clear. There wouldn't be a girl in Middlefield so well blessed.

Rose rode the bicycle home to show it to Dad when he came in for his dinner and, after the whole family had ridden it up and down Wells Road in turn, Dad sat at the table to read out Uncle Patrick's letter.

Rose could barely concentrate. Uncle Patrick was moving on again, by Canadian Pacific to Quebec . . .

'The train is enormous,' Dad was reading, 'bigger than any you've ever seen. It is almost a quarter of a mile long with an eight-wheeled engine like a great iron monster that towers above the platform. Each wheel is taller than a man and the driver has to clamber up six steps to reach it.'

What an adventurous life Dad's brother had, Rose thought as Dad turned the pages over and continued, 'Steamers on the estuary of the St Lawrence . . . the great grey citadel . . . Quebec . . .' Uncle Patrick always finished by asking for all their news, asking for snapshots of the family, enclosing pictures of himself and Alan's uncle.

What would high school be like? She'd read about girls' boarding schools, where they had midnight feasts and tuck boxes and played lacrosse and tennis. Middlefield High taught hockey and tennis. Middlefield High was a day school and therefore not as grand as those she'd read about

129

but the fees were high, the entrance examination was tough and it was recognized as the best school for miles around. High-school girls walked to school or came in by train from the country. Everyone in town recognized their distinctive uniform of navy blue and gold. Rose knew she'd love wearing hers.

But when the clothing list arrived by post, she and Mum read it with amazement and horror.

'We'll never be able to get all this, Mum,' Rose breathed as her eyes ran down the long catalogue of necessities. 'I have to have three of everything: dresses, gymslips, blouses and cardigans.'

Mum had fallen silent.

'And a velour hat, a Panama, winter coat, summer blazer, and a gabardine,' Rose's eyes were like saucers. 'A tennis skirt, hockey skirt, dancing slip, hockey stick and tennis racquet, satchel, pencil box, purse, black shoes, sandals, plimsolls, dancing shoes. They even tell you what kind of stockings and knickers to buy.' She sat down with a bump, on to the wooden armchair.

'Are there really people in the world who can afford to buy all those things? All new? All at once?' Rose read it again.

'What will we do?' she asked. 'You can't spend all that much. And look. It says here that I have to go to the school next week to be measured for them. So we can't make do with just one of everything. And you'll not be able to make a coat, will you?' Rose couldn't bear to see the look of disappointment on Mum's face. She swallowed hard and fought back her tears. 'I'll go to the Catholic senior, Mum,' she said. 'I really don't care which I go to.'

Mum gave her a great big hug and, when she spoke, her voice sounded as if it were about to crack. 'Don't get upset about it, Rose,' she said. 'Wait until I've spoken to Aunt Carrie.'

Aunt Carrie paid for everything, even the Cash's name tapes.

★

But there were times, once she was actually there, when Rose wished she'd gone to an ordinary school. For here all the girls were rich, or so it seemed to her. Their parents paid fees for them, every term. It was only the three scholarship girls who got in for nothing. And they were treated differently.

It seemed to Rose that scholarship girls were despised because they didn't live in grand houses, with parents who were important people. The girls always asked 'What does you father do?' as soon as they met a new girl and Rose, who was so proud of Dad, the best insurance salesman the County Insurance had ever had, had to endure their puzzled expressions and undecided air when she answered them.

Her worst moment came right at the start, on the first day when she put up her hand in class and before she could think, heard herself saying, 'Please, Sister . . .' The girls didn't even try to hide their mirth. She felt a burning wave of colour spread over her cheeks when even the form mistress began to laugh.

But it was worse for the other scholarship girls. One of them had no father, the other's was a labourer.

It was a whole year before she lost the feeling that she was a girl apart and found that she was becoming popular; found that the teachers liked her for her intelligence and the girls for her ability at games. Swots were looked down upon. But if you could score more goals than anyone else on the hockey field, even at centre half and had once taken the tennis coach to three sets you were revered.

She made one particular friend, Norah Blackford; one of the scholarship girls. Norah vied with Rose for top marks but otherwise they appeared to have little in common. Norah had a solemn, interesting face, a square but unathletic body, hair of dull blonde and was the most observant character Rose had ever met. Norah was poor, more so than Rose, and yet she had a quiet pride and a deadly determination never to be scorned. She was the

131

kind of girl, Rose discovered, who always found the right answer to a spiteful remark, and found it as soon as it was uttered. Rose, conversely, always thought of them afterwards.

The only thing Norah never spoke about was her absent father. Norah lived with her mother, a hard-working woman who worked long hours in a mill. Like Aunt Carrie, Mrs Blackford did not encourage Norah's friendships but, unlike Aunt Carrie, she was never rude or overbearing.

Perhaps, Rose thought, that's why Norah and I get along so well; we both understand the embarrassment of not being able to bring friends home. But it was not that, for Norah was not in the least troubled by her mother's taciturn manner.

'It's Hell being thirteen, isn't it?' Rose said as she and Norah ploughed through the park on their way home from school. They always took a short cut through the trees and shrubbery behind the tennis courts.

'Can't say it's bothering me,' Norah answered slowly. 'Do you want a game of tennis tonight? Here?'

'Could do. I'll meet you after tea. Say six o'clock?'

'Six o'clock,' replied Norah drily.

'You are an ass, Norah,' Rose giggled. 'You know what I mean.'

'Have you any money?'

'Three ha'pence. Have you?'

'No.'

'We'll climb over the wall then. The park keeper'll never see us. He's always half asleep when you want to pay.' Rose changed her satchel to the other shoulder. 'I'll have to be back for seven. Aunt Carrie's a bit tricky sometimes. She thinks it's immoral.'

'What is?'

'Showing your legs in public,' Rose laughed. 'She thinks that the sight of a bit of leg will drive men silly. I don't care if men go silly, do you Norah?'

'I think they start off with a big advantage anyway,' Norah answered. 'They're half daft to begin with.'

They had reached the park gates, where their ways parted.

'See you later, then.'

'All right.'

Rose ate her tea as quickly as she could. 'I'm playing tennis tonight with Norah, Mum. I want to be gone when Aunt Carrie gets here,' she explained. 'I'll change into my tennis dress and go.'

She buttoned the canvas cover over her racquet and placed two newish balls in her string bag. 'I've put my white skirt on over my tennis dress. In case Aunt Carrie sees me,' she called from the hall to Mum who was still working in the kitchen. 'Bye!'

When she reached the park gates Norah was waiting.

'Did you get the tuppence ha'penny?' Rose asked her.

'No.'

'We'll go over the wall then. Come on,' Rose encouraged her. 'Let's run up the avenue and climb into the courts that way.'

They knew the exact spot on the high brick wall where their feet would find purchase between the bricks. Once on top they had to sit astride the coping stones and shuffle themselves along until they were above the courts. Then they would drop straight down on to the spectators' area and wait until a court was free. Nobody checked, once you were in.

Rose gave Norah a leg-up on to the wall and clambered up after her friend. 'Phew,' she said when they were safely on top. 'Push on, Norah, before we're seen.'

'The courts are empty,' Norah called over her shoulder.

'Get down quickly and bag the one nearest the gates. If anyone asks for our money we can run for it,' Rose answered. 'Go on. Jump!'

Norah heaved her right leg on to the inside and dropped heavily to the ground, right on the spot that Rose herself was heading for. She tried to swerve in her leap, struck her foot on Norah's shoulder and felt her left thigh tearing on the gravel.

'Dash,' she said, lifting her skirt to inspect the damage. There was an ugly scrape, right at the top of her leg, at the back. It was bleeding, but not too badly. Her tennis skirt must have flown up.

'What a cheek!' Norah remarked with a solemn face. 'I can see half your bum. Pull your skirt down.'

Rose pulled at the leg of her cotton knickers, covering the spot. She winced but ended up grinning at Norah. 'You are funny, Norah,' she said. 'Come on. I'm not going to let it stop me.'

Because her leg smarted so Rose lost the first game to Norah. She hoped the graze didn't have dirt in it. She'd have a good wash when she got home.

Norah won the next game, through sheer determination. After that Rose started to win them all, but not too easily. Norah, scowling with concentration, would hardly let a ball pass her, returning even the ones that would probably have gone out.

Then the courts began to fill up and soon, Rose knew, somebody would come to claim theirs. 'Last game?' she shouted over the net. 'I'll buy a lemon cordial between the two of us from the refreshment place.'

'Right.' Norah slammed her last four services straight into the net and it was over.

Rose pulled her long skirt over her tennis dress and they walked, tired but happy, to the refreshment stand.

'What time is it?' she asked.

'Quarter to eight,' Norah replied. 'We'd better run.'

As soon as they had finished the cool drink they left one another, Rose running like the wind before Aunt Carrie could start fretting about her.

She had no idea why Aunt Carrie was so strict but the interrogations were becoming a perfect pest. Anyone would imagine she'd something to hide. As she ran she anticipated Aunt Carrie's questions and prepared her answers.

Where've you been? To the park. To the park? What for? To play tennis. Who do you play tennis with? A friend from school. Have you come straight home? Yes.

She turned into Wells Road, red-faced, gasping for breath and reached the gate of number 23 just as Aunt Carrie came to the front door

'Where've *you* been?' Aunt Carrie asked.

'To the park,' she replied, leaning on the gate, panting.

'What for?'

'Playing tennis,' she said. 'With a friend from school.'

'Did you come straight home?'

'Yes, Aunt Carrie,' Rose said wearily. 'And I'm dying for a sit down and a cup of tea.' This was cheeky and she knew it was. It implied that she wanted nothing else, not even to answer Aunt Carrie's questions.

Aunt Carrie let her go ahead into the living room but no sooner was Rose inside than she heard her aunt's high pitched voice at it's most annoying.

'What's that on your skirt? Blood?' she demanded.

Oh. Help. Now Aunt Carrie would want to know how it got there. She'd be livid if she knew that she'd climbed over the park wall. Rose began to think fast but no explanation came.

'What? I – I didn't know there was anything on my skirt,' she stammered. She turned her head and looked at the back of her long white skirt. There was a large bloodstain, more of a streak than a spot.

'Oh,' she cried, in mock alarm. 'I don't know how – don't know what I've done.'

'Oh, please,' she prayed, 'don't let me blush.' But she felt hot colour rise into her face as Aunt Carrie held her by the elbow.

'You don't get blood all over your skirt without knowing where it came from.' Aunt Carrie was almost

screeching. 'What have you been doing? Go on. Tell me.'
She was shaking Rose's arm now.

Rose cast pleading eyes on Mum. 'Can I have a cup of
tea, Mum?' she asked. 'I don't know where the blood's
come from. Honest I don't.'

She hated lying to Mum but now she just couldn't tell
anyone. If she told Mum she'd hurt herself, then Mum
would want to see where. And 13 was much too old to
show your bottom to anyone, even Mum. Tears were
stinging her eyes. 'Please, Mum! Make Aunt Carrie
believe me! I don't know!'

'That's enough, Carrie,' Mum was saying. 'She's done
nothing. You know as well as I do what it is.'

'You don't know, Mum! I haven't done anything! I
haven't!'

It wasn't even as if she were telling Aunt Carrie a real
whopping lie. Why did Aunt Carrie always question her
so? She dropped into the armchair and put her hands over
her face so that Mum wouldn't see that she was lying. Sobs
were shaking her now. She'd have to get out of this.
Maybe if she said she felt ill then Aunt Carrie would feel
sorry for her and stop haranguing her.

'Oh, oh,' she cried. 'I don't feel well. Can I go to bed?'

Suddenly Mum was at her side, her arm around Rose's
shoulders. 'Where's the pain, love?' she asked.

'In my stomach,' Rose lied. She knew that they'd let her
go to bed if she had stomachache.

'Get upstairs, pet. I'll bring you a cup of tea and a hot-
water bottle,' Mum said.

At her words of comfort Rose broke into loud sobbing
and hurled herself through the door and up the stairs. In
her bedroom she pulled off the stained skirt. There was
nothing on the short tennis dress but her knickers were
caked in blood. Mum was bound to see it. She ran to the
bathroom and washed her leg, rubbing furiously until all
the dried blood had gone and only the tiniest cut could be
seen. Then she coated it with Snowfire cream and talcum

powder so that it would be invisible and returned to bed, lying quietly, as if she really were ill.

After Mum had brought her the drink and the hot-water bottle and taken away the bloody knickers and stained skirt Rose began to feel calm again. She could hear Mum and Aunt Carrie arguing in the next room. They were trying to keep their voices down but if she strained she could hear every word.

'You know what it is, Carrie,' Mum said.

'She's too young,' Aunt Carrie answered. 'She's only just thirteen.'

'Some girls start at ten. So I've heard,' Mum's voice came clearly.

It was peculiar, Rose thought. Fancy making all this fuss about a drop of blood. And what did they mean? Start?

'You didn't. And I didn't. We're late starters in our family. I was seventeen when I first had mine,' Aunt Carrie was saying, her voice no longer angry. 'And you'd been married two years before yours started. That's why I was so against it.'

'That's not to say that Rose'll be the same.'

Of course it wasn't. Mum was right, Rose thought. She had no intention of getting married when she was young, whatever might start two years later. She wished Aunt Carrie would just stop talking like this.

'She's not even developed yet,' Aunt Carrie was saying. 'She's got no bust. Nothing. For all we know someone could have been tampering with her.'

Rose felt herself blushing again. She had got a bust. Only it was still very small. There were hard lumps where before it had been flat. They hurt her, especially if she forgot they were there and bumped them up against things. She always wished the earth would swallow her up when Aunt Carrie talked about her; about her body.

'You'd better talk to her then,' Mum said.

Rose heard their footsteps, heard Aunt Carrie's hand

turn the doorknob. She'd pretend to be asleep.

'Rose?' Aunt Carrie's voice was soft and wheedling. 'Rose?'

'What?'

'This blood, love. In your knickers. It'll happen again.'

The tears were coming. Rose fought them back with tight-shut eyes.

'It won't Aunt Carrie,' she whispered. 'I promise. It won't ever happen again.'

But Aunt Carrie was not to be stopped. 'And when it does, love, you mustn't cry. You must ask your mother for some boiled napkins. And fold them up and put them in your knickers. And ask your mother for a clean one when it's full. She'll wash them and put them in your drawer for you.'

Silent sobs were taking her now. Her shoulders were heaving under the covers. It must have been true. All those things the other girls said. Was that what they meant when they sat out of games? Was that why they cast their eyes up to heaven and said they were 'unwell' when asked for an explanation? She didn't want to bleed.

'Does it happen to boys?' she sobbed.

'No. Only to young women.'

'Why?'

'You'll know when you're older,' Aunt Carrie said.

'Who'll tell me? Will you?' She blurted out the words in her embarassment. 'And when?'

'You don't want to know all that,' Aunt Carrie's voice was sharper now, exasperated. 'It's better if you don't know. Just don't let anyone near you. Understand?'

'I think so,' she whispered, though she didn't understand at all.

'You must know so. If I ever thought anyone was going to touch you, I'd have him locked up! That I would.'

She was getting into one of her tempers now. I'd better say the right thing this time, Rose thought. Anyway, what did she mean 'touch you?' People touched each other all

138

the time. It wasn't a sin. How could it be wrong?

'I won't, Aunt Carrie,' she promised. 'I won't do anything you don't want me to do.'

'There's a good girl.' Aunt Carrie got to her feet, as if she were pleased. 'Just remember what I said. That's all'

When she had gone Rose lay, wondering what it all meant. All this bleeding and touching.

'I know,' she whispered to herself. 'I'll ask Alan. He knows everything.'

CHAPTER NINE

Alan made the run up to the wicket. His bowling had not been brilliant all day but he knew this was a good one as soon as the ball left his hand. A yorker! He heard the crack of hard leather on wood as the leg stump lifted and cartwheeled out of the ground. St Joseph's had won by twenty runs. The wicketkeeper raised his arms and it was all over.

There were a couple of house matches still to go and if he could manage to bowl a few more like that one he'd be in; the only 16½ year old to make it to the first eleven for ten years. Dad would be pleased, though cricket wasn't his game. Dad had been a rugby player in his youth.

Applause was coming from the stand beside their pavilion and he heard the light laughter and enthusiastic whooping from the girls who had turned out to support St Joseph's. Alan pushed his damp hair back and glanced across at the group in their pale dresses, wondering if he had the nerve to ask Gerald's sister to go to the Picturedrome tonight. She was about a year older than himself but he knew she liked him. He could just make out her dark hair. He'd been helping Dad at the Swan for a year, so he had some spending money; enough money to take her to the cinema. If she agreed to go he'd reserve one of the double seats on the back row.

She was standing next to a red-headed girl in a yellow dress who waved a hat towards the field, yellow ribbons fluttering in the spring sunshine.

The umpire handed him his pullover and Alan followed the team, sixth formers mostly, to the pavilion where the girls waited for their brothers and their brothers' friends. This was it. Gerald's sister would be asked by the captain if he didn't get to her first.

The red-haired girl was standing on the veranda in front of the pavilion with the captain talking to her. The captain always tried to play the charmer. Alan saw him put his hand under her elbow as if to steer her towards the tea-tent. She waved again – to him.

It was Rose. He crossed the last few yards of the green and looked up at her. She stood, holding on to the white-painted rails.

'Were you watching the match?' he asked.

'Yes. I've been here all afternoon. Didn't you see me?'

'Did you come alone?' He wasn't panting for breath any more. He climbed the wooden steps and saw that the captain had moved away from Rose's side and was giving him envious looks.

'No. There are one or two other girls from school here,' she said. 'One of them said you were playing for the firsts so I thought I'd come and watch.'

Alan was taken aback by the transformation in her. He'd seen her a couple of weeks ago when she'd come round after school looking, as she usually did, ruffled and untidy. But it was no wonder he'd not recognized her. Her long plaits had been cut off leaving her hair a bright haze of reddish-gold about a heart-shaped face. She'd discarded the thick stockings and black laced shoes and here she was, silk-stockinged, sandalled and looking grown-up.

'Let me change then we'll have tea. Grab a table and keep a chair for me,' he said. 'In there.' He pointed towards the door at the end of the veranda, where Gerald's sister stood watching them.

The captain was untying his spiked boots when Alan reached the locker room. He didn't look up, but as Alan leaned across to unlock his door, said, 'I don't know how you do it, McGregor. Half of those girls are here to watch you.'

'I wish they were!' Laughing, Alan took off his boots. Then he said, hoping the captain would lay off her, 'I like Gerald's sister, though. I think I'll ask her to go out somewhere.'

'Who's the red-head? The one in yellow?'

'Who?' Alan stuffed his boots into the locker and reached for a towel. He tried to appear nonchalant and used to it in the presence of these older players. 'Oh. You mean Rose – Rose Kennedy.' He stood at a washbasin next to the captain's and pulled the white cotton shirt over his head. 'She's a friend of mine.'

'How old is she?'

'Fifteen, I suppose. Too young for you.' Alan had to bend at the knees to look in the cracked mirror.

The captain gave him a knowing look. 'I'd wait a few years for her. What a knock-out she'll be!'

Alan had never thought of Rose as a knock-out. He wondered what her reaction would be when he told her that the captain of the first eleven thought she was pretty. Still, he had to admit that she looked very pretty, dressed up. He'd not get a chance to talk to Gerald's sister with Rose there.

In the tea-room Gerald's sister sat with her brother and two other girls. Alan saw her brown eyes follow him as he took his place next to Rose. He had changed into flannels and a blue shirt and he dumped his bag of cricket whites under the rattan table.

'You look nice,' he told her. 'It's the first time I've seen you in a proper dress for years.'

'Aunt Carrie bought these things for me,' she said.

He liked the short hair. It suited her. She had pale skin and a long slender neck which he'd not noticed before. The yellow dress was edged with a rolled-back collar of plain silky stuff and it dipped in a low vee at the front making him aware of the shape of her.

'Your aunt? Has she had a seizure or something?' he asked.

142

Rose laughed. She had a low, attractive laugh and Alan saw the captain, who had found a place at the next table, look at her with interest.

'No. She's taking me away. On holiday!'

She leaned forward and lowered her voice. 'I've got to tell you something, Alan. I'm really worried. Can I come round after supper?'

Alan knew that the captain was listening to every word. He frowned, as he thought, significantly, to warn her to keep quiet until they were alone. Rose had a disconcerting habit of blurting out whatever was troubling her, regardless of where they were.

'Shh,' he said, trying to warn her that they were being overheard.

'But, Alan!' the pitch of her voice was lifting now and Alan knew that the captain's eyes had never left her face.

'Rose, shut up, will you?' he said. She was impatient and impulsive and he was forever telling her to hold her breath and count to ten before she spoke or acted. She never heeded his advice. Now she was about to explode into one of her confidences, oblivious of the other people.

'Alan! I've been waiting for hours to ask you something and it's really, really important.' Her eyes were starting to brighten.

He pushed back his chair and got to his feet. 'Come on,' he said. 'Tell me on the way home. I can do without the tea.' He led the way and noted that Gerald's sister turned her head to watch him as he steered Rose towards the door.

They had to walk round to the front of St Joseph's, the long red-brick and limestone school, along the wide gravel path which bordered the quadrangle. Gowned masters crossed from the staff door to the boarders' entrance and Alan knew that a good number of the younger boys would be watching from the refectory.

'Alan!' Rose sounded anxious.

He didn't want her to tell him here, where the juniors

were peeping at them from an upstairs window. He walked faster.

'What?' he said.

'Can I tell you now? Something really private?'

Alan looked behind them. 'Wait until we're out of the gates, will you?' he said.

'Come on then. Run!' She speeded her pace, overtaking him. 'Hurry up, Alan. It's vital.'

They were outside in the tree-lined avenue. The great wrought-iron gates were behind them. Alan leaned against the high stone wall. Now she could say what she liked.

'What is it?' he asked, and he smiled at her and tried to make amends for being short-tempered. 'Tell me.'

Rose's face, normally so pale, was bright pink and her eyes were troubled. 'Can you get a baby from kissing?'

The question was asked in such a rush that Alan was not sure he'd heard her properly.

'What?' he said.

She began to cry. Her wide mouth was being pulled downwards at the corners and soft, snorting noises came from the back of her throat.

'Can you get a baby? From kissing?'

'Of course you can't.' He couldn't bear to see her crying. He never could. When she was little he used to feel at a complete loss if she cried; he never knew what he was supposed to do about it. He fished in the pocket of his blazer for a handkerchief. 'Here,' he said, offering it into her hands. 'Stop crying. Tell me all about it.'

She fell into step beside him, alternately sniffing and blowing her nose. 'A boy kissed me, Alan,' she said. 'He held me down and kissed me.'

'Who did?' Alan felt a quick surge of anger towards the boy.

'I don't know his name,' she said and the awful crying threatened to come over her again.

'Well, how?' Alan demanded.

'You know the way I come home from school – we can

144

cut through the park or walk down Victoria Road?'

'Yes.'

She stopped walking and turned to face him. 'These boys jumped out – they pulled us, Norah and me, into the bushes in the park and . . .' The sobs were starting again but she blew her nose loudly. 'The one who'd caught me put his hands behind my head so I couldn't move away, and . . .'

'He kissed you?' Alan finished the sentence for her.

'He pushed his great fat tongue into my mouth, Alan.'

Her voice was getting louder but it didn't matter, the road was empty. She was looking at him with such indignation that all at once he had an urge to kiss her himself.

'His spit went in my mouth, Alan,' she wailed, 'and . . . and . . . I swallowed it!'

He knew she meant it. But he could hardly believe his own ears. 'Surely you remember what I told you?' he said.

'Yes, but are you sure? How do you know? Who told you?'

This was ridiculous. How could she doubt it? It was plain old common knowledge that had never been hidden from him. And he'd told her all she'd wanted to know, ages ago. 'I've known as long as I can remember,' he said. 'And I told you two years ago.'

'I know! But you told me all about sheep and cows.' She was looking at him with pleading eyes. 'And we had a lesson at school. We had to have signed permission to go to it,' she said, trying to hold back her tears.

'Well? You know, then. What did they tell you?'

'They told us all about rabbits. How they grow inside the female.'

'Well?'

'And the males. They make the seeds.' Now she was staring at the path, not looking at his face.

'So what makes you think you can have a baby from

145

kissing, Rose?' He could not understand it. 'You're not a fool.'

She looked up after a moment's hesitation. 'The biology teacher didn't tell us all of it. Nor did you. She never told us how the seeds got inside the female. We knew she didn't want to tell us. I thought it was only me who didn't "twig it" but Norah doesn't know either.'

'But we're just the same as the animals,' he said with a sigh of bewilderment. 'You've seen animals. Dogs and cats.'

She pressed her mouth into a firm line and gave him a starchy look. 'We are not animals,' she said. 'We are "set above the animals" according to the nuns, Alan.'

Her obstinacy made him speak sharply to her now. 'Listen,' he said. 'I've helped Nat Cooper for years. There's only one way you can get a baby.'

'Doing It?' she asked. 'Like the animals do?'

'Yes.'

She began to walk slowly and he kept pace beside her again. It was a few seconds before she spoke. It was as if she were thinking it over. 'Oh,' she said at last. She cast a shy, sidelong look his way. 'I never . . . never made the connection, somehow.' She turned her gaze on to her feet as she walked beside him. 'I suppose it's obvious really. Sometimes I just don't see the most obvious things,' she went on in a mournful voice. 'I don't seem to think in straight, logical lines. I always look for great complications.'

'Don't you believe me?' he asked earnestly.

'That means that Mum and Dad have Done It. At least three times.'

He smiled. 'That's what people get married for,' he assured her.

'I thought it was a sin.'

'It is, if you're not married.' He was trying not to laugh now.

'It isn't afterwards?'

'No. People get married so they can do it.'

146

'They must both want to Do It, then,' she said at last. 'I can't imagine why.'

She was beginning to smile again then all at once went serious and looked at him accusingly. 'You thought girls had periods, didn't you?' She stopped walking. 'Every month?'

'Yes.'

'I had one, two months ago,' she said, 'and no more after that.' She scuffed the toe of her sandal in the gravel.

'And you thought you were going to have a baby?'

'Yes.'

'Look at me, Rose.' He took hold of her hand and turned her to face him. Her dark blue eyes were misted under wet black lashes. 'You can't get babies any other way. Not from kissing. Not even from French kissing.'

A smile of mischief was breaking through, he saw, and he went on, holding her hand firmly. 'Perhaps girls' periods aren't regular right at the start. And Rose?'

'Yes.'

He didn't want other boys to kiss her. It had given him a quick jealous shock when she'd told of the boys who had waylaid her. 'Don't let anyone kiss you.'

'I hated it, anyway,' she said emphatically. 'I hope nobody ever tries it again.' She began to walk ahead of him, carefully placing one foot on the grass verge, one on the footpath as she went.

She was beautiful, slender and graceful. He wondered how it was he'd missed seeing it in all the years he'd known her. 'You won't say that in a few years' time,' he said. 'The captain of our first eleven called you a knock-out.'

She stood stock-still and looked at him with incredulous eyes. 'The silly ass!' she said.

One minute she was his friend, the next she was like the older girls. Alan knew that their childhood friendship was over. He'd have to start treating her like a young woman. But how?

'Come round after supper?' he said.

'All right. But I'll have to be home for nine.'

'Aunt Carrie?'

'Yes.'

She had forgotten her fears now. Now she was going to tell him all her news. It would come tumbling out; all she'd done at school and at home since she'd last seen him.

'Wait until I tell you what happened yesterday,' she said.

When she went round to Alan's house later, Rose told him what she'd heard the evening before. She had been weeding her patch of garden ready for the pansies and asters she wanted to plant out. It was eight o'clock and there was hardly any daylight left but, bent double, under the window of the living room she worked fast, loosening and pulling long runners of couchgrass that had spread from the lawn into the small, brick-bordered square of soil.

Aunt Carrie was inside and Rose heard her say in a startled voice. 'He wants what?'

Rose could hear her aunt clearly through the closed window. She kept her head down. Aunt Carrie had always been easily upset and she had no intention of being a witness again to one of her aunt's outbursts. In a minute she'd slide along under the window, let herself in at the front door and go up to her room.

'He's coming here.' Mum sounded determined.

Rose stopped weeding and listened. They must be talking about Dad's brother. He had sent them a telegram from Dublin to say that his wife had died. Uncle Patrick and his wife had never lived together, Dad had told her. The marriage had been a mistake from the start but when he heard that she had died he had come over from Canada to Dublin to see the relatives.

'He can't.' Aunt Carrie's voice had gone high. It had a note of fear in it. Rose knew every inflection of her aunt's voice.

'You can't stop him, Carrie.' Her mother's tone had taken on the placating note she used to her sister. 'His wife's dead. He'll only be here for a week, until the boat sails from Liverpool. He wants to see her.'

Rose kept as still as she could. Which one did Patrick want to see?

'When is he coming?' Rose heard Aunt Carrie get to her feet. Chairs were scraping along the floor. All at once she was afraid that she'd be seen and she crouched lower and pushed her back against the wall of the house.

'The week after next.'

'You two can entertain him, with Mary and Vivienne,' she heard her aunt say. 'I'll take Rose to Southport.'

Rose and Aunt Carrie were to catch the early train to Southport in the morning and Rose, for the first time was to sleep overnight at her aunt's. She had not minded being the one to miss the visit of Dad's brother. She was sure that he hadn't specially wanted to see her. And this was to be her very first holiday.

Aunt Carrie's sitting room in the Temperance Hotel was cluttered. In contrast with their own house in Wells Road which had Dad's drawings in the hall, Mum's flower pastels and some pictures from abroad in the front room and, in the living room, a holy picture and a print of *The Boyhood of Raleigh*, Aunt Carrie's room was like a gypsy's den. There was barely an inch of wall that wasn't covered in pictures; there was hardly space on top of the furniture for more than the china figures, porcelain vases and silverware they already held. Most of it, Aunt Carrie told her, had come from her old home; the rest she'd collected.

'But you've no room to move about in, Aunt Carrie,' Rose said. 'I'd get rid of most of it, if it were mine.'

'No you wouldn't. Not if you knew what it's worth,' Aunt Carrie said. 'They're worth more than the house, Rose.' She looked hard at Rose and lowered her voice, as if afraid that the neighbours might hear her. 'And when they come to you, mind you don't let them go,' she added, smiling mysteriously.

Rose couldn't imagine that she and her sisters would want to hang and display the things Aunt Carrie thought of as works of art. Aunt Carrie was funny; she turned her back on love and friendship yet gloated over her little knick-knacks.

'All right,' she answered, trying to ignore the look in Aunt Carrie's eyes. 'I'll see they're taken care of.'

For as long as she could remember she'd had this sense that Aunt Carrie was only a few yards away, watching her; she had always felt that every decision regarding herself had to be approved by Aunt Carrie. When she was younger she used to look first at Aunt Carrie after she'd spoken, knowing from a movement of the lips or eyebrows whether or not her aunt was pleased. It had seemed as if Mum faded into the shadows and let Aunt Carrie take charge.

If the moment ever came when she'd have to stand up to Aunt Carrie, she'd do it. But today, with Aunt Carrie in such a changed mood she'd better not spoil things.

'Where's the case?' she asked. 'I've brought all my stuff round in a parcel. I haven't a bag of my own.'

'I'll buy you one, in Southport,' Aunt Carrie replied. 'Put your things in the case next to mine.'

It felt odd, packing her things in the heavy leather case of Aunt Carrie's. She folded her clothes: slips of patterned artificial silk, skirts and blouses she'd made on the treadle sewing machine from material bought in the market, her navy-blue bathing costume with a red stripe that went from her left shoulder to her right thigh and the new sandals and dress Aunt Carrie had bought for her.

She wanted to giggle when she saw Aunt Carrie's deep pink corsets with the long strings wrapped around them. Aunt Carrie didn't need corsets, she was slim and straight and it made Rose want to laugh, thinking of her holding her breath and pulling the laces tight. Next to the corsets,

150

even funnier, were Aunt Carrie's silky vests and pink silk bloomers with elasticated knees.

But Aunt Carrie was taking all the nice-smelling stuff off her dressing table and Rose knew her aunt would let her share them. She loved Aunt Carrie's scented things. The Floris Gardenia was her favourite. Like her aunt she was revulsed by certain odours that others scarcely seemed to notice. She held her breath when she passed Potts' shop on coffee-roasting days and she dared not enter Cartledge's, where sacks of smelly meal for rabbits and things stood around the floor.

She and Aunt Carrie shared the same tastes in food too. Neither of them could eat meat that hadn't been prepared at home and sometimes they would both crave the same things on the same day. 'I need to eat something dark green,' they had said almost in unison, one spring morning.

Rose could not help out at church rummages where old clothes were brought for sale, for, even though they had been washed, there was a sour smell to them that turned her stomach.

But her aunt was packing the Elizabeth Arden face cream, the Pond's cold cream and two new pieces of Cuticura soap. It was baby-soap really; Aunt Carrie said it was the only stuff that didn't irritate her sensitive skin.

'Where will we stay?' Rose asked. 'Is it near the sea?'

'A woman at chapel told me about it. I've only been to Southport once, on a Wakes Monday trip. We'll get a taxi from the station.'

Aunt Carrie had one tiresome fault in the eyes of Rose and her sisters; she talked about money too much. The Kennedys never spoke about money. Aunt Carrie spoke about little else but the need for thrift, though she was given, now and again, to wild extravagances. Rose wondered at her aunt for going to the expense of a taxi. It'd cost her a shilling, at least.

Rose was as excited as a child. She lay wakeful all night

151

in one of the attic bedrooms, trying to imagine what Southport would be like. She knew that there was a pleasure ground, a long pier with a tramway and parks and gardens galore. Her friends at school had told her that there were glass canopies in front of the shops and that the shops were full of beautiful clothes, even better than those in Lewis's of Manchester. Rose made her own dresses by copying the clothes she saw in Lewis's. Southport had sea-water baths and an outdoor bathing lake, a boating lake, a miniature railway and wide streets with even bigger houses than those of Lincoln Drive. She wanted to see everything.

Whilst Rose was lying in her bed imagining the delights of the seaside holiday, Carrie, in her bedroom, could not sleep for the palpitations that made her heart feel as if it were throbbing in her throat.

It was because she was afraid, she knew. Patrick Kennedy was on his way to Middlefield and she had to leave town until he was gone. She could not have faced him in front of Jane and Danny. And Rose.

Ever since her first letter had flitted its tentative way over the seas they had corresponded regularly and, to Carrie's unease, secretly. For he never mentioned in his letters to Jane and Danny that he wrote to her. And he should have done. She had not asked him to make a secret of it though he'd have known she could not, herself, justify writing to him after all this time.

If he had been a gentleman, she reasoned, he would have said in his letters to Jane and Danny something like, 'I have written to Carrie and hope she replies'. Then, for her part, she could have announced that she had heard from him. But, no, he'd made it all undercover, so that now it was like a conspiracy from which she could not withdraw; so that now she never dared say anything when Jane and Danny spoke about him, in case she tripped herself up.

But the most unsettling thing was that before their

correspondence started she had managed to subdue her passions. Since, with every letter, the old feelings were evoked and her treacherous mind seemed bent on remembering their lovemaking. She had to remind herself, every time she held a letter in her hand, that he had deceived her and led her from the paths of righteousness. She tried to order her pulses not to race as she opened his letters.

And, right from the start, he had not acknowledged that he was the father of Rose. She remembered his reply to her first letter. 'The photographs are very good and are much appreciated. Rose is a lovely child with the Kennedy look about the eyes and mouth, don't you think?'

She had been disappointed. She'd wanted proof; proof to show to Danny if ever he said those wicked things again. In the letter he'd gone on to talk about himself and John McGregor and their great adventures in the Canadian Arctic where they'd spent a winter fur trapping with the Cree Indians. He'd enclosed a photograph of himself skinning a fox, just to disgust her she thought.

She had written straight back, asking why he had not put it in writing that he was Rose's father, and his answer, which had taken three months to reach her said 'Stop this, Carrie. Rose is Jane and Danny's daughter. All that which is the child's natural love for her parents belongs to them. I have to think of her as theirs. Don't you see that?' Then again he'd gone on to write about how the fur trade wasn't for him and that he and John McGregor were going back to Quebec. But it was a kind of admission.

Since then his letters had been shorter versions of the ones he sent to Jane and Danny and perhaps to the McGregors since he was Alan McGregor's godfather. And always, in his letters to her, there was a paragraph right at the end where he came out with something double-edged with meaning. It was always there. It was as if he couldn't end his letters on the simple, friendly note he started with. And every time a letter came, every time she saw that handwriting, her heart started beating faster, just as it used to do when he came near.

Tonight she couldn't sleep for thinking about him. There were times when it came over her again, like a recurrent illness. They said that malaria was like that, striking out of the blue, making you feverish. There were times like tonight when, if she didn't control her imagination, she would be back, lying, naked, in his arms.

And she didn't want to think about him. What was done was over and done. He had been her downfall but she had risen above it. She was a respected, respectable woman now. A single woman could never aspire to the heights of importance that a married one could; not in a town like Middlefield. But she had her place here. She told herself she should be content. And she feared that she was not.

She got out of bed and went to the wardrobe where she kept the ebony box in a drawer, lest Rose should come across it. It was light outside and she took his last letter to the window and read it again.

'Here is a photograph of myself and John McGregor, timber felling,' he had written. Carrie put on her glasses and peered again at the two men whose faces were nearly obscured by their steel helmets. Patrick, recognizable in the foreground, was holding what was evidently the focal point of the picture, a large unwieldy power saw that looked like an engine. He was cutting into the massive trunk of a pine tree.

She had felt a wholly irrational stab of jealousy, she remembered, on seeing the same picture, only larger, on the Wells Road mantelshelf. It seemed he was beginning to settle to something at last. He and John McGregor had been loggers for a few years. Patrick was the manager of the company now.

Then, here it came in the last paragraph: 'Is it satisfying, Caroline Aurora? Your hidebound existence behind closed gates? Does seeing the Kennedy girls every day meet your own needs? Are you getting enough out of life?'

How could he ask such things? Satisfying? Get enough out of life? Needs? Did he ask these things deliberately, to unsettle her?

She stared into the empty space around her, and pulled the angora bed-jacket closer, over the top of her cold arms. He knew. He knew it wasn't enough. It was not even enough that she would have Rose to herself for two weeks.

She forced herself to think of Rose, not of herself and the longings, the sinful lusts of the flesh, that Patrick called needs.

Rose was growing up and looking ahead to her own future; a future, modern girls being what they were, in which parents would not loom large.

The papers were full of the carryings-on of the young women in London, the Bright Young Things they were called. It would be a while before it spread up to Middlefield but Manchester wasn't far away. Manchester was never far behind London. Rose was going to take her School Certificate examination and was beginning to talk about going to a college in Manchester.

She'd got that from him. From Patrick. He'd been educated. Patrick had been to a good college, Danny boasted. Well, it hadn't done him much good. Apart from writing a good letter. and they were good. They made Canada come alive for everyone who read them. Apart from his vivid descriptive powers he'd wasted all his learning. He should stick to writing about the lovely places he'd seen, instead of upsetting her with questions like that; making out her life was empty.

Her life was full.

She would stop thinking about him. She would not think about his questions. And she must see that Rose was put to something. If she wanted to train for a job she could be apprenticed to a dressmaker since she liked sewing. Or take up shorthand and typing, here in Middlefield. If Danny and Jane encouraged her to go to that college in Manchester then who knows who she'd meet. Rose must only meet the best people. She was a cut above the rest.

When she was older, Carrie herself would introduce her to some nice young people from respectable, chapel-going families. There was to be no more talk about going away to college. If Rose had got that from him an' all, the wandering streak, she'd have to squash it. Oh, dear, her thoughts were back with him again. Her daughter must be a credit to her. Looked up to. Particular.

She went back to bed and concentrated her mind on planning for their holiday. She would not, dared not, imagine the gratifying of her needs and wants.

CHAPTER TEN

The two train journeys were thrilling. When they arrived in Manchester Aunt Carrie took her to a cafeteria; the first one Rose had seen. She was so bewildered and tempted by all the dishes set behind the glass, took so long to make up her mind which food to choose, that the people behind her complained and received the sharp end of Aunt Carrie's tongue in reply.

Aunt Carrie was beginning to smile. She'd closed her eyes on the second train and taken her glasses off and Rose had seen that her aunt was relaxed and happy. It was also the first time she'd ever seen real beauty in her aunt's face and the thought came to her that her aunt was really quite a good-looking woman. If she smiled more often, didn't need those ugly glasses and wore pretty colours she'd look much nicer, she thought.

And they were here, following the crowd out of the station and waiting in a long line for a taxicab. It would be her first ride in a motor car.

'Oh! It's beautiful,' she said when the taxi turned on to Lord Street's wide boulevard. 'Look at those shops, Aunt Carrie! And the trees! Imagine the lucky people who live here!'

The taxi stopped outside a terraced house, not far from Lord Street and the driver carried their case into the tight little hallway. The lobby, Mrs Bloor called it.

Mrs Bloor was very old. She was a quiet little woman who provided, for eight and sixpence a week each, what she called Rooms with Service; a bedroom with two iron-framed beds, washstand and wardrobe and, downstairs, a sitting-dining room.

They ate in the sitting room. They ate their own food which Mrs Bloor cooked for them, the way Aunt Carrie told her to; and they ate the kind of rich food Rose had seldom tasted before. It was as if Aunt Carrie didn't want to lose face. Every day she shopped in the morning for thick rump steaks and new potatoes or fresh salmon and garden peas and every single day they ate strawberries and cream with bread and butter for their tea.

Aunt Carrie was never like this at home. In Middlefield she complained if Mum bought too much stewing meat or more than enough fish to go round. And here she was spending as if she had no end of money.

Every morning they'd wash in the water Mrs Bloor brought up to the bedroom and not even bother to empty it into the pail under the washstand. There was no bathroom at Mrs Bloor's house and Rose felt sorry for the frail old lady having to lift the heavy china washbowl. But as soon as she went to pour it away on the first morning Aunt Carrie stopped her.

'Leave it,' her aunt ordered. 'We're paying her to do it.'

When they were dressed they went downstairs and took grape nuts and butter out of their cupboard and Mrs Bloor brought toast, fried bacon and eggs and a large pot of tea. They didn't have to 'side the table' as the girls did at home but left the little house, to shop and amuse themselves all morning.

The first two mornings Rose spent in choosing heart-shaped brooches for Mum and her sisters from a shop that sold mother-of-pearl. Dad was to get a stick of pink peppermint rock and a pipe-rack with his initials done in poker-work.

It was hot, even for Southport in July. Everyone said so. Rose swam in the sea-water lake every afternoon. She wanted brown legs, so she lay on her towel, facedown, then faceup for an hour afterwards before joining Aunt

Carrie at the military band concerts round the Lord Street bandstand. She had to stand behind her aunt's chair as the session was nearly over. Even though Aunt Carrie was spending so much money it seemed that she baulked at the wastefulness of paying for a seat that would only be used for ten minutes.

It was funny, too, the things that Aunt Carrie was doing here in Southport. Things she never did in Middlefield. They went to the cinema here every evening yet Aunt Carrie always had something to say if Mum and Dad took them to the pictures too often at home. Dad always told them, laughing, that Aunt Carrie went secretly, by herself, sitting in the best seats with a box of chocolates but Rose had never believed him, until now.

Here, they laughed uproariously at Charlie Chaplin in *Modern Times* and held their breath with excitement, seeing Robert Donat in *The Thirty-Nine Steps*. There were thirteen cinemas in Southport and with the programme changing twice a week it was hard choosing which to go to every night. They went to the Trocadero at the end of the first week to see *The Scarlet Pimpernel* where Rose sighed every time Leslie Howard came on to the screen; she would be madly in love with him for days afterwards.

She noticed Aunt Carrie's eyes brightening when the man who played the organ went into the haunting tunes of *These Foolish Things* and *The Touch of Your Lips*. So Aunt Carrie did have a romantic side to her, Rose thought; glad of the cool evening darkness where she tried not to let the deep plush seats scratch her hot legs which, so far, were only freckled.

They had been there for ten days when Rose took sick. After the shopping in the morning, as was the pattern of their days, they had taken the tram to the top of the pier and watched the pierrot show. Rose knew by heart all the songs the Follies sang. She was going to teach them to Vivienne when she got back.

The pier was long and hot and on the return it felt as if

they would never reach the end. Rose asked Aunt Carrie if she could have an ice-cream with lemonade in the great glass pavilion at the pier entrance. It seemed as if Aunt Carrie could refuse her nothing and Rose, when she had finished the ice cream, asked for a tub of shrimps from the kiosk they passed on the way to Mrs Bloor's.

There was a chocolate shop on the corner of Lord Street and in the window a display of chocolate rabbits in a green velvet field. Aunt Carrie bought one for her, making her promise not to eat it until after their meal but Rose surreptitiously ate the head as they walked along under the trees, almost fainting in the heat when they turned the corner.

'It's a nice bit of roast lamb, today,' Aunt Carrie told her. 'And I've asked her to do a tray of roast potatoes with it and a rhubarb tart and custard, while she's got the oven on.'

'I don't feel very hungry,' Rose ventured, hoping that, for once Aunt Carrie would let her leave her dinner.

'You've got to eat,' Aunt Carrie told her in the voice Rose used to think of as demanding, though now she knew that her aunt was trying to be motherly and matter of fact. 'What d'you think would happen if you didn't eat? You're too thin as it is. I want to see you looking well when we go back.'

She couldn't eat a bite. She pushed the meat around her plate, willing it to disappear. She took a forkful of chopped spinach and felt her knees go weak. She clutched at the tablecloth and saw that Aunt Carrie had put down her own knife and fork. But Aunt Carrie's voice was coming from far away.

'Why, child, you're as white as death,' Aunt Carrie was saying. 'Are you feeling ill?'

Rose felt as if the floor were coming up to meet her and she was falling backwards.

The chamberpot was being held under her chin and Aunt Carrie's hand was around her waist. Her head was hot and yet she was shivering. She couldn't get warm and she couldn't be sick. She pushed the pot away and fell back on to the bed. Her breath was coming fast and her teeth were chattering. And as well as this Aunt Carrie was starting to have one of her horrid turns.

'Mum! Mum!' Rose found herself crying. Hot tears were coming from her dry, prickling eyes.

'I'm here, love. I'm here!'

Aunt Carrie's voice was high and hysterical and her outburst so unexpected that Rose's tears stopped for a moment as she looked at her aunt. Aunt Carrie had taken off her glasses and was sitting, one hand under her nose, the other clenching and unclenching around the bedcovers and her eyes were staring and terrified.

'You'll be all right. I'm here. Do you hear me, Rose?' Aunt Carrie was beginning to cry. Rose found it made her feel even worse.

'I want my Mum, Aunt Carrie. I feel awful. Awful,' Rose managed to tell her but she was holding her stomach now and bending over as great knots of pain grabbed at her insides.

'Mrs Bloor's sent for the doctor. Oh, God. I wish he'd come quick.' Aunt Carrie was crying again, rocking herself back and forth but stopped in a few seconds, abruptly, as the door opened and an elderly man with a small moustache was shown into the room.

'Is this the patient?' The doctor approached the bed but before Rose could answer Aunt Carrie had grabbed his arm.

'It is! Don't let her die! Save her!'

She was being more silly than Rose had ever seen her. Rose pulled her knees up again as another sharp pain went through her.

'I want my Mum,' Rose said. 'I want my Mum, not you, Aunt Carrie. I'm not going to die. I just feel horrible!' And she started to cry again.

The doctor spoke kindly to Aunt Carrie. 'Will you help me with the examination, Miss Shrigley? Unfasten your niece's buttons so that I can feel the abdomen.'

Aunt Carrie managed to pull herself together and take the sticky cotton blouse and skirt off her. Rose reached for her aunt's hand as the man gently pressed her stomach until she bit her lip with the sharp stabbings his touch brought. Aunt Carrie's other hand was stroking Rose's forehead but her eyes never left the doctor's face.

'What is it, Doctor?' she said when he finally drew the sheet over Rose's bare stomch. 'Is it a Pendicitis?'

The doctor smiled. 'It's not her appendix, Miss Shrigley. She's suffering from sunstroke and the effects of too much rich food.'

Relief flooded Aunt Carrie's features. She dropped Rose's hand and reached for her glasses.

'Give her plenty of boiled water. Put a pinch of common salt into it and if she begins to vomit come round to my surgery and I'll have the dispenser make up a bottle for her.'

Rose spent three days in bed. For three days Aunt Carrie sat in the darkened room with her, talking to her, bringing cool drinks, sponging her down to cool the reddened skin which had blazed forth from under the freckles. And Aunt Carrie spoke to Rose more kindly and with more understanding than she had ever seen her show.

'You'd have made a good mother, Aunt Carrie,' Rose said on the last evening. 'Did you ever want to get married?'

'I did, once,' Aunt Carrie answered softly. She had a faraway look in her eyes, Rose thought, as if she were remembering something lovely.

'What happened? Won't you tell me? You never talk about when you were young,' Rose said. Aunt Carrie could fly into a rage at anyone's questioning but she appeared to want to talk tonight. They were sitting companionably on the wooden framed seat with cushions that ran under the window of the sitting room. It was growing dark and Aunt Carrie's face was in shadow.

'I know all about Mum and Dad. How they fell madly in love when Mum was young. How they eloped, married and had to come rushing back from Ireland so I'd be born in England.'

'Is that what they tell you?' Aunt Carrie interrupted.

'Yes, and I often wondered why you didn't find someone to love and get married to and have children with. Like Mum and Dad did. You could have been happy, like them.'

Aunt Carrie made no reply but Rose felt that underneath her aunt's silence a struggle was being waged. She knew her aunt too well to mistake a withholding of herself for the buttoned-tight reserve she usually adopted.

'Do you have any regrets, Aunt Carrie?' she asked.

The scene was one she never forgot and Rose could have sworn that her aunt was on the point of tears, her voice was so different, almost strangled as she replied.

'Only one regret, love. I once gave away something very precious.'

'Can't you buy it back?' Rose asked, disappointed that her aunt's regrets only extended to property.

'No. I gave up all rights. It was the most beautiful . . . the most beautiful thing that ever belonged to me. And I gave it away.'

'What was it?' Rose begged. 'Tell me.'

'I can't tell you, Rose. It belongs to someone else now.'

'Will you ever tell me?'

Aunt Carrie got up from the seat and went towards the door. 'You'll know when I'm dead,' she said with finality. She then indicated, with a nod of the head that Rose was to follow. 'Come on. Let's start packing. We'll catch an early bus to the station tomorrow.'

Rose followed her up the stairs to the bedroom, reluctant to drop the subject. 'I've got a regret,' she said, hoping to please Aunt Carrie. 'I wish we weren't going back tomorrow.'

'You're happy, aren't you?' Aunt Carrie turned and

spoke sharply once the door was closed behind them. 'Your Mum and Dad are good to you aren't they?'

'Of course they are. I've got the best Mum and Dad in the world,' Rose answered quickly. She had only meant that she was enjoying the holiday. Aunt Carrie mustn't think she was glad to be away from her family. 'I think it's a pity you never found love, that's all,' she said.

It had been a mistake. Aunt Carrie's mellow mood had gone. 'Love?' she said. 'What's love? There's no such thing as love.'

'Then why did you want to marry, like you said, once?'

'I was daft, Rose. Young and daft.' Aunt Carrie looked hurt; she looked both hurt and angry. She paused for a moment then said, 'Don't you ever be beholden to a man.'

'Don't you want me to get married?' Rose asked.

'I do. But you must keep yourself for the right man. Do you know what I mean? Keep yourself?'

Rose didn't like the turn the exchange had taken but she dared not refuse to answer. 'I think so,' she said quietly.

'You must know so, Rose. If I ever thought anyone would take advantage of you, I'd . . . I'd kill him!'

Aunt Carrie's eyes were gleaming behind the lenses. Rose wanted to calm her down yet she also wanted to let her know that she was not going to put up with her interference in the future.

'Don't be silly, Aunt Carrie,' she said. 'It's 1936, not 1836. Girls don't need chaperones these days. Girls can look after themselves.'

'Ha! Girls might have changed. But men haven't,' Aunt Carrie answered in the voice she always used when she was being unreasonable.

Rose made another attempt to calm her. 'I want to get married one day, Aunt Carrie. And I want my husband to be my friend. Like Dad is,' Rose told her.

'Friend! There's no such thing as friends. You've only one friend in this world. And that's your pocket. Your money! Do you hear me?'

'I hear you. But it's not true,' Rose knew her aunt would be furious but she couldn't stop. 'I'd rather have friends. I'd much rather be with Alan than have a lot of money. Anyway,' she added, 'I'm going to earn my own money. I'm going to college to be a teacher. So I'll be rich.'

'Who says you're going to college?' Aunt Carrie seemed to be as upset about college as she was about her friendship with Alan.

'I say. Mum and Dad say. Dad wants us all to be able to earn our own livings. He's always told us that.' Rose began to take clothes out of the wardrobe and lay them on the bed. Aunt Carrie didn't seem to be doing anything to help.

'I want you to come and live with me, love.' Aunt Carrie's voice had a wheedling tone now. 'You'd not want for money if you came to live with me. I'd give you money. You'd not have to go away, anywhere.'

Rose tried to disguise the look of horror that she knew her face showed. She didn't mean to hurt her but how could her aunt ever dream that she'd leave her Mum and Dad and the Wells Road house to live with her?

'I'm going to college. When I've finished I'll be a teacher. Then I'm going to give half my wages to Dad so he and Mum can start to enjoy themselves,' Rose told her.

'Enjoy themselves?' Aunt Carrie's voice was becoming high pitched again. 'They've done nothing but enjoy themselves all their lives.'

Evidently she was outraged at the suggestion that Mum and Dad could need more than they had. Rose must try to get her to understand.

'Yes. Dad hates the insurance company. He's always hated the work. He says he likes doing things with his hands, making things, building. He built our house, he told us. He says we girls are never to do something we don't like. He says we can hold our heads up if we can earn our own livings, doing what we want to do,' she said emphatically.

'They've given you big ideas.'

Aunt Carrie was no longer trying to win her round. She was her usual cynical self and Rose was relieved to see the severe look return to her aunt's face. She didn't know how to deal with her aunt when she was trying to be pleasant.

A heap of letters was waiting for her on the hall table when Carrie returned to the Temperance Hotel.

'Put them on my table in the sitting room, Maggie,' she said to Mrs Bettley. 'I'll go up and unpack. Will you make me a pot of tea?'

Maggie scuttled off, nodding in agreement, glad that she was back, no doubt. She was a good worker, was Maggie Bettley. She'd looked after the place very well Carrie noticed as she went upstairs; the stairs had been polished, brass doorknobs gleamed.

Carrie closed her bedroom door, put her case on the bed and began to empty it, hanging her good dresses up and dropping the used clothes into her linen basket. Oh, it had been a lovely holiday, just herself and Rose. How proud she was of Rose. What a ladylike manner her daughter had.

She must be the nicest girl in the whole of Middlefield, Carrie thought. Nowadays you see girls no older than Rose, hanging about street corners with lads. There'd be trouble before long with Brenda Gallimore's girls. They painted themselves up like actresses. The whole town talked about them. She, Carrie, would never allow that. And neither would Jane and Danny, she was sure.

It had been a wrench sending her back home, seeing her off in a taxi at the station, jealousy striking again when she saw Rose's eagerness to get back to the family and tell them all about the holiday.

She hadn't wanted to send her back and find herself alone again, feeling lost. Carrie dropped the lid down on the empty case and snapped the locks to, chiding herself for foolishness as she did so. Here she was, a woman of 42, a woman who had always taken charge, feeling sorry for herself because she'd had a lovely holiday and it was over.

She had better start counting her blessings she reminded herself as she poured water into the china bowl and began to wash herself. 'Count your Blessings,' her father used to say. Mind, that wasn't one of his own sayings, it was from a hymn. She began to hum it as she lathered her soap in the cool soft water; the words ringing around in her head.

'WHEN UPON LIFE'S BILLOWS YOU ARE TEMPEST-TOSSED, WHEN YOU ARE DISCOURAGED THINKING ALL IS LOST . . .'

She wasn't discouraged. And she hadn't lost everything. In some ways life was getting better. For one thing, her eye-sight was improving. It was strange how she'd always been short-sighted and now, the optician told her, she was going long-sighted. He said that in time both faults might even compensate one another. One day she might have perfect eyesight.

'COUNT YOUR MANY BLESSINGS, NAME THEM ONE BY ONE . . .'

There were her savings and her property. She'd enough money to last her out and enough to leave Rose provided for. Then there was her health. She was as strong as a horse, always had been, so that now she didn't look as old as most middle-aged women. In fact, she suspected, the years were being kind to her looks, such as they were. She'd never been a beauty of the conventional, chocolate-box or film-star type but here she was, unwrinkled, straight-backed and no sign of a thickening waist.

She peered at her face in the glass above her washstand. No, there were no wrinkles and her teeth were white and straight, none missing. And her hair, a bit faded now, more auburn than red, was thick and soft, not dry and grey like most women of over 40.

'AND IT WILL SURPRISE YOU WHAT THE LORD HAS DONE.'

She left the water for the girl to empty and began to dry herself and rub Glymiel jelly into her hands to keep them soft. She massaged her feet and legs with Pond's cold cream to keep them from going dry. It was supposed to be face cream but she had some expensive stuff for her complexion. She put on clean underwear and a spotted-silk afternoon-dress, slid her feet into the glacé, kid shoes which matched the lace collar on the dress. She then fastened her pearl necklace.

Tomorrow she would not go to chapel. She would go to the service at St Michael's instead. It would have seemed like heresy to her father, she knew, but she was becoming a bit more tolerant these days. She had been to St Michael's once or twice – to the Service of Remembrance, when they'd asked the Choral Society to sing, and to sing duets with Douglas McGregor at their Harvest and Carol services.

There were some occasions when a bit of pomp and show didn't go amiss. It was nice to put your best hat on, so's you'd look as good as anyone, to put two half-crowns on the plate with a bit of a gesture, to have some of them – them as thought of themselves as top-drawer – coming up to talk to you outside, afterwards.

'COUNT YOUR MANY BLESSINGS, NAME THEM ONE BY ONE.'

To be honest, that wasn't the only reason she sometimes missed chapel. The truth was that Cecil Ratcliffe was becoming a problem. Ever since his wife had died he had been paying her a lot of attention. He deferred to her, hanging on to her every word, agreeing with her opinions. Most people thought him an imposing man with his height, good looks and silver hair; a presence. She didn't.

He'd bought a Humber saloon car; a big black shiny one with the palest fawn leather inside. Nobody went in for displays of wealth at the chapel but he justified it by saying that, with all the claims on his time, the town council, the shop, his good works and his preaching duties, it was essential. He was the only person she knew who had a car. He looked important behind the wheel, even a bit arrogant and aloof. Many a woman would think him quite a catch. There were quite a few widows and some ageing spinsters at chapel who acted silly whenever he talked to them.

Maybe it was because she didn't welcome his attentions that she seemed to have inspired them. Some men were like that, she'd noticed; a slight from a woman was seen as a challenge. He'd begun to find excuses to come to Waters Green; accompanying visiting preachers who were to stay overnight at the Temperance Hotel. Twice he'd given her a lift home after a service. He'd said he was offering to drive her because it was raining and he'd given some of the others a lift as well, but she knew what he was after.

'AND IT WILL SURPRISE YOU WHAT THE LORD HAS DONE.'

He'd bring himself to ask her, she just knew he would, as soon as his wife had been dead a year. Cecil Ratcliffe would start in earnest then and the thought worried her. Though, why should it? She was 42; Cecil Ratcliffe was nearly 60. He'd not expect anything . . . anything carnal at his age. It would be a marriage of . . . of . . . what did he expect? Not money for she'd outlive him. Companionship? He'd not been good company to his wife. He had a daughter, but she'd caused a lot of scandal by 'upping and off' as soon as her poor mother was laid to rest. What did he want?

He was an alderman. That would be it. He'd want someone at his side for all the banquets. She could picture their photographs in the *Middlefield Times*: Alderman and Mrs Cecil Ratcliffe.

No, oh no! There was something about him. Something about his buttery voice that she had never taken to. Voices were important. She liked to hear a man with a deep, resonant voice. Cecil's sounded wrong; as if he'd tried to iron out his original speech and ended up with something that sounded empty and affected. And, though he was good-looking, there was something a bit posturing about him. There were times when she had, to her discredit, wondered if he were a secret drinker for his face went florid when he got excited.

Oh, it was wicked of her to think badly of him. After all, he did good. He did a lot of good for no reward on the board of guardians of the girls' Borstal. The reformatory they called it. He helped rescue those bad girls; he preached to them. He was well thought of, held in high regard in Middlefield where he knew everyone and knew everything that was going on.

She went downstairs and sat at her octagonal table in the window. And there it was. A letter. Irish postmark, so he'd posted it before he'd come to Middlefield. Before she'd fled to Southport out of his way, frightened of seeing him, knowing she'd not be able to act normally in front of everyone.

Her heart was thudding as she slit the envelope. It was the sight of his bold, careless handwriting again that started it off, she was sure.

'Darling Carrie,' he'd written. 'I shall ask you this but once and never again. I am not a man who will pursue a cause when all is lost but I am sure that you have not lost your love for me. I have only ever loved one woman in my life – you. Come with me to Canada – you and my Rose. We can be married out there. I need you and want you and I believe that when we meet next week you will say the words I long to hear. Our boat sails from Liverpool on the twentieth of July.'

Why did her heart go thundering? She was middle aged. She was past all that. Women in middle age didn't think about men and love. And why were the tears pouring down her cheeks? Why was she having to fight with herself? Why did she long to throw her clothes back into that case and run, run like the wind to him. The boat went tomorrow. There was time . . .

It was crazy. Impossible. How could he think that she

would give up everything, come clean about their sin, tell Rose, leave Middlefield, her position, her livelihood?

She snatched the handkerchief from her dress pocket and pressed it hard against her eyes. Maggie Bettley might come in at any minute.

He must be mad to write such things. And she must be mad even to read them. She folded the letter with shaking hands and replaced it in the envelope. She would take it up later and put it in the ebony box.

Rose, when she arrived home, was met with a bombardment of news and excited gabbling as soon as the taxi had set her down.

Mary, normally so quiet and calm, pulled her by the arm into the living room the minute the front door was closed. 'Mum and Dad have gone shopping. They'll be back soon,' she said, then, as if trying to get the words in before Viv could take over. 'Uncle Patrick went back yesterday. He was disappointed you weren't here, Rose.'

'He's good fun,' Viv butted in. 'He's very handsome. He looks like Dad, only he's bigger.'

'And older . . .' Mary added.

'Not much older,' Viv said. 'And he speaks American.'

'Canadian!'

'It sounds like American, anyway,' Viv raced on. 'He says he's been to "Tronta" when he means Toronto.' She let go of Mary's other hand and began to dance around the room. 'And he's been to Hollywood, Rose. He says if we go and visit him he'll take us to see where the "Movies" are made.'

Mary was laughing, trying to say something without spoiling Viv's performance. 'He brought presents for us all,' she managed to say whilst Viv stopped tripping about and rushed to the cupboard.

Mary carried on, carefully reciting the list, 'Fur hats for Mum and Dad.'

'And fur ear-muffs!' Viv squealed.

Rose found herself swept along with the gaiety of it all. 'A fur hat? For Dad?' she said. 'Ear-muffs? What are they?'

'Yes!' Viv pulled a large parcel from the depths of the cupboard and pushed it into Rose's hands. 'And wooden dolls for us!'

Rose looked incredulous. 'We're too old for dolls.'

'They are lovely,' Mary said gently. 'More like ornaments or keepsakes really. Open it!'

Rose tore at the paper. It was a carved wooden doll with jointed arms and legs, a delicately painted china head and masses of curled fair hair. 'Fancy him buying us dolls,' she said. 'Doesn't he know we're grown-up?'

'Yes,' Mary answered. 'He does. He bought us writing sets last Christmas. He said he couldn't resist buying three beautiful dolls for three beautiful young girls.' She brought her own doll from its hiding-place behind the curtains. 'See,' she said, cradling it as if it were a baby. 'I've made clothes for mine and Viv's.'

'Uncle Patrick sounds nice,' Rose said.

'He is. He went to the antique shop and bought something for Aunt Carrie,' Vivienne told her eagerly.

'Guess what it is?' Mary said.

'I've no idea.'

Vivienne delved under the table and brought out a large flat parcel that was wrapped in brown paper. 'We hid everything – to surprise you,' she explained as she struggled to untie the string. 'Close your eyes!'

Rose obediently closed them tight, hearing Vivienne prop a picture against the wall.

'Open your eyes!' Vivienne cried.

'Golly!' Rose stared at it, astonished. The pictures he'd sent to them over the years were of snow-capped mountains and deep green forests.

It was a big painting in glowing colours. The great canvas was filled with beautiful, half-dressed nymphs and gods. Apollo, it said underneath, was the god who held the reins of a chariot drawn by restless, eager white horses that were charging towards the sun, whilst veiled Aurora, the rosy-fingered goddess of dawn, held open the Gates of Morning.

'What will she think of that?' Mary was saying. 'She has no room on her walls.'

'And she only likes landscapes and still lifes,' Viv added.

'I think she'll love it,' Rose told them. 'She's quite a romantic old thing, underneath.'

Mary carried the bag Aunt Carrie had bought her up the stairs to Rose's bedroom.

Viv followed them, still chattering. 'We had a party. In Alan McGregor's garden. Our Uncle Patrick is Alan's godfather you know.'

Mary dumped the bag on the counterpane and began to help Rose unpack.

'There was dancing at night, Rose,' Viv went on, ignoring them in their task, bobbing her face in front of Rose's at every turn, making them laugh and have to push her aside. 'It was a party. A lovely singing and dancing party. In Alan's drawing room.'

Rose began to wish she had been there, or that at least they could have waited until she returned. She took out the little packages and handed them to Mary and Viv.

Mary opened hers, smiled shyly and kissed her big sister on the cheek. 'Thank you,' she said. 'It's lovely. I need a brooch to go with my new blouse.'

Viv hadn't even opened hers but was tugging at Rose's arm to get her attention again. 'You should have seen Dad and Uncle Patrick doing the Irish Jig,' she went on. 'And I danced the veleta with Alan McGregor – and the sailor's hornpipe on my own . . .'

'And all the men sang.'

'Ooh, it was spiffing.'

CHAPTER ELEVEN

A year later Douglas sat on the wooden bench in front of the Swan. There were ten minutes to go before opening time – just enough to read Patrick Kennedy's letter before he pushed back the heavy oak door. The market square was sunny and the stall-holders were doing a brisk trade this warm June morning.

He slit open the envelope. 'Dear Douglas and Alan,' the letter began, 'Congratulations, Alan, on getting a place at medical school. I'm sure you will enjoy every minute of university life. But what will your poor old Pa do, with you gone to Edinburgh?'

Douglas smiled to himself. He was going to enjoy himself too. In the courtyard at the back of the Swan stood a new car – a red Lanchester. A couple of stables had been knocked into one to make a garage. Motoring was going to be his new pastime.

He looked absently across the bright, busy stalls. He had not found a motoring companion yet but there were one or two single ladies of his acquaintance . . . He must not give any of them ideas but it would be nice to have someone to take for a country drive, afternoon tea . . .

He went back to the letter. 'John McGregor wants to buy a small farm, probably in Calgary. John, as no doubt he'll have told you, has marriage in mind and we have decided to go our separate ways. I think it is time I put down some roots and will look for a place in Vancouver.

'We have travelled all over Canada in the last few years and a journey by C.P.R. would seem like home-from-home to you, Douglas. There are so many places with

Scottish names: Fraser Valley, Craigellachie, Banff, Fort William. I hope I can show it to you some day.'

There followed another two pages of Patrick's description of a motoring trip he and John had taken through the Rockies and then . . . A smile crossed Douglas's face as he read the last paragraph. 'I sent a five-page piece of writing to one of the big newspapers in Vancouver, and – would you believe it – they paid for it and asked me for more. I was paid more for an evening's relaxation than I have ever earned in a week's hard work. I'm going to send some articles to the other big dailies to see if the first was a flash in the pan. Who knows? This might be the start of a new way of life.'

Douglas was pleased for him. Patrick had always had a gift for communicating. He replaced the letter in its envelope and put it in his breast pocket. He'd show it to Alan later.

Across the bustling square he caught sight of Miss Shrigley and Rose talking to Nat Cooper. Rose Kennedy, red-haired and beautiful, was a girl who was all unconscious of her charms. Douglas smiled now, seeing her attracting the glances of all who passed by, unaware of their interest, deep in conversation with Nat. She had grown up in the last year; she was tall, not unlike her aunt in build.

They were all growing up, Rose, her sisters, Alan. Alan would be leaving home in a few weeks' time and he would have to mark it in some way. Yet, proud as he was of Alan's achievement in passing the examinations, his father was stumped for a way to celebrate it. Alan hated fuss yet Douglas wanted to mark his leaving, with a party if possible.

They had not had a good celebration since Patrick Kennedy had come over from Canada last year. That had been a spontaneous event and everyone had enjoyed it. This time he would have to organize it in advance and he was at a loss as to how he could make it appear casual.

175

He waved to Rose and to Nat Cooper who, badly injured some years ago, was limping across the square. Nat would be in the bar soon. Every Saturday Nat stabled the horse round the back of the Swan in one of the old loose-boxes. The young farmer made a day of Saturdays after his morning milk-round, driving his horse and cart back up to Rainow farm late on, after he'd spent the evening at a cinema or whatever it was he got up to.

Douglas stood and went to bolt back the heavy oak doors. He went inside to get the bar ready. Alan would be down soon to help.

Nat Cooper, 24, sandy haired and oddly shy in spite of his big smile and deep country voice, limped across the square.

Middlefield market square, a cobbled rectangle, was the best part of an acre he supposed, if you counted the grass and the four sycamores behind the stalls. He bought pipe tobacco for the weekdays, matches and a packet of Craven 'A' at the tiny tobacconist's next door to the Swan. Girls liked you to buy them cigarettes and once he'd had a few pints to get himself talking he was going to ask the girl who worked at Lipton's to go to the pictures with him tonight.

The bar was already filling up when he arrived and Nat watched Mona Siddall as she served. Her movements were fast and accurate and she kept the men in place with a sharp word when they tried to order out of turn. She'd a lot about her, had Mona Siddall, he thought. A farmer could do with a wife like that.

But it was no good thinking that way. He'd liked Rose Kennedy for so long that he'd wait a bit longer, until he either plucked up the courage to ask her out when she was old enough, maybe next year, or saw her courting someone else.

'Hello, Nat,' Douglas greeted him. 'Do you want a drink?'

'Aye.'

'I saw you talking to our Rose,' Douglas said. 'She's a bonny lass.'

'Oh, aye.' Nat answered.

'She's got all the heads turning,' Douglas grinned. He looked at Nat across the bar. 'Beer?'

'Please,' Nat replied.

'Aye. She's a bonny lass,' Douglas continued. 'Haven't you found yourself a lassie, Nat?'

'I don't meet that many,' Nat hedged.

He'd never tell Douglas or anyone else that he'd been in love with Rose Kennedy since she was a 14-year-old kid. He'd been running the farm since his father had died, and was 21 when he first noticed her, cycling to the high school every morning, her satchel slung over her shoulder, pretty face peering under the brimmed velour hat of navy blue. He'd been annoyed with himself, been a little ashamed of himself, for falling for a schoolgirl.

She'd been full of fun and laughter. She brought a carrot or an apple for Dobbin every morning and the big horse got to know and wouldn't pass the end of Wells Road without a bit of shouting when she wasn't there. And Nat hadn't told her to stop; he never told her that horses were creatures of habit and that Dobbin still stopped in his tracks whenever he saw her. He'd got as bad as the horse; looking for her, thinking a day without sight of her worse than a field of weeds.

Sometimes, when she walked to school, she'd climb up beside him on the milk cart, taking the reins, and he'd watch her face light up with pleasure at Dobbin's clopping pace through the quiet morning streets. It had been a while since that had happened though.

'Alan's going to university in September,' Douglas said. 'Did you know?'

'Aye,' Nat smiled back. 'What are you goin' to do with yerself, eh?' he asked. 'You'll miss 'im.'

'I've plenty to do,' Douglas said. 'I've bought a car. I've

got the choir. I'll be all right.' He leaned over the counter and lowered his voice. 'I want your advice, Nat,' he began.

'What's up?'

Douglas slid a foaming pint of best bitter over the counter. 'I want to give a party for Alan,' he told him. 'You're his friend. You'll understand the problem,' he said. 'I can't let him think it's being held in his honour.'

'Eeh,' Nat smiled. 'I dunna know how to organize 'em. I've never bin to a party . . . A proper party, like.'

'You're twenty-four,' Douglas said. 'It's time you had a bit of fun.'

'I 'ave a bit o' fun, Douggie,' Nat answered. 'But I've never been asked to a party.'

'Alan's not to know I'm giving it for him. He wouldn't want that. How can I get round it?'

Nat took a deep draught of the ale. 'Tell 'im it's for the end of 'is schooldays. For 'im and 'is friends.' He took another drink before continuing. 'If you ask me, I'd say, tell 'is friends' mothers and dads and get 'em all involved in it.'

He drained the glass and placed it on the counter. 'There's a few of 'em from 'is school going off to university, isn't there?'

'Aye,' Douglas said. He refilled Nat's pint mug. Nat wanted to get a couple of pints down quickly before he went to sit down with the last one.

'We can give them a good send-off.' Douglas seemed to like the proposition.

'Hire a band, why don't yer,' Nat was saying, warming to his idea. 'Yer could open them French winders on to t'veranda and roll yer carpets oop.'

'I'll put coloured lights in the trees if we get the weather,' Douglas went on.

'If you 'ave yer party afore t'next moon you'll be all reet for weather,' Nat said solemnly. 'There'll be no more rain until t'moon shifts round.'

Douglas lifted his eyebrows as if questioning Nat's weather forecasting.

'I'm like me Dad was. Never far out. And if yer don't shurrup,' Nat said, 'yer game'll be oop. Your Alan's just gone past t'winder.'

'Keep him talking then,' Douglas said. 'While I go in and make out the list. Alan can look after the bar. If it's to be before the moon goes down I've no time to waste.'

Douglas went into the back parlour to make his plans. He took pencil and paper from the dresser and began to list the people he'd ask: Gerald and his sister. He'd tell Alan about the party as soon as he had the agreement of the other families. They were sure to give it.

He would string lights on the apple and pear trees, place picnic tables on the lawn, with lanterns on them. Danny Kennedy would help with that.

It was a pity Patrick Kennedy would not be here to see his godson's farewell, but it couldn't be helped. He'd book someone from the photographer's to take pictures; send some to Canada.

He would invite some of the people from the Middlefield Choral Society. It was to be a real Scottish party. A good mix of young and old. He'd hire the town's best band. They could play for the dancing on the veranda he'd had built across the back of the house. They could play the latest swing tunes for the young ones and accompany the choral singers between dances.

It was going to be a grand summer party. And the first ever for young Nat Cooper and probably the Kennedy girls' first.

On the night, Alan stood on the veranda and looked over the grass to where his friends were gathered in colourful groups around the tables, laughing and talking.

The weather was perfect; the sun had gone down, leaving an indigo velvet night that was warm and sweet scented. The garden looked magical, lit by lamps that

179

were strung in the trees, lanterns set on tables and hanging lights swinging from the canopy of the wide, wooden veranda.

The girls had dressed up for the occasion; they brought to mind bright butterflies, fluttering their hands whenever a remark amused them; flattering the men with their attention. Most of the men, like himself, were wearing flannels with sports jackets. Some wore cricket-club blazers and all had crisp white shirts that shone under the lights.

Most of them, Alan noticed wryly, appeared very sure of themselves with the girls who were clustered around them.

He wished he were like his friends, confident and assured. He didn't lack confidence in other ways. Or with most girls. But Rose wasn't most girls. Rose was beautiful. She was charming. She was full of life. She was intelligent. In fact every man here tonight wanted her; he knew it. There was no earthly reason why she should look at him. She could take her pick of any of the handsome chaps who were surrounding her.

Behind him the French windows had been flung back making drawing room and veranda one dancing area where at this moment a five-piece band was playing *Why Did She Fall For The Leader Of The Band*.

The music was being ignored by his friends in the garden, Alan noticed, though inside the house Danny and Jane Kennedy and some other couples were dancing.

Over by the potted geraniums on the far corner of the veranda, Vivienne Kennedy had Mary by the arm as she attempted to teach her wide-eyed sister the intricacies of the quick-step.

Alan watched them; Vivienne's feet quick and light like the girl herself. She seemed to anticipate the beat whilst Mary's big eyes moved from her sister's feet to her own as if willing them to catch up with her vivacious partner's.

Nearby, their Aunt Carrie sat with Cecil Ratcliffe, sipping fruit cup. Alan passed her chair to tell the barman not to confuse the cold punch, which contained two bottles of good brandy, with the fruit cup Dad had ordered for the teetotal members of the Choral Society.

As he went past them he amused himself with the thought that she might already have taken some of the strong punch unwittingly, for the normally uncommunicative Miss Shrigley, eyes firmly fixed on Gerald's sister, was saying to Ratcliffe, 'Look at that girl's dress! She wants her bottom smacking! She's plastered with lipstick and eye-black.'

A trestle table, covered with a white damask cloth had been set on the opposite corner to the one where the girls were dancing. Glasses and punchbowls were placed along the length of it with dishes of fruit and sweet almonds. Alan told the barman not to confuse the drinks.

Dad and Nan Tansley were at the moment checking with the catering people in the kitchen, ensuring that the sherry trifles were kept apart from the ones made from crushed fruits.

Alan went down the veranda steps. Rose was talking to Nat Cooper, Gerald and Gerald's sister. Rose looked more beautiful than ever tonight, in a clinging, silvery dress that stopped just short of her ankles. He knew she had made it specially. He hoped he appeared unruffled but his heart came up into his throat every time he looked at her. Nowadays she was always surrounded by a crowd of admirers. He went across the grass to them.

He poked Nat's arm in fun when he reached them. 'Enjoying it?' he asked.

Nat, though Alan knew he felt uncomfortable in his new suit, with his sandy hair pasted down, looked as if he were having a good time. His cheeks were bright pink. 'Aye,' he said, in his deep, slow voice. 'This punch is right good stuff. It's fair mekkin' me talk.'

Gerald's sister, in a short green dress with a frilled hem, was ogling Alan. Her dark eyes were fixed on his face.

'Want a cocktail?' he asked her.

'Ooh, goody,' she squealed. 'I'd rather a Pimms, if you have it.'

Alan beckoned to one of the waiters. 'What about you, Nat?'

'Give us a beer, will yer?' Nat said. 'Ah'm not used to them fancy things.'

'Rose?' She was smiling at him now, as if relieved to see him there. His heart lurched again.

'Is Aunt Carrie looking?' she asked.

Over his shoulder Alan saw that her aunt was still talking with unusual animation to Cecil Ratcliffe.

'Your aunt seems to be giving all her attention to a man, on the veranda,' he answered with a smile.

'Aunt Carrie? Talking to a man?' Rose was laughing softly back.

Alan moved closer to her and whispered into her ear, 'I'll bet Cecil Ratcliffe goes down on one knee at any moment.'

Rose turned to look, narrowing her eyes, but Alan knew she'd not be able to see from here. 'She looks as if she'd rather he didn't,' he told her. 'But I don't think she'll notice what you're drinking.'

'Then I'll have a Pimms as well. I can always say it's fruit cup, can't I?' she said.

Alan gave their orders to the waiter and turned back to Nat, trying not to show his annoyance when Gerald took hold of Rose's elbow to say something to her. He knew that he himself didn't stand a chance. Rose wouldn't look twice at him. After all, he was the boy-next-door, not handsome. Much too ordinary for a girl like Rose. But Gerald wasn't anything special either.

Alan turned back to Nat. 'How are you getting back, Nat?' he asked. 'Is Dad going to drive you to Rainow? Have you seen his car?'

He tried not to keep glancing over Nat's shoulder to see what Gerald was up to now. Gerald was always bragging about his being irresistible to the girls. It was not surprising, Alan thought sourly, if he held on to the girls the way he was doing with Rose.

'No,' Nat was saying. 'Ah've left t'cart behind t'Swan. Th'horse is stabled. He'll see me home, will Dobbin.'

'I'll go with you. Help you with the milking. But I'm going to enjoy this party first.' Now he nudged Nat again and said, as quietly as he could, 'Ask Gerald's sister to dance. She keeps giving you the glad eye.'

'Eeh,' Nat grumbled, blushing, 'I canna do them fancy dances.'

Alan saw that his friend was red-faced with embarrassment and, sorry that he'd been the cause of it, turned back to the group who were gathered in a laughing, chattering semicircle around Gerald.

Rose was so beautiful. She had fastened a corsage of flowers on to the shoulder of the silvery dress. Her long legs with their fine ankles were encased in pale silk stockings and on her feet she wore silver dancing shoes with a wide instep strap. All the time she was laughing with Gerald her foot was keeping time to the music.

Her hair, polished bronze under the lights, kept falling across her face and he saw that as she pushed it back with slender fingers her bare arm brushed against Gerald's sleeve.

Alan knew a surge of jealousy. She was his – not Gerald's. Why was she smiling at Gerald? Why was she avoiding his eye? The band had finshed the fast dance tunes and was starting to play the first few notes of *I've Got You Under My Skin*.

He couldn't let Gerald take Rose on to the floor for this one. If he didn't ask her first though, he might be too late. He'd never lacked courage. He moved quickly towards her.

'Rose?' His hand closed around her narrow wrist. 'Come. Dance with me. On the veranda.'

And she was laughing and running with him before the music could start properly. He tugged her up the veranda's wooden steps, stood before her and held out his arms.

And he didn't know – didn't care – whether they were trying to foxtrot or tango to the music for she was in his arms and his hands were shaking, holding her.

But their feet fitted and her face was inches from his and he felt such a rush of longing for her that it was all he could do to remember that everyone was watching.

'SOMETIMES I WONDER . . .' the music went. He must not give in to the urgent desire to kiss that wide, generous mouth that was mesmerizing him as she spoke.

'Will you miss us all, Alan?' she was saying.

He managed to make his voice sound normal. 'I'll be home at Christmas.'

'Are you going to take up flying?'

'Yes,' he answered.

Someone indoors was singing the words. The smell of night-scented stock was heavy in the soft air.

'Rose?'

'What?'

'I want to kiss you,' he whispered. He felt the pressure of her fingers tightening around his; saw with delight that she had felt it too, for she had stopped the bright chatter and was looking into his eyes as the music ended and the band began to play *Smoke Gets In Your Eyes*.

She was humming along with the music, close to him. But others were crowding on to the veranda to dance and he knew she need not worry that Aunt Carrie's warning looks would be directed towards her.

'THEY ASKED ME HOW I KNEW . . .' She was singing the words, careless of their effect on him; smiling into his eyes. Her breath was sweet and warm. He drew her closer, letting his hand rest on her bare shoulder.

Her aunt had gone indoors. She and Dad were going to sing a duet next. Alan pulled Rose closer so that he could feel her body, long and slender against himself as the music swept along. Their feet were barely moving. His head was dizzy with the sight and the sound of her as the music came to an end.

They began to play his favourite song. Nobody would see them if they danced round the corner, behind the big ferns. And she knew. Her feet were following his as he led her through the crowd. His heart was thumping. Her hand was warm in his.

Now he held her in his arms, leaning against a wooden pillar.

'WHEN THEY BEGIN . . . THE BEGUINE . . .' Her arms were around his neck, her fingers threading in and out of his hair . . . and his mouth was crushing down on her soft, open lips.

Then she pulled away, blushing furiously and slid out of his arms to go back, before they were seen, into the throng of dancing couples on the veranda.

Alan watched her slip away; saw her go into the drawing-room; saw her seek out her Aunt Carrie and stand by the haughty woman's chair; watched her whisper something into her aunt's ear; saw her aunt's smile as she patted Rose's hand.

'Damn! Damn!' he said under his breath. 'I've scared her. She'll never let me kiss her again.' He tore a leaf from a giant fern and broke it angrily in his fingers.

Carrie had wondered, when she awoke with a splitting headache on the morning after the garden party, if there had been something peculiar in the fruit cup. It had taken her breath away. It had tasted very different from the squashes she always made from thinly sliced oranges and lemons. She'd put it down, the next day, to the fact that Douglas McGregor's offering had been made with pine-apple juice. It had had a metallic taste to it. The trifle, too, had tasted strange, as if it had almond essence soaked into the sponge at the bottom.

A week had passed since then but it had given her a lot to think about. Today she was sitting in her private sitting room, as she usually did for an hour in the afternoons and still dwelling on it. She had never been to a party before, a party with singing and dancing. At first she'd been sure she was going to hate it. She'd only accepted because Jane and Danny and the girls were going.

Still, she had sung well, better than she'd ever sung before. She and Douglas McGregor had been asked to do four encores. It was funny the way she and Douglas McGregor could sing together. They knew one another's voices so well that all they needed was a score and a half-good accompanist and they could make any song sound good.

Mostly they sang oratoria but last week after she'd sung *Early One Morning* he'd asked her to sing *Who is Sylvia?* as a duet. Then he'd sung *A Wand'ring Minstrel I* and she'd sung *My Ain Folk* every bit as good as Miss Nellie Melba used to, they'd said.

She couldn't remember the last time she'd enjoyed herself so much. She couldn't remember much about getting home, except that Cecil Ratcliffe had driven her back after the singing. She hadn't spoken more than a couple of words in the car, she thought, and those rather curt.

Now she remembered. She'd said that Gerald what's-it's sister wanted her bottom smacking, carrying on the way she did. It was right common the way she made a display of herself, hanging on to lads' arms in public. 'You'd think her mother would have sent her home in disgrace,' she'd said to Cecil. 'I would have,' she'd said. 'I'd have given her a good spanking.'

She'd gone straight to bed. She hadn't asked him in for a cup of tea but, ever since, Cecil Ratcliffe seemed to think he had some kind of claim to her.

Carrie turned down the radio when she heard a rapping at the front door. Maggie would answer it, but she could not justify to herself her enjoyment of listening to the BBC. She had no idea why she should feel so guilty about it, or about enjoying the party. Perhaps it was her up-bringing, being taught that simple, godfearing pleasures were all that were permitted. With all that dance-band music nobody could call the wireless a simple pleasure.

Her father would have been horrified at the thought that a private sitting room in the Temperance Hotel was filled with sound, afternoon and evening. For, these days, now Rose was nearly grown-up, she only went three or four nights a week to Wells Road and never at weekends.

Maggie's footsteps were coming along the corridor, followed by a man's. Carrie turned the set off. 'Come in,' she called.

It was Cecil Ratcliffe. 'Er – I was wondering, Miss Shrigley,' he began in the halting voice he only used for her benefit. When he preached he wasn't hesitant. He was fluent, unctuous, when he preached.

'Thank you, Maggie,' Carrie said quickly. Then, to Cecil, 'Come in. What is it?'

This was his fourth visit in a week. He'd driven her home from the party, then from chapel the next day. He'd called in on his halfday-closing with a pair of shoes she'd ordered and now here he was again.

'Did you want to see me, in particular?' she asked, smoothing down the pleats in her navy-blue dress with a sharp, impatient movement.

'It's the Sunday School anniversary and treat tomorrow.'

'I know.'

'Well, er, I was . . . I wondered if you'd do me the honour . . . er, allow me to . . . the charabanc is not really the same . . .'

'You want to take me in your car. Is that it?'

He was determined. She'd give him that. He'd had little encouragement but she'd known that once his year of mourning was up she'd be pestered by him.

'All right.' She found the hesitant manner irritating. But she knew that he was a little in awe of her. She would not for a minute let him think he was getting any nearer to his heart's desire. But the charabanc was not the same as travelling in style. She was becoming quite fond of being chauffered from the chapel.

'Will you call for Mrs Tatton as well?' she demanded. 'We can hardly drive up to Rainow in your motor car and let our good superintendent's wife ride with the children on the charabanc.'

'Of course. And will you sing for us at the concert, Miss Shrigley?' Cecil Ratcliffe placed his bowler hat on the small table at the side of his chair, nipped and lifted the creases of his trousers and seated himself.

Again his mannerisms annoyed her. Carrie went to the door and rang the bell for Maggie who answered the call immediately.

'Bring a tea-tray, Mrs Bettley,' she said. 'With scones for Mr Ratcliffe.'

Maggie gave her what Carrie thought was a knowing look before she went off to the kitchen. Carrie hoped Maggie Bettley wasn't going to start imagining things, or, Heaven forbid, hinting to the neighbours. She turned back into the room.

'Will you sing, for us?' Cecil repeated.

'You needn't ask, Mr Ratcliffe,' she answered sharply. 'I always sing. It's expected of me. It was my grandfather who built the chapel.' Carrie pulled herself up to her full height and, since he was still seated, looked down at him, hoping to intimidate him.

'What are you singing?' he asked in that artificial voice.

'I'm singing, *What A Friend I Have In Jesus*.'

'Wonderful,' Cecil exhaled as he said it. 'And appropriate. After all, Miss Shrigley we all ought to be aware, in these troubled times, of the very real presence of Our Lord.' He looked at her with a hopeful half-smile. 'Jesus comes to us in many . . .' he began again.

'Yes, yes,' Carrie interrupted. In a minute, she knew, Cecil Ratcliffe would be inviting her to join him in a quick burst of prayer. Prayer was never far from his lips. Yet she

188

thought him insincere. He could sound sanctimonious at times.

'And I shall lead the prayers,' he was saying. 'Such an important day in the life of the chapel – the anniversary.'

Carrie stifled a desire to laugh as he sat looking up at her with his pale blue eyes shining behind the gold-rimmed glasses he had recently affected. He was trying to look 'fetching', the old fool. His face was flushed bright pink with excitement, his thinning hair had been greased and spread carefully across the freckled baldness of his scalp. And he smelled of Atkinson's Lavender Water. She couldn't abide scented men.

'Are you preaching on Sunday?' She managed to make the enquiry sound polite. 'Your name's up on the board.'

It was the wrong thing to say. He was beaming back at her, evidently flattered by her interest. 'I am, Miss Shrigley. And may I say that before another year is out I venture to hope that . . . That the board at chapel will give notice that . . .'

Maggie Bettley saved her from any more embarrassment by tapping with the toe of her shoe on the sitting-room door. Carrie meant to tell her about that. She'd done it before. Old retainer or not she would not allow Maggie Bettley to become overfamiliar. Carrie opened the door but did not take the tray from her hands.

'Put it on the table, Mrs Bettley,' she said with studied politeness. 'And wait in here until Mr Ratcliffe has finished.'

She turned to look into Cecil's disappointed face and said, 'You'll have to excuse me. I have an appointment at three o'clock.'

Cecil Ratcliffe leaped to his feet.

'No, no,' Carrie said. 'Don't apologize. Enjoy your tea. My fault, my fault entirely.'

She left him to Mrs Bettley and went to her bedroom. That would teach him. Though she knew that by the time he drove away from the hotel Cecil Ratcliffe would have convinced himself that she was even more desirable as the future Mrs Ratcliffe. He'd want a wife who could act high-handed. He'd hinted as much.

She sat, a little way back from the window, waiting to see him depart, asking herself how she could rebuff his advances. He would ask her, outright, soon. He'd gone all around the subject – telling her that when he remarried his wife would be respected – looked up to. She'd have every comfort money could buy. She'd have an important position in the town. He'd even said that he'd expect his future wife to give up any interest, any business, of her own. He'd said his wife would have servants to help her run his home. And a nice big house he'd got. He didn't live above the shop.

She heard the slam of his car door and waited until she heard the engine start before looking out to see the Humber turning up the Wallgate.

Why hadn't she simply told him not to make a fool of himself – that she had no wish to marry? Was it because she was prepared to think about it? Was she afraid of living and dying an old maid? Ought she to consider it? Was she too fastidious?

She'd try to imagine herself as an alderman's wife – the mayor's wife even. Yes, that was better. If only she didn't have to imagine Cecil Ratcliffe beside her.

She went to her dressing table and scrubbed her hands with the scented soap to take away the sticky feeling.

The following day dawned grey and overcast. Carrie had thought it over. She would make it clear to Cecil that she did not want his affection. When he came for her she would sit in the back of the car and let Mrs Tatton take the front passenger seat.

She looked as far into the distance as she could see from her bedroom window. With those heavy grey clouds it would certainly be wet in the hills at Rainow. She went downstairs, in her black dress, to supervise the serving of breakfasts and to write out the bills for the guests who were leaving.

She was always down there before the daily woman came in. They thought of her as austere and difficult, she knew, but they knew where they were with her. And so did the guests.

Today though her mood was irascible. More than that, she knew herself to be in a shocking temper. There were times when she couldn't bear to be crossed; times when nothing would give her more satisfaction than to swipe her tormentor across the face; times when the very thought of Cecil Ratcliffe brought out the worst in her.

She had her work cut out to finish in time. There were orders to be given to Maggie Bettley and the bedroom girls, the grocery order to be made out, for there was no work done on Sundays and a lot of preparation went into that.

At last she was satisfied that the women had everything under control and she went upstairs to change her clothes. She chose a grey suit and an ecru silk blouse, to match the sky and her mood. She would wear her flat, lace-up shoes with it.

As she was pulling on the hat that matched her blouse – a brimmed style that dipped over to one side and flattered the shape of her face – she heard the Humber draw up. She went quickly downstairs and answered the door herself.

'Oh. You're ready, Miss Shrigley,' he said as she went out and closed the door behind her. He looked disappointed, as if he'd been hoping to be asked in. But she wasn't going to spend any time alone with him.

She walked in front of him towards the car, Cecil's long feet snapping behind and around her in a smart five-four time as he tried to reach the front passenger door ahead of her.

'Where's Mrs Tatton?' Carrie peered into the back seat of the saloon. It was empty but for a cardboard shoe box.

'Are we picking her up next?' This was a set-back. Now she'd have to sit beside him.

'Er, I believe that dear Mrs Tatton is indisposed,' Cecil was explaining apologetically.

Carrie let him settle her into the front, stiffening as he fussed over a travelling rug which he tried to tuck around her legs. 'I don't need that,' she said sharply. 'Come along. We don't want to arrive after the others.'

He looked conspicuous today; as if he were making even more of an effort to please her. He was wearing a check plus-four suit and a flat cap – the sort she always referred to in a disparaging manner as a ratting-cap. He should stick to dark colours and bowler hats, not dress up like a country squire. He was only an alderman.

'Very well. All set then?'

He was trying to be flirtatious – smirking all over his reddening face before he pressed the starter button with a flourish. He seemed in an excited mood – missing the Buxton Road turning.

'Which way are we going?' she asked. 'You've gone the wrong way.'

'Miss Shrigley,' he began, turning his head to stare.

Carrie kept her eyes looking straight ahead.

'Miss Shrigley, what do you think?'

'What?'

'They've cancelled the picnic. The field at Rainow is flooded.'

Anger was rising in her. Her voice went high. If he were not behind the wheel of the car she'd have hit him. 'Then why didn't you say so, Cecil Ratcliffe? Are we going to the chapel hall?'

'No.'

'Where then?'

'I've got you all to myself. Until we go to the concert. I'm going to take you to Chester.'

He'd tricked her. 'You'll take me right back!' she blazed. 'How dare you!' She snatched the travelling rug off her lap and threw it on to the rear seat. 'Turn this car around,' she demanded.

He kept on driving. He made no move to indicate a turn but spoke to her in that sermonizing way, his skinny hands jerking up and down on and off the wheel.

'I believe the good Lord is directing me, Miss Shrigley,' he said. 'In all my actions I am guided from above.'

'And the good Lord is directing you to Chester, is he?' Carrie raged.

'Just as He directed you, when you told me to wait for your answer,' he replied.

Carrie was shocked into temporary silence. Had she said that? That he must wait for her answer? To what? What had been the question? She could hazard a guess.

'I? I told you to wait?' she said. 'I don't believe you. When?'

'At Douglas McGregor's. Last week.' Cecil Ratcliffe was looking sure of himself again. 'We'll be back in time for the concert,' he said. 'Have no fear, Miss Shrigley.'

'Don't you lay a finger on me, Cecil. Don't so much as lay a finger on me.' Carrie found herself saying before she could think of something cutting.

'Unless you wish it, my dear,' he said. He was starting to look pleased with himself. 'Do I understand that we are now on first-name terms, Caroline?'

'You understand no such thing. Turn this car round!'

They had passed beyond the shops by this time and were approaching the edge of the town, where the houses began to be spaced farther apart. Ahead, on the left was a small wood. Cecil Ratcliffe slowed down and turned in. Carrie saw that there was a narrow pathway leading into the heart of the wood, between beech trees whose heavy branches overhung the way.

He pulled the car to a halt and let the engine stop. Carrie turned to face him. 'Well,' she demanded. 'Are you turning back or what?'

To her horror Cecil Ratcliffe leaned across and, flushed

pink with excitement, placed one thin hand round the back of her head and drew her towards himself as if to kiss her. At the same time he clutched at her left hand and squeezed it so hard she thought it would snap.

'Oh, oh, Miss Shrigley,' he breathed. 'Let me . . . Only let me . . .'

Fury rose in her as she wrenched her hand away and with strength she never knew she possessed, she hit him full force across the face. His head seemed to strike the window before he righted himself by clutching wildly at the steering wheel, letting his head drop forwards before it struck the wheel and he pulled himself into a sitting position again.

She felt, as she had on the other two occasions when she had hit someone in temper, a sudden wave of shame and remorse; not for having responded to his vile approach with anger, but because she had acted on impulse and her impulse had been of such a violent nature.

This feeling was immediately followed by one of satisfaction when she saw the expression, a hang-dog expression, on Cecil Ratcliffe's face. She tugged at the handle and the door flew open. Carrie got out of the car quickly and then, with great dignity picked up her handbag and began to walk back down the path, her head held high.

She heard him getting out, heard his feet stumbling along behind her. She would not look back. She was not in the least afraid of him.

'Miss Shrigley. I deserved that,' he was saying, right behind her. Now he had caught up with her. 'Stop. Please stop,' he said.

Carrie stood still and looked at him. She didn't know what to make of it. Her anger had gone. 'What ever got into you, Cecil Ratcliffe?' she demanded. 'Have you taken to drink? Taken leave of your senses?'

'Hit me!' he said with great urgency. 'I asked for it. I beg you, Miss Shrigley. Caroline. Hit me again! As hard as you like!'

She looked up at him and all at once felt sorry for the man. Then to her astonishment, he smiled, and it seemed to Carrie that he was not apologizing but that, in some way, he had enjoyed it. She must be imagining it. How could a man enjoy being struck and scolded by a woman?

'If I ever do a thing like that again, Miss Shrigley, then please, I beg you . . .' Here he broke off and looked longingly into her face. 'There are times, my dear, when a man needs . . . Needs to be put in his place.'

'What do you mean "Put in your place?"' Carrie snapped. 'If you ever do a thing like that again, Cecil Ratcliffe, I'll . . . I'll horsewhip you!'

She had never said a thing like that before. It wasn't an expression she'd used, though she heard it said. But it had the desired effect on him.

He seemed to make another tremendous effort to control himself; straightening up, swallowing nervously and finally half-bowing to her.

'Will you allow me, my dear, to make amends,' he said. 'I have taken the liberty of reserving a table for lunch at the Blossoms Hotel in Chester. In the back of the car I have a gift, a small token of my regard.'

Before he could start to pontificate again Carrie cut him short. 'Don't make a fool of yourself,' she said, turning back towards the car. 'You don't have to crawl. I'll go to Chester with you. I can't very well go back home now.'

He ran, almost leaped, she thought, back to the Humber, held open the door and once she was seated got in and reached over to the back seat for the shoebox.

'Here you are,' he said, handing it to her. 'I know that your birthday is around the time of the anniversary.'

It was a pair of court shoes, good quality leather; navy-blue-and-white lattice-work uppers and a navy-blue heel. They were her size, made by the best shoemaker. She didn't know what had possessed him, thinking she'd accept a gift like this.

She looked hard at him, 'Why?' she asked. 'Why did you think I'd let you buy shoes for me?'

'I . . . You buy your shoes from my shop. I've had them in stock for a time. Won't you accept them?'

He'd apparently not seen anything untoward in his actions for he went on, as if he'd not seen her hesitation. 'There is much, much more I could do for you, if you would allow it.'

'What are you talking about?'

'Oh, nothing improper. Nothing like that.' He was smirking now. 'What I meant was: I am in a position to be of help to you, my dear, in your business.'

'I have managed my business, run the hotel, without any help up to now, Cecil Ratcliffe. I am not a novice, you know.'

'I know. I know,' he said smoothly. 'But there may come a time . . . Should you want anything . . . Want to buy anything . . . A word in the right ear, at the right time, can save you a lot of money and aggravation.'

There was nothing he could do to help her in her business affairs, but he obviously thought he could help. And that she should be pleased to hear him say so.

'All right, Cecil,' she said with a weary sigh. 'That's enough of that sort of talk. Now start the car and let us go to Chester.'

He wasn't going to be a problem after all. If ever he started pawing her again he'd know what to expect. She could deal with Cecil Ratcliffe and his nonsense; and it could turn out to be very enjoyable, receiving gifts, being driven about in the lap of luxury.

CHAPTER TWELVE

Alan had decided not to get serious about girls. He would not forego flirtations or the enjoyment of feminine company but until he qualified he would take these pleasures lightly. He had years of study ahead of him and there was only one girl he would ever consider seriously, and she was too young, too far away and, as far as he could tell, she was not interested in him as anything other than a friend.

But tonight he must write to her.

'Dear Rose,' he began. 'You asked me to write to you, so here goes. Medical School and Edinburgh is all I hoped for. The work is not a problem.'

He chewed the end of the pen for a few moments and then continued. 'Dad gave me some money just before I left home, to pay for my flying. I didn't expect it. As you know I have always worked in the Swan for my spending money so I was touched – and grateful. Anyway, I joined the University Air Squadron and last week flew solo.'

He put the pen down on the blotting paper for a few minutes and stared out of the window, thinking back.

The squadron demanded as high a standard as the RAF and he had been impatient for his first flight. At last, after hours of theorizing and hours of drill he was given his flying kit.

'See if they fit,' the instructor said. 'Report to the hangar. We're going up for half an hour.'

It was a clear, bright morning towards the end of October and the wind was a good south-westerly – perfect flying conditions.

Everything fitted and he ran, awkward in the boots, towards the airfield where the instructor waited in front of the hangar. Alan strapped himself into the rear cockpit, outwardly calm yet inwardly tense as the propeller spun and they went bouncing over the grass.

Then there was nothing beneath the wheels and the ground was falling away. The wind was stinging his face as they soared upwards and the instructor was shouting at him as he made the manoeuvres.

'Stick forward – the nose dips.' The ground appeared to rise to meet them.

'Stick back – watch it rise.' The wing tips lifted and dropped.

They circled the airport perimeter slowly, swaying a little when they turned from the wind and it seemed that, no sooner had they got into the air than they were coming in to land. The instructor made a perfect landing. Alan was sure he would never acquire the same skill.

But after only ten hours' dual flying, when he expected to leave the aeroplane after another perfect landing, without warning the instructor turned to him.

'Get into the front seat and take her up,' he said. 'Look after her.'

He had no time for doubt or nervous tension and he knew that, had he been warned, he might have suffered both. He was in the front seat, opening the throttle and easing her into the lift-off. Then he was up in the crystal air, circling, glorying in the lonely freedom of flight and the machine like a living thing beneath his hands and feet.

He had brought her in, flattening her, holding off until her tail came down and she touched the ground in a perfect three-point landing. The instructor had smiled and said, 'Not bad, not at all bad.' And he'd done it.

Martin Forsyth, his student friend and room-mate, was waiting for him on the grass behind the low huts. He'd blown part of a legacy on his flying and a seven-year-old car. He sat, the hood rolled back, engine turning over, grinning as Alan swung himself over the door into his seat.

'Good landing.' Martin pushed the Riley firmly into gear and headed for the camp gates.

'Thanks,' Alan answered. 'Did you go solo?'

'Yes.'

'Does it call for a celebration?'

They sped towards the city on the wide, straight road from the airfield.

'Café Royal?' Martin asked, at the top of his voice.

'Shall we ask the two nurses we met last week?'

'The infirmary's a bit out of the way,' Alan said. 'We'll give the Ferguson girls a ring.'

He wouldn't tell Rose about the girls, of course. He was not that much of a fool. He took up the pen again.

'I am bringing a crowd of friends down to Middlefield over the Christmas holidays. I hope to introduce them to you. We will be returning to Scotland for the New Year. They make much of Hogmanay and first-footing up here.'

He wished she were older; wished she might be with him; wished he wrote a better letter.

'I hope everything is going well with you. I will see you when I come home.'

He didn't know whether he should write, 'Love from Alan,' or just, baldly, 'Alan.' In the end he put 'Love to you and all the family, Alan.'

Rose worried that she might inherit the short-sightedness that ran in the family for, when she pored over her books in the front room, away from the noise of the family, her eyes were held very close to the page.

Alan had gone to medical school in Edinburgh the autumn before and though she had had a letter from him and had seen him once or twice in the holidays it seemed to her that he had changed. He no longer shared his time with her but spent days with Nat Cooper at Rainow Farm or else he helped his father run the Swan.

Then, when she had been shopping in the market a few days before New Year she had seen him walking towards her, a darkhaired girl at his side, and a wave of jealousy had swept through her, frightening her with its force, making her feel weak and angry.

She pretended not to see them as they made their way towards her across the busy Churchgate but Alan saw her and called her over to be introduced. Rose did not even hear the girl's name. She blushed and stammered an excuse for not wanting to talk, then she hid her burning face from him and walked away, knowing that she wanted Alan McGregor to herself; knowing that she'd never feel this kind of love for any other man.

She was 17 and she knew she was attractive to the young men she met in the Milk Bar on Churchgate, where she and her school chums gathered on Saturday afternoons. Many of these friends had brothers who contrived to be going her way when she came home from school. Alan's friend, Gerald, made sheep's eyes at her across the aisle in church and waylaid her afterwards on the pretext of discussing the problems of the geometry paper.

When she and her sisters went to the Picturedrome she always seemed to find Gerald sitting a few rows away. Men tried to catch and hold her glance in the street and this annoyed and upset her.

Rose would have none of them. She'd get her certificate and become a teacher. She knew she was not a girl with much ambition. She wanted to be a teacher for only two reasons; the first, that she loved children, and the second, that she would be able both to support herself and be worthy of Mum and Dad's faith in her.

There was an obstinate streak in Rose that would not allow her to be deflected, once she had set her mind to anything and now she kept her aims in view. She'd go to college, she'd stand firm against Aunt Carrie's opposition and she'd pray that the silly passion for Alan which had grown out of a childhood friendship would no longer trouble her. Most of all, she hoped Alan never guessed at her feelings.

Aunt Carrie did all she could to dissuade her. She came to the house with offers of work in lawyers' offices and she made appointments with bank managers which Rose refused to attend.

Rose knew that her aunt wanted her to go and live with her. She could not understand why Aunt Carrie would want the company of an unwilling niece or why her aunt didn't want her to go to college and become a teacher.

Talk of impending war must not deter her, she decided. Mum and Dad tried to pretend that it wouldn't happen but people were talking now about when, not if, the country would go to war. There had been a piece in the *Daily Express* about Air Raid Precautions; they had practised for an air raid in London and men were being recruited as ARP wardens at £3 a week.

Aunt Carrie said she had seen it all before, but Aunt Carrie always looked on the black side of life and was now, it seemed, eagerly awaiting Hitler's next move.

It was a cold May evening only weeks before the big exam, and the fire she'd been allowed to light had not had time to heat the front room. Her hands were cold and she found her attention wandering from the textbook.

On top of the piano was a letter from Uncle Patrick. Such wonderful letters he wrote. Mum or Dad usually read them out. He had always been a paragon in Dad's eyes and his letters were read and re-read. He was a respected journalist and often sent cuttings from the daily papers when he thought the article would interest them. She wondered if Dad had forgotten to read this one to them.

She had lost her concentration. She went to the piano and pulled the pages from the envelope.

'Dear Family,' she read. He always called them that. 'I want you to think very seriously about sending the girls to me. You cannot close your eyes to it. There is going to be another war in Europe. It will be far, far worse than the last one. Germany has re-armed. Their führer is rounding up Jews, persecuting and murdering them. Every week I hear from our European correspondents and what I hear frightens me.

'I have a home here, for all of you. Come quickly, before it is too late. If you two and Carrie won't come, just send the girls.'

Rose felt a shiver go through her. Dad wouldn't send them away, surely? Were things really so bad? Would it be a dreadful war? Would she be able to qualify as a teacher?

Aunt Carrie's voice was coming through the thin walls.

'Here it comes,' she cried. 'Listen to the news, will you.'

The wireless's battery needed charging and Rose heard the room fall silent. She could not make out what was said but evidently it was bad. Dad gave a low whistle of surprise. Rose dropped the letter from her cold fingers and went to join the others.

In the living-room they were all crowded round the set where it sat on the windowsill. Mum put her fingers to her lips as the last words died away.

'Germany's on the march! What did I tell you?' Aunt Carrie clapped her hands together in horror but her eyes were alight behind the thick lenses. Her high-pitched voice rose. 'Austria today! Czechoslovakia next! Then it'll be our turn! He'll not be satisfied till he rules Europe. It will be like the last time. A generation will be wiped out. All the young men will be killed.'

She saw Rose standing in the open doorway and a smile crossed her face. 'You'll not be able to go away now, lass. Not with a war on,' she said.

'I'll do whatever I like, Aunt Carrie.' Rose shouted the words as if to change the air of foreboding that had settled over the family. 'I'll do what I want to do, no matter what you say.'

She ran from the room and threw herself on to the bed as sobs of rage and fear overcame her. She wouldn't go downstairs until Aunt Carrie had gone home. Then she would ask Dad to explain Uncle Patrick's remarks.

The evenings, when Aunt Carrie wasn't there and her sisters were in bed, were some of Rose's most precious times. She, Mum and Dad would sit and talk, drinking cocoa and eating sandwiches around the fire.

The front door slammed with vicious force. Rose heard Aunt Carrie's sure tread as she made her way along Wells Road. She would lie here a little longer, thinking; thinking about Mum and Dad.

Dad was the rock of their family. He was the only man in it but theirs had never been a household run as some such families were with lots of loose gossip. Dad would not have any of them speak unkindly of people. He was a man whose satisfaction came from his family life; whose pleasures were homely. He'd told them that after the war, which he always referred to as The Great War, he'd had only one aim in life; to lead a decent, peaceful life with a wife and family. Then he'd say that he could not have been better blessed than he was with them all.

Rose smiled to herself thinking about them. Dad and Mum were ideal partners. They had always done everything together. From the first day they met they had never spent a day apart. They did the shopping together, cooked the Sunday dinner side by side in the kitchen, giggling and laughing like a couple of newly-weds: not only had they never slept apart, they even went upstairs to bed together.

Dad liked to draw, to read, to make things with his hands. He was lovely company but he could be caustic too. He was, at times a bit cynical about Aunt Carrie, pointing out ulterior motives or any falseness in Aunt Carrie's assertions. Mum always stopped him with a quick, sweet word and then he'd laugh and say something that only he and Mum understood.

She must have fallen asleep and, when she awoke, it was dark and she heard the whisperings of her sisters in the next room. Mum and Dad were downstairs. She could hear their low, earnest voices. She would go down and ask them about Uncle Patrick's letter. It was worrying her.

As she went into the living room, Mum gave a startled little jump, before saying, 'You missed your supper, Rose. Shall I get something for you?'

'Sit down, Mum.' Rose closed the door behind her and went to sit on the rug at Dad's feet. 'I'll wait for the cocoa.' She looked at Mum. 'What was all that about in Uncle Patrick's letter?' she asked. 'Why didn't you show this one to us?'

Dad put his hands on her shoulders and squeezed them. 'We didn't want you to be upset, love,' he said. 'All that talk about war and emigrating.'

Rose looked into Dad's face. 'He said, "Send the girls to me." You wouldn't send us away without you, would you?'

'He's a very deep feelin' man, Rose,' Dad told her. 'Your uncle thinks of you as his girls. He has no children. You are all – we are all, all of us – his family. He's frightened for us.'

'Have you written back? Have you told him we are going to stay here?' She didn't want Dad to consider, for one minute, sending them away. 'It would be like . . . Like rats leaving a sinking ship, wouldn't it? Running away?'

Dad said in a slow voice, 'War isn't glorious, Rose. It's degrading and evil. It's something the rest of the animal world has never sunk to.'

'But man has always fought,' Rose said. 'You did, and our Uncle Patrick . . .'

Mum had gone to stand behind Dad's chair, leaning over his shoulder and reaching out for his hand.

'I know, love. We had to. We wanted to . . .' Dad was patting Mum's hand to comfort her as he tried to explain something he couldn't understand himself. 'But I want to think that those things could never happen again. Especially to you young ones.'

'Oh, Dad,' Rose said. 'I'm sorry. I wish I hadn't been rude to Aunt Carrie tonight.'

Mum stood straight and put her shoulders back. 'I'll go and make the cocoa,' she said.

Rose got up and sat opposite Dad. 'I'll pull the stool up for myself when you come back, Mum.'

Dad had leaned forward in the armchair and was filling his pipe from a leather pouch, stuffing the tobacco into the bowl deftly.

'What were you and Mum talking about? Before I came in?' Rose asked.

Dad looked up from his pipe-filling and smiled. 'Your Aunt Carrie,' he said.

'What about Aunt Carrie?'

'I think there'll be a wedding soon,' he answered. 'Your aunt is being talked about all over the town as the future wife of an alderman; as Mrs Cecil Ratcliffe.'

Rose stared at him. 'It's not true. It's not!' she said. 'She couldn't. She couldn't marry him. He's a . . . He's a snake.'

'It's not for us to criticize,' Dad said. Dad now had that teasing look on his face. 'If Aunt Carrie wants a man, then who better than that esteemed old . . .'

'Dad!' Rose stopped him there. Sometimes Dad went too far. 'I know . . . I just know she won't marry him.'

Mum had come in with the plate of sandwiches and placed them on the table. Rose turned to her. 'Dad says Aunt Carrie wants to marry Cecil Ratcliffe,' she said.

Mum shook her head. 'She hasn't said so, Danny.' She gave Dad a look of warning.

'She hasn't said so, Jane. Not to you or me,' Dad answered. 'But everyone else has. Don't forget I meet her chapel people and the townsfolk every day.'

Mum's face was going pink and exasperated. 'Danny! You know she wouldn't. Why would she?'

'What else is there for her?' Dad asked, putting the match to the bowl of his pipe, drawing it over and over the surface whilst he sucked and puffed. Mum made a quick tutting noise before, half-smiling at Rose, she went back for the cocoa cups.

Rose pulled up a stool to place the cups on and sat on the fender, her arms around her knees. 'I know she won't marry Cecil Ratcliffe, Dad.'

'There's nowt so queer as folk, lass,' Dad answered, trying to do the local accent, making her want to laugh. Then he looked up. 'How do you know?'

'She couldn't bear to touch him,' Rose began. 'She's like me. We're very alike. I know her. I can't bear to touch some things; can't stand certain smells; I'm revolted by some foods.'

Mum had come in with the cups and saucers. 'You know that, don't you, Mum?' Rose said. 'Aunt Carrie's the same. I used to think I was odd; different. But now I think I know what's right for me, instinctively. I trust my instincts. If I sense that something doesn't agree with me then it probably won't. That's true, isn't it, Mum?'

'Well,' Mum answered as she handed the cup to her. 'You always used to say, "If I eat that, I'll be sick," and if you did, you were.'

Rose passed a cup to Dad who was smiling fondly into her eager face. 'Aunt Carrie's like that,' she said.

'There are some people who have a . . . an – I don't know – a kind of aura, an atmosphere about them. And with them you're either repelled by it or drawn to them,' she went on. 'And Cecil Ratcliffe's atmosphere is horrible.'

Dad was trying not to laugh. 'And what sort of aura has your Aunt Carrie got about her then?' he asked. 'A halo?'

They all laughed together at the thought then Rose became serious again. 'When I was little,' she began as soon as they were listening again, 'Well, let me explain. You know how the children used to play that game; they hold hands and make a circle around someone, then they call out "Who d'yer favour?"'

206

She saw Mum smile again, remembering. To Dad, who still didn't understand some of the local dialect, she explained, '"Who d'yer favour?" means "Who do you look like?"' She took her cup of cocoa and settled back on the fender. 'I always used to copy their voices, to be the same as them. I'd shout out, at the top of my voice, "Me Antee Carr-ee!" because I looked so like her.'

She had expected Mum and Dad to be in stitches of laughter at her but they didn't even smile. Perhaps they didn't like to be told how she used to talk with the strong, north country accent when she was at elementary school. 'I'm glad I never really spoke like that, though,' she said quickly. 'I'm glad you taught us to speak properly, Mum. It will be much better, for a teacher.'

Mum leaned over, ruffled her hair and smiled, pleased with the compliment. Rose hadn't told them, as she had meant to do, that the second question the children chanted before they would release their little captive was, 'Who d'yer go with?' and she always used to shout, 'Alan McGregor!' The children, satisfied that they had forced a confession of love, would squeal with delight, scatter, giggle and then take the victim into their circle before moving on to find another child to trap.

But she had 'favoured' Aunt Carrie. They were very much alike. Neither of them could eat liver, or kidney, or tripe and onions like the rest of the family did. It made them ill. They both held their breath when they smelled coffee roasting, though Aunt Carrie assured her she'd enjoy drinking it when she was older.

And she knew, too, that both she and Aunt Carrie were secretive people. They weren't deceivers in the sinful sense but neither of them felt the need to talk about their hopes and fears to anyone. They could both let the world think they were doing and saying one thing when they were really engaged in quite opposite thoughts and deeds.

She was sure too, though it was never spoken of, that Aunt Carrie shared her awareness of an atmosphere, an aura almost, about some men, that made you recoil from contact. You couldn't bear them to lay a finger on you. And Cecil Ratcliffe had that aura. He was false. And Aunt Carrie knew it.

Dad was sipping his cocoa, making soft, quick, slurpy noises before saying, 'The thing that worries me about it is that I believe Cecil Ratcliffe wants Carrie to sell the Temperance Hotel and put her money in with his.'

'No, Danny,' Mum interrupted him. 'Carrie told me that he keeps hinting. He wants her to put her money in the bank. He wants her to give up the hotel and have an easier life.'

'Jane,' Dad said, 'Do you realize what will happen if she sells up and marries Cecil Ratcliffe? All her money – everything will go to him when she dies.'

Mum was getting quite cross now, pink-faced. 'But he's old, Danny. He'll die first. And Carrie would never let everything go like that.'

Dad wouldn't be stopped. 'I know all about it. I'm an insurance man. I see it every day. Cecil Ratcliffe wants to get his hands on your sister's property. And your father, though he left it all to Carrie, meant you to benefit as well.'

'Danny! Please!' Mum was really mad with him now, Rose saw. 'Think what you're saying. She's always said she'd leave it all to Rose, to the girls. She's no fool. And she's had a hard life. She deserves a bit of happiness.'

'Well, she won't find it with him.' Dad's jaw was set in the firm line which meant he was not teasing. 'He's a nasty bit of work,' he said. 'I don't talk about people behind their backs and I don't let people tell me their tales, but there are rumours that persist so long you have to take account of them.'

'What rumours?' Mum asked.

'They say he was warped when he was younger. Unnatural. And this guardian work at the girls' reformatory. Do you know who metes out the punishments? Cecil Ratcliffe!'

'They have to be punished, Danny,' Mum said. 'They've done wrong.'

Dad looked quickly from Mum to herself, Rose saw, as if wondering if he should tell them all he knew, then he went on to say, 'They are girls, Jane. Young girls. He takes them into the punishment room and it's said he beats them.'

Mum and she had fallen silent. They were both shocked, though it was well known that the reformatory girls had to be corrected.

'Somebody has to do it,' Mum said in a small voice. 'We don't believe in corporal punishment, I know. But they've always done it in schools and reformatories.'

'He enjoys it. He likes punishing them. Then he makes them kneel and pray for salvation.'

'But, Dad?' Rose asked. 'What have they done to deserve it?'

'They've done no more than any young girl wants to do, love. They want to wear lipsticks and fancy underclothes. And these things are forbidden in there. And to the likes of Cecil Ratcliffe frippery is the mark of a Jezebel.'

'Oh, Danny,' Mum said. 'It gives me a queer turn, just thinking about him.'

'And by all accounts,' Dad added, 'he was cruel to his wife and daughter.' He knocked out his pipe slowly. 'I'd never allow a man like that to have authority over my girls.'

'Well, that's not likely to happen anyway,' Rose said.

'Carrie says he wants someone at his side. For council dinners and all that,' Mum explained. 'He doesn't want a real marriage. She wouldn't tolerate that.'

'If she can have Cecil Ratcliffe within a yard of her she can tolerate a lot more than you think,' Dad answered with a cynical edge to his voice.

Rose knew there was no point in expecting Dad to see how preposterous was the idea of Aunt Carrie marrying. Dad and Aunt Carrie had never been soulmates. But she'd never speak to Aunt Carrie again if she married Cecil Ratcliffe.

Three months later Rose gained distinctions in her Higher School Certificate. There was a place for her at teacher training college and, although it gave her satisfaction, the ebullience she'd felt at winning the scholarship did not return to her on the morning the results came out.

Mary and Vivienne were upstairs in their bedroom, sorting through Vivienne's dressing-up clothes, an assortment of costumes she used when she gave impromptu 'concerts' in the back garden for her friends.

Rose smiled to herself at the girls' cries of delight and the occasional shout of rage when Vivienne found she had outgrown one of last year's creations. Her sisters had one overriding interest in common and that was – Vivienne. Viv had asked to be sent to dancing lessons almost as soon as she could speak and went to Miss Barton's Dance Studio four times a week, accompanied by the devoted Mary who sat out and watched her sister through lessons in tap-dancing, ballet, country-dancing and acrobatics.

Mary, lovely Mary with her talents for drawing and sewing, had no higher aim in life than to be Vivienne's handmaiden despite Mum and Dad's hopes for her. Mary was 14. She should be spending every spare minute working for her School Certificate. Instead, she altered the costumes which Vivienne shamelessly begged from dancing troupes; searched for bright pieces of satin and lace in the market; found an occasional tuppeny treasure in the pawn shop sales – a broken mother-of-pearl headdress, sparkling glass necklaces and old-fashioned long kid gloves. Her reward for her labours was a share in her sister's glory and small supporting roles in the one-girl pantomimes.

Now they called downstairs to Rose, 'Alan's here! He's coming up the road. Rose!'

Rose watched him turn in at the gate. He was six feet

tall, dark and very slim with an easy, loose-limbed walk. Today he wasn't wearing the baggy old trousers and pullover he wore to work on Nat Cooper's farm. He was smartly dressed in grey pressed flannels and a green Harris tweed jacket. The very sight of him nowadays made her heart turn over.

She went to the door and opened it before he could knock. His face had lost its soft edges but not the boyish grin that spread across his features as she let him into the hall.

'Well?' he asked. 'Have you got the results?'

Rose handed the letter to him, trying not to give away anything by her expression but her eyes never left his face as his brown eyes flew over the page. He looked at her, grinned and threw wide his arms as if inviting her to be hugged. Rose smiled but made no move towards him. She was afraid that if she allowed herself to be held by him then the feeling of closeness might overwhelm her and she'd do something silly, like cry.

'Are you going to college?' he asked. He was still smiling, as if he'd not seen her hesitation.

'Yes,' she said. 'I've never been away from home before and I'm nervous.'

'Don't be. You'll enjoy it,' he said. 'I'm going back to Scotland in a couple of weeks to do a bit of flying.'

He followed her through to the living room where Mum was ironing at the table. Rose had felt shaky, alone with Alan and she was comforted when she watched Mum's quick movements; as the flat-iron hissed over a starched tablecloth.

'I've come to ask you to have dinner with me on Saturday,' Alan said. 'I thought we'd take Dad's car and drive out to a roadhouse I know where they have dinner-dances.'

Rose felt a great flood of colour rise to her face. He was asking her out. Was it a date? Did he want to reward her for passing the exam? Oh, she couldn't, not yet. She'd

211

make a fool of herself. He was used to taking girls out. She had never . . . never even been out with a boy. She'd have to refuse him. She took a deep breath and clenched her hands together.

'I'm sorry, Alan. I can't.' Her voice sounded strained and unusually high-pitched, false to her ears. If only he had given her warning, she might have worked out a way to accept, to deal with the banging of her heart and the jelly in her legs. Why was this happening to her?

It was too late. She wanted to change her mind when she saw his expression change. Now he looked the way he did with strangers, distant and polite. The smile had gone. It was as if the light behind his eyes had been put out. He turned towards the door.

'Write to me, Rose. Let me know how you like college, will you?' His voice was quiet and cool with a new formality.

She followed him to the front door. 'I will,' she said, 'and thank you. Thank you for being pleased.'

Alan looked hard into her face for a few seconds. 'We're still friends, aren't we?' he asked.

'Yes.' Rose felt a great knot in her throat. If he had only put his arm around her then, as of old, she knew she'd have been lost. But he looked at her with a serious kind of expression she had not seen before, making her look straight back into his eyes.

'I'll ask you again,' he said, 'when you are older.' Then he turned on his heel and walked quickly down the street. He did not look back. He did not see her biting her lip, raising her hand as if to call him to her again.

She ran back into the living room and flung her arms around Mum.

'Oh, Mum,' she wailed, 'why did I say no?'

Mum held her at arm's length and looked into her eyes with perfect understanding. 'You've fallen in love with him, haven't you Rose?' she said softly.

'Yes,' Rose answered as tears began to roll slowly down

her face. But she wanted to smile with happiness as well as cry. 'I've sent him away, Mum. Do you think he'll ask me again?'

It was a fortnight before she heard from him, when she received a letter telling her that he had joined his friend in Edinburgh in advance of the new university year. After that his letters began to arrive regularly.

Aunt Carrie gave up her attempts to keep her at home, prophesying that war would be declared at any moment and that the universities and colleges would be closed down but Rose began her studies in September at the college in Manchester.

There too, it appeared that nobody thought of anything but the worsening situation in Europe. Lectures often ended early, in discussions with senior lecturers about the inevitability of war. Outside, on hoardings, posters urged 'Don't Leave it to Others. Serve to Save. You're Wanted. ARP.'

Every evening, in her digs in Levenshulme, they listened to the wireless. At the cinema she saw Neville Chamberlain, whom she thought of as a true, honest Englishman, waving aloft a piece of paper on his return from Germany, which, he said bore Hitler's signature as well as his own, promising that their two countries would never go to war again.

'Peace in Our Time,' he declared.

Most people believed he had been duped. For, if war was not expected, why had 38 million gas masks been issued? Why was everyone urged to carry them at all times? Heavy objects in cardboard boxes with a string that constantly broke.

Rose had a black, imitation-leather, carrying case for hers and wore it slung across her shoulder over the blue tweed coat Aunt Carrie had bought for her. She took it everywhere at first but soon found it an encumbrance, as did her friends, and abandoned it.

On Friday nights, when she returned to Middlefield for

the weekend, she was in the habit of calling in at the Temperance Hotel when she got off the train, to have a cup of tea and a chat with Aunt Carrie before walking the mile and a half to Wells Road.

Always, Aunt Carrie told her which of the mills had switched over to making munitions and which were making shirts and uniforms for the services. She told her the names of the boys who had joined up. Gerald was in the army. She told her that the mill boys were waiting for their call up; that the country was re-arming as fast as it could; that she was buying tinned food and half-hundredweight bags of sugar, to store in her attic.

CHAPTER THIRTEEN

It appeared that Aunt Carrie had foreseen events. On 15 March the following spring, news came through that the president of Czechoslovakia had signed away Bohemia and Moravia to Hitler. Hitler had not consulted Neville Chamberlain and the good man was forced to admit, 'We have been deceived.'

Rose would finish her first year at college, she knew, but she had accepted the fact that she would not complete the course. In any case, she wanted to do her bit if it came to war.

In April all fit young men of 20 and 21 who were not exempt were called up. Many had already joined the services and some of the older lecturers had gone too, to replace the schoolteachers who were in the forces.

By May everyone was reconciled to the prospect of War. It was all that anyone talked about. Dad had dug an Anderson shelter in the back garden and, in the washhouse next to the back door, he kept a stirrup pump and buckets filled with sand and with water.

But it was Rose's eighteenth birthday week and she was home for the weekend. Aunt Carrie always made a fuss of their birthdays so, on the Saturday morning, she went down early to the Temperance Hotel.

All thoughts of war were absent today. She felt as if she were walking on air. Her feet hardly touched the pavement in Churchgate for, in her pocket, she had a letter from Alan which he had tucked inside her birthday card. She knew it off by heart and kept recalling it, word for word, as she glanced, unseeing at the shop windows as she passed.

'Dear Rose,' he'd written, 'I'm sorry I won't be home for your birthday. I am staying in Edinburgh for an Air Squadron course and will not be in Middlefield until mid-September. I enjoy reading your letters so much. Do you think you could write more often? Once a week?'

Here, the handwriting changed. It was as he'd broken off, thought a bit, plucked up courage and started again, for the writing was faster, untidy. 'I have no right to ask you to wait for me, I know. You are eighteen with no doubt half of Middlefield at your feet, but would you, could you, be my girl? I can't wait a week for your answer, especially if it is yes, so please telephone me,' – here he had given a number – 'on Saturday night. Yours, in hope, Alan.'

What a wonderful, beautiful day it was. She was Alan's girl. She was going to speak to him tonight. She'd be with him again in September. And she was glad, so glad that she had waited until Alan had asked her. She was glad she hadn't had lots of boyfriends.

Were other girls like this? Rose didn't think so. There were girls who could kiss anybody – the more the better it seemed. You saw them linking arms with one boy one day then another – and another the next and the next again. She could never do that. She had only been kissed twice. That horrible first time in the park when she'd felt ill for days afterwards and that summer, that wonderful summer when Alan had kissed her at his farewell party. She'd had to tear herself away that time, before she fainted clear away from all the lovely sensations that had swept through her.

She reached the top of the Wallgate and hardly remembered getting there. As she went down towards Waters Green she reminded herself again of what a lucky girl she was; she was going to see Aunt Carrie, who would make a tremendous fuss of her. Later she would buy chocolates on her way home and call for Norah, her old schoolfriend, who was coming for tea. And tonight she'd talk to Alan on the telephone and say, yes, yes, yes.

She saw Nat Cooper in Waters Green and stopped, to stroke the horse and talk to Nat.

'Goin' to see yer auntie, are yer?' Nat said, smiling widely at her. 'Watch yer frock. Old Dobbin's goin' to tek a chunk out 'o it if yer dunna watch out.'

Rose laughed and stepped back before the horse, rattling his bit, drooled all over her green print dress. 'It's my birthday, Nat. I'm eighteen,' she said.

'By gum,' Nat answered. 'I thought you was younger'n that.'

Rose laughed out loud. 'Do I look old?' she teased, then wished she hadn't for Nat, unused to that kind of thing, blushed bright red before leaping on to the front board and taking up the reins.

'You look luvly,' he managed to say, before urging the horse into a walk and turning his head towards the Co-operative Dairy. 'I wish yer many happy returns.'

Rose watched him go and looked down to check that her dress hadn't been given a wetting by the faithful old Dobbin who seemed to know everyone and every stopping-place in the town.

It was then that she saw Cecil Ratcliffe's car parked a little way up from the Temperance Hotel. It was the first thing to cast a cloud over her happy mood. What was he doing here? Aunt Carrie had refused to talk about him when Dad had questioned her and they had all assumed that old Ratcliffe had been sent packing.

Mrs Bettley opened the door to her. 'Come in and wait,' she said. 'Your aunt's upstairs, talking to someone. She'll be down in a minute,' before she scuttled off down to the kitchen.

Rose did not want to go into the residents' dining room in case any of the guests were still eating so she opened the door to the glass-fronted cubicle her aunt used as an office. She had never been in here before though Aunt Carrie had not forbidden it.

Everything was neat and tidy. It was a dark little cubicle, tucked into and under the curve of the staircase with a good view, through the glass above the desk, of the front door and hallway. There was just room for the roll-top mahogany desk, a chair and a drawer cabinet. The desk lid was rolled back. Set upon the top of the desk were a leather-bound blotting pad with a clean sheet of blotting paper upmost, a round jar of sharpened pencils, an inkwell in a silver holder, a wooden stationery holder with neatly stacked headed notepaper and envelopes and three pen-holders with shining clean J nibs.

The only disordered note was struck by the heap of just-delivered letters the postman or Mrs Bettley had dumped on the ledge in front of the little glass window. Rose picked them up to put them into a tidy pile. And what was this? She could not believe her eyes. A blue envelope, the so-familiar handwriting, a bulky number of pages inside evidently. A letter from Uncle Patrick. Aunt Carrie had always given the impression that she had no time at all for Uncle Patrick. What did it mean?

She felt guilty, as if she'd been prying. She put the letters back, as they had been, untidy; the Canadian-stamped letter underneath and went to open the door.

No sooner had she turned the handle than she heard Aunt Carrie's sitting-room door, right overhead, open; heard her aunt saying in a quiet, confidential voice, 'I don't want you to announce it or anything Cecil. Especially not at the chapel. I'll not tell my sister and her husband until I'm ready.'

'Very well, my dear,' Cecil Ratcliffe answered.

'If I sell, I want to get a good price for the hotel. If it is like the last time, if they want to commandeer it for a ministry, then it's better I'm compensated for a going concern.'

'I understand. We'll announce it in the New Year, shall we? It's only six months away. I've waited all this time, Caroline.'

To Rose's horror she heard what she could only assume was a kiss; Cecil Ratcliffe making sloppy noises and no sound at all from Aunt Carrie.

'Oh, God,' prayed Rose. 'Don't let them see me.' She pressed her back against the stair-wall panelling and edged her way towards the kitchen. The door was ajar and inside, at the far end of the big stone-flagged room, Mrs Bettley and a kitchen maid were standing, chattering, drying a pile of wet dishes with carefree unconcern.

'There you are, Rose,' Mrs Bettley said. 'Is your aunt down yet?'

'I don't know. I – I was in the – the – dining room,' Rose stammered weakly. 'I was j–just looking round.'

Aunt Carrie came into the kitchen, dressed severely in a plain black dress with cross-over fastenings, not a hair out of place. She looked just as she always did. Not in the least like a woman who had just been kissed by that disgusting man.

'Why, Rose. I didn't hear you come in, love,' she said, smiling. 'Happy birthday.'

'I – I only just got here,' Rose said.

Aunt Carrie didn't seem to have noticed her confusion.

'Come on then, love. Come upstairs. I've a present for you. Bring us a tray of tea, Maggie.'

'Yes, Miss Shrigley,' Maggie said.

Rose followed Aunt Carrie through the hall. The letters were gone. Upstairs, there was no sign that anyone had been in the room, no tea-tray, no disturbance of the cushions, nothing. It was as if she had imagined it, Rose thought, were it not for the fact that in the pocket of Aunt Carrie's light wool dress she could see the outline of the envelope she had held in her hands a few moments ago; the one from Uncle Patrick.

Aunt Carrie closed the door and handed Rose a parcel and an envelope. 'Here you are,' she said.

Rose's fingers were shaking. She hoped Aunt Carrie would think it was excitement that made them awkward as she pulled the string away from the little package.

It was a watch, a pretty, rectangular wristwatch in gold. It had black numerals and hands and a band of woven gold threads with a paler gold, Greek key design along its length. It fastened with a clever clasp.

'Thank you. It's lovely,' she said.

'Open the card.'

Rose slit the envelope and took out a little card, silvery embossing with satin violets arranged in its centre. The card itself was delicately scented. Inside, folded, was a cheque. Rose opened it out. 'Pay to the Bearer the Sum of One Hundred Pounds,' it said. She was speechless.

Aunt Carrie was saying, 'Well?'

Rose sat down with a bump on to the nearest chair. What a lot of money. She was rich.

'I don't know what to say,' she said.

'Say nothing, lass. Take it to the bank and put it in your account. If you want to leave college you needn't worry about money.'

'Oh, thank you.' Rose took her aunt's hand in hers, stood up and kissed her cheek. 'I'm going to carry on at college for now, Aunt Carrie, but – thanks.'

She left the Temperance Hotel before twelve, so that she could get to the bank, she told Aunt Carrie. But she needed to think, to puzzle out what was going on. Aunt Carrie was keeping to herself the fact that she was writing to Uncle Patrick and was not telling anyone about her intention of marrying Cecil Ratcliffe in the new year. Rose knew she would not dare to mention it at home.

Tonight, after she had telephoned Alan, she would take her sisters to the Picturedome. The new film was *Swingtime*, with Fred Astaire and Ginger Rogers. They would forget all about war and trouble and the thing Aunt Carrie was planning to do in 1940.

After she'd been to the bank, Rose walked down Church-gate and turned into the side lane where the *Middlefield*

Times Office was. Norah Blackford was a junior reporter there and would be finishing for the weekend about now. She pushed open the door and entered the tiny office. Behind a counter which divided the room into two narrow strips of space, Norah sat, slamming stamps on to a stack of letters. She looked exactly as she had when she was a schoolgirl; fair, solid and serious.

'Nearly done,' she said. 'You're early.'

'I thought we could go to the Milk Bar first, then up to Wells Road,' Rose said. 'Are you the last one here?'

'Yes. Stick some of these down for me.' Norah pushed a heap of envelopes over to her and Rose sat on the counter and began to work her way through them.

She grimaced at the fishy taste of the glue. 'Do you like being a reporter, Norah?' Rose asked her friend. 'Will you join up if war's declared?'

'I don't think they'll take me. I've still got asthma,' Norah smiled her slow smile. 'I like my job though. It's very appealing to nosey types like me.'

Rose grinned at her. 'Why?' she said. 'What do you know that we can't ferret out for ourselves?'

Norah went quiet again for a moment. 'I've not been told to keep it quiet,' she said, 'so I don't suppose it matters but . . .'

'What?'

'Put the bolt on the door, will you?' Norah said, serious again.

Rose did so and gave Norah an enquiring look.

'Do you want to see the old papers. In the cellar?' Norah asked, all in a rush, as if afraid.

'Do you keep them?'

'Yes,' Norah answered. 'They go back fifty years. I found out all about my father by looking through.'

'I thought he was dead, Norah. You never said . . .'

'My mother won't talk about him,' she said. 'I wanted to see what I could find out.'

'And?'

'I don't know if I ought to tell you.'

'Why?'

'Well, there's something about your family in the same paper.'

'Oh, Norah. You'll have to tell me. I'll have to know, now.' Rose's heart was going fast with anticipation.

Norah opened the door and let her into the office. 'Mind your clothes,' she said. 'It's full of dust and cobwebs.' She opened a second door which led directly on to a flight of stone stairs and felt with her hand along the wall for the switch.

Rose saw a deep cellar that went beneath both the outer office and the inner, editor's room. The layout was the same as above except that, below, there were no doors and the walls were lined, floor to ceiling in both rooms with strong oak shelves stacked with newspapers and labelled with their dates.

The two rooms were lit, dimly, by electric lights that hung on twisted and knotted flex low down, at about waist height.

'I'd be scared to come down here, Norah,' Rose said, recoiling from the musty airless atmosphere.

Norah was ahead, swinging the light about until she found what she was looking for. 'Don't be scared,' she said. 'It looks a bit of a muddle but they're all in order. Here they are.' She turned, with a pile of old papers in her arms. 'There are no mice or anything. Sure you want to see them?'

'Yes.' Rose answered firmly. Of course she wanted to see them. 'Shall I carry some?'

She took some of the papers and went ahead up the stairs to the outer office again.

Norah followed and quickly found what she was looking for. She opened an old yellowed paper out on to the counter.

'Look.'

Rose glanced at the date – 21 January 1921. 'Safebreakers

get fifteen-year sentences,' the headline said. Rose read the report. 'Three local men were sentenced at Chester this week to terms of imprisonment totalling forty-five years for their part in the robbery at the Regional Bank last October.'

She looked at Norah. 'It doesn't mention a Blackford,' she said.

'Mother went back to her maiden name and moved to Middlefield from Gawton where they'd lived before,' Norah explained. 'The name on my birth certificate is the name of the – the ringleader.'

'When were you born?' Rose wanted to know.

'January the twenty-first.'

'So your mother was having you at the same time your father was being jailed?'

'Yes. I'd never have known if I hadn't found my birth certificate and searched through these papers and old court records.'

'When did he come out of prison?'

'He didn't. He died there.'

'Oh, dear, Norah!' Rose didn't know what to say. Norah didn't look particularly upset – not like she would be if she found that her father had been to prison. 'Does it make any difference?' she asked at last.

'It's better – knowing. I always knew there was something. I think children do, don't you?'

'I expect so. Though I think every family has something it wants to hide,' Rose agreed.

'Look,' Norah said, pushing another paper towards her. 'It's on the centre page.'

Rose felt shaky now. She would much rather have walked away, out into the fresh spring sunshine, away from dusty cellars, old newspapers and family secrets. But she could not help herself. Nervously she glanced at Norah before opening it.

It seemed to leap off the page at her. 'Patrick Kennedy sent to Strangeways.' She read on, underneath. 'Deceiving

Miss Caroline Shrigley, Middlefield hotel-keeper led Patrick Kennedy, a jobbing builder to five years' penal servitude for fraud and deception. Kennedy, an undischarged bankrupt, defrauded Miss Shrigley of her home and life savings when he persuaded her to purchase the building company which he declared was his own property in September last.

'Miss Shrigley sold the Temperance Hotel in Middlefield's Market Square, and gave the proceeds to Kennedy in return for promissory notes giving her title to the unfinished houses. The accused, however, had no title to the properties. There were outstanding loans on these and other properties and an unanswered charge of bankruptcy in the Irish Republic. The court granted the said Miss Shrigley title to the properties when creditors were paid.'

'I had no idea,' Rose whispered. She folded the paper with shaking hands. 'Dad never told me.'

'They don't want us to know,' Norah blurted out. 'I'm sorry if it has upset you.'

'It hasn't.' Rose knew that she was not speaking the truth. She was upset, but she wouldn't show it.

'You're as white as death.'

'It hasn't sunk in, Norah,' Rose said.

'Let's put these papers back.' Norah began to collect and fold the papers. 'We can talk about it outside if you want to – or perhaps you'd rather . . .'

'I'd rather not.' Rose brushed her hands with her handkerchief, as if to take away the feel of the paper. 'Let's get out of here. We'll have a milkshake and a sandwich then we'll go home. I don't know what to think.'

They left the office and sat for an hour in the Milk Bar, drinking banana-flavour milk shakes and talking to friends, but Rose could remember little of the rest of the afternoon. All the time she was acting normally the questions were going round in her mind but she knew that she would not ask her parents for an explanation this time.

The newspaper could not have lied. If Mum and Dad had hidden from them for all these years the skeleton in the family cupboard, and if that skeleton was the fact that Uncle Patrick, their hero, had cheated Aunt Carrie out of her savings, then they would not want her to uncover the truth.

Why, she would only have been . . . No, Mum had not given birth to her at the time. She was not born until May 1921. Uncle Patrick was sent to prison almost four months before her own birth. So Mum and Dad must have run away to Ireland before all this took place.

Why had Aunt Carrie given him the money? Was she foolhardy in those days? Did she expect to make a fortune from the deal? It was not the action of the Aunt Carrie she knew. Aunt Carrie today would never be induced to sell her hotel and give her money to anyone. Would she? But wasn't she going to do that very thing again if she married Cecil Ratcliffe?

But only today she had seen a letter from Uncle Patrick addressed to Aunt Carrie. Aunt Carrie had always appeared uninterested in the letters he wrote to them all. Why should he write to her at all? Was there perhaps some connection? Something to do with the houses? Or the Temperance Hotel? Did Uncle Patrick still have some kind of share in the property? Did Uncle Patrick own anything here? Their own house. Dad and his brother had built it but now Dad paid rent for it. Had Aunt Carrie been obliged to tell Uncle Patrick that she was planning to sell the Temperance Hotel?

There was a connection somewhere that she was failing to make. She could not think straight and logically no matter how she looked at it. No matter how she tried to reconstruct the tragic events of the past she could not find, in spite of all she already knew, the link between the Aunt Carrie of yesterday that the old newspaper had revealed and the efficient business woman she now was. It was like a jigsaw puzzle with half the pieces missing.

Rose told herself, finally, to stop trying to guess what had happened. It was all in the past. But now she understood what Mum meant about Aunt Carrie having had a hard life. For the life of her she could not see why Dad was not as tolerant.

She got through the rest of the day and nobody noticed any difference in her. Then at last, tea was over and she could think of nothing but the fact that she would talk to Alan soon.

They were going to the cinema tonight; herself, Norah, Vivienne and Mary. They would go to the second-house showing. The others could queue for the tickets – she would make an excuse – she'd say she was going to the sweetshop for a bag of Palm toffee – she had no qualms about keeping it secret – and she'd slip up Rivergate to the telephone kiosk in the marketplace.

And she was there, a purseful of pennies and threepenny bits to hand, dialling the operator. 'Please put fourpence in the box.'

She was put through.

'Hello. Hello. Rose?'

'Alan?'

'Yes.'

There was a pause before he spoke again. 'Rose, will you? Will you?'

'Yes. Yes!' Tears of happiness were filling up in her eyes, making the booth, the numbers, everything blurry before them.

'I can't get to Middlefield to see you – not for months.'

'It doesn't matter,' she told him.

'To me it does.'

'I'll write,' she said.

'Can you come here? To Edinburgh?'

Could she? She'd have to deceive everyone. 'I don't know.'

'Think about it.'

Aunt Carrie would be horrified. If she went she couldn't

tell Mum and Dad, for they would not want to lie to Aunt Carrie. 'When would you want me to come?'

'I'm going to Kent next week for eight weeks. I'll be back at the end of July. Try to come. I'll only have two or three days – the journey takes a day each way.'

'Where will I stay?'

'Mrs Forsyth – my flatmate's mother – she'll put you up. Will you?'

'Yes. Yes!'

'Promise?'

'Honestly, Alan. I'll be there.'

'Shall I send money for the fare?'

'I've got money.'

There was another silence, when it seemed neither of them could think of anything to say.

'Rose?' Alan said. 'I'm longing to see you.'

'Me too.'

'Write to me?'

'Every day.'

Rose put the telephone back on its rest and ran like the wind, back down Rivergate, to find Mary, Viv and Norah waiting outside the Majestic for her, the queue gone.

'Hurry up, Rose,' Norah called.

'We'll miss the beginning,' Vivienne said crossly as she came, panting to a halt.

'Where are the sweets?' Mary asked.

'I couldn't get any. I was talking to someone.' It wasn't a lie and she was not going to tell anyone her lovely secret. Rose took her sisters' arms. 'Sorry! Come on. The big picture won't have started.'

They squeezed along the row to their seats whispering 'Sorries' as they went. They had missed the cartoon and the trailer. The newsreel was about to start.

A hush fell immediately the Pathe News cock began its crowing. And there he was, with his wicked eyes and small moustache, wild look and hysterical voice, the masses of Germans soldiers goose-stepping and 'sieg-heiling' for

227

him. It sent a shiver down Rose's back; it was hypnotic watching him rage and the whole auditorium felt it, sighs escaping from hundreds of lips as the screen image cut away into news of familiar, home events.

Alan waited on Waverley Station for the train. He liked the hustle, the air of expectancy, the great engines heaving away, porters, laden with luggage, moving quickly amongst the crowd.

Today it seemed that every train from Manchester and London was filled with troops or drafted men on their way to training camps. He felt himself to be part of the frenzied world of imminent war; knew that he would soon be uniformed and serving. He had no doubts now, only fears; only fears that he would not live up to it. It was only a matter of weeks. All the university squadron were waiting for the call.

'The train now approaching Platform One is the ten-thirty from Manchester Exchange,' the announcer was saying, and here it came, steaming slowly towards the platform.

Over the heads of the crowd Alan saw her; her flaming hair flying in the breeze, the navy-blue, pill-box hat held firmly in place with a gloved hand. The very sight of her was like an electric charge to him and, as he pushed his way through the crowd, he had to remind himself not to alarm her with a great display of affection.

He stood before her. God, she was beautiful. 'Let me take your luggage,' he said, reaching for her zipper-bag. 'Was it a good journey?'

She smiled back, a little shyly, he thought. 'Yes. I loved it.'

'Did your mother and father see you off?' He wanted to take her hand but thought it better to wait.

'I didn't tell them I was going to Edinburgh,' she answered, shouting a bit, to let him hear above the noise of the crowd.

Alan was surprised. 'Why not?' he asked.

'I – I said I was going to Manchester. To my digs. To see to things.' She was looking to him for re-assurance. She didn't like lying.

'Would they have minded?' he asked.

'Mum and Dad wouldn't. But Aunt Carrie might have asked where I was.' She laughed here. 'I'm still under her thumb, aren't I?' she said. 'Come on, Alan. Don't stand there staring as if I've come from Mars. Which way do we go?'

He led the way up the station approach. The pavements were too crowded to walk side by side and he turned every few yards to check that she was still there and to look at her.

'Soon be there,' he said. 'It's just up the hill.'

So, she was prepared to mislead her family, to see him. That put a different complexion on her being here and raised his hopes once more. Then he reminded himself not to move too fast. Apart from her agreeing to come she had given no indication that she was interested in anything other than his friendship. Her letters were long and confidential but in them she steered short of anything even ambiguous. She could be writing to a schoolfriend for all he read between the lines.

She was at his side again, at the top of the rise, looking towards Princes Street and the gardens. 'What a city, Alan,' she said. 'You never told me it was beautiful.'

'Wait until you see it from the Forsyth's flat. You can see for miles,' he answered, taking her hand now. She didn't take it away.

'What are we going to do?' she asked. 'Have you anything planned?'

'I'm taking you to the theatre tonight,' he told her, 'with Martin, my flatmate, and his latest girlfriend. Afterwards we'll dine at the Café Royal, then back to the flat.'

'Heavens!' she said.

He had planned it all. Tomorrow they would explore

the city together in the morning and take a tram down to the fun-fair at Portobello in the afternoon.

'Here we are,' he said. They had arrived at Ramsay Gardens and he was eager now to show her off to the Forsyths.

Afterwards, Alan thought, it was as if they had caught the mood that was spreading throughout the country. Everywhere, everyone was saying 'It might be the last time we can do this for a while.' Mrs Forsyth had excelled herself in her welcome to Rose. There was hardly a minute that was not filled with pleasure.

They had seen the variety programme at the King's Theatre. Martin had been at his most amusing when the four of them dined at the Café Royal and Alan had wished he were as debonair, as carefree as his friend whose lack of reserve seemed to hold both girls' attention. Then, in the middle of one of Martin's outrageous stories Rose had reached for his hand and tucked her arm in to his as if it belonged there and a great warm feeling of proprietorship and love had come over him.

The weekend flew by in a whirl of activity. They had not been alone together for more than a few minutes at a time when, on the Sunday morning, he stood with her at the station on the crowded platform.

He turned her to face him and clasped his hands together behind her waist. 'Thank you for being here,' he said. 'I wish you were not going back.' He wanted to hold her, to keep her here. When would he see her again?

'It was the best weekend of my life,' she answered.

'It might be our last meeting for a time,' he said.

The train had pulled in. People were pushing towards the platform's edge.

'You'll go into the RAF as soon as it's declared, won't you?' Her eyes were full of anxiety. 'I'm afraid for you.'

He pulled her close. 'I'll be all right,' he said. 'Take care of yourself.'

Then he was kissing her; hard passionate kisses,

oblivious of the crowd that was jostling them. She seemed to be melting against him, as eager as he was. Then she pulled back; breathless, pressing the palms of her hands against his chest and he saw that her blue eyes were huge and bright with unshed tears.

'Go now,' she whispered. 'I can't bear goodbyes.' She grabbed her bag and ran for the open door of a third-class compartment.

Alan stood watching her as she found a seat; saw an elderly woman speak to her as she sat down and resolutely turned her face away from the window.

CHAPTER FOURTEEN

Carrie woke seconds before the alarm went off. She always did. The alarm spring was permanently wound tight, only the lever which set and turned it off was ever used.

She reached over and turned the lever to 'off'. It was seven o'clock, Friday, the first of September and a beautiful sunny morning, as warm as any in June.

There was no need for her to rise early, for the lodgers did not take breakfast, but it was a lifetime's habit. Only two bedrooms were let and those to two elderly refugee couples – one Czechoslovakian, the other a German Jewish pair. Cecil had recommended them to her. Cecil had influence. He was on all the committees he could get on to.

She wished that she could look forward to marrying Cecil. Why did she still find herself unsure? He'd done nothing to make her uneasy. He was in every way most attentive and considerate. And there had to be a future for herself. She couldn't contemplate growing into an old and unwanted woman. She had always had someone to look after. Somebody had always looked to her for support. First Jane, then Rose.

Never had she been, never had she liked, the kind of clinging, simpering woman who let a man take charge of her life. She had always made her own decisions. But there were times when even she longed for a strong shoulder to lean upon.

She lay a little while longer, remembering the day he had proposed. It had been after chapel, nearly four months ago.

He'd given the sermon; a good one on the sin of David

with Bathsheba. At every 'smote' or 'smitten' Cecil had beaten his hand on the edge of the pulpit to make his point. And when he said that David lay with Bathsheba he seemed to linger over the words. All the members had congratulated him on the sermon so it must only have been herself who felt that Cecil overdid it at times.

He'd driven her home and she'd asked him in for a cup of tea. There were no live-in servants at the Temperance Hotel so no-one could gossip about it.

He always followed her into the kitchen, and this particular evening he had a high colour from the excitement of his preaching and the members' congratulations.

There was a little scullery off the kitchen. She used it mainly as a private wash-room. It had a sink with a gas water-heater above it. There was no hot water in the big kitchen. She didn't want him hanging about too long so she filled the kettle with almost boiling water at her geyser. And when she turned round he was behind her.

'Get out of the way, Cecil,' she said. 'I'm making the tea in the kitchen. Sit down at the table.'

He sat, on the edge of his chair, waiting for her to seat herself and begin pouring.

'You must know by now, Caroline,' he'd begun.

'Know what?'

He came right out with it. 'That I want you to be my wife.'

It was not a surprise. Carrie poured the tea and handed his cup and saucer to him. 'I've never much fancied marriage,' she said. 'I couldn't stand all that . . .' She took a deep breath. It had to be said, straight out. 'I couldn't stand any intimacy, Cecil. I'm not that kind of a woman.'

He put down his cup and to her consternation came round to her side of the table and dropped to his knees in front of her.

'I need you,' he declared. 'You are my salvation.' He reached for her hand and took it in both of his. It was not romantic or silly, the way he did it. His voice was a bit overwrought but, to her dismay, she saw his eyes fill with tears.

She pulled her hand away from his fondling fingers, just before he could press it to his lips. Where did he get the idea that a woman liked to see a man grovelling on the floor?

'What are you doing?' she said with as much spirit as she dared show, under the circumstances. It was unnerving, seeing a man who was usually proud and arrogant on his knees before her. She didn't know what to do.

He looked up at her with longing. 'I have no appetites, Caroline,' he told her, on his knees still. 'I need a woman who is strong, who will smite as she would a beast of the field a man who . . .'

'Stop it!' she ordered. 'Stop it this minute.'

He pulled himself to his feet and appeared to shake his head as if he'd been in a trance. 'I apologize,' he said. 'I have offended you.'

'I don't know what gets into you,' she said at last. 'You act so silly at times.'

'Can't you bear to have me touch you?'

'No.' She had better explain what she meant. 'I don't want that kind of thing. Not from any man. If I did marry, Cecil, it would be for position, security, for companionship and that would not be enough for you.'

Then he was down on his knees again, on the cold floor.

'It is enough,' he said with great sincerity. 'If you'll have me.' There were tears in his eyes and he looked so, so pitiful and humble that her heart was moved.

How could she refuse a man who said he needed her as Cecil did? And if she did marry him she would be a woman of rank; a woman of importance in the town. And he would stop all this . . . this self-abasement.

She looked at him with eyes full of compassion. 'I'm not ready. I'm not ready to decide, yet, Cecil.'

'But you will consider it?' He got to his feet.

'Yes.'

'When can I expect your answer?' He was smiling now, as if she had indeed accepted him.

'Give me until the end of the year,' she'd said. Was she hoping that he would tire of her before then? Or did she think he would withdraw his proposal? 'I know it's a long wait for you, but your wife has only been gone two years and there are a lot of things to take into consideration. The hotel. I will not sell the hotel unless I can get a good price for it.'

And that had been it. The proposal. After that he never again dropped to his knees. He sometimes kissed her hand and although she didn't really like it – he kissed the palm of her hand, wetly – it seemed a small price to pay for his evident enjoyment. She also had his protection, the little civic favours an alderman could arrange, her good, respectable refugees and the big black Humber to be driven around in.

But another consideration, and the one that finally won her over, was that Cecil would drop a hint here, an advisory word there, on the means by which she could make a great deal of money. He, himself, was not rich. He had only been able to make a comfortable living from his shop, he told her.

She had always put her money into property. Wells Management drew rents from all over the town without anyone knowing that she was the sole owner for she kept the deeds and the account itself at a Manchester bank. There were too many nosey people in Middlefield.

Cecil had advised her to buy empty premises that he said would be needed by a government department. She had questioned this; it did not appear to her to be above-board, but he had laughed and assured her that, since it was going to be bought, someone would make a profit. Why not herself? When she asked how he knew she was in a position to buy he'd told her that, though he would never break the confidence, his office – his official duties – gave him access to copies of all the deeds of sale of Middlefield properties. He knew what she already owned. So far she had bought well. He would see that everything she bought from now onwards was a sound investment.

Then there had been the empty flour mill which he had persuaded her to lease. She was now drawing ten times as much in rent since it had gone over to munitions.

As for his peculiar ways, the hand kissing and the occasional frenzied outburst of religious zeal, for all she knew most men behaved in this manner. She knew little about the workings of men's minds and cared even less. But she would not allow him to speak of it to anyone yet.

She got out of bed and went to the washstand. In the mornings she always had a quick, cold wash before dressing, standing naked at the table no matter what time of year it was. It was good for the skin; it toned the breasts so that they would never sag; and it gave her a delicious quick feeling of desire that she liked to deny.

She could hear the Singers, moving about upstairs. She did no cooking for them. Mrs Singer, the Jewish lady, cooked dinner for herself and her husband in the evening. The other couple ate their dinner at midday, as Carrie always did so that their arrangements were not at all inconvenient. In fact, Carrie thought, life was a lot easier with permanent lodgers. Both couples had impeccable manners and behaved both towards one another and towards herself, the men in particular, with extreme formality, courtliness almost.

Carrie dressed in her black working things, pulled back the curtains and looked out over Waters Green. An early stallholder, the baker, was setting out his stall. Nat Cooper was delivering milk at the far side, near the bus station.

She could not pronounce the name of the Czech couple so she always referred to them as Mr and Mrs Terry Chenko. The husband, who was getting on, about sixty, Carrie guessed, had found work in one of the mills. His wife spent her mornings cleaning the bedroom.

Mr Singer had started a little factory. The Jewish people

were very enterprising in Carrie's opinion. She had a great deal of admiration for them; in fact she'd set them as high in her estimation as the Salvation Army. Mrs Singer, who spoke no English, spent her day tearing up lengths of silk for her husband's cutters.

Carrie always thought of her as something like the poor girl in the Rumpelstiltskin story. Mr Singer brought in sacks and sacks of stuff and his wife worked away, not turning them into gold exactly, but getting through the work as fast as she could. All the little ends and pieces she kept in a large bolstercase and when it was full she presented them, miming ceremoniously, to Mary. Mary cut them or stitched them together into patchwork quilts, dolly dresses or frilly bits and pieces for Vivienne's dressing-up clothes.

She went down to the kitchen and turned on the wireless. It took a minute or so to warm up so she filled her kettle and set it on the stove.

'German troops this morning attacked Poland. Warsaw is under heavy bombardment,' the newsreader said.

Carrie turned it up. '. . . that if German troops are not withdrawn within forty-eight hours . . .'

So it was here. War.

Carrie filled her teapot and set it upon the scrubbed wooden table. She heard Nat Cooper coming up the entry, the alleyway that divided the Temperance Hotel from the next house, and went to open the back door.

'Have you heard the news?' she said.

'Aye.' Nat handed over a quart can of milk. 'All t'lads at Brocklehurst's mill have got their call-up papers.'

Carrie emptied the milk into a tall china jug and went to the sink with the can. 'You'll not be going then?' she asked.

'I canna. They're not tekkin cripples,' Nat answered.

'You wouldn't have to go anyway.' Carrie handed him back the rinsed can. 'They'll need farmers. What does your mother think about it?'

Nat grinned. 'She's gettin' the spare bedrooms ready for th'evacuees. She reckons she can tek four.' He swung the can around his fingers. 'Are you tekkin some?'

'I don't think so. I've two spare rooms but they might billet a ministry on me.'

She closed the door when Nat had gone. She was glad that she had Cecil on her side. He'd make sure she didn't have to take evacuees. She knew she couldn't cope with children. She found Mary and Vivienne too much for her. She always had.

She sat down at the table. She was relieved, in a way, that it had started at last. They said that an expeditionary force had gone to France. They'd have learned a lot from the last war. The French had their Maginot line. They would soon put Hitler to rout.

It was what would happen here that was alarming everyone. They all knew that this war would be waged against civilians. There would be bombing of all the towns and cities and wholesale gassings. Hitler would try to crush the British from the air since he couldn't march in.

'Mothers and children are being evacuated today from London . . .' the voice went on. 'All families who have been told to expect . . . gather at assembly points as instructed . . .'

She wouldn't take children if she could help it. Cecil had fixed it for her. Since he'd been on the committee the authorities had told her to keep a room free. With hers and the two refugees' rooms that only left the old maid's room and one attic bedroom and that was already half-filled with cans of corned beef, pineapple chunks, sugar and a chest of tea. She was only stockpiling the stuff that had to come in from abroad. She would not be caught out like last time.

She heard the postman at the front and went to the door. There was one from Canada – they wouldn't be able to get through soon – and a card, with a picture of a windmill and a woman with clogs on, from Cecil. He was in Holland. They were big chapel folk, the Dutch. He'd be on his way back now.

She had not missed him for a single minute of his absence. In fact it had been a relief when he'd left. Now that it was about to be declared, war would postpone any wedding plans they might have made. She could not think about marrying him until it was over. Everyone knew it would not be a long war, not like the last. Cecil would understand. He was a patient man. She respected him. And he'd respect her over this.

She slit open the letter from Patrick with shaking hands. It was as if her hands had a life of their own for they always shook when they held a letter from him before she even knew what the contents were.

'You should be here, all of you, out of harm's way before the war starts. You are an obstinate woman, Caroline Aurora. Rose does not need your supervision. She is eighteen and has her own life to lead. You are wasting yours.' Why did he say such things to her? What did he mean by them?

Of course her daughter needed her. Rose was talking now about leaving college. She had spent a weekend in Manchester last month, tying up loose ends, as she'd put it.

Rose said that she was going to go back this term but Manchester was no place to be when there was a war on. Carrie hoped she would be able to influence her. Hoped that Rose would not do anything rash, like join one of these new womens' services as she'd hinted she might. If she felt that way then she must take a course, become a First Aider or a VAD nurse.

Rose arrived home on Christmas Eve. She couldn't carry on with her studies when every pair of hands would be needed to help win the war. She'd done a year and a term. It would count when the war was over. Now she had to make a decision. She had been turned down for the

239

services as her eyesight was not good enough. They had advised her to wear glasses all the time, not just for reading as she did now. She would try to get work in Middlefield.

She was tying packets of sweets to the branches of the Christmas tree. Mary and Vivienne, inseparable as always, were sorting out paperchains and the tin bells they were going to pin to the curtains.

Mum was at church, setting up the crib in readiness for midnight Mass. Dad had gone to meet her.

Outside was the ever-constant reminder of almost four months of war. The Phoney War, the Americans called it. It might seem phoney to them, Rose thought, here it seemed real.

They had all been given identity cards and ration books. So far only sugar, bacon and butter were rationed. Aunt Carrie was looking smug about her stock of sugar. Any day now the air raids might start. All the windows in Middlefield were blacked out. No lights showed. A few older men of the neighbourhood patrolled the darkened streets, tin-helmeted and important in the officious ways of the ARP wardens.

Inside it was as it had always been; warm and secure, well loved and familiar. Rose had missed it badly when she was away and was glad to be home again.

The tree was almost done. In a minute she'd go upstairs and change out of the old green skirt and jumper she was wearing. She could put on her navy-blue dress ready for midnight mass. She looked over and smiled at her sisters.

'Have you made your mind up yet?' Mary lifted her head from the tangle of paper-chains and lanterns she was making.

'About college?' Rose asked.

'Yes. Are you coming home, or what?'

'If it were me, I'd go on the stage and dance for the soldiers,' Vivienne exclaimed.

'I'm leaving. I don't know what to do though. I've been turned down for the WAAF.'

She looked at Mary. 'What about you? Are you staying on at school to do your School Certificate? You sit the exams in May, don't you?'

'I won't pass it, Rose,' Mary said in a worried voice, 'and Mum and Dad will be so disappointed.'

Rose looked at Mary's sweet face. 'Shall I talk to them about it?' she asked. 'If you're sure . . .'

'I want to leave now,' Mary said. 'Before I fail. I could work in a shop, or one of the mills.'

'I don't want you to work in a mill,' Rose told her. 'You are too young.'

'Well, a shop then. The Co-op's looking for girls.'

Vivienne piped up, 'Do you still write to Alan?'

'Yes. He's hoping to get leave over New Year. I heard from him yesterday.'

'Ooh,' Mary sighed. 'I do think Alan is handsome.'

'What's that?' Rose jumped to her feet. There was somebody at the front door.

'What?' Mary dropped one of the paper lanterns.

'Someone's at the door. We must be showing a light,' Rose said. 'Come with me.'

Mary and Viv stood behind her as she opened the door a little way and peered into the pitch blackness, at first not able to adjust her eyes to the uniformed figure.

'Miss Kennedy?'

She recognized the police sergeant's voice and widened the door so that the light from the hall fell on his face. He didn't smile. He had the air of one who is trying to show sympathy and Rose clutched at her sisters' hands in sudden fear.

'Mum and Dad are out,' she said.

He seemed to hesitate. 'I'm afraid I have bad news. May I talk to you inside?'

They stood back, pressing themselves against the wall

to let him walk ahead into the front room.

'I'll not sit down, Miss. Thank you,' he said. 'I'm sorry to have to break it to you like this. There was an accident. Tonight. In Rivergate . . .'

Rose felt the blood drain from her face. She felt herself go faint as he spoke.

'They were killed outright. It was a heavy truck. The brakes failed. Your mother and father have been taken to the mortuary.'

Afterwards she tried to remember their reactions but all that returned was the cold feeling of unreality. She could not remember putting on her coat. She must have told Mary and Vivienne to stay at home. She remembered following the sergeant to the single-storey brick building that was set apart from the magnificent Infirmary.

She remembered walking behind him, following the lowered torchlight beam and she remembered, afterwards, how she had chattered, the words tumbling nervously as she tried to sound cheerful – how dreadful she'd been, as if it couldn't possibly be true if she behaved normally – lest the policeman saw the terror that had gripped her when he said, 'I'm sorry, but I have to ask you to accompany me to the mortuary, Miss Kennedy. It's your duty, as the eldest, to identify your parents.'

It was impossible to believe that they were here. An hour ago Dad had knocked out his pipe and put on his tweed overcoat and leather gloves. 'Don't let the fire out, Sweetheart,' he'd said. 'We'll be back before nine.'

Everything was waiting for them at home; the presents were round the tree. In the kitchen the stuffed chicken was in it's tin, mince-pies were cooling on a tea-towel. Mary and Viv had prepared the vegetables; they were set out in the saucepans ready for Mum to cook tomorrow. How could they be here, so far from home, lying on raised slabs, draped in purple sheets, white and still?

'Yes. It's them,' she whispered. The man held her elbow to steady her but Rose dared not let him see her

242

tears. She pulled her arm away and ran from the faintly-lit room, sobbing and stumbling as she fled back to the house.

Carrie had been told just after it happened. She was in the middle of taking a hot-pot out of the oven. It was hard to see if it was done, the light was so bad. There was only a single bulb under a white metal shade; the shutters were closed and the blackout curtains drawn.

The girl who came in every night to serve the lodgers – two ministry men for whom she cooked in the evenings – said, 'I think that was the door, Miss Shrigley.'

'You'd best go and answer it then,' Carrie answered sharply. 'And don't waste time.'

She placed the deep brown pie-dish on to the scrubbed table and closed the oven door before turning to see that the girl was back, an ARP warden behind her. She knew, before he spoke, that something awful had happened. She never showed a chink of light so it must be . . .

'Miss Shrigley?'

'Who is it?' she almost cried. It wasn't Rose, surely. She was coming back from Manchester tonight. 'Who's dead?'

'Your sister. And her husband. They were killed on the Chester Road, just half an hour ago. Run over by an army lorry.'

A wave of horror, mingled with relief swept over her at his words. Thank God it wasn't Rose. The warden was still talking to her. His voice seemed to be coming across a great distance. She clutched at the edge of the table.

'A lorry . . . The blackout . . . They wouldn't have known a thing about it . . .'

It was a moment or two before she found her voice again. 'Thank you for coming. You can go now,' she said. She turned to the girl. 'Finish off for me. I'll get my coat.'

Outside it was pitch black. There was no moon yet she managed to walk almost as quickly as she would in broad daylight. She knew every paving stone, every step of the way.

All the panicking feelings which, she thought, over the years she had conquered, rose up in her as she went. What would she do? She didn't think she was capable of looking after three girls. If it had been only Rose who needed her. How could she bring up the other two?

She had finally stopped going round to Wells Road in the evenings, with the excuse that it was madness to go out in the blackout. She had expected Jane and Danny to protest. After all she had been their main support all their lives, she believed. She had brought Jane up. Jane had always needed her sister's guiding hand. They had depended on her, always had. Danny had never earned a big wage.

Since the war had started she had taken to visiting Jane in the afternoons. Her sister needed her. But there had been no incentive, without Rose, and she had been unable to put up with the other two, especially Vivienne. Jane and Danny had spoiled them, letting them get away with far more than they or she had ever allowed with Rose.

And now Jane and Danny were dead. She couldn't help but think they had been careless. They'd done everything together from the day they'd met. It was just like them to die together.

'Oh, God. Forgive me,' she whispered. 'I didn't mean it. I've never been able to face death and devastation. I can't deal with this.' She was almost there and she waited for a few minutes, leaning against a wall in the darkness, saying a prayer.

'Dear Lord,' she said under her breath, 'Let me do Thy will. Send Thy guiding hand to me. Make me capable and fearless; Strong in Thy sight. Thy will be done. Amen.'

She felt better as soon as she had finished. Now she knew what she must do. She must be what they would expect of her; be as she had been when Jane was young; a solid, capable woman. She would have to make the decisions. She must not let them see her doubts and weaknesses. If there was a job to be done, she'd do it. No ifs and buts. With the good Lord's help, remembering her own father's strictures, she'd have to manage.

She opened the door to find Rose waiting for her. She could hear Mary and Vivienne crying in the living room.

Carrie took off her coat and hat in silence and went ahead of the sobbing Rose into the living room where Mary and Vivienne were huddled together in the big chair with wooden rails. Each had an arm across her sister's shoulder and their eyes were red and swollen.

'Stop it,' she ordered. 'Stop crying. Pull yourselves together.' They looked up at her, desolation in their faces. What else could she say to them?

'Three big girls? Crying? I looked after your mother when we were left orphans. She was a lot younger than you.'

Carrie hoped to give them courage by her example but the girls were now looking at her as if they hated her. 'There's a war going on and a lot more'll die before it's over,' she said.

'Oh, please God,' Rose was crying hysterically now, wringing her hands. 'Please let me wake up. Let it be a nightmare.'

'It's not a nightmare.' Inside, Carrie was in turmoil. But whatever she said seemed to increase their agitation. She made another effort to assume control. 'We'll have to work something out. I can't think what to do when you three are carrying on like this.'

'Don't you care?' Rose's voice seemed to be coming from another person. 'Mum and Dad are dead! They're lying there. Dead!' She dropped on to her knees on the hearthrug and put her arms around her sisters' legs, sobs tearing through her. 'I don't know how to live. I don't know what I'll do, without them.'

Carrie flinched at the despair in her voice. She made a move towards the weeping girls but drew back. It was vital she didn't lose control of herself. She must be practical. 'I'll make the arrangements,' she said. 'I'll have to let your Dad's brother know. I'll send it by cable but he'll not get here.' Then she added, 'You'll have to leave that college, Rose.'

Vivienne gave her a look of pure loathing and began to cry louder.

'Don't talk about arrangements,' Mary begged. 'Please. Don't.'

'Your Dad won't have provided for you,' Carrie added. 'There'll be nothing in the bank.'

'We'll manage, Aunt Carrie,' Mary wailed.

'Manage? Manage?' Carrie felt her control going. Her voice was high and harsh now. 'What on, Miss Clever?'

It was no good letting them think they could get along by themselves. She'd make that plain right from the start.

'You'll all come and live with me,' she said.

The cemetery was half a mile from their house in Wells Road and the day of the funeral clear, with a brittle frost. Rose had been trying all day to steel herself; now she felt herself quivering inside from the strain as she followed the back of Aunt Carrie along one of the narrow gravel paths.

Father Church led the straggling procession to the Catholic section of Middlefield's burial ground. The sun sparkled off granite chippings and lit upon white china flowers under glass domes as they trod on crunching feet. She had got through the requiem mass at St Alban's. It had been followed by a short service in the Catholic chapel of the cemetery. It had all seemed unreal; a few prayers, a few words, nothing to confuse or upset mourners from other religions; tiny vases of snowdrops the only adornment. Could the lives of the most wonderful Mum and Dad anyone had ever had end this way? And where were they, the bodies?

Aunt Carrie's long, black-coated back obscured the way ahead, delaying the shock until she halted, moved to the right and revealed the horror of newly dug red soil heaped beside the yawning grave, of the waiting priest, the two polished coffins.

Mary and Vivienne began to cry. Loud sobs broke the still air as they faced each other and clung together, comforted in shared misery. Aunt Carrie's expression was grim and dark with disapproval of the Catholic presence and the betrayal of her sister's non-conformity.

Rose had no-one now. She began to shake convulsively. Her arms would not stay at her sides and she pressed black-gloved hands against her thighs to steady them, making her rigid and attentive as the priest intoned, 'Ashes to ashes, dust to dust . . .'

From the little crush of neighbours and friends who stood respectfully apart, Alan moved to Rose's side. She had not seen him. The faces opposite were a blur but, as she felt his strong arm around her shoulders, she sagged against him with relief. She heard her aunt's quick intake of breath but did not pull herself away.

'Thank you for coming,' she whispered.

White satin ribbons were tied to the coffins' brass handles and one of them slid into the waiting ground as she watched. Rose reached for Alan's hand and gripped it as the hard lump in her throat pressed against her windpipe, stopping her from crying, from dropping to the icy ground and weeping until she was spent.

'Will you be all right, Rose?' Alan spoke softly. She heard the anxiety in his voice. 'I don't want to leave you. But I have to go back tonight.'

'Yes,' she managed to say.

'If you need anything,' he said, 'go to the Swan and speak to Dad. He'll tell me.'

She felt the tears coming, hot into her eyes, wanted all at once to bury her face in Alan's chest and cry herself out. She fought again for control, fought back the terrible gulping sounds that were coming from deep inside.

'I'll be all right,' she said, strangling her grief. 'Just hold me, until it's over.'

Four days after the funeral, an hour before Aunt Carrie

would arrive from the Temperance Hotel, Rose sat at the breakfast table, Dad's open cash box before her.

Aunt Carrie had been right about the money. There was none. But money or its absence had never troubled their parents.

'There's enough to go round,' Dad used to say and when he sold a big policy there was money for the treats Aunt Carrie disapproved of; dancing shoes for Vivienne, crash linen and embroidery silks in shimmering colours for Mary and the money for Rose's books and her digs in Manchester.

They'd never felt poor even though Aunt Carrie would sniff and say that a fool and his money were soon parted. 'The day of reckoning'll come,' she'd tell them grimly, 'then you'll not see hide nor hair of your priests and nuns when you've nothing to put on the plate.'

But Father Church and the nuns had been there. They had come round to offer comfort and arrange the burial.

'We have to leave Wells Road.' Rose closed the rent book, Penny Bank book and Co-op dividend card.

Mary and Vivienne were looking at her expectantly.

'I'm going to work in the factory near Aunt Carrie,' Mary said. 'They're training girls as machinists, making silk parachutes.'

'So'm I,' Vivienne added. 'I'm nearly fifteen.'

'We'll give you our wages – and if you get a job as well – we'll stay here,' Mary said, as if it settled the matter. 'We can pay the rent.'

'Aunt Carrie says the landlord won't pass the tenancy to us,' Rose told them.

She shuddered, remembering all that was said last night. How did you tell your sisters that they had to leave the only home they'd ever known, the house they'd been born in?

'Who is the landlord?' Mary took the rent book and studied the cover. 'Who are Wells Management? I thought Dad built the houses in Wells Road.'

'He did, but not for himself. He built them with Uncle Patrick and they had to sell. They sold them to the company we rent it from.'

'Aunt Carrie could ask them if we can have it,' Vivienne said. 'They'd not say no to her would they?'

Rose wouldn't tell her sisters that Aunt Carrie owned, had always it seemed owned, their house. 'She says she's asked them and they want us out.' She gathered up the books and placed them in the metal cash box. She was filled with pity now; pity for Mum and Dad who had worked so hard to give them a happy home; pity for her sisters who must leave that home.

Remembering last night she had no pity for Aunt Carrie.

'Aunt Carrie's not our mother,' Mary said.

'She's our guardian. And we have to do as she says,' Rose answered.

'She could live here with us.' Vivienne sounded resentful.

'We're to move into the Temperance hotel. We have to sell the furniture and everything,' Rose told them firmly. It was no good giving them hope. 'It's no good arguing. There's no other way.'

'There's no room in her hotel,' Mary said. 'It's full.'

'We're to have the spare attic bedroom.'

'Does it have to be Aunt Carrie? Do we have to listen to her nasty tongue all day long?' Vivienne asked plaintively. 'Will I still get my dancing lessons?'

'I'll pay for your lessons when I get a job.' Rose held out a hand to Viv. 'I'm seeing the manager at the Regional Bank this afternoon. They're taking girls on now some of their men have gone.'

'Sister Theresa says it's wicked to hate people, even the enemy,' Mary said. 'I told her that Aunt Carrie hates everyone, especially Catholics.'

'Don't talk like that.' Rose stood up and began to collect the plates. 'Go upstairs, make the beds and tidy up. I'll clean the grate and wash the dishes.'

'We could go to St Alban's and live with the nuns, couldn't we?' Viv asked. 'I'd sooner that than live with Aunt Carrie.'

'She'd never let us go there,' Rose told them, 'but we'll get away from her as soon as we can. When I'm twenty-one and the war's over I'll rent a house and we'll all live in it. I'll take care of you.'

She had tried to tell them the truth but things had been said last night that her sisters must never know. She felt no anger, more of an aching pain, recalling her confrontation with Aunt Carrie the previous evening, when her sisters were asleep.

Rose had gone into the kitchen to tidy away the supper things. Mary and Vivienne had gone early to bed. The days since the funeral had exhausted them all. Rose, too, wanted to sleep. She was bone-tired but she had first to talk about their future with Aunt Carrie who was at that moment sitting by the fire in the living room, waiting for her.

Rose put her head round the kitchen door. 'I'm putting some cocoa on,' she said. 'Don't get up, Aunt Carrie. It won't take a minute.' Aunt Carrie was sitting in the armchair, her face expressionless.

Rose put the dishes away slowly. She wanted time alone, to think, to decide what was best for her sisters. For herself she would not plan. It would be enough if she got the job at the bank and could maintain the roof over their heads. She had prayed for strength and a mass had been said. Keeping going was as much as she could hope for.

She felt she had aged. Two weeks ago her hopes and fears were all for Alan's safety. Now she must think and fear for her sisters as well. Would there be enough money coming in from a bank clerk's wages? Would Mary earn much at the Co-operative? Would Vivienne be able to contemplate a life without her dancing and her dreams of fame?

She hoped her aunt was not going to be difficult. Aunt

Carrie had been coming to the house daily since the accident, every day making reference to the near future when they would all live together. Mary, Vivienne and she could not think of living with Aunt Carrie and, eventually perhaps, with her and Cecil Ratcliffe. Surely Aunt Carrie would see that it was out of the question.

She had done all there was to do whilst she was trying to think of the best way to say what was in her mind. At last she placed the cocoa and biscuits on a tray, squared her shoulders for what she expected would be a battle of wills between them and went into the living room.

'I'll have to sort things out, won't I?' she said as she put the tray on the table, assuming an air of stating a fact rather than asking a question.

'You can start packing what you want to keep,' Aunt Carrie answered sharply. 'Have it sent down to the hotel.'

Rose took a deep breath. 'I have decided not to,' she said evenly. 'We are going to stay here.'

'You can't.'

Aunt Carrie was going to be difficult then. Rose knew she must not give in.

'I am going to get work,' she said. 'I've an interview at the Regional Bank tomorrow. Mary will get a job. I've got a bit in my savings . . .'

'Don't you tell me what you'll do!' Aunt Carrie's voice was rising ominously. 'I'm telling you. You will all come to live with me.'

'Please see reason, Aunt Carrie.' Her aunt had never been reasonable but at all costs Rose felt she now had to show her that it was not unrealistic for them to try to keep their own roof over their heads. 'I don't mind being responsible for Mary and Viv. We'll be all right.'

'You've no idea, girl. No idea what it takes to run a home and bring girls up.'

'I want to try.'

'You can't stop here,' Aunt Carrie said.

'Why not? I can pay the rent.'

'The landlord wants you out.'

'Who is the landlord?' Rose appealed to her. 'I'll go and see him.'

'I'm the landlord.' Aunt Carrie said it with horrible finality. 'You're to be out by next week.'

Rose saw that it had been a futile appeal. She made one last attempt. 'But we don't want to leave here,' she pleaded. 'I'm nineteen. I can take care of everything. I can pay the rent if you need the money.'

'That's what happened to me,' Aunt Carrie said, so bitterly that Rose believed she must have resented every hour she'd spent looking after Mum. 'You aren't going to go the same way.'

'But Aunt Carrie,' Rose said. It was useless. She saw fury on her aunt's face. Aunt Carrie was going to explode into a really violent rage, she could see.

'Your parents appointed me your legal guardian!' Aunt Carrie cut in. 'You're not stopping here! You've no money and you're not entitled to Relief. I'll have to pay for everything. I always have.'

'I can . . .' Rose started to say. But it was too late; Aunt Carrie would not be silenced.

'So you either come to live with me or I'll have you and your sisters put in a home,' she added.

It was as if she'd been slapped in the face. Always Aunt Carrie had done this, dictated to them, attempted to control them. Did her aunt have the right to impose her will? Didn't she and her sisters have any rights? She felt her face growing pale.

'I am going to find out about this,' she said coldly. 'I am going to see a lawyer. Surely I have rights of my own.'

'You have no rights to anything!' Aunt Carrie's eyes were ablaze. She looked as if she were about to strike her.

Rose was not afraid. She stood her ground against Aunt Carrie for the first time in her life. 'You don't have the right to tell me what to do.'

'I have every right!'

Rose closed her eyes for a second so as not to see the high spots of colour, the blazing eyes of Aunt Carrie. 'I know you were appointed our legal guardian but my father would never have done it if he'd known you were going to marry that, that man . . .'

'What?' Aunt Carrie was on her feet. 'Who told you?'

'I heard you. I heard you myself. Dad suspected. Dad would have changed the guardianship, given us to Uncle Patrick, if he had thought you'd marry him.' Rose felt herself close to breaking down but she could not stop herself, seeing Aunt Carrie's face, distorted with anger, glaring at her across the table. 'My mother is dead,' she started to say.

'You fool!' Aunt Carrie moved swiftly across the room. She took hold of her arms; shook her as if she were a rag doll then brought her face close to her own as she declared in a wild, furious voice,

'I AM YOUR MOTHER!'

If she had felled her, the blow could not have been more shocking. Aunt Carrie's iron grip loosened the moment the fateful words were uttered. She let go of Rose, who momentarily lost her balance and steadied herself against the table.

'You?' Almost inaudibly Rose whispered the words, 'You? My mother?'

There was no need to doubt it. Aunt Carrie had paled. The heat of her anger had left her and yet a change had come over her, Rose saw. She had softened, as if all her life she had waited to say it.

She pulled one of the dining chairs forward and sat down heavily, facing Rose. 'Yes,' she said. 'I am. I hadn't meant to tell you like this.'

A new feeling grew in Rose at that moment. She felt it; it was anger flowing in her veins. How could Aunt Carrie – she would never, never be able to think of her as a mother – how could she tell her the truth now?

'I wish you hadn't,' she said. 'I truly wish you hadn't!'

Aunt Carrie had not seen, or chose that moment not to believe that Rose had spoken the truth, for she went on, with a self-pitying air, 'I couldn't bring you up, love. I should have done. I regretted it . . .'

'Stop it! Stop it!' Rose heard herself shouting. She put her hands flat against her ears. 'I don't want to hear any more.'

'I want to explain.' Aunt Carrie began to tap nervously with the palm of her hand on the table top.

'Don't explain!' The words were choking in her throat. 'My mother is dead! You are nothing to me! Nothing! Don't ever say that you are my mother again.'

Aunt Carrie was on her feet, an arm around her shoulder. 'You will understand one day,' she said.

Rose looked at her. The angry redness had left Aunt Carrie's face. She was pale now, tears were sparkling in her eyes. But rage, impotent fury was still boiling within Rose. It was a new emotion. She had never felt it before. She wanted nothing so much as to hit Aunt Carrie, to hit her until she withdrew the terrible, the terrible truths she had been telling. She had no doubt at all that it was the truth and that Aunt Carrie wanted her to acknowledge it.

Instead, she pulled back, out of her aunt's hold and looked at her, unmoved. 'I don't believe you,' she said. 'My mother is dead.'

'Jane wasn't your mother,' Aunt Carrie said in a gentle voice. 'I am.'

'Exactly what kind of a mother are you?' Rose demanded, contempt in every syllable. She almost spat out the words.

At that moment she hated Aunt Carrie.

PART TWO

CHAPTER FIFTEEN

Pilot Officer Alan McGregor floated above the airfield, waiting for his signal from Control.

'Hello Red Four. All clear to land. Runway Two-Seven.'

He was coming in well; down to nine hundred feet. He slid back the perspex hood and put on his helmet and goggles, raised the seat, leaned out for a quick look and started the circuit of the aerodrome.

Losing height . . . reducing speed . . . a hundred . . . the tail was lowering nicely. Ninety . . . eighty . . . a few feet from the ground now. There, she was down.

The small wheels of the Spitfire touched the runway and began to squeal and tear at the grass as he braked. The long raised nose of the little fighter blocked the forward view and he had to steer a zig-zag course, following the signalling flags until he taxied in behind Martin Forsyth and George Jeffreys.

Switch off. Brakes on.

The rigger put the chocks on as Alan released the side flap and unfastened his harness. He edged out of the cockpit on to the wing, dropped easily to the ground and pulled off the leather helmet.

The cool air rushed against his sweaty scalp. He always had the same feeling; a feeling of relief with a tight thread of tension that would not be broken. The others had it too. The tension on the one hand begged to be broken and on the other made him want to get back into the machine; to climb skywards and feel the steady throb of the Merlin engine and the swift, responsive controls.

So far their guns had not been used in battle. They had practised; firing at a towed drogue or a white marker on the sea. Daily, they expected the call to action. For himself he was also nervous, and afraid that he was alone in this. The others seemed louder and bolder than himself. Martin in particular was thirsting for battle.

'Flight Lieutenant wants to see you, Alan!' Martin called to him as he headed for the Ops room.

'Right-o. It'll be about my leave.' Alan ran, heavy-footed in the flying boots, across the grass to his friends. 'You haven't forgotten? The car?'

'No. She's all yours. It's outside the mess with the hood down,' Martin said. 'You'll have a good run home in this weather.'

The other pilot, Jeffreys, had caught up with them. 'How long will it take you to reach Middlefield?' he asked.

'Five hours if I average forty.'

'What are you going to do? Sleep?' Martin asked.

'No! I'll spend a day with my farmer friend – and the others with my girlfriend,' Alan said.

'Are you still seeing the one you brought to Edinburgh?' Martin grinned at him.

'Yes.'

'What's she like?' Jeffreys wanted to know.

'Like Rita Hayworth! She's got red hair and a figure that would knock you cross-eyed.' Alan laughed at the expression on Martin's face. They had been to see *Fallen Angel* last week for the flying scenes.

'Go on!' Jeffreys evidently thought he was joking.

'Wait till you've met her!' Alan said.

Martin gave him a broad wink as they went to report on the morning's duty.

In the office a few minutes later Alan snapped to attention and saluted.

'You've four days leave, McGregor?'

'Yes, sir.'

The Flight Lieutenant ran his finger down the desk

calendar in front of him. He looked up quickly. 'Due back Tuesday, the fourteenth of May. Twenty-three hundred?'

'Yes, sir.'

The senior officer smiled. 'Sit down, Alan.' He pushed cigarettes and lighter to Alan who relaxed, long legs stretched out beneath the desk. 'It looks as if things are moving. You and another six men from this squadron are going into action when you get back.'

Alan felt the bubble of excitement that lived in the pit of his stomach begin to grow.

'Good show, sir.'

The Flight Lieutenant smiled back. 'It's confidential, Pilot Officer. Tell your family you're going to another unit. That's all.' He stood up and Alan rose to his feet. 'Good luck. Enjoy your leave.'

Alan went to the hut, threw his spare uniform into a case and, thirty seconds later, dropped it on to the back seat of Martin's Riley. It was the same 1928 model, converted from a saloon to soft top, with spoke wheels, a raised bar in front of the radiator and a long leather strap holding down the hinged bonnet. But it went like a dream when it was warm and Alan could feel the wind whipping his hair back as he headed out of camp, north to Middlefield, his father and Rose.

Nan Tansley would have his suit and flannels pressed and ready. She'd be glad to do his two uniforms as well.

'Tralaa, tralala, tralala, tralalaaaaah,' he sang. In his wallet were two tickets for Manchester Opera House and a performance of *La Traviata*. He hoped his letter had reached Rose and that she was expecting him.

He was glad not to be spending another evening in the mess. He always joined in with the others in the boisterous sessions; he could balance a pint of beer on his head and do the backwards crawl. He could roar with oafish laughter at the dreadful jokes. He enjoyed it all.

But he also understood the clinical, the psychological, reason for this unnatural behaviour. He knew what lay behind the hilarity and he often felt envious of the men who went home at night to a wife or girlfriend. He'd find himself lonely in the midst of the fun. He'd find himself longing for Rose, his studies and normality.

He'd been back only once since the beginning of the year and that at short notice. He'd contrived to meet her, but it had been on the day of their removal from Wells Road to the Temperance Hotel and they had not been alone together. But he'd seen in her eyes and knew from her letters that she was beginning to miss him and he believed now that at last he could declare his feelings.

He smiled to himself, thinking about her. Rose was unaware that, when she walked by, men's eyes followed her. She didn't know that men hoped for a smile from the wide mouth or a glance from deep blue eyes that could delight with their look of quick intelligence or make a man weak with longing at the unconscious look of invitation.

He'd known for a long time that one day, when he qualified, he'd ask her to marry him. But now, with a war to fight and his medical training postponed, could they afford to wait? And would she have him? A good number of the men he knew were marrying, making the most of the only time they were sure of – the present. 'Good God,' he thought realistically, 'I'm thinking about marriage and I've only kissed her twice.'

He raised his hand in a derisory gesture as he overtook an army lorry and he laughed aloud at the driver's two-fingered salute and blast of the horn.

'Tra la la, tra la la, tra la laaaah.'

The three spires of Lichfield Cathedral were behind him. He'd be home by five. Tonight he and Dad would have supper and a couple of bottles of wine at Lincoln Drive. Dad was going to volunteer for Coastal Command, if they could use him, he'd told Alan. It might be their last few days together for a while.

By four-thirty the Riley was skimming the last few miles to the Cheshire boundary under a clear, warm sky. Alan slowed to a snorting rattle behind a queue of traffic that waited to take the narrow bridge over the river Hollin, then started the steep climb up Rivergate.

The market square was busy. A policeman waved him into Churchgate, narrower than Rivergate and lined with shops. He passed the Picturedome and turned uphill again into Chester Road. There was nobody he knew outside St Alban's, though he saw the back of Father Church disappearing into the presbytery.

He was in Lincoln Drive at last, parking the car at the top of the short driveway, stretching muscles that had been tense for hours. He ran up the six wide steps of his home.

Rose shared a bedroom at the Temperance Hotel with her sisters. Aunt Carrie said that in case of air raids they would be safer downstairs and they had persuaded her to let them have the big room that would have originally been the servants' quarters. It was reached by a narrow staircase from the back porch, beside the kitchen door.

It was Saturday morning, a few days before her 19th birthday and she was dressing for the halfday of work. Mary had gone to the mill. Both she and Mary would be home at midday. Vivienne was asleep. As she pulled the hairbrush through her thick hair Rose looked in the mirror at the reflection of the sleeping Vivienne. She could hear Aunt Carrie in the kitchen.

She could not think of her aunt as anything other than she had always known her. Certainly not as a mother. Rose knew, had known from the moment her aunt had told her, that she had spoken the truth. She knew too, that Aunt Carrie had expected a very different response from her. Aunt Carrie had expected what? What had she thought?

Over and over it went in her mind; the same questions, the same reasoning. 'How can it matter now? I was brought up by Mum and Dad. They were my parents. That's what's important. I can't transfer all those feelings

261

to Aunt Carrie. Is that what she wants? Is that why she wouldn't allow us to stay in Wells Road? We had a right to live there. If Aunt Carrie had given Mum an allowance then it was no more than Mum would expect since she was bringing up Aunt Carrie's child. Bringing me up. Me!'

And again she thought, 'What is the good of telling someone – an adult – telling me "I am your Mother!" A mother is loved unconditionally when her child is young. Did Aunt Carrie expect me to fall down and worship at her feet because she gave birth to me? Has Aunt Carrie confessed because she wanted to unburden herself? Am I to share Aunt Carrie's guilt and carry my own burden of secrecy? I cannot tell anyone. She has told no-one but me.'

She picked up the clothes brush from the windowsill and swept it over the black jacket she wore to the bank and tucked her blouse firmly inside the waistband of her grey skirt.

She could not bear to think about it any longer. If she did accept her new, secret status then she could not logically leave it there. Too many questions remained to be answered and she did not want to confront Aunt Carrie again with the one she had refused, on the fateful night, to answer.

If Aunt Carrie was her mother, then who was her father? Was it the man she had once professed to want to marry? It could not be the soldier who was killed at the Dardanelles for she, Rose, had not been born until 1921.

Surely it had not been Cecil Ratcliffe? He was showing a lot of interest in her and her sisters, trying to ingratiate himself.

There was also a part of herself that did not want to know; a part that told her that it would have been better never to have been told; a part that could not countenance any more revelations.

Now, when it seemed she would be left alone with her aunt she deliberately left the room. She could not risk her aunt's tempers. The day would have to come when they told one another all that was in their hearts but not yet.

Now, she and Aunt Carrie treated one another with a kind of watchful politeness. And neither Mary nor Vivienne had noticed the difference.

She took a last look in the mirror. She looked all right. Then she ran as quietly as she could down the stairs through the door that led into the hall and out on to the pavement in front of the Temperance Hotel, to wait in the May sunshine for the postman. She did not want Aunt Carrie to know how many letters she received from Alan.

She tried to keep the paperboy talking until the postman rounded the corner from the steps.

'*Daily Express* and *War Illustrated*.' The lad handed the papers to her. On the front was a photograph of Nazi soldiers taking cover from Norwegian sharpshooters, yet the battles of Norway were over. Last night's news had been of the advance of the German army against the Netherlands and Belgium. She'd prayed, as she did every day, that Alan was not in danger.

She tucked the papers under her arm and looked over the boy's shoulder at the postman who had stopped at their door. 'Anything for us, Tom?'

She tried to sound casual but the old man must know; he'd brought her two or three letters every week since they'd come to live here. He'd seen her slip them into her pocket before her aunt's suspicions could be roused.

'Two for Miss Shrigley,' he said.

He was teasing her, she knew. Tom put his hand inside the canvas satchel and produced the hoped-for letter with a wink and flourish.

Rose took it from his hand and slid it inside the wristband of her white blouse before retreating behind the heavy oak door.

Her aunt sat at the table in the kitchen, drinking tea.

'Here's the post, Aunt Carrie,' Rose said as she dropped letters and magazine in front of her. 'I'll be off then.'

She put on her black jacket and looked quickly at her

aunt. 'I'll be home this afternoon,' she added with a smile. But the smile went unanswered. Aunt Carrie had turned her attention to the papers.

Rose left the hotel, turned the corner and ran up the ancient Hundred and eight steps. The steps were shallow and worn and their twenty feet of width were flanked by stone walls against which were fixed iron handrails that shone from the constant polishing of passing hands. It would only take two minutes to reach the Regional Bank so she halted under the church, in the shadow of the towering limestone wall and read Alan's letter.

How would she get through the morning's work with her insides turning somersaults?

'Rose Kennedy, please.'

The Chief Cashier was rapping on the glass panel in a high screen of polished mahogany that hid the Bank's depths from the eyes of the customers.

'Coming, Mr Wilson.' Rose blotted a current account ledger, closed it and slithered from a high stool; her black cuban heels clattering on the oak block floor caused the elderly Miss Thompson, who was entering figures in another leather-bound ledger, to lift her eyebrows in annoyance.

'Count Mr Cooper's cash, please,' Mr Wilson lifted the battered money-bag and carried it to a cubicle for her before returning to his position at the counter.

'Pretty as a picture, isn't she?' she heard him say to Nat Cooper.

'Aye. She's all right,' Nat replied bluntly.

Rose blushed for Nat, knowing how embarrassed he'd be by Mr Wilson's manner.

'I said to the manager,' the Chief Cashier went on blithely, 'that the only good thing about the men being called up is that the bank will have to employ young women.'

'Oh. I see,' Nat's tone was noncommittal.

Lack of encouragement would not stop Mr Wilson. He

was talking like this for her benefit, not Nat Cooper's. Through the plain glass window of the cubicle she saw Nat's weatherbeaten, freckled face.

'And we've got the prettiest girl in Middlefield, don't you think?' Mr Wilson didn't wait for a reply but added, 'It's given the old secretaries high blood-pressure, you know.'

Rose knew what Miss Thompson would think of that remark. She was sure it would not go unheard but she concentrated on counting. Eight half-crowns to the pound: she stacked and counted five silver columns into each bag of buff-coloured paper. The pennies and halfpennies took longest and Nat had collected hundreds on his milk-round. Rose shovelled the copper into strong linen bags and finished off with the envelopes of sixpences.

The bank's door was set diagonally across the corner of the building and, from where she sat, Rose could just see the stalls in the crowded square. She glanced at the clock. They'd be closed soon. Saturday was a halfday. The big doors would be shut in ten minutes and she'd be out there in the sunshine.

She might even catch sight of Alan in the square, unless he was helping his father at the Swan. Rose thought again of the letter.

'Dearest Rose. Please keep Saturday night free. I'll pick you up at five o'clock. I have four days, Martin has lent me his Riley and I want to spend my leave with you. Love, Alan.' That was all it said – but she knew – she'd read the thoughts behind the words in his last letters. He didn't see her as a schoolgirl now.

'Oh, Alan. You could have had any girl in Middlefield and you've chosen me,' she whispered to herself before carrying Nat Cooper's takings to the first till positon.

'There you are, Mr Wilson.' She put the bags on the shelf and gave him the credit slip, self-conscious as she turned the brass handle and made her exit from under his openly admiring gaze.

Miss Thompson no longer sat at the bank of ledgers. Rose put her pen and pencils in the drawer, screwed up the scrap paper she'd used, dropped it into the tall wicker basket and made her way to the ladies cloakroom. She walked through the empty back room where Sylvia and Pamela normally worked, listing cheques and totalling day books and cash sheets on two mechanical adding machines that whirred and clashed as the girls keyed in figures and pulled the operating handles as fast as the mechanism would accept them.

The tall, cast-iron monsters which were bolted to the floor were silent now, covered over with canvas hoods, and the girls had gone upstairs to a hastily-converted corner of the stationery store that served as a cloakroom for the lady clerks.

Sylvia and Pamela's expensive education had not prepared them for real work but they were, in their own ringing words, 'Making the jolly best of it.' Rose liked them; they included her in their conversation but quickly lost interest in her as they horsed around, sharing jokes, their talk punctuated with references to Cook, Nanny and 'going to the country'.

'What are you doing this weekend, Syl?' Pamela, tall, fair and ungainly, whom finishing school had not cured of a built-in clumsiness, slooshed water all over the floor as she scrubbed her long hands vigorously.

'Exercising Shamrock, I suppose. Poor old thing's not had a decent ride for ages.' Sylvia, dark and fiery in appearance, was gentle by nature. She rubbed lotion into her hands and looked at Pamela. 'War's a bugger, isn't it? What are you doing?'

'Going to the cottage. Mummy's says there'll be no ruddy petrol soon, so we're making the most of it.'

Both girls had an air that Rose wished came naturally to herself. It was something to do with the way they expected to be heard, she thought. They'd tilt their heads backwards and looked confidently at whoever was speaking to them. She heard the sniffs of disapproval from Miss Barclay and Miss Thompson at the girls' bad language. In case the older women were looking at her she smothered a smile as she checked her face in the mirror.

'What will you do, Rose?' Pamela asked. 'Take your sisters to the Picturedrome?'

'No,' Rose said. 'My friend. He's a pilot. He's coming home on leave . . .' She filled the washbasin with water and began to soap her hands.

'A pilot?' Pamela's voice lifted at least an octave. 'You lucky dog. Fancy not telling us you had a boyfriend.'

Sylvia stopped brushing her hair. 'Is he good looking?' she asked eagerly. 'You're a dark horse!'

They were curious and interested but Rose didn't want to give them the idea that it was a serious love-affair. Alan had never spoken about love.

'He's a friend I kind of grew up with. He lived in the house at the back of ours. The house in Wells Road. The one we lived in before,' she told them.

'Go on,' Pamela urged. 'Is he good looking?'

Rose found herself colouring again, wishing she could be like them, sure and unembarrassed. 'He's tall, thin, dark haired and sort of serious looking. Not what you'd really call handsome,' she said.

'How old is he?' Sylvia demanded.

'Twenty. He's . . . He was a medical student at Edinburgh and he'd joined the University Air Squadron. So he joined up,' Rose told them. 'Honestly, there's nothing more to tell.' She tried to sound as casual and sophisticated as they were and was relieved to see that they were satisfied.

Rose reached for the towel and dried her hands before putting her jacket on and going towards the stair door.

Pamela called after her. 'Have a good time!'

'Tell him to bring two pilots home for us next time,' Sylvia added, oblivious of the outraged looks of Miss Thompson and Miss Barclay.

267

Rose slipped out at the side door into the narrow street. When she reached the steps she stood and looked down on the iron-railed cattle pens, the roofs and chimneys of the mills and beyond them the foothills of the Pennines where the houses thinned out along the old road that climbed from Middlefield to Derbyshire through wild purple moorland. The only nice thing about living here was the view; the hills beyond the town and, away to the left, the flat plain of industrial land that stretched from Middlefield to Manchester.

Three markets were held each week at the top of the steps and a cattle auction weekly at the bottom. Cattle and sheep were driven on foot. The shouts of drovers and shepherds filled the houses in Waters Green and the cries of street sellers, rag-and-bone men and the squabbling children in Churchwall Street, behind the hotel, seemed never to be absent. Even the town sirens sounded from the cotton mills opposite.

Rose walked down the Hundred and eight steps. Mary and Vivienne were half-way down, sitting on top of the mountain of sandbags which were packed around the entrance to the crypt of St Michael's.

'Are you taking us to the pictures tonight, Rose?' the girls chorused, 'the Fred Astaire film at the 'Drome?'

Vivienne's lips were bright red.

'You've been putting lipstick on Viv!' Rose stood before them, hands on hips, squinting up at the impudent pair. 'You're not old enough.'

'Mary does. So I can. She's only eleven months older than me.' Vivienne tucked an arm into Mary's. 'Tell her it's all right,' she said as she nudged Mary.

'It's all right, Rose. We'll wipe it off before Aunt Carrie sees it,' Mary said defensively, swinging her solid legs in time with Vivienne's slim ones.

'It looks common,' Rose told them. 'You don't want to be like the girls round here. Do you?'

'We won't put it on to the pictures, will we Mary?'

Vivienne conceded. 'Are you taking us?' she added eagerly.

'I'm going out.' Rose gave them a hand each and they jumped down beside her. 'With Alan.'

'Ooh. Is he coming home?' Mary's big round eyes widened. The three of them had the same colouring but Mary, as she had grown up, had developed a heavier bone structure which gave her a practical look, making her seem older than her almost sixteen years.

'I want to see Fred Astaire. Will you and Alan take us to the pictures?' Vivienne asked insistently. Rose could not remain cross with Viv, the real beauty of the family, she believed. Vivienne had chiselled features, a graceful body and a wildness, almost a wanton look about her; a girl for whom excitement was a drug and as necessary as air and water.

'If you take that muck off your face, I'll pay you both in,' Rose said. 'Where's Aunt Carrie?'

'In the market,' Mary replied.

'Good. I'll have a wash before she comes back, while I've got the scullery to myself,' Rose said.

She went down the rest of the steps to Waters Green, turned into the entry and let herself into the back door of the Temperance Hotel. The kitchen was empty. Off the kitchen a latched door led into the scullery, two steps down. The tiny room, stone-flagged, cold, smelling of damp and gas, overlooked the yard.

A brass cold-water tap was set high above a shallow, brown slopstone-sink which held a white enamelled washing bowl with chipped and rusty edges. Beneath the sink a yellow curtain concealed a matching pail and jug. Rose set them on the wooden draining board and lit the gas. A tiny window, pasted with a lattice-work transfer to make it opaque and criss-crossed with sticky tape against bomb-blast, when it came, gave poor light to the little room.

Rose filled the bowl with hot water, put the catch on the

door and slipped out of her clothes. She'd wear her best dress, a blue crêpe-de-chine tonight. It had a sweetheart neck and a little fall of pleats over the right hip, covered buttons with loops all down the back and tight bands at the wrists. She'd wear her barathea jacket over it and the black hat that fitted the crown of her head so that her hair curled around it. There was about half an inch of Evening in Paris perfume in its navy blue bottle on her dressing table. She loved its heady scent.

She'd have to tell Aunt Carrie she was going out with Alan. There might be a scene, but she was prepared for it. Mum and Dad wouldn't have minded and, she reminded herself, 'I'm almost nineteen. Aunt Carrie can't run my life.'

Then as she thought about Mum and Dad again, all the same questions rose to torment her. Was there a man somewhere, at the moment, in Middlefield who knew her to be his daughter? She tried to press the facts she knew into the history of her birth and found again that too many other questions were raised. There were some pieces of the puzzle that didn't fit. It was like a detective story without the clues. And always there was the suspicion that again she had failed to make the logical connections. That the answer was staring her in the face and she simply couldn't see it.

What did she know? She knew that Mum and Dad had fled to Ireland to marry, three months before her birth. Mum had been 15 at the time, that much had been revealed with the discovery of the certificates in Wells Road. Aunt Carrie, at the same time, had lost her home and her money to a man who had smooth-talked her out of them and was in the throes of a legal battle to salvage their inheritance. And she was pregnant. With her.

Did Aunt Carrie share the same medical history as she and Mum had shared. For Mum had told her that she was not able to have many babies.

Had the man, her true father, deserted Aunt Carrie?

270

Why had she not married him? Was he dead?

And how, most of all, could Aunt Carrie, a woman she had always thought of as most like herself, deny her strongest instinct, her maternal feelings, and give her baby to Mum to bring up?

She must really have hated me, Rose thought.

Rose had no doubt that Mum and Dad had done it gladly. She had always known herself to be loved and, in some way, special.

Sometimes, she thought, she would go mad, thinking in this way. She must try not to do it. She concentrated on her preparations.

In a few hours she would be going out with Alan. Where was he going to take her? Her stomach gave a funny lurch when she thought about him. She'd only seen him once since the funeral.

Nat Cooper crossed the square from the Regional Bank to the Swan. The Swan was the busiest pub in Middlefield and the bar smoky and crowded when he arrived. Stallholders leaned against oak pillars, old men exchanged experiences with young soldiers from the training camp a mile or so out of town; and Nat went up to the bar and watched, admiringly, Mona Siddal as he always did.

'Hello Nat,' Douglas McGregor said cheerfully, 'You'll have to stand for a wee while. Your table's occupied.'

The shyness that had overcome Nat when he'd seen Rose at the bank fell away as he ordered his first pint.

'Alan's home this weekend. Did you know?' Douglas said.

'He's got leave, then?' Nat drank half of his pint at one draught, smiling hugely when he put the glass down. Then the smile left his face as he asked, 'Did you 'ear t' news, last night?'

'Aye. They'll not stop until they reach the coast,' Douglas said grimly. 'I think it will be a while before Alan gets leave again.'

'Will 'e come up to Rainow d'yer think?'

'I'm sure he will. He'll want to see you and your mother. And you know he likes the farm.' Douglas pulled the beer pump's china handgrip and filled tankards for two soldiers who stood to attention, smart as paint in new uniforms.

'He likes flying, doesn't he?' Nat asked. 'He'd rather that than be a farmer.' Nat looked down at his right leg which was a good half-inch shorter than his left and prevented him from playing his part in the war. The accident when he was 14, his leg crushed between the shaft and wheel of a haycart, had left him with a limp that a built-up boot could not disguise.

A working farmer need not expect to be called up but Nat would happily have turned the place over to an older man for the duration of the fighting if he'd been able to pass a medical test.

Douglas leaned over the bar. 'He enjoys reaping a field of wheat as well as he likes flying over it. Will ye take a dram?'

Nat grinned. 'Ta,' he said, then casually added, 'I saw Rose Kennedy in the bank. She must have left college afore she qualified. Proper shame, that is.'

'Aye. She's a bonny lass,' Douglas replied. 'Have you found a lass, Nat?'

'No. Not yet,' Nat said. He couldn't pluck up the courage, that was the trouble. How could he go up to her now? Him a twenty-six-year old farmer and her a pretty little nineteen-year-old bank clerk? How could he tell her that he wanted a wife and she'd spoiled him for anyone else? That even now, after all these years, any girl he met seemed a simpering idiot beside her?

'You could do with a wife though. There's a lot of work to be done on yon farm and your mother's getting on,' Douglas continued.

Nat looked at the face of the big Scotsman. 'I canna ask a girl to start courting and tell her about the 'ard life of a

272

farmer, now, can I?' he said. 'Any road we've got three landgirls since the elder Gleave brothers went. Gimme another pint, Doug.'

Nat took his pint glass and found a seat at the table just inside the door. Two young women were drinking port, their vermilion-painted lips streaking their glasses, their bright red nails flying up to their hair or tapping on the table. They were well known in Middlefield for their habit of spending every Saturday moving from pub to pub, assessing the company they were likely to find that night. They were a loud and cheeky pair and Nat would have avoided them if he could but theirs was the only table with a spare seat. They stopped talking as he sat down and Nat tried not to look at them but looked instead at his square hands where they lay across his muscular thighs.

It wasn't that he lacked the confidence to talk to girls, rather the opposite. He could get a girl interested, buy her a few drinks; maybe a plate of fish and chips in the little café on Rivergate, take her to the pictures, see her home. Then if he was lucky . . .

He'd been doing it for years: coming down to Middlefield on a Saturday, his shoes and trilby in the wooden box beside the milk churns, his best clothes under the linen coat he wore on the round. He'd leave Mam and young Jimmie Gleave to do the afternoon milking and return, steadily climbing through the sweet-scented night, the three miles to Rainow by the light of the lanterns that swung from the front of the cart; humming if he'd struck lucky, singing tipsy songs in his tuneful baritone if he'd spent the evening in the Swan.

The blackout restrictions didn't stop him. Where the car drivers had to manage on half-blacked headlights, if they were brave enough to chance the roads, a horse would return the way he'd come and Dobbin knew his way back to Rainow, lanterns or no.

No, he didn't lack confidence. It was just that he'd

never found a girl he'd wanted to ask out twice. And he didn't have the nerve to ask out the one he wanted, even once.

The two floosies, as he thought of them, were scraping back their chairs, pushing by him to the signalling soldiers. Nat stood up to let them pass and as he did so, saw Alan, in flannels and an open-necked shirt, making his way towards the table through the crush.

'Nat!'

'Alan. Good to see yer.' Nat shook his hand warmly. 'Is this yer furst leave? Sit down. I'll get yer a beer.'

'It's all right. Dad's sending two over,' Alan said. 'Yes. My first. I've got four days. Can I come up to Rainow on Monday?'

'Aye. Be glad to see yer. What are you doing tonight then?'

'I'm taking my girlfiend out. To the theatre. To Manchester.'

'Oh. This is something new,' Nat laughed. 'Who's the girlfriend?'

'Rose. Rose Kennedy.'

Nat stared for a moment then felt the colour drain from his face. What a fool he'd been, imagining all these years that he might, one day, stand a chance. He must not let Alan see that his words had had any effect on him. He'd have to put all thoughts of Rose Kennedy from his mind now. What a good thing he hadn't asked her. He fumbled in his pocket for a handkerchief and blew his nose thoroughly and noisily.

'What about yourself?' Alan was saying. 'Are you fixed up for the evening?'

Nat stuffed the handkerchief back in his pocket. 'Not yet,' he said. 'But I'm going to ask your barmaid out as soon as I've had another pint.'

Mona was looking at him, eyebrows lifted in questioning.

'Another two pints, Mona,' Nat called to her. Then he gave her a wide smile and a broad wink. 'Please.'

He'd have to mind his manners with Mona if he wanted her to go out with him. She wasn't an ordinary sort of girl.

CHAPTER SIXTEEN

Outside, in the market square, Carrie shopped for some vegetables for the weekend.

'Two pounds of carrots, please,' she said to the stall-keeper. 'I don't suppose you've any Spanish onions?'

Already she could see what rationing was going to be like if things got worse. Some shopkeepers were acting as if they were the masters and the customers the servants. And you had to keep a civil tongue in your head or they'd never give you anything that wasn't on show. One or two had taken to keeping stuff under the counter for their favourites.

Good. The woman had found her some onions off the back of the stall. 'And ten pounds of potatoes,' Carrie added. She handed over the brown Rexine bag Mary had made for her. 'Put them in here.'

Mary was no trouble. She had taken a job at the mill, making army shirts. Mary was the one most like Jane had been. It was lovely having Mary around; it made up in a way for the loss of Jane, to whose death she had not yet become reconciled. It was peculiar, the way she thought Jane was still there.

'And a white cabbage, please,' she said. She'd told Mrs Chenko she'd get her one. They seemed to use a lot of white cabbage, these foreigners. Mr Terry Chenko had turned out to be a lively, talented man. He was musical. He had taught music at an academy in Danzig. When the piano had been brought from Wells Road and set up in the lodgers' dining room he'd asked if he could play it. He was a good pianist, playing by ear. And he could play the fiddle too. You only needed to hum a tune and he'd got it. It was as if he knew every piece of music that had ever been written. It was a gift, like singing was.

Vivienne wanted to ask him to play tunes for her to dance to. But she'd told her. 'no.' She didn't mind Mr Chenko playing music for singing to. But she wouldn't encourage Vivienne to keep her head full of that dancing nonsense.

Vivienne was a thorn in her side. If she'd had charge of her from the start, Carrie knew, she would never have been so wayward. Still, she could leave school soon; go to work in the mill; use up her energies. She was nearly 15. Jane and Danny wanted them to take their school certificates but their two, Mary and Vivienne, weren't clever. There, she was doing it again, thinking Jane and Danny were alive. Was she going mad?

Sometimes she believed that she was indeed going mad. The strain between herself and Rose was something she could not get used to. It was destroying her.

Since the night she could hardly bear to remember, when she'd told Rose the truth she had not been able to sleep properly. She lay, hour after hour, her thoughts in total confusion, asking herself if she had been right to tell her? Why was Rose behaving this way? Why had Rose turned against her?

Jessie Burgess was coming across the square to talk to her. She had on the brown coat and hat she'd worn for years. Carrie went towards her. 'Hello Jessie. Where's your Ronnie?' she asked. 'Is he still in France?'

'As far as we know, Miss Shrigley,' Jessie answered.

'It must be a worry for you.' Their Ronnie was the apple of Jessie Burgess's eye. She had three more sons but Ronnie had always been her favourite. 'He's always in our prayers at chapel.'

'I know. I haven't been to chapel for a week or two,' Jessie was saying apologetically. 'We've got me mother with us now. She's a lot of work.'

'It's six weeks,' Carrie said, 'or more, since you were at chapel.'

'How are you managing, Miss Shrigley? It must be hard for you. Bacon and butter being rationed. They say it's only a matter of time before meat . . . But then I expect that – you and Mr Ratcliffe being – promised-like, he'll be a big help.'

'I manage,' Carrie interrupted her.

So. They were all wagging – all the tongues – about herself and Cecil. He must have let it slip at the chapel, that he'd asked her. After Jane and Danny had died she had told him that any wedding plans would have to be set aside, at least until the war was over and he had agreed.

'I can remember the last time.' She looked Jessie Burgess straight in the face. 'I once paid twenty-two and six for a chicken in 1918.'

'Well, I suppose . . .'

Jessie looked worried sick. Carrie felt sorry for her. 'They're being fair this time, Jessie. It doesn't matter who you know. My knowing Mr Ratcliffe makes no difference. There's no such thing as influence. They'll ration everything fairly. No-one will get more than their share.'

'I hope we can manage,' Jessie said. 'I wanted to get some oranges . . .'

'They've got some in Marks and Spencer's,' Carrie said. 'Hurry up. There was a queue an hour ago.'

Jessie hurried away. Carrie watched her go, fast as a little mouse she was, her shopping bag bobbing along, nearly touching the cobbles.

Carrie took off her glasses and looked again. Her eyes were improving. She could still see Jessie Burgess. She had stopped for a word with someone. It was Cecil. He was coming towards her now. Carrie fought down the sudden impulse she had to turn her back; to walk away; to pretend she hadn't seen him.

'Aha! Miss Shrigley!'

He always called her Miss Shrigley when they were out.

She had asked him not to use her Christian name in public. It had seemed petty even as she'd requested it but he'd taken it well. He seemed to think it was more highfalutin.

He stood before her, hand outstretched. She put her own out and he took it. His hand felt limp.

'What are you doing here?' she asked.

'I'm on my way to buy our tickets for tonight's concert,' he replied. 'You hadn't forgotten, had you, that we are going to the town hall?'

'I remembered,' she answered. 'But you won't need to buy tickets in advance.'

'I have other work to attend to as well,' he said. 'There are consignments of rationed goods coming to Middlefield. I'm in charge of the allocations.'

He was smiling all over his face; that knowing smile that she distrusted.

'I hope you do it all fairly. Fair and even-handed,' she said. 'You have to be careful. You have to be seen to be careful as well.'

'Of course. Of course,' he assured her. The smile left his face. 'You don't think ill of me, do you?' he asked quickly and anxiously.

He seemed to be becoming more, not less, dependent on her good opinion of him. Sometimes he got all worked up if he thought she was not pleased with him. And, at the same time, he appeared to be more fanatical in his religious zeal and even more involved with the affairs of the town. She did not understand his behaviour at all.

'No. I'm sure you'll do right, Cecil.' She gave him a frosty smile. 'I'll see you later.' She left him and went towards the Wallgate.

Cecil was a help to her. It had got so that you needed permits for everything. She'd wanted two sinks and two lavatories put into the hotel and, without his interceding for her at a planning meeting, she'd have had to wait years. He'd prevented them from requisitioning the house in Wells Road. She should be grateful.

He'd let a ministry take over his shop. He didn't know if he'd want it back after the war he said. He'd see. He'd see how she felt about it. About him and her running it.

He was kept busy these days, on one committee after another. It was Cecil who had set up the Food Office. There was going to be a Ministry of Food he'd told her. They'd open it soon. And he wanted her to buy a house in the town centre and rent it to one of the ministries until after the war. He'd see she 'came out smiling' he'd told her. She had snapped at him, asking if the war effort was meant to be a golden chance for opportunists. He'd laughed.

They weren't alone so often since the girls had come to live with her, but she didn't mind not seeing him alone. She was glad they weren't alone too often. He came to the Temperance Hotel, dropping by before or after the meetings which were held in the town hall, to let her know about the civic decisions.

It was embarrassing though, the way Rose behaved when Cecil came into the kitchen. She'd look at him as if he had a nasty smell about him.

Carrie knew that the three girls didn't like Cecil though he tried to make them like him. He'd given them presents. Shoes – old stock admitted – but they were ungrateful. Poor Cecil did his best to please them. He offered them lifts in his car. And they said they'd rather walk.

Rose was being so – so disdainful. She wished she knew what to do about it. She had acted in Rose's best interests. What did the girl want? Why did Rose avoid being alone with her? Why, whenever there was an opportunity to thrash it out, did she choose to sit with her sisters in the bedroom?

Was it because she wouldn't tell her who her father was?

They had heard from Patrick soon after they had buried Jane and Danny. Terribly upset he'd been. She had replied, explaining their new arrangements and asking him to address his letters to herself and the girls.

She had said, 'We are all well. Apart from those worries which the whole nation shares we have no worries. It is better if you address your letters to Miss Shrigley and the Misses Kennedy. Please make no more reference to either my own feelings or my future, as you so often, gratuitously, do.' It was a good word, gratuitous. Cecil used it.

'You will be interested to know that I plan to marry a very respected man. Cecil Ratcliffe is an alderman and expects to become mayor of Middlefield one day.

'Once the girls are established in their own lives we will get married. I had to ask Cecil to wait and he has agreed to do so. It would be too upsetting for the girls, to lose their mother and father and for their aunt, who is legal guardian, to tell them that she is going to be married to a man, to bear on top of everything.

'I got myself into the middle of a sentence there that I could not get out of. I am sure that, being a writer, you understand the meaning.'

His reply, addressed to them all as she'd requested was full of his usual talk about Canada. What Canada was doing for the war. How Canadian boys were joining up, coming over here as pilots and everything. How he wished he could do something. Then he had put, right at the end. 'I think I remember Cecil Ratcliffe. Wasn't he a big noise in your little chapel? I wish you both a long and fruitful life together. May all your troubles be little ones.'

The last sentence was sarcasm she suspected though perhaps it was meant as a joke. He'd know that it wasn't going to be that kind of a marriage

By half past four Alan had polished the Riley inside and out. It stood behind the Swan, in front of the loose-box where Nat's horse, Dobbin, chomped contentedly on a rackful of hay. The chromium-plated headlights and radiator grill shone in the afternoon sunshine, the chrome rim of the windscreen was bright and shiny, the wooden panel gleamed and the tan upholstery had had a rubbing-over with saddle-soap. There was petrol in the tank and a fringed rug for Rose's legs if they drove with the hood down, as he'd done.

He didn't know if she liked opera, but he thought she would. She used to know all the Gilbert and Sullivan songs and play them on his wind-up gramophone in Lincoln Drive. Rose had a good singing voice. Something deep inside tightened into a knot at the thought of her singing.

He walked across the unswept square, now littered with wilting cabbage leaves. The traders packed up early to avoid blackout and this and the piles of sandbags was the only change in the life of Middlefield. It was hard to imagine that the terror of war was raging in Europe, that ships in the North Sea were being sunk, when here the tulips beamed their welcome under the trees behind the stalls.

Young boys hid behind headstones in the little church-yard and dropped with wild screeches from overhanging trees to the high stone wall and on to the narrow flags. Their sisters solemnly chalked lines and squares on the same pavement and hopped and jumped as they neatly kicked a broken tile from square to square in an age-old order.

He leaned over the wall, high above the cattle market. Rose was expecting him at 5 o'clock and there were five minutes to spare. He looked down on to the rooftops and considered the hard struggle their aunt had imposed on the Kennedy girls. She was an obstinate and guarded woman. He had never felt comfortable in her presence when he was a child. Now he knew he'd have no patience with her.

Alan walked down the steps to Waters Green and rapped at the door of the Temperance Hotel.

Carrie Shrigley answered his knock and peered at him through bottle-glass lenses that made her eyes look like pinpricks.

'Is Rose ready?' Alan asked in a brusque manner. Since he'd been in the RAF he hadn't much tolerance; short-fused he supposed would best describe his temperament.

'Where do you want to take her?' she snapped the words out quickly, as if suspicious of his intentions.

'We're going to Manchester. To the Opera,' Alan told her. Alan hoped Rose would appear and put an end to this nonsense; being questioned by the old tartar out in the street as if he were a child who had broken a window.

'In that motor car? The one you had parked outside the Swan?' She had a high-pitched voice for such a big woman and her every word implied criticism.

'Yes. It's not mine. It belongs to a friend,' he found himself telling her. Then he was annoyed with himself for explaining.

'I should think it's not. Not yours. What'd you be doing running around like a wild thing in a sports car?'

The woman talked nonsense. The conversation might have been funny, had not every word been uttered with such bitter resentment. But Rose was behind her now and his face softened as he held out his hand to her. 'We may be late, Miss Shrigley. Don't worry. I'll take good care of her.'

She moved aside to let Rose pass. 'Just see you behave yourself,' she said. 'That's all.'

Mary and Vivienne were with the Gallimore girls at the corner, by the steps. As they approached them Alan was aware of their eyes on him and aware too of Rose as she glanced sideways at him, hoping he didn't mind their attention.

'Let's give them something to talk about,' he said, taking her hand and pulling her towards himself. 'Pretend we haven't seen them.' He slid an arm across her shoulders and began to whistle nonchalantly. Rose returned the pressure of his hand. Mary's eyes were big and round and Vivienne's quick and observant as they passed the watchful group.

'How are your sisters, Rose?' he asked in as casual a tone as he could manage.

'They're fine. They're out, somewhere,' she replied and he saw that she was doing her best not to laugh until they reached the top of the steps. And he knew that she had been nervous, afraid of finding him changed, and that she was relieved that their shared fooling had brought them close again.

The Riley ran smooth and speedy. Middlefield was behind them and Alan wished he could point the car in the camp's direction and show off the pretty girl who sat beside him. Her eyes, dark blue as a twilight sky, were narrowed against the sun. She'd been attractive as a child, but now . . . He glanced at her profile, her straight nose, wide mouth and the bright hair blowing against the side of her face, a sheet of bronze silk. She was thinner than she'd been and he wondered if the changes of the last six months had taken their toll.

'Do you like the bank?' he asked. 'Is it a let-down after college? It must be dull. All those old fogies.'

'The old fogies aren't so dull when you get to know them.' She laughed and turned her face towards his. 'I enjoy it. There are two girls about my own age, Sylvia Wright and Pamela Tannenbaum. They're good fun. Pamela's father's a consultant at a Manchester hospital.'

'That's a German name, Tannenbaum.'

'I know. But they're English. Her father was in the army in the Great War,' she went on. 'Pamela keeps inviting me to tea. Only I can't go. Not now.'

'Why not?' Alan asked.

'I can't ask her back. Not to Aunt Carrie's,' she said.

'What do you do all day? Count the money?'

'Yes. And ledger work,' she said. 'What about you? Do you like the RAF?'

'Yes. There's so much to tell you but if I started you'd still be listening next week.' There were no flag indicators on the Riley, unlike the new cars and Alan had to give hand signals as he turned off the Middlefield Road on to the straight run into Manchester.

'What I'd have liked is to join a service,' Rose was saying, 'but my eyes weren't good enough. Then after . . . After Mum and Dad died I thought I'd better stay with my sisters.'

'What do you think of living at the Temperance Hotel?'

'Hate it.'

'Why didn't you stay in Wells Road?'

'Aunt Carrie owns the house, it appears. She said she couldn't spend any more money on us.'

Alan was surprised. His father spoke as though Carrie Shrigley had money. 'I wonder what she's going to do with it all?' his father had said, when he heard that the girls were moving. Perhaps Dad had been mistaken.

'What about your sisters?'

'I don't think they mind as much as I do but I want them to have something better than living there and working in a mill.'

'Ambitious little thing,' he teased. 'You're not turning into a snob, are you Rose?' He smiled as he said it, but he saw her cheeks flame.

'It's not snobbish. Mum and Dad were ambitious for us. I'm not. It's just that I can't bear to see them changing. The Gallimore girls run wild and Mary and Viv are talking like them already. Viv's going to start work in the mill with Mary soon, and she seems hard to keep down.'

'It's not your place to keep them down,' he told her. 'Mary has got a sensible head on her shoulders and Vivienne – I can't see Vivienne missing out. Vivienne will get whatever she wants, rich or poor, war or no war. Is your aunt kind to you?'

Rose put her face down. 'No,' she replied with a hard little laugh. 'She's never had a good word to say about anyone as long as I can remember. We're a burden to her.'

'You were always close. What's gone wrong?'

She didn't answer for a moment. He looked at her

285

again. She looked as if she were longing to pour out her heart to him as she used to do when she was young.

'Come on,' he said. 'Tell me.'

'I . . . she . . . She gets on better with Mary and Viv, now,' she began. 'It's odd. I thought they'd never hit it off. I thought there would be ructions, especially with Viv.'

'And?'

'She hasn't been hard on her, yet.'

'What about Mary?'

'Mary's got a job at the mill, sewing. She's got a happy nature. She cooks and bakes in her spare time. And she's got Viv.'

'What have you got?'

'Oh, Alan. I wish I could tell you everything.'

He glanced at her again.

'Did you know,' she said, turning to look at him as if waiting for his reaction. 'Did you know that she's going to marry Cecil Ratcliffe?'

'No.' Somehow the thought of her aunt marrying anyone seemed ridiculous. She didn't need a husband; least of all a man he privately thought of as shifty and untrustworthy.

'What do you think of it?' he asked. 'Do you like him?'

'Good Lord, no.' She sounded indignant. 'He's the most – the most obnoxious man I've ever met.'

'What's she thinking of? She doesn't need a provider or anything. She can't love him.' He had to look ahead now; the traffic was heavier here.

'She got angry when Viv asked.'

'What did she say?' He could not imagine what the woman was thinking of, bringing a man like that into the girls' lives.

'She snapped her head off. She said it was nothing to do with us. She said we'll marry and go away and leave her.'

'And will you?' he asked quickly, suddenly afraid that she may have met someone else.

'I won't,' she said.

He glanced at her serious face, relieved that she had spoken so vehemently, laughed softly and reached for her hand. 'I bet you will. You'll marry and have half a dozen children when the war's over.'

'I don't think I will.' She spoke quietly and he heard the quick leap of pain in her voice. 'I can't have children, Alan.'

He remembered the last time she had pronounced on reproductive facts and wanted to smile at her, but he knew that she was quite serious. 'Why do you say that?' he asked in a serious voice.

'I . . . I've never . . .'

He looked at her. She had stopped speaking. She was blushing furiously.

'Well, only four times,' she said.

He saw he would have to draw it out of her. 'Look, Rose. I'm halfway to being a doctor. You can tell me anything.' She seemed to be about to reply and he added, 'You've always told me your troubles. I know everything else about you.'

'You remember when I was fifteen. When I told you . . .'

She had picked up her gloves and was nervously twisting them. He would have to try a professional manner with her. 'We're talking about your periods, Rose. They're not regular, is that it?'

'Yes.' She looked relieved once she had begun. 'I used to pretend. When I was at school I used to sit out of gym every month, to be like the other girls. But I didn't need to. I only had mine once a year. Once a year since I was fifteen.'

'Have you spoken to your doctor?'

'Yes.'

'What did he say?'

'He told me not to worry. He said I was perfectly normal in every other way and that he didn't want to tamper with my glands. He said I'm to see him again after I'm married. He said it was unusual.'

It was unusual, but not unknown. Practically every lecture from any doctor he'd ever heard had stories to tell of women patients who were convinced that they were made quite differently from the rest.

'It's unusual, but not unknown,' he said. 'It doesn't mean you'll never have a child but you may have a long wait. Sometimes it rights itself after a first baby. Anyway, there is a lot of research being done. I'm sure you'll be all right.'

He grinned at her. 'I've learned a lot since I washed your knee, haven't I?'

'Fancy remembering that.' She laughed with him now.

'Put my scarf round your hair. I'm going to put my foot down,' he said. He moved the advance lever and accelerated. The Riley leaped forward. Rose had braced her feet against the dashboard shelf and was holding on to the leather door strap.

'You're not scared are you?' he shouted above the engine and wind noise.

'No! It's terrific ! Go faster!'

'Ever been in an aeroplane?'

'No. This is only the second time I've been in a car.'

CHAPTER SEVENTEEN

Six o'clock was striking as they followed the tramlines through Piccadilly and Deansgate. Alan parked the Riley behind a line of cars.

'Let's have tea at the Kardomah. We'll have a meal after the opera.'

The cafe was busy, crowded with soldiers and their girls, and they had to wait in line for a table. Alan reached for her hand and Rose felt happiness flood through her, looking into his face and listening to the chattering voices behind them as they reached the top of the queue and were led to a table by an elderly waitress.

The tea came in a silver teapot and they ordered sandwiches and toasted teacakes. She felt happy and confident now. She was not going to think any more about Aunt Carrie. Here she was, in her city with the man she loved. She wanted him to see her as adult and capable.

'What's it about? *La Traviata*?' she asked as she poured the tea.

'It's the Lady of the Camellias story. About the courtesan, Violetta,' Alan started to tell her.

'What is a courtesan, exactly?' Rose interrupted.

'She's a kept woman. Not a prostitute. I suppose you'd say she was the mistress – the mistress of a man of the court – a man of rank.'

Rose felt herself blushing. She wished she had half the sophistication of Pamela and Sylvia. They'd have known what a courtesan was. They'd never have made fools of themselves by asking. She could have kicked herself for not even looking the word up. She'd come across it many a time, in books.

'What does *La Traviata* translate as?' she asked.

'It comes from the verb *traviare* – to lead astray. The feminine form,' Alan told her. 'The sinner, I suppose, would be the nearest.'

'Of course. I should have known that.' Rose felt more foolish than ever. What on earth would he think of her? He'd think she was stupid, she was sure. She finished her teacake and began to re-arrange the dishes, to pour more tea. She glanced at Alan. He had not noticed her confusion but was beginning to relate the story for her.

She hardly heard a word he said, so entranced was she just to be there, listening to him. He had filled out, grown broader, from the training she supposed. His face was tanned and had a rugged look that was new. His brown eyes were lively and amused as he looked into hers and a smile kept breaking over his face every time he paused for breath between the tragic scenes of the story.

'And as she dies, the opera ends,' he said at last. He brought a cigarette case out of his pocket, lit a cigarette for himself and grinned at her. 'You'll love it. The music's wonderful and we've got seats near the front.'

They were three rows from the front. Rose sank into the red plush seat and watched the opera house filling up. There were uniforms and afternoon dresses amongst the taffeta gowns and evening suits and Rose tried to memorize every little detail of the evening, to tell to her sisters. The violins were tuning up, the lights dimmed and the conductor bowed to the audience before they began to play the first slow notes of the overture.

For two hours there was no war, no blackout, and, as the little tragedy unfolded before them, the audience seemed to hold its breath at one moment and break into a riot of applause the next. Rose held on to Alan's arm, a tight knot in her throat at the beautiful Violetta's grief.

She was spellbound with the gaiety of the ballroom

scene and cast down by the terrible confrontation between Violetta and her lover, Alfredo.

Rose was living it with them, at one with audience and performers alike. At last, when Violetta crumpled to the floor and the final emphatic notes died away there was silence, as if nobody could break the spell, before a storm of clapping and cheering filled the theatre.

Her hands were sore. It was a relief to see the company lined up and know that Violetta had been acting. She'd remember all this – how the people stamped and clapped, bringing them back time after time – and how strange it felt to adjust to the cold black Manchester night when their heads were ringing with music.

There was a corner table reserved for them at a smart little restaurant and a French waiter took her jacket as if it had been fur. There were candles and flowers on the table, and white wine in a yellow bottle, wrapped in a snowy napkin. And Alan, treating her as if she were something precious, looking at her as if he were as besotted as she was. What a wonderful day it had been.

When they drove back into Middlefield Alan parked the car behind the town hall, where they would not be seen. The air was fresh here, cool and clean after the city. The square, in full, brilliant moonlight, was empty, silent, like a black and white photograph. The distant mountain range was not visible and Alan, the church and square the only reality for Rose.

'It was the most wonderful night of my life,' she sighed. 'Thank you for taking me.' The outline of his profile, strong against the pale silver of the wall gave her the same, familiar jump of pleasure. 'I'll never forget tonight.'

Alan turned to face her. 'Will you remember me, Rose?' His arm was across her shoulder and he drew her towards him. 'When I'm away, will you think of me?'

'I always think of you,' she said in a low, serious voice. 'I think about you every day of my life. I always have.'

Then his mouth was on hers and her mouth and her

body were leaping in response to the taste of his kisses and the hands that caressed her. She had never been kissed like this before. It left her shaking and breathless and a look, a movement was all it took for them to fall into one another's arms again. She wanted time to stand still for them, wanted Alan's arms round her for ever, wanted to hear him saying her name, as now he was doing.

'Rose. Oh Rose. I want you.'

And his hands were under her coat, sliding over the blue bodice of her dress, making her weak, making her seek his mouth, hungrily, letting her tongue move against his until he pulled away from her and held her by the shoulders and looked hard into her widened eyes and watched her as she lay back against the seat, her breath coming fast.

'We must stop,' he said. 'Come on. I'll walk to the steps with you.'

They stood on the steps at the corner of Waters Green, formal now in case Aunt Carrie was watching from her sitting-room window.

'Tomorrow?' Alan said. 'Wait for me after early mass. We'll drive into the hills. I've something important to tell you.' And he was gone, loping with easy stride up the steps.

Rose heard the Riley's engine jerk into life as she went down the entry, heard the soft rumble of tyres over the cobblestones as she turned the handle of the back door.

Aunt Carrie was sitting beside the fire in the darkened kitchen.

'Were you waiting up for me?' Rose asked gently. 'You needn't have. You could have gone to bed.' She hoped the note of apology was evident to her aunt. She longed, suddenly, to share the spilling happiness of her day with Aunt Carrie, all at once sorry about the gulf that lay between them, the unspoken words. She could bear it now, if Aunt Carrie wanted to talk. 'Shall I make you a cup of tea? Or cocoa?' she asked.

Aunt Carrie came quickly across the dark room. The dying firelight was behind her and Rose could not see her aunt's expression. She was unprepared for the slap. She felt a sharp stinging against her ear as the force of it sent her reeling, crashing into the corner of the table.

'Get out of my sight!' Aunt Carrie's voice was high and hysterical. 'You're behaving like a cheap little harlot! I saw you! I saw you making a display of yourself in the market place.'

She raised her arm again. Rose dropped to the floor in terror. She had never been struck in anger. Panic made her slide along the floor, out of reach. The pain in her ear was spreading down into her neck and shoulder.

'We weren't doing anything wrong,' she said through her tears. 'He kissed me. That's all.'

— 'All? That's all, is it? Well, there's to be no more of it. Do you hear me?' She had dropped her arm and turned to stand over Rose's sobbing form and it seemed to Rose that there was hatred in every word.

'You think you can go and confess it all, don't you? Say a few Hail Marys and forget?' She was spitting out the words. 'You'll learn, my girl! But don't bring your shame to me when it's got a bonnet on and its fine Catholic father's nowhere to be found!'

'Don't. Please don't!' Rose put her hands to her ears to shut out her aunt's words with the dreadful interpretation of what she had witnessed ringing through them. 'It's not like that,' she wept. 'I love him, Aunt Carrie. I love him.'

'Love? See how far that'll take you.'

Rose felt the scorn and rage as a physical assault. She knew now that Aunt Carrie would never understand an emotion she couldn't feel. She stayed, crouching on the floor until Aunt Carrie left the room, until she heard her aunt's tread on the stairs and the creaking of boards overhead. Then Rose pulled herself wearily to her feet and into the scullery, where she ran cold water over her shaking fingers and tried to scoop it into her open hands and cool her burning face.

Then, weary and dejected, she climbed the stairs to the

room where Mary and Vivienne slept, untroubled.

Rose lay wakeful and afraid, for the last few hours before dawn. When light crept into the room she quietly took pencil and paper and left a note for her sisters.

> Tell Aunt Carrie I'm going to see Pamela from the Bank. She's asked me to spend the day with her. I'll be back before dark. Rose.

Now she was being forced into deceit, but there was nothing for it. She would have to live here for the time being. She had nowhere else to go. But she vowed to herself that she would never let her aunt treat her like that again. She would ask for nothing, tell her nothing. She had tried to love her aunt, she'd felt ashamed of herself for not feeling any affection for her but now she didn't care.

She'd not tell Alan. He'd have plenty to worry him without her troubles.

St Alban's church, where Churchgate became Chester Road and the shops alternated with town houses, was gaunt and smoke-blackened. It was set a little way back from the road and a little lower, so that it appeared much smaller and plainer than it was.

It was a beautiful church. Stained glass windows, small and high, depicting the stations of the cross ran, six each side down its length, giving an impression of great height, as did the towering stone columns supporting the roof and painted ceilings. There were twelve columns either side of the aisle and, at their bases, carved oak doors opened into high-fronted pews. At the top of the nave, the great window cast a rainbow of light on the high altar where Father Church intoned the Mass.

Alan did not see Rose immediately but the flicker of anxiety was stilled when he saw her follow four nuns to the altar rail. He knew she had to bear her aunt's disapproval every time she came to church and he loved her the more for her endurance.

She waited for him outside, dressed in a light-grey coat. She had removed the lace square she'd worn in church over hair that was a blazing halo against the plain clothes. Love and desire for her leaped in him as he walked towards her.

'The car's round the corner,' he said quietly when he reached her side. 'I'll be there in a minute. I want a word with Father Church.'

He stood at the church gate and watched her graceful walk as she rounded the corner.

'Can I see you tonight, Father?' he said when the last parishioner had shaken the hand of the young priest.

'Of course, Alan.' The priest's Irish lilt was more pronounced when he spoke to the young people of the parish and Alan sensed the warmth behind Father Church's quiet smile.

'Come to the presbytery after nine, will you? We'll be able to talk then.' He chuckled and fell into step with Alan the few paces to the Chester Road entrance. 'She's a lovely girl, our Rose. You're a lucky man.'

'How do you know, Father?' Alan asked, pleased at the priest's perception. Perhaps the father had seen something he'd missed, for he was not at all certain that Rose felt as he did, though he'd known, last night, that she wanted him.

'It's as plain as the nose on your face, boy. To one who's lookin'.' The priest's hand fell on Alan's shoulder. 'Why, she can't take her pretty eyes off you.'

'Thanks, Father.' Alan, hope rising in his heart, ran to the car, opened the door and dropped into the driving seat. 'I put the hood up in case it's cold. Are you comfortable?' he asked. She had taken off the grey coat and he saw that she wore a skirt of fawn check with a pretty crimson jumper. It was the first time he'd seen her wear make-up and the bright lipstick made her skin look pale and her teeth, when she smiled were like white porcelain.

'Where are we going?' she asked.

Alan pressed the starter button and the Riley sprang into life. He had taken out the side windows so that he could lean out and give hand signals and he waved some cyclists on before replying.

'We're going over the moors. Nan Tansley's made up a picnic basket for us.' He looked at her and impulsively took her hand for a moment. 'We'll eat beside the river in the Goyt Valley. I want us to be all alone. I've something important to tell you.'

'Lovely.' She turned the dark-blue gaze on to him. There was reserve there, in those blue depths and yet he saw the fire beneath that had burned for him a few hours ago.

They drove through the quiet town, over the bridge behind the cattle market and began the climb to Derbyshire, Alan stealing glances at her, watching the rise and fall of her breasts beneath the clinging jumper, the angle of her face as she watched the passing scene, smiling when she caught him looking, pleased at his attention.

He stopped the car at the top of the hill by a stone wall that separated tilled fields from the wild, rock-strewn moorland that lay ahead. They could see the whole of Middlefield, spread out below them like the view from a cockpit. The sun was warm on their backs and the scent of peaty heather drifted in the silent air.

'Look,' she said. 'How clear it is. I can see the steps from here.' She extended an arm towards the distant town.

'I'd rather look at you,' he said in a low voice. 'Rose?'

'Yes?' She had narrowed her eyes and was leaning forward on the wall as if to get a better view.

Alan put an arm across her shoulder. Maybe last night's response had more to do with the magic of the occasion. But no, she was moving closer to him and turning her face to his. He wasn't mistaken. He half-lifted, half-held her as his lips met hers, gently at first, then sensing the response in her, with urgency. She clung, eager and fiercely to him with a desire that matched his, a desire that was filling and beginning to overtake him.

He pulled himself back, breathing deeply to regain control of himself. He must restrain himself; he meant to talk to her, to court her with words and yet her nearness was putting thoughts and words from his mind.

He assumed an air of authority he did not feel. 'Let's get moving,' he said.

The road ahead was straight and empty. Alan held the Riley at a lazy speed and fondled Rose's shoulder inside the wide neck of the knitted jumper. She leaned a little towards him, letting his fingers fall on to the full roundness. She wore nothing beneath the jumper and he felt her breast firming under his hand as it strayed. He wanted to stop the car and hold her. He looked at her quickly, saw that she was aroused by the brief contact. Her breathing was faster and her eyes huge and dark-centred. He took his hand away and put it back on the driving wheel.

They headed away from the moors, through a deep pine forest that descended gently to the still valley. Alan drew the car in to the side of the road that ran along the riverbank. Under the trees the spring's warmth had turned leafmould and pine needles into a brown resilient carpet and pale new leaves caught the sunlight overhead, dappling the ground and the tumbling water.

An ivy-covered ruin, surrounded by rhododendrons and laurel grown luxuriant with neglect, faced them across the quick shallow river and they carried rugs and the picnic basket over the rotting bridge that had once served the old mansion. Alan led her to a tiny clearing, spread the rugs and lay, watching her as she unpacked the hamper.

The crimson jumper had risen above the waistband of her skirt, revealing the pale skin of her back as she knelt and reached, placing crockery and napkins on the check tablecloth she'd laid on the grass. He had planned to talk of love, of waiting, of a future for them when the war was over. But now, seeing her near, when every movement of her, every glance from her filled him with aching need he knew that they had no time for talk, for waiting, for a future that might never be theirs.

He leaned back on his elbows and closed his eyes. 'Leave that, Rose. Come here.' He felt her light feet on the rug, felt her drop to her knees beside him.

'What is it?'

Her hair brushed his face as she bent over him and he caught her scent of shampoo and young flesh.

'Marry me.' He sat up and looked into her startled eyes, inches from his own. Then his arms were around her and he was pressing his face into her slender neck, kissing her ears and throat and his hands were sliding inside the crimson jumper.

'Will you marry me, Rose?'

Her eyes gave him all the answer he needed. Her hands were linked behind his neck and she was pulling him down on top of her, answering him with closed eyes and quick little cries.

There was a hard demanding need in him now and he forced himself to deny it. He felt the warm pressure of her breasts and he took her arms from his neck and laid her back gently on to the rug. 'I love you, Rose,' he said. 'I always have. Say you'll marry me.'

'I love you Alan,' she whispered. 'So much.' Her eyes were shimmering and her breath was soft on his cheek. She raised her arms to him and pulled him down until his mouth was on hers again and he was drowning in its warm sweetness, feeling the thudding of her heart under his hands.

And again he lifted his face and looked into her deep-blue eyes. 'Rose? Will you marry me?'

'Yes, I love you. Yes I'll marry you,' she answered, reaching out for him as if she could not bear to lose the feel of his mouth on hers; looking at him through the dark lashes, making desire surge through him until he could hold back no longer.

'I want you, Rose,' he was saying, urgent and insistent now in his need of her. 'I want you now. I want to make love to you. Will you . . .'

She was trembling under his touch and he knew with sudden joy and certainty that he was going to take her, to make her his, here in this quiet, hidden glade, so far from war and fear of death. She was charged with a passion as strong as his own. He knew that the eyes that were holding his were repeating the urgent longings of her body as it thrust itself against his, imploring him to fulfil it.

'Alan, I love you so much.' Her voice was soft and low and pleading. 'I want to. I want you to. Don't hurt me. Alan, love me. Now.'

Then he covered her face with kisses whilst his hands pulled away her crimson jumper and she slid her white arms from the restricting garment. And his own need was hard in him as he held her, his mouth moving to her firm breasts, making her call out to him.

She needed him. She was moving her body, pushing into him as he raised her to her knees and slid the fawn skirt over the slope of her hips, her silk knickers falling away easily as he released the button that held them.

'Alan, Alan,' she whispered. 'Now. Quickly.'

Her breath was coming fast on his neck as he unfastened his clothes and pushed them aside. Her hands were moving over him, drawing him down until she lay, waiting for him.

His fingers parted the soft folds and moved inside her hot, slippery body. Oh, God. He must be quick, for her sake.

Every sense in his body was clamouring for her, yet she was a virgin and he knew he must be careful. As swiftly and firmly as he could he broke through, into her, taking unexpected pleasure in her sharp gasp of pain and the soft moan that followed his slow, deepening movements.

He watched her face, the fine beading of sweat on her upper lip, the tip of her tongue caught between her teeth, excited by her low murmerings as new sensations inside her grew stronger.

Then her legs were up around and gripping him and he was pushing deep, deep into her as her movements came together with his and their bodies were as one in sliding, flowing tension. Inside her he felt strong muscles pulling him in, heard the rasping breaths that were his own, and hers quickening in time with his. And when her cry came he covered her mouth with his, tasting her sweetness in the soaring abandon of her.

At last she lay beneath him, relaxed, her breathing deep and regular, returning the little kisses he placed on her lips, on her chin and her half-closed eyes.

He watched her face as he stayed inside her, stroking her white, lightly veined breasts, gently caressing her pink nipples until they rose and became rigid and she caught her breath. She was trying to conceal the signs. But her fragile control was going even as he watched. Her body was obeying his touch. He saw her eyes widen in surprise as she felt the stirrings of desire deep inside herself again and slowly he covered her open mouth with his own and felt the response in hers.

Her hands began to move over him. She was whispering words of love to him, telling him she loved him, that she needed him and wanted him. Her hips were moving, circling around him, her fingers hard on his hips.

And he was full again and needful and had no mind to play or take her gently. He thrust himself hard and furiously into her until she cried out. He wanted her to share this fast ascending ecstacy of his. His fingers were raking through her tangled hair and he was calling her name and forcing her flat against the hard grassy ground to still her, silencing with his mouth her wild cries as he came pouring and streaming inside her to the very entrance of the womb he could feel against him in the farthest reaches of her. And she gave a long-drawn cry and held him fast inside in her involuntary muscle contractions.

Then they lay, damp and weak, his weight on top of her, his head on her breast and her hands light and loving on his arm.

Then at last he looked slowly into her eyes and brushed his lips with great tenderness over her own. 'Did you think it could be like this?' he asked her quietly, 'when you imagined love?'

'No.' She pushed him on to his back, spreading herself across his chest, her eyes soft and luminous. 'And you? It wasn't new for you, was it?'

'Oh, yes. It was.' He spoke the truth. 'It was my first time. I've been near, been tempted, but I always found it easy to hold back.'

'I'm glad,' she said fervently. 'I couldn't bear to think you had. I couldn't bear to think of you doing that with another girl.'

Alan laughed softly at her serious expression. 'Oh my!' he said. 'What a wife I've got! What an ambitious, fierce little female.'

'Do you suppose that having a baby feels like that?' she asked, teasing him, twisting little strands of his black hair in her fingers.

'Like what?' He sat up, grinning at her and the serious look on her face.

'Like Doing It.'

'No. It would be much, much worse.' He laughed, then asked seriously, 'You didn't think it was awful, did you?'

'No.' She was smiling a satisfied and knowing smile.

'Did it hurt when I broke the hymen?'

'Oh, Alan!' She was laughing. 'You're so damned clinical. You give everything it's proper name. I'll bet that all the time we were Doing It you were thinking of those Latin words.' She had sat back on her heels, her hair tousled and wild from her exertions.

'No,' she explained with the most preposterous piece of illogical thinking Alan had ever heard. 'I just thought that if you get anything as wonderful as a baby for Doing It, then having a baby must be like it but more so.'

She was so beautiful. It sent a shiver of fright through him to think of leaving her. Alan put his arms around her and pulled her upright. 'You are going to marry me, aren't you?' he said.

'Yes,' she answered gently. 'How could I not? After today?'

'You love me?'

'Oh, yes, I do. So much. There could never be anyone else.'

He could not doubt her. Her love for him was lighting her face. He thrust his arms quickly into his shirt, sharply aware all at once of time that was slipping away from them. 'Put your clothes on. We'll go back and tell them. I'll get a special licence. We'll be married on my next leave.'

She was still, her face suddenly drained of colour. 'Aunt Carrie'll never give her permission. I'm under twenty-one. I'll need her consent,' she told him in a distant voice.

'I'll speak to her. I'll make her see.' Alan saw the quick look of fear that crossed her face.

'No,' she said. 'I'll ask her myself. It's better that way. She'll be angry if she hears it from anyone else.'

'I must tell my father. And Nat,' Alan said. He knew that he was strong-willed but there was a reckless streak in him that made him impatient with delay. 'They'll have to know.'

He stopped, looked hard into her eyes and gripped her shoulders to emphasize his words. 'You're mine now. My wife in all but name. I won't let anyone come between us. Your aunt won't stop us. I'll not stand any opposition. She has to let you go. For your sake I'll not speak. But you must. You will leave her and live in Lincoln Drive if necessary.'

'I don't want her to hear it from anyone else. I'll go for the forms myself and ask her to sign them. We'll ask for a special licence.'

'Do it soon. God knows where I'll be sent or when I'll get leave. I want to get married.'

'And you don't mind about the children? That we might not have any?'

'No. When the war's over we'll go to the best specialist in the country. If it's possible we'll put it right. If not, we'll face it together.' He rolled up the rugs. 'Come on. We've only a few hours left.'

CHAPTER EIGHTEEN

When Rose returned to the house Aunt Carrie was at chapel and Mary and the Gallimore girls were in the yard. They had placed stools and wooden lemonade boxes in a row and were seated there, in shadow.

Rose saw them as soon as she pushed open the back door.

'Come and sit here,' Mary called. 'Push up, Flo. Make room for our Rose.'

'Where's Viv?' Rose asked.

'Coming down in a minute. We're giving a concert. We're going to sing after Viv's turn,' Mary added cheerfully.

'It's getting dark. She'd better be quick.' Rose perched uncomfortably on the box next to Mary. The seats were arranged against the rough brick wall. The two WC's at the far end of the yard were to be the backcloth, Rose saw. The girls had swept the cracked flagstones and draped tired-looking curtains over the doors of the old privies – no longer in use since Aunt Carrie had had indoor lavatories installed.

'Here she comes.' Mary clapped encouragingly as Viv ran on to the imaginary stage.

Vivienne's hair, which she normally wore pinned into an untidy bun was fanned out about her shoulders, a soft, moving flame of light bronze. She wore a long, black dress in the Spanish style which clung to her slim, childish body until it flounced out in a froth of red net from a point above her knees.

'Ooh!' the girls sighed.

Vivienne poised with her hands above her head for a few moments before snapping her red tap shoes against the stone. The girls, taking their signal, began to clap slowly as the youngest amongst them started to dance.

Rose could not take her eyes off her sister. Vivienne's body twisted and held in the defiant postures of the Flamenco. Her feet made the rapid-fire sounds rise and fall, offset against the slow handclapping of the watchers. The glowing hair leaped and swung as the girl, with half-closed eyes, moved in time to the music that sang in her head and when, finally, with a series of quick steps she stopped, her body erect before them, Rose applauded as enthusiastically as the others.

The singing and recitations of Mary and the Gallimore girls were good-natured and a little tiresome. They didn't need an audience, satisfied as they were to amuse one another. Rose slipped back into the kitchen.

She pulled the blackout blinds before switching on the light. The girls had left the kitchen in a mess. She began to clear up but stopped for a moment when she thought she heard the sound of crying from their room, then continued when she decided she was mistaken.

As she began to take away the dirty dishes that had been left from tea she listened again. There it was. And it was coming from their bedroom.

She went to the bottom of the stairs. 'Vivienne?' she called softly. The crying ceased.

No. It was louder. Rose ran up the narrow staircase and pushed open the bedroom door. Vivienne lay on the bed, still wearing the Spanish dress, her shoulders heaving as great sobs shook her.

'What is it, love?' Rose put her arm across Viv's shoulders. 'Tell me.'

'It's Aunt Carrie. I hate her!' Vivienne turned her face towards Rose; a red-eyed angry face that was so different from the dreamy dancer of five minutes past that it took Rose all her time not to smile.

'I shall hate the job in the mill,' Vivienne cried. 'The only thing I live for is dancing. Why can't I go on having lessons? I want to be famous. I want to be a film star!'

She sat, dry-eyed, gripping Rose's hand. 'And now she says I have to give it up.'

'Why does she say that?' Rose knew how much it meant to Vivienne. Her sister had little talent for anything else. Dancing used all her energy. It gave her an outlet for the wildness that was in her.

'She says we're all going wrong and she'll not have it.' Tears began to fall again. 'It's your fault, Rose. She said she saw you slopping all over Alan MacGregor in the middle of the street where everyone could see you.' She picked up the corner of the counterpane and dabbed her eyes before turning a pleading look on to Rose. 'Don't do it again, Rose. Don't let her see you. She'll take it out on us.'

Rose felt a cold shiver run down her back. 'She must really hate me,' she said quietly. 'She doesn't want me to be happy.'

'She does! She does hate you. She's always going on about you.'

'Where has she gone? To chapel?'

'She's not coming home until late. There's a meeting after chapel,' Vivienne said. 'Don't annoy her, will you Rose? Not until I get my dancing lessons back?'

Rose forced a smile. 'Don't worry. I'll say nothing to make her angry. I'll talk to her tomorrow.'

'As if nothing's happened?' Viv added urgently.

There was a weight on Rose's heart. A certain knowledge that she dared not speak of marriage to her aunt. 'As if nothing's happened,' she agreed.

Vivienne combed her hair and ran a cold damp flannel over her face, standing at the sink in the corner of the room, all traces of tears gone. 'I'm glad we've got this room,' she said. 'We can come up here whenever we want to. Imagine, Rose, if we were next to Aunt Carrie, or in an attic.'

'I suppose we do have some privacy up here,' Rose agreed. 'Come down, Viv. Help me with the dishes before she . . . Before Aunt Carrie gets back.'

'Will Cecil Ratcliffe be bringing her home?'

'Oh, I hope not.'

'He gives me the jitters,' Vivienne said. 'He gives me the creeps.'

'Same here,' Rose said.

Vivienne followed her down to the kitchen where they found Mary piling cups and saucers to drain on the metal draining board.

'Thanks,' Rose said. 'Mary?'

'What?'

'Do you like Cecil Ratcliffe?'

'I'm scared of him,' Mary answered quickly.

'Scared?'

'Yes. He stands too close,' Mary began.

'And lays his hands on our arms, doesn't he, Mary?' Vivienne added.

'Ugh!' Mary said. 'I try not to let him. I keep out of his way.'

Vivienne didn't want to let the subject drop. She tugged at Rose's sleeve. 'He only does these things when Aunt Carrie isn't looking,' she said earnestly. 'He's cunning.'

Mary tipped the water out of the enamel bowl, wiped it carefully with the dishcloth and propped it, end up, behind the brass tap. She said in a worried little voice, 'He says things like, "I wonder if Mary would go to my car" and sends me chasing off for something.'

'And as soon as she's gone he asks Aunt Carrie for a cup of tea saying "I'd like to hear what dear Vivienne is doing at school,"' Vivienne said, curling her lip scornfully in a way that would normally have made them all laugh.

It was worrying. They couldn't laugh. Rose frowned as she said, 'You aren't making this up, are you, Viv?'

'No!'

'No! She's not, Rose,' Mary was quietly insistent. 'We

307

can't tell anyone. We can't tell Aunt Carrie. But he makes us feel on edge. We're a bit scared of him.'

'You must tell Aunt Carrie not to leave you alone with him,' Rose said.

'I can't!'

'Neither can I,' Mary said.

'I'll try to speak to her,' Rose said. 'But I don't think she'll believe me.'

'Let's go up to bed,' Mary said. 'We can talk up there and we'll not be around when they come in.'

'All right,' Rose agreed. 'You two go ahead. I'll make some cocoa and bring it up.'

When her sisters had gone upstairs Rose wondered how she was going to tell Aunt Carrie about the way the girls were being frightened by Cecil Ratcliffe. Aunt Carrie would make a terrible scene. She'd give them all the third degree, Cecil Ratcliffe too. And then there would be no peace in the house.

Perhaps it would be best if she told Mary and Viv, to keep right out of his way. After all, Cecil Ratcliffe might imagine that he had to bring about a closeness, an understanding between himself and the three of them. He might be trying to worm his way into their favour and merely being clumsy and inept about it.

The presbytery, a three-storey house, was the first in a long row of stone-faced terraced property adjoining the churchyard of St Albans. Alan rang the doorbell and was admitted into the gloomy passageway by Father Church who led the way into his plain, tidy little study at the back of the house.

'Come in, my boy,' he said when he had closed the door behind them. 'Sit down.'

Alan remained standing. He was not in the mood for talk of the parish. He wanted to have it all settled; and soon. 'Father, I want to marry Rose Kennedy,' he said in a voice which sounded, even to himself, unnecessarily abrupt. 'She's underage. And her aunt's no friend of the church.'

'You've spoken then? She'll have you?' The priest's face broke into a smile. 'Congratulations, me boy. You don't want to wait until she's older, I take it?'

'In the eyes of God she's my wife already, Father.' He was relieved now, to tell the priest and he watched his face for signs of reproach.

Father Church's hand fell on to his shoulder in an attitude of understanding. 'And what about babies? There'll be children comin' and you two not married. Is that it?'

'No, Father. Rose can't have children. Not yet. She may need an operation. We've no fears that way. But we want to marry. Will you marry us when we've got her aunt's permission?'

'Oh, I will that. Sit down, Alan. Will her aunt agree to it? Rose being so young.'

'Rose is going to speak to her,' Alan told him before he decided to add, by way of explanation. 'She didn't want me to go to Miss Shrigley myself. She seems to be afraid of her.'

Father Church leaned against the leather back of his chair and it seemed to Alan that he was silent for a fraction too long. Did the priest know something he didn't? He felt the knot tighten in his stomach. 'What is it, Father? There's something behind her aunt's antagonism isn't there? Something beyond intolerance? She'll not give her consent, will she?'

'I think she'll not.'

He had no time for slow, ponderous talk. 'Can you tell me why she'll object?' he asked sharply.

The priest did not want to say more. Alan could see that the father was having a struggle with himself and he rose to his feet and spoke angrily. He had no time to waste, beating about the bush.

'I've told you what we've done. In the eyes of God, in

my eyes, she's my wife. I've got to marry her in the church.' He hesitated before lowering his voice and looking hard into Father Church's eyes. 'I may not survive the fighting, Father. I tell you, though I am under an oath of secrecy, that I am joining an active unit on Wednesday.'

Father Church moved his hand quietly. 'I think ye'll have to ask your own father, Alan. He knows all the facts.' He looked at him steadily. 'Shall I go to see her?' he asked. 'Miss Shrigley, she might be persuaded to sign the forms, if I ask her myself.'

Alan shook his head. 'I don't think she'd give you a hearing. Thank you for offering,' he said. 'I'll ask Rose to apply to the court if I have to.' He went towards the door, the priest, looking sorrowful, following him to the street. Alan shook his hand. 'Good night.'

He would ask Dad to tell him the whole story tonight.

When he got home he found that Nan Tansley had left supper ready for them: the table set and the oven on low. Nan, in her sixties now, had gone to her room. She would not consider retirement and Alan and Dad were content for her to stay. They too believed her to be indispensable. Tonight she had laid places for them on the low, wheeled table at the living room fireside.

There was a letter from Patrick, propped against the clock over the fireplace. Beside the clock was John McGregor's wedding photograph. In it the bride, a woman of about 30, smart in a long, high-necked gown and holding a bouquet, was posed between the two men who were standing, straight, unsmiling and formal. It reminded Alan of a Victorian wedding.

The letter read, 'Dear Douglas and Alan, You must wonder what is happening here as it is so long since you heard from me. I am waiting to hear where I will be sent since I applied for, and was given, the job of foreign correspondent. Apparently forty-nine, my age now, is too old to be made war correspondent but I am not over the hill yet. I shall not be sent to cover the fighting in Europe but there is every chance that I will land up in Scotland to cover troop activities in Britain. So we may meet again, Douglas, on those bonny banks. You will be aware of course that I am not allowed to say more.

'If I am sent I'll contact you by telephone and arrange a reunion.'

Alan put the letter back in the envelope. It was the first they had received for months; a miracle really, that it had got here at all. It would be marvellous to see his godfather again. But he wondered if it would come about, with Dad going God knows where and himself on active service.

Dad came in at eight, and when they had done justice to Nan's stew and dumplings and cleared almost every homemade cake on the stand, Alan got to his feet and stood with his back to the fireplace.

'Pour us a couple of whiskies, Dad,' he said. 'We've something to drink to.'

Dad went obediently to the cabinet, poured two whiskies into cut glass tumblers and placed them on the high marble mantelshelf. 'What is it?' he asked with smiling curiosity.

'I've asked Rose to marry me,' Alan announced. He'd meant to put a serious expression on his face but a broad smile of happiness could not be held back. 'And she's accepted.' He watched Dad's face and saw with delight the look of pleasure in his father's eyes.

'That's wonderful news, Alan,' Dad said. He put a hand out and Alan grasped it. 'I couldn't be more pleased. She's a bonny girl. You've loved her for years, haven't you?'

'How did you know that, Dad?' Alan grinned. 'I only asked her today.'

'Aye. But ye've been thinking that way for long enough.'

'You are right,' Alan answered. 'But I didn't think she was thinking the same way. Until today.'

'Here's to your marriage, then.' Dad clinked glasses and they both drank.

311

'Ye'd better bring her here tomorrow, Alan,' Dad said. 'We'll have a proper celebration. We'll drink to your happiness in champagne.'

Now was the time to ask to be told all Dad knew. Alan put down the glass and spoke thoughtfully. 'Rose doesn't want me to tell her aunt. She needs her consent, being under age,' he said. 'I've spoken to the priest and he says Miss Shrigley won't give it.'

Dad looked serious now. 'He may be right, Alan.'

'What's behind it?'

'Sit down, son,' Dad said. 'Pour yourself another glass. I'll tell you all I know.'

It took Dad an hour to tell him everything he knew of the time when Rose's parents ran away to Ireland, leaving Carrie Shrigley to face Patrick Kennedy, his own godfather, in open court.

When he had finished it seemed to Alan as if an old quarrel had been kept alive. 'How can the events of the past, between Miss Shrigley and Patrick Kennedy, have any relevance to Rose and me?' he asked at last. 'Rose is only her niece. What possible reason could she have for preventing her from marrying?'

'I don't know, Alan.' Dad gave him a puzzled look and said thoughtfully, 'Though at the time it was a terrible business. It was a foolish thing that Patrick did; he was more foolish than wicked. But somehow I have always had the feeling that it could have been avoided. I always felt, though I don't know why, that Carrie Shrigley was as much to blame as himself. For it was not at all like her to be reckless and it was not at all like Patrick to go like a lamb to the slaughter. He put up no defence against her.'

Alan had listened carefully. 'Rose knows nothing of this,' he said. 'They have kept it from her and her sisters.'

'It's not something they would boast about, son.'

'All the same, if it were me I think I'd rather have known.' He was thoughtful for a few seconds longer. 'What do you think I should do?' he asked at last. 'I won't

312

tell Rose of course, that her uncle, my godfather, was a swindler . . .'

'He wasn't.' Dad spoke sharply. 'He's one of the finest men I've ever met. I'll never think otherwise.'

'All right. I'm sorry I used the term. I've certainly never had any evidence that he was crooked.' He puzzled over it for a few moments longer. It certainly explained what he saw as Miss Shrigley's bitterness, but he could not see how it would affect her attitude towards Rose.

Dad spoke again. 'You'll have to wait,' he said. 'Rose will be twenty next summer, won't she?'

'Yes. But I think we should apply to the court. Get a special licence. I've told Rose so.' Alan stood, leaning his elbow on the mantelshelf. 'The balloon's gone up,' he said. 'I don't know when I'll be home. I'd like to have it all ready. I want to marry her immediately.'

Dad said, 'Your mother and I were married on one of my leaves in the last war. But then, in Scotland ye can take a wife at sixteen.'

He got up from the chintz-covered settee and went to the corner cupboard where the family treasures were kept, brought out a little square box and handed it to Alan. 'Your mother's ring,' he said. 'Give it to Rose.'

Tears were glistening in Dad's eyes when Alan opened the box and carefully withdrew the circle of gold with its cluster of diamonds. It was a good ring. Alan was sure it represented many a week's catch of fish for Dad would have been a poor fisherman when he bought it.

'Thanks, Dad. She'll love it,' Alan said. 'I'll give it to her tomorrow. I'll bring her here in the evening after she's finished work. We'll celebrate. I'll ask her to go for the forms but I'll wait if she can't face appearing in court.'

Half an hour later, in bed, Alan lay on his back, remembering Rose and their loving and thoughts of her sent such a wave of longing through him that he knew he'd not be able to close his eyes until he saw her again.

★

And yet, it was morning and the alarm at his bedside startling him out of sleep. Six o'clock. He was meeting Nat at seven, in the square.

His running feet echoed through the empty streets and he reached the market place just as the milk cart turned the corner from Rivergate.

Nat slowed and Alan climbed up and took the reins from him. 'Was that your last call?' he asked.

'Aye. I don't have such a big round now. I sell most of it to the bottling plant at the Co-op. Head for Rainow. Mam's got us breakfasts waiting.'

Alan urged Dobbin, flicking the reins across the old boy's flanks and the horse, eager to return to his paddock, jingled his harness as he broke into a lively trot.

'Did you take the barmaid out on Saturday?' Alan asked.

A slow grin spread over Nat's ruddy face. 'Yep! She's all right is Mona,' he answered. 'I've asked her to keep next Saturday free.'

Alan laughed. 'You'll be settling down soon. Will you?'

'I dunna know about that. What about yerself?'

They were climbing the road out of Middlefield, the road he and Rose had taken yesterday. In half a mile he would make a left turn and leave the main road, still climbing to the lowest of the Pennine foothills where Rainow Farm snuggled between soft meadowland and the hillier reaches of low mountain slopes. Already the clean air was singing through him.

'I've asked Rose Kennedy to marry me,' he said. 'And she says yes.'

Dobbin needed no more urging. They had turned the corner on to the hawthorn-hedged lanes. The carthorse knew he was on the homeward stretch and the cart rattled over the stony road that led, another mile up the hill, to the farm. Alan had to raise his voice to be heard against the noise of the empty churns as they lifted and banged together. Nat appeared to have fallen quiet.

The road, steeper now, wound sharply right and Alan

held on to the wooden seat as Dobbin rounded the corner and made the turn through the narrow gate.

'He never makes a mistake, does he?' Alan said. 'I hold my breath when he turns in. There's only an inch or two of clearance.'

'They never forget,' Nat called back.

Alan could see, over the tops of the drystone walls, the fields and woods. There was something reassuring and unchanging about this farm. Meadows and coppices followed the lie of the land. The back of the house faced the downslope of an ancient meadow, where a stream divided it from the old road and the woods. From the farmhouse kitchen Ma Cooper would have been watching their approach. The front door and tiny flower garden faced the hill. Alan had never known the front door to be used. The living room and kitchen were at the back where a long flagged terrace, edged with a stone wall, ran the length of the house from the cobbled, enclosed yard into which they had now pulled up.

Nat climbed down and unhitched the cart whilst Alan held on to the horse's bridle. As soon as he'd done Nat said, in a voice that sounded almost nonchalant, 'Don't say anything to Mam. Don't say, owt about . . . About you getting engaged to Rose Kennedy – will yer?'

Alan was not fooled by Nat's air of unconcern. He looked quickly at Nat's reddening face.

'She'll only start on at me,' Nat explained.

Alan felt a quick rush of sympathy. His news had affected his friend. He'd thought, when he first spoke, that Nat had been shaken by his announcement. He had not thought that Nat was touchy about his single state. How insensitive he'd been, boasting about his good fortune. He'd have played it down if he'd had any tact.

'I'll say nothing,' he promised and added, 'Anyway we have to get her aunt's permission and I'd rather it wasn't talked about until we get that settled.'

'Hang Dobbin's harness up and put him in't paddock.

Will yer?' Nat said. 'I'll rinse these churns in't dairy. Tell Mam I'm ready for me breakfast.'

When Dobbin was released, Alan crossed the yard that was bounded by the house, shippon, stone barn and dairy. He passed under the stone archway that linked the dairy and house and saw Ma Cooper waiting for him with outstretched hands.

Alan bent and kissed her rosy, unlined cheek. She was tiny, plump and lively and full, even in her advancing years of an energy that outstripped everyone.

'Eeh. Alan. Come in love,' she said. 'Eeh. It's good to see you. Come on. Take your boots off. You know I won't have mud on my kitchen floor. Leave 'em under the bench by the wall. It's not raining.'

He obeyed, smiling, and followed her into the long, low, beamed kitchen where everything gleamed and shone. Every surface; dresser, table, wooden mantelshelf and windowsill was covered first with a thick plain cloth and topped with a starched, lace edged and embroidered cover. The cooking range, blackleaded and polished was on the far, narrow wall and took up its whole width. There was a small window above the deep white sink, hung, half-way down with a muslin curtain, and, at the side of the sink, a fine iron water-pump, rubbed and polished until the cast iron shone like steel. The wooden draining board was scrubbed daily until it was as white as bleached bone and not a crumb or speck sullied the red quarry tiled floor.

Ma Cooper beamed at them both when at last they were seated. 'I picked some mushrooms this morning,' she said. 'Do you want some with your ham?'

She had already filled the big plate with fried eggs and thick ham, fried bread and kidneys but Alan knew that protests would be ignored. 'Just a few, Ma,' he said as she placed a heaped ladle of wide flat field mushrooms on to his plate. 'Give the rest to Nat. He's always hungry.'

Nat grinned as Alan went on. 'You ought to ease up a bit, Ma. You still keep everything spotless don't you?' He knew she loved to be praised, he loved to see her face light up in response to the appreciation she seldom got from her son.

'I'll ease off when our Nat fetches a bride home.' She nudged Alan with a conspiratory chuckle and cocked her head towards Nat. 'He goes a-courting every Saturday night but he's never brought her home yet.'

'I have a different one every week, Mam. I keep tellin' yer.' Nat replied crossly.

'You don't,' she cried happily. 'I know what you're like. You're close. Like your father was.' Her ready laugh pealed through the kitchen. 'You'll fetch a wife here one day. I know you will. Eeh! I'm that eager. I'd love a nice girl to keep me company. And grandchildren.'

'You'll have a long wait, Mam.' Nat, evidently irritated by his mother's talk, handed Alan an earthenware half-pint mug of tea. 'Get that down yer and we'll put the cows out. I can't listen to much more of Mam's nonsense.'

Alan was enjoying himself. Ragging Nat was irresistible. 'Have you still got all your baby things, Ma?' he asked, keeping a straight face. 'All those pretty clothes you've kept?'

It was difficult to keep the straight face when Nat was groaning and rolling his eyes heavenwards.

'Eeh. I have that. I get them out every spring and wash and starch them, Alan,' Ma answered eagerly. 'Do you want me to fetch them down and show you?'

She wiped her small hands on the pinafore and untied the knot that lay over her round stomach.

'I'll see them later. When the work's done,' he assured her. 'Perhaps the sight of them will spur Nat on.' He glanced at his friend's crestfallen face and could not hold back his mirth any longer, remembering Nat's embarrassment every time his mother showed off her hoard of tiny garments.

Nat left the table and went to the door, jerking his head for Alan to follow. 'You want to give 'em to a museum,

Mam,' he called over his shoulder as they sat on the kitchen step pulling on their boots.

Then as they rounded the corner of the house, out of sight of his mother, Nat gave Alan a playful shove, sending him helpless with laughter over the low stone wall of the dairy.

'Yer great gowk!' Nat said. 'She'll have the flaming lot out when we go back in. We'll have the whole ruddy family history an' all. How her great grandmother put the lace on the daft caps.'

It took Alan minutes to control the gusts of laughter that Nat's outraged expression brought.

'Come on then,' he said at last. 'Let's get the cows out.'

'Aye. Then we'll take a look at the sheep on th' hill after we've done the cows. After we've had us dinner.' Nat began to smile again. 'If we can get away from Mam and her ruddy hope-chest,' he said.

CHAPTER NINETEEN

When she woke on Monday morning Rose lay for a few minutes. Mary had gone to the mill and Vivienne, who had an hour's walk to the Catholic secondary school, had left. The sun was streaming in at the window; she was warm, luxuriant, enjoying the rare solitude of the quiet room and very aware of her body.

Last night she had been asleep when Aunt Carrie came back from chapel. They had not faced one another since Aunt Carrie had struck her. They would have to talk soon but now Rose was even more resolved never to allow Aunt Carrie any authority over her. She wanted to clear the air between them; to ask her to allow Vivienne's dancing lessons to continue and had decided, if Aunt Carrie's mood was propitious, to talk about marrying Alan.

She got out of bed and sat for a full five minutes, looking at herself in the mirror on the dressing table; looking to see if her face had changed. She thought perhaps it had, making her look older, wiser, now she was . . . What was she? No longer a virgin. A woman perhaps? Or was she just a girl who had Done It?

No, she wasn't going to use that expression any more. It didn't do justice to the way she felt. She saw a pale face looking back at her, with dark shadows under the eyes which she'd not noticed before. What were they from – worries or just excitement? For she felt them all.

The first worry – the new standing she meant to establish with Aunt Carrie – would be dealt with later; this evening, perhaps, when she came home. The worry for Alan's safety she could do nothing about. She must keep these fears to herself, not let him return to his squadron burdened with her terrors. Last night, instead of dreams of bliss she had been tormented with fears.

Perhaps the sound of night-flying aeroplanes passing low over the hills had disturbed her slumber, for she had woken with a start from a nightmare, hearing Alan calling to her from a great distance and, unable to see him, she had been running along a seashore, screaming his name to an empty, darkening sky.

But there was excitement in her too. The remembering of his arms around her, the weight of his body on hers, the slightly bruised sensation that reminded her, with every movement, of their love-making. They had twenty-four hours still.

She stripped, went to the washbasin, filled it with cold water and lathered herself, using the last piece of scented soap she had. She was accustomed now to washing in cold water. The scullery was the only place with hot. When she had done she put on her dressing-gown, tied the cord tightly around her waist and descended the stairs, to make tea and toast. Aunt Carrie was not there. It was eight-thirty. Perhaps she had gone early to the market.

She'd be late for work if she didn't hurry. And she had to leave a note for Aunt Carrie, if she wasn't in the kitchen when she came down next time, telling her that she would be coming home at half past ten, when the pictures came out. She'd say she was going with Pamela and Sylvia.

And what was she to wear? There was a green crepe blouse that had been Mum's. She'd wear that with her best grey skirt. She had a pair of silk stockings and would put them on instead of the rayon ones she usually wore. From one of the tiny drawers of the dressing table where she kept her brooches and beads she brought out her little box of Poudre Matite. She kept it hidden from Vivienne who would have used it without a qualm. She dabbed an extra covering under her eyes, then, after staring at her reflection for a few seconds longer she took out her lipstick and applied some with the tip of her little finger, rubbing it in well before pressing her lips firmly together to colour her whole mouth.

She smiled to herself at her boldness. Miss Barclay and Miss Thompson would have something to click their tongues about this morning.

She left the Temperance Hotel and ran up the steps to the square where she let herself into the side door of the bank.

Pamela and Sylvia were leaning over the handrail on the little landing outside the cloakroom, waiting for her.

'Tell us all about it, Rose,' Pamela demanded, following her through to the cloakroom. 'Where did he take you?'

'Has he gone back yet?' Sylvia asked eagerly, her dark eyes lively with curiosity.

'No. He's still here. I'm seeing him tonight,' Rose told them as she hung the black jacket on her peg and turned to face them. 'He took me to the opera.'

'Phew!' Pamela sat down quickly on a chair, arms flopping over the side, gawky legs outstretched, pretending astonishment. 'I've never been taken to the opera by a man. Only Daddy.'

They heard the back door slam; heard the noise of one pair of pattering feet and one heavy clumping pair in the corridor.

'That'll be Woof-Woof and Tombstone,' Pamela said, making them explode with laughter. 'Look tragic before they get here. It will ruin their day if they think we're enjoying life.'

'Tell us all about it in the back room, Rose.' Sylvia pulled Pamela to her feet. 'Come on, you idiot.'

Rose winked at them as Miss Barclay and Miss Thompson came into the cloakroom. They were asking for her friendship. 'I'll be down in a minute,' she promised.

The machines were clattering and clashing when she reached the back room. Pamela and Sylvia entered figures at great speed, their fingers flying over the keys and bashing the long bar whilst with their free left hands they turned over cheques, memorizing and entering.

'Come on,' Sylvia said. 'Tell us.'

Their eyes darted quick looks between times as they encouraged her to tell them all about her date.

'What time are you seeing him, tonight?' Pamela urged her on.

'He's taking me to the Churchgate Cafe for tea at six o'clock.' Rose had to raise her voice against the noise. 'Then we're going to his house afterwards.'

Pamela stopped still, the motor of her machine whirring and wheezing as it ran down. 'He's taking you home already? That means he's serious.'

Rose laughed out loud at Pamela's expression. 'Yes. You are a fool, Pamela.'

'That's funny.' Pamela kept her face straight as she glared at Sylvia as if daring her to contradict. 'We're going to the Churchgate cafe for our tea tonight. Aren't we, Sylvia?'

'No. Yes. Are we?' Sylvia's bright eyes flew from Pamela to Rose so quickly and with such alarm that the three of them laughed until they were weak.

The door opened and Miss Thompson crossed the room on quick feet. 'Concentrate on your work, girls!' she snapped. 'And you, Miss Kennedy. Come along. You are keeping the chief cashier waiting.'

Despite her earlier feeling that the hours would drag until she saw Alan, it was a quarter to six. She had been upstairs and made herself ready and her heart was starting the pounding that the very thought of Alan set up. She would be with him a few minutes from now.

The banking hall was at the far end of the tiled corridor from the back room where she was helping the girls to tidy date stamps, pens and papers. Out of hours, when the heavy doors were closed, staff used the side door which was reached from the yard. It was not possible to open it from the outside and a knock, as now, at this time of the afternoon, was a nuisance.

'Damn,' said Pamela. 'I'll go.'

They heard her open the door and her clear, carrying voice saying, 'You must be Alan. Do come in.'

She put her head round the door and made an appreciative face. 'Rose,' she called loudly, as if the place had not fallen silent. 'Someone to see you.'

Why had he come to the bank? Rose pulled wide the door.

He was in uniform. He stood there, tall, dark and straight in the well-fitting suit of airforce blue. He seemed to fill the narrow hallway. She had never seen him in uniform before and for a second could not speak. He looked so different; distant, dedicated and so very handsome. There was a strange taste in her mouth, a sensation like butterflies in her inside as she gathered herself and made the introductions.

'Pamela; this is Alan MacGregor. Alan – Pamela Tannenbaum.'

Pamela was utterly composed. 'You were a medical student, Rose tells us,' she said as she shook his hand confidently. 'Which branch of medicine do you want to specialize in?'

'Obstetrics.' Alan smiled at her.

'Daddy's a consultant obstetrician,' she said. 'In Manchester.'

Rose interrupted her to introduce Sylvia to Alan and all the time she could see that Alan was impatient to speak to her.

'Do you think I could have a word with you alone, Rose?' he said as soon as he had shaken Sylvia's hand.

'Go into the back room,' Pamela said. 'Be my guest. We're going upstairs now, aren't we Sylvia?'

'No. Yes. Oh, yes,' Sylvia replied, bewilderment in her face again.

When the door closed behind the girls Alan took her hand in his.

'What is it, Alan?' Rose asked. But she knew, before he spoke, what he would say.

'There was a telegram for me when I came back from the farm,' he said. 'I've to be back tonight. It looks as though things are moving.'

She heard the excitement in his voice; knew he was eager to go, to join the action. A cold shudder of fear went through her yet she made her face bright for him lest he should leave with a shadow of anxiety for her. She fought back her impulse to hold on to him, to beg him to stay.

'Have we any time?' she asked.

He gripped her shoulders and looked into her eyes. 'Only enough time to tell you I love you,' he said. 'And to give you this.'

He took a small box from his pocket and opened it. The diamond cluster caught the light as he withdrew it and held out his hand for hers. The ring slipped easily on to her third finger.

Rose lifted brimming eyes to his and saw that his too were glistening with tears.

He held her then in a grip of iron and his mouth came down on hers with a fierce possessiveness she'd not felt before. And her heart was crying inside her, Don't Go. Please Don't Go, whilst her arms were around his waist, feeling his slim, strong body under the rough serge tunic that encased him.

And then, as if he needed to do it this way, he released her. He looked hard at her, his eyes searching her face as if he wanted to memorize every detail of it and before her tears and the naked fear for him could overwhelm her, abruptly he turned, and was gone.

Pamela was holding her now, steadying her as sobs shook her and, in the loyal way Rose would come to rely upon, offering friendship and strength to sustain her.

'Wash your face, Rose,' Pamela said when the shaking

ceased. 'Brush your hair. We'll go out to tea anyway, the three of us. Alan's a British pilot. He's got to do his duty. We can't let the side down, girl. Keep your chin up. Press On.'

Carrie regretted it now. Regretted losing her temper, striking Rose. After she'd done it she had gone upstairs and cried. It was years since she'd last been driven to tears, but – seeing her there, in that car with Douglas McGregor's lad – and Cecil there too.

He'd seen it – Cecil. He had parked his Humber in front of the town hall before the concert and rather than move it he had said he'd walk with her down the Hundred and eight steps after the recital. They had passed right beside them. Bold as brass they had been – Rose and Alan McGregor. She could almost swear they had never even seen her and Cecil walking by.

Cecil had hurried her along, muttering, 'Don't look,' in an urgent voice. Immodesty in a woman was offensive to Cecil. He preached against it at the reformatory. She had looked. Of course she had looked. And she'd been sick to the stomach.

She had asked him to leave her at the door of the Temperance Hotel. She couldn't excuse or explain Rose's shameful conduct to Cecil. She had gone inside to wait.

And, as she'd waited, all the memories of her own downfall had risen to confront her. Surely Rose wasn't going to do the same as she had done? It wouldn't be adultery of course, in Rose's case. Not as it had been with herself and Patrick Kennedy.

She had only waited ten minutes before Rose had come in but as soon as she'd spoken all the rage, all the uncontrollable rage that was in her, had risen to the surface and she'd not been able to stop herself from striking out.

But she regretted it. She would have to make peace between them.

She had hardly slept that night and the night since. For the first time in her life she was tormented about whether she was doing right. Before she'd had the girls she had never doubted herself. Always she used to ask herself what her father would have done. And until now she had had her answer. But how would her father have dealt with all she had to contend with? She truly didn't know. She found herself spending more and more time alone in her sitting room, thinking and asking for guidance but, all at once, it was as if there was no-one there.

Last night she'd hardly slept for thinking about it all. What Rose might have done, what she, Carrie, and Patrick Kennedy had done. She had been awake since five o'clock this morning, had gone downstairs at five thirty and had made the girls' breakfasts for them when they came down to the kitchen at seven.

Vivienne had been in a better mood. Since she'd put her foot down over the dancing lessons she'd calmed down a lot – been more eager to please. She'd give her another week or two before she reconsidered the lessons.

Now she walked up the Wallgate to the market. It was a beautiful morning. There were quite a few people in the market square and it was only eight o'clock. She'd get some meat if the butcher had anything. The ration was only one and tenpenceworth a week each and she wanted a joint for weekend. The butcher opened at eight and the greengrocer at half past. By the time Frank Cartledge opened at nine she'd be ready to go to him and ask for a packet of his sleeping-powders.

When she had finished the shopping she went to Frank Cartledge's. There was no-one else in the shop so she could speak out. He was white haired now. His son, another Frank, had qualified as a proper chemist and he'd make up a cure for anything.

'I'm not sleeping well,' she told the senior Frank. She had to lean over a sack of something that smelt malty. It made her feel sick. 'And I keep – I know it sounds daft – I keep bursting into tears. For nothing.'

He frowned, thoughtfully. 'How's your appetite?'

'It's going.'

'Do you get faint?'

He was clever. He was as good as a doctor – better in fact. Fancy knowing that she felt faint. She'd forgotten to tell him that.

'I get . . . kind of . . . what you might call mazy bouts, Frank. I go all mazy and have to grab on to things. I can't concentrate any more.'

He had gone into the back and dispensed some medicine for her, a ruby-red colour it was. He said it would help her to sleep and that she was to take a tablespoonful, in water, after food. She felt a bit better just knowing there was a cure for it.

On her way down the Wallgate she bumped into Brenda Gallimore and her Flo, coming up.

'Aren't you working, Flo?' Carrie said. 'I thought you were at Brocklehurst's.'

Brenda Gallimore looked fat and frumpish these days. She'd let herself go, had Brenda. She couldn't keep control of them, her girls. She gave Carrie one of those looks of exasperation as she answered for Flo. 'She's got a bellyache. We're goin' to get some of that white medicine from Cartledge's.'

'Has Vivienne started work yet?' Flo asked in the cheeky way she had. She didn't sound as if she had a bellyache.

'She's at school,' Carrie answered.

'They've settled down well, haven't they?' Brenda said. 'You must be proud of them. Everyone says what little ladies they are.'

'They're no trouble,' Carrie answered, feeling a warm flush of pride.

Flo sniffed. 'Well I think your Rose is stuck up,' she said.

Brenda Gallimore clouted her across the ear. 'That's not a nice thing to say.'

Flo grimaced, clapped a hand to her ear and answered her mother back. 'She gives herself airs and graces, anyroad. I can't stand her.'

Carrie didn't mind in the least if Flo Gallimore thought Rose stuck up. Just as long as she never behaved like Flo. Flo Gallimore was common.

'She walks past yer and never says a word. She dun't even pretend to see yer,' Flo was going on.

'She doesn't wear her glasses. That's what's wrong,' Carrie answered before leaving them and continuing down the steep incline to Waters Green.

She was relieved at what Flo had said. At least it meant that the Gallimores hadn't seen Rose and Alan McGregor in that car on Saturday night.

When she got in she saw the note on the kitchen table. 'I am going to the pictures after work, with Pamela and Sylvia. Back at eleven, Rose.' It wasn't even addressed to anyone. She looked at it, knew perfectly well that Rose was lying – she'd be seeing Alan McGregor again – and made up her mind to talk to her, tonight.

In the middle of the morning Cecil called to tell her that the council had agreed to pay what she privately thought was an exorbitant rent for the town property. She had bought it on Cecil's own recommendation so she made allowances for his excitable state. He had to keep dodging out of the way in the kitchen. Mrs Tereschenko was bustling about, preparing a goulash at the time.

'Don't forget zee muzik,' she kept reminding them.

'I haven't forgotten,' Carrie answered. She turned to Cecil. 'Mr and Mrs Chenko are having a musical evening,' she explained. 'It's a Polish festival.'

Mrs Tereschenko nodded and smiled at them. She understood a little English now. She couldn't follow conversations but she could ask for what she wanted in the shops. She must have persuaded the butcher to let her have two weeks' meat ration. They would be living on fish and liver or sausages for the next fortnight by the size of the dish she was using.

'Mr and Mrs Singer will be coming downstairs as well,' Carrie went on. 'We are going to have it in the dining room.'

'Be sure that it is not an . . . an idolater's festival,' Cecil warned without lowering his voice, as if sure that he would not be understood. 'Remember, these people have not been saved.'

'Of course it's not. And don't you start all that. They are nice people.' Here Carrie smiled encouragement again at Mrs Tereschenko and saw by her expression that the woman hadn't understood a word Cecil had uttered. She felt herself going mazy again.

'Will you allow her – your niece – to join the celebration?' Cecil asked her, in an undertone.

'What are you talking about?' Carrie pulled herself together and looked at him closely. He looked the way he did before he gave a sermon; a bit inflated. 'Which niece?'

'Has she repented? Have you chastised her?' Cecil came closer and reached for her hand.

Carrie pulled it from his grasp. 'That's enough!' she said. Then she said, so that Mrs Tereschenko would not think anything was amiss, 'Get back to the council meeting.' Her expression, she knew, was forbidding.

Cecil picked up his coat. '"Who can find a virtuous woman?"' he proclaimed. 'Ecclesiastes – one. "For her price is far above rubies."'

'I said, "That is enough," Cecil,' Carrie said. 'Don't assume any rights in this household. I'll deal with the girls in my own way.'

'I make applestrudel, yes?' Mrs Tereschenko asked.

'Yes. Yes. Anything you like,' Carrie said. 'I'll see you to the door, Cecil.'

He left, after kissing and nearly crushing her hand. He had a grip of iron when it suited him. It was most unpleasant. She climbed the stairs to her sitting room. She had a bit of a headache. Maybe if she soaked a pad of cotton wool in eau-de-cologne, put it over her forehead and lay on her settee for half an hour it would go.

Lying there she reflected on the feeling of unease that the touch of Cecil gave to her. It was odd, for she reacted with such delight when Mr Tereschenko took her hand to his lips. He had spoken to her yesterday, when she'd come in from Sunday School.

'Mees Shriglee,' he'd begun, taking her fingers lightly in his and raising them to his lips. She had found herself feeling regal, exalted; not at all offended as she sometimes was when Cecil touched her. 'Mees Shriglee. Irina . . . my wife . . . and I ask you and your most lovely girls to take zee . . . zee supper . . . if eez posseeble . . . in your dining room for zee lodgers.'

'What a charming idea, Mr Chenko,' she'd replied, all girlish and silly under his flattering gaze. His eyes held hers but there was nothing but admiration and, yes, respect in them as she smiled back at him. 'When?'

'Tomorrow. At eight o'clock.' He had bowed again.

She was surprised, in view of the note, when Rose came in at half past six, saying that she had had her tea.

'Can I talk to you, Rose,' Carrie said. 'Mary and Vivienne are in the room. Getting ready. I want a word in private with you.'

Rose nodded. She looked pale and a bit puffy-eyed but it was impossible to guess at her mood.

Carrie went ahead, up the stairs. 'Close the door,' she said when they were inside the sitting room. 'And sit down.'

Rose shut the door and followed her to the octagonal table in the window. 'We can't go on like this,' Carrie began. 'Not talking.'

'I think we've said too much already,' Rose answered, not looking directly at her.

'I have,' Carrie said quietly, fighting back the tears that

threatened. 'I know I have – said too much. I'm sorry. I'm so very sorry I hit you.'

Rose still didn't look up.

'I . . . I don't want the same thing to happen to you,' Carrie went on. 'You are my daughter and . . .'

'Don't! Don't start again,' Rose said; quietly pleading with her. 'I know. I know it's all true. It's just that . . . I can't . . . can't think of you that way – not yet.'

She was crying, quietly, desperately crying and her tears were not to do with what they were saying. Carrie pulled a handkerchief from her dress pocket and held it out to her. 'Here. Use this.'

Rose put out her hand for it. Her left hand. Carrie saw the ring. It had gone that far then. She struggled again to keep down her tears. She had better try to be tactful.

'I see he's put a ring on your finger,' she said, trying to keep up an appearance of calm. 'When did he do that?'

Rose snatched the handkerchief and stood up as if to leave the room. 'Today,' she cried. 'He's gone back. God knows where he'll be sent to.'

'You're not hoping to marry him, are you?'

'Why would I wear the ring if I didn't want to marry him?' Rose demanded.

'You must wait. I don't want you rushing into anything.'

Rose just stood there, staring at her, tears rolling down her white face, refusing to add anything. There was still a great gulf between them. Carrie did not know how to breach it. It was plain that Rose wanted nothing from her: not advice, not comfort, nothing.

'Pull yourself together,' she said finally. 'There's nothing you can do. We'll forget our differences.'

Rose ran from the room, still crying.

Alan swung the Riley through the camp gates at ten-thirty, reported to Ops five minutes later and went to the mess where he found everyone in high spirits.

'Good leave?' Jeffreys joked, as the steward brought

their drinks. 'Was she waiting for you? Your English Rita Hayworth?'

'Yes,' Alan said as he drained the glass and signalled to the steward for more. 'What's the flap about? Have you been told?'

'We've been on readiness all weekend. All leave has been cancelled. Everyone recalled,' Martin said. He gave Alan a knowing look. 'That's knocked your romance through the window, hasn't it?'

'Oh. I don't know . . .' Alan wanted to keep it to himself a little longer but now Jeffreys had that wolfish look in his eyes and had nudged him knowingly.

'I think we'll be sent up at dawn.' Martin was raising his voice against the noise of a group of pilots whose raucous laughter was filling the room. 'I want to get up there and at 'em. Bloody Jerries. We've not even seen a Messerschmitt so far. Did you ask her?'

'She said yes,' Alan said, grinning at his friend.

'Congratulations. Did the car run all right?'

'Super. She's behind the mess.'

'Rose is?'

'The Riley, you clown!' Alan laughed. 'Order another, then I'm going to get my head down.'

The tension was getting to him again; the nervous energy they all displayed was like an infectious disease. He could only take so much of it before he had to get away from the crowd. He finished his drink and went to the hut, to write to Rose. Tomorrow they could be tangling with the enemy and have no chance to write.

But the following day they were sent on patrol when other squadrons were in action. What had the training been for if they were never to be tested? The war would be over soon. There was little enough happening.

There were times when he wished he'd joined the navy. His father would be seeing action before he would if Dad's orders had come through. It was more than a week before the call came.

'Wake up, sir. Wake up.' The light was on and Alan's shoulder was being shaken.

'What time is it?' he snapped at the airman.

'Three-thirty, sir. Take-off's in half an hour.'

He was wide awake now, heart thumping, struggling into his flying gear, sipping steaming hot tea. They were going into action at last and his heart was pounding with fear and excitment.

He ran outside and on to the tarmac where flight mechanics were warming up the Spitfires.

He ran towards the group who stood around the squadron leader in the pale grey light.

'Where are we going?' he shouted to Martin above the noise of the revving engines.

'Dunkirk.'

'What the hell's going on there?'

'They're evacuating or something,' Martin said. 'Squadron Leader's about to give us the details.'

They crowded round the senior officer. 'They're on the beach,' he was telling them. 'Thousands of our men. Being strafed and bombed. We've to protect the boats. Knock their bombers out of the sky. It's the biggest rescue operation ever. As soon as I say "Take Action," go for it.'

'There's the phone!'

The orderly poked his head out of the door.

'Scramble!' he yelled.

Alan raced across the grass and leaped into the narrow cockpit. He clipped his harness straps and pressed the starter, the procedures fixed in his mind. Last minute checks. Flaps and ailerons were adjusted. Test r.p.m. Push forward the throttle lever. And he was moving forward to take off behind the leader.

At eighty-five miles an hour the Spitfire was airborne and climbing. Then they were in formation in the still air, flying eastwards towards the dawn and the coast of France, voices on the R.T. headphones; instructions; Control; the leader's asides.

They flew over Dover, the steady note of the Merlin settling into cruising, the even tones of their unperturbable leader somehow inspiring. He felt calm now; cool-headed and ready.

Then he looked down on to grey sea. From bays and little coves and harbours along the coast boats were moving out to sea joining a line that stretched towards the continent. Destroyers, paddle steamers and yachts, pleasure boats and tugs, lifeboats and fishing vessels all were heading out to the Channel, merging, joining a straggling line that appeared to reach all the way to France.

Minutes later they neared the French coast.

Beneath them, like ants, black moving dots on the sand were unbelieveably, men; thousands of them. From the water's edge to the boats in the shallows threading, black lines of men were wading out to their rescuers.

Behind the beaches battle smoke obscured the town. Flashing gunfire could be seen and further on a plume of black smoke from blazing fuel tanks was being thrust skywards. The smell of burning oil was filling his nostrils even from that distance.

The R.T. crackled.

'Enemy aircraft ahead. Enemy aircraft ahead. Take action!'

The metallic taste of adrenalin was in his mouth. Ahead he saw, coming towards them, barely three miles ahead and high above, a slanting line of bombers; about fifty in number and, above the bombers, fighters.

Messerschmitt 110s were overhead seconds later. He saw their twin fins glinting in the sun; saw the black crosses of the enemy, their load of bombs. They were climbing to avoid a fight.

They were going to bomb our men below. He felt a surge of hatred for them; a hot thrill of hatred such as he had never felt in life before.

He veered sharply to the right, nose up, closing on the 110 he'd selected as his own. The squadron was hurling around the sky; he could hear them, a fury of voices in his ear but he was above and behind his Messerschmitt as it dipped and wheeled to avoid him.

The voice in his ear. 'Red Leader calling. Watch your tail, McGregor. Bandits at four o'clock.'

He saw the grey shape of the German fighter as he glanced back. Two Spitfires were streaking towards it, engines screaming as they dived. The bomber was in his sights.

The sun glanced off perspex. His thumb jabbed at the button and the Spitfire's guns tore out in an angry roar over the huge wings that were filling his windscreen.

His blood was still running hot with rage. He fired again, aiming at the cockpit and the pilot's leather helmet. Power seemed to be running through him.

He heard the rattle of his guns tearing into the 110, felt the recoil; saw pieces of metal flying; saw a burst of flame that glowed red and spread along the wing. Then the wing folded, dropped and was gone.

He glanced in the little mirror above his head as he opened the throttle and lifted the mullet head of the fighter. The 110 was spinning crazily, aflame in front of a fast-lengthening ribbon of smoke as it went down into the sea.

Blood was pounding through him now. He was exultant. He'd got one. He had not let anyone down. He'd done it. In his first action, he'd got one.

Ahead the sky was empty. He glanced in the mirror and saw, just above his rudder, the nose of a Messerschmitt 109. He turned steeply, the cold chill of the hunted replacing the heat of the hunter.

White tracer streamed from the 109. He dived. It was still behind him, and firing. He steep-turned at the same moment that he was hit.

The impact was terrific. His shoulders were thrown forward against the harness straps that seemed to be taking his full weight. Something must have gone.

He was momentarily calm as the aeroplane lurched and there was no response from the stick that fell loosely against him. The nose was pointing down and the engine roaring. He was falling; the altimeter unwinding rapidly. His eyes went to the mirror.

The tail had gone.

There was no sign of the 109.

Smoke was coming from the engine, filling the cockpit. He must get out. He pulled at the rubber ball overhead and felt the hood tear away; heard the screaming wind and the protesting engine. The wind was dragging his breath away. The noise was deafening. Tearing at his helmet to dislodge it he pulled himself upwards. There was no time. Flames were leaping out behind the cockpit. He kicked against the bucket seat. He felt a blow, as if he had been struck by a wall. Then his body slewed into the air and the burning aircraft dropped beneath him, plunging downwards like a flaming, disintegrating cross.

Coldness was whipping his legs. He pulled the D ring and heard the crack of air against the opening parachute as his body was jerked from its fall.

He was being held, floating beneath the billowing white mushroom above his head. A thousand thoughts and prayers crowded into his mind. He was alive. Amazingly, he was alive.

'Please God, let me land safely. Let Rose know I am alive.'

The prayers ran repeatedly through his mind. There was searing pain in his legs. He looked down. His trousers were ragged shorts with tattered strings of charred material flapping like a crazy fringe round his thighs. The skin was blackened but his legs were there. He must have freed himself with only a fraction of a second to spare. And below him, only feet below, trees.

The 110 had gone down in the sea. He could not be far inland. He was coming down fast. He missed the trees by inches and saw grass rise up to meet him.

He landed badly, heavily, jolting every joint in his body as he pitched forward, rolled and was dragged, cutting shins and knees, ripping elbows on the tussocky ground that was dotted with sharp-edged little boulders.

The parachute dropped to earth, billowing slowly and rising until the air was out, falling again in a tangle of cord and cloth where it caught on the stones.

And again the prayers. 'Thank God I'm alive. Thank God. I am alive, Rose. Rose I'm alive.'

His reflexes were normal. Alan unfastened the harness with desperate fingers. Ignoring the sharp pain that was now shooting through his right foot he slid along the ground to free himself. At any moment he would hear shots, or at least the raised voices and barking dogs of a search party.

There was nothing. Not a sound. Only the shallow river behind him, gurgling carelessly.

Had he been seen? Had the Spitfire gone down in the sea? He'd got out just in time. Another minute and he'd have burned with the aeroplane. Had nobody seen the 'chute open? There was a farmhouse nearby. He'd seen it just before he dropped in front of the trees. Surely someone had been watching the fighting above their land.

There was silence. In the distance a cow was lowing. But there were no human noises.

He struggled to his feet and tried to walk. His big toe was swollen to twice its size. It was probably broken but there was nothing to be done. And now another pain. Sharp; scorching pain that stretched from his ankle to the top of his thigh. He winced and, taking all his weight on his left leg, barely able to put the right to the ground, he ran to gather the parachute.

He folded it into an unwieldy bundle and, hopping and falling, made for the water. The river was about twenty feet across; the water waist-high. He plunged into the chill depths, feeling smooth, weed-slippery stones under his feet and the water a blessing, numbing the burns on his legs.

Then he was over and stuffing the parachute bundle deep into a clump of brambles at the edge of a copse.

He found a hiding-place in the thicket and at last dropped to his knees, feeling the creasing of his burnt legs an agony that made him grip his hands together to prevent himself from making a noise.

When it was dark he'd move. He'd make for the farmhouse, scout around for clothes and food, try to talk himself into the favour of the French farmer who might be prepared to assist him. He would try to get to the coast. It was not far. Not Dunkirk. He was not going to walk into enemy lines. Perhaps further south where he could find a boat?

First, he would have to get down to the water again as soon as he was sure the coast was clear. He must bathe his legs; he must examine and cool these burns.

CHAPTER TWENTY

Rose was in the glass-fronted cubicle, counting the ten-shilling notes when Mr Wilson tapped on the door. She looked up quickly. Mr Wilson, normally so nonchalant, looked grim. His face was pale and set. He beckoned to her. Alan's father, looking ashen, was behind him.

'Mr McGregor wants to talk to you, Miss Kennedy,' Mr Wilson said. 'You can go to the accountant's room.'

Rose felt her knees go weak. Her legs did not seem to be strong enough to carry her towards the office. Before anything was said she knew what she would hear. Something had happened to Alan.

Mr Wilson closed the door for them and Alan's father, having difficulty holding himself in check, turned to her.

'Alan's plane was lost over France – yesterday,' he said in a tight voice. He pulled from his jacket pocket a yellow telegram envelope and handed it to her.

Rose put out her hand slowly. She knew that she too was as white as death, but from somewhere strength came to her. She withdrew the paper with it's pasted-on message strip and read.

'. . . regret to inform you that your son, Pilot Officer Alan McGregor, is missing . . . believed killed . . . 28 May.'

She looked up after reading it and saw Douglas McGregor's face, lips pressed hard together, jaw clenched.

'A senior officer came to the house – shortly after,' he said. 'He told me not to give up hope. He said it's possible that Alan baled out. Nobody saw a parachute – they saw the Spitfire go down in flames . . .'

A wave of horror washed over her but it was swiftly followed by another feeling which she knew she would never be able to explain rationally.

Alan could not be – was not – dead. She would have known it.

'He's alive,' she said with quiet assurance. 'I know. Don't ask me how, but I know he's alive. I feel it. He is injured. But he's not dead.'

Douglas reached out a hand to her and she took it in both of hers. She had to pass on to him this conviction – that Alan would return. She held his large hand in her little warm ones and very gently she repeated. 'I know. I just know he'll come back.'

'I wish I shared your certainty, Rose,' was all he said in a quiet voice.

He let go of her hands and staightened his shoulders, then turned from her, going towards the window to look out over the market square. 'I'm leaving Middlefield.'

'Leaving?'

'Yes. It's only a matter of time before all the men under fifty will be called up. I volunteered for Coastal Command. My orders came through this morning.'

'Where will you go?' she asked.

'North. To Leith or Aberdeen,' he said, still without looking at her. 'I report in Edinburgh on Tuesday.'

'And the Swan? Is it to be closed?'

'Commandeered,' he said. He glanced at her. 'The bar will stay. I've got a manager. The accommodation will be used for officers from the barracks.'

'And the house?' she said.

'Mrs Tansley will live there.'

'Mr McGregor?'

He turned now, quickly, to look at her. 'You would soon have been calling me "Dad" wouldn't you?' he said, smiling a sad, rueful smile.

'I will. One day,' Rose answered softly. 'Will you write to me? When you hear where Alan is?'

340

Douglas came forward. He looked slowly into her eyes for a moment, then sat at the big leather-topped table that nearly filled the room. He took a sheet of paper out of the wooden stationery stand, dipped a pen into the inkwell and began to write as she watched.

'Mrs J.R. Forsyth.

Ramsay Gardens,

Edinburgh.'

Then he added a telephone number and the address of Coastal Command.

'The mother of a friend of Alan's,' he explained.

'I know,' Rose said. 'I've met her.'

He didn't ask for explanations. He was a kind, understanding man. Rose wanted him to go to his own service as sure of Alan's safety as she was. She hoped she was giving to him her faith that Alan would be restored to them.

'If you need to get in touch with me,' he said, handing the paper to her.

Then he stood and placed his hand on his shoulder. It was not a hug, not even a pat, just a message of affection. 'I shall be back when the war is over.'

'Thank you.' Rose had a great lump in her throat. She wanted, all at once, to hold him, to comfort him. But this was the wrong time, the wrong place.

How long would it be before she saw him again? It felt as if another part, another good part, of her life was leaving with him. He was a part of her experience. A part of her childhood. 'Don't despair, Mr McGregor,' she managed to say. 'We'll have Alan back.'

He shook her hand, very formal now.

'Goodbye,' he said.

When he had gone, Rose went back to the cubicle. It was as if a great heaviness had come upon her. She could not have explained it but she felt detached; felt she was spectating on all that was going on around her. The news had spread like wildfire amongst the staff and it seemed that they all wanted her to know that they felt for her.

Pamela and Sylvia were the first to come to where, head bowed, she went on counting the money, trying not to consider the possibility that her faith in her instincts had deserted her. He lived.

'Rose?' Pamela whispered as she opened the door.

'It's all right, Pam,' she answered. 'He's not dead.'

Pamela – bold, confident Pamela – had tears streaming down her cheeks. 'Sure?' she asked in a choking voice.

'I'd know it. If it were true.'

Pamela ran from the cubicle before the frightened face of Sylvia appeared in Pam's place. 'Keep your pecker up!' she said. 'A lot are coming back.'

'I know.'

'Have you read the papers?'

'No.'

Sylvia handed over a newspaper. 'It's all over the front page,' she said. 'The evacuation. Small Boats Brave Fire and Shells. Taking the soldiers off the beaches.'

Rose noticed that Sylvia's hands were shaking, though she hadn't cried. Sylvia's uncle had gone out with the British Expeditionary Force. They'd had no news of him. 'Read on, Sylvia,' she whispered.

'Warships are standing off,' she read. 'The Royal Navy puts up a halo of fire.' Her voice was faltering.

Rose read it. 'Please God,' she said. 'Let them all get back.'

At last the day was over and she went back to the Temperance Hotel.

Aunt Carrie was waiting for her at the far side of the kitchen. She stood by the dining table which was now placed in the big alcove. Mary and Vivienne, looking uncertain, stood by her, one either side. So they all knew.

'I'm sorry, lass,' Aunt Carrie began. It seemed to Rose that Aunt Carrie had rehearsed for this moment. She looked neither sorry nor distraught.

'There's no need to be.' Rose had not meant to sound

342

curt but the words had come out that way. Aunt Carrie had made it plain that she did not care for Alan. She need not pretend concern. 'I know he's alive,' she said, louder.

Aunt Carrie was coming towards her, arms out-stretched. She couldn't bear it. She didn't want comfort. She took a step backwards, towards the door she had just entered.

'And I want you all to believe it!' she cried, and turned, stumbling to reach the stairs and run to her room where, now there was no-one to see, she fell on to the bed and cried herself into a short, fitful sleep.

She must have slept for about an hour. When she awoke she went to the washbasin, splashed her face with water and rubbed it vigorously with her towel. Then she took a deep breath at the open window. She could face them now. She went downstairs, calm and composed.

Mary and Vivienne were at the table with Aunt Carrie. The table, as ever, was covered with a starched, em-broidered cloth. They all fell silent as she entered. They had stopped eating.

Rose pulled up a chair and forced herself to say, 'Don't look at me like that, all of you. I know he's alive. I don't want anyone to talk about it. That's all.'

Mary pushed across the big china plate. Butter mixed with margarine was spread thinly over the thick slices of homebaked bread. She took a piece in silence then gave Mary a forced smile.

Vivienne handed the Wedgwood jar that was filled with Aunt Carrie's blackcurrant jam. Rose took a spoonful, placed it on the side of her plate and nodded to Viv to take the thing away. 'She never gives up,' she thought to herself. No matter that there were only the four of them and that their tea consisted of bread and butter and jam and a piece of cake. The silver teapot was used, the second-best china service, starched white napkins and the four evenly-cut wedges of her homemade ginger cake were placed on a silver cakestand with a crocheted lace mat beneath them.

Sometimes, she thought, but not at this moment, she wanted to scream, seeing Aunt Carrie and all the silly consolations she surrounded herself with to make up for the great yawning gap in her life which she had never filled with the love and affection she was capable of giving.

I hope I never, never get like that, Rose thought as she ate quietly under Aunt Carrie's watchful gaze. I could have relied on Mum to help me now. For, though she knew absolutely that Alan would come back to her, she felt inside herself something changing, stirring and sickening her and she did not know what it could be.

'I don't want a cup of tea,' she said, putting out her hand to prevent Aunt Carrie from filling her cup. The mere imagining of its hot sweetness had turned her stomach. 'I'll just drink milk for now. If we've got enough.'

'Yes. We've plenty,' Aunt Carrie said quickly and eagerly as if she was glad there was something she could do. 'I'll order an extra pint from Nat Cooper. You are three growing girls. You need milk.'

'I'm already grown,' Rose snapped. 'Don't worry about me.'

She saw and recognized the hurt look on Aunt Carrie's face but it seemed she was unable to prevent herself from rebuffing all her aunt's overtures.

Aunt Carrie rose from the table. Rose saw her straight, dignified back as she left the room and a sense of hopeless weariness descended upon her again.

'There was no need to be rude to her,' Mary said quietly when they heard their aunt's footsteps in the corridor. They heard her take her coat from the hall stand; heard the front door slam. 'We're all upset about Alan. It doesn't make it any easier . . .'

'I know. I'm sorry,' Rose said, her eyes still on the open door. She was sorry, but she couldn't go to Aunt Carrie. She couldn't have run after her to apologize. Not now. Not with Alan lying injured somewhere and Aunt Carrie wishing him ill.

'Then I think you should tell her so. She's done nothing to hurt you,' Mary added.

Mary was so like Mum had been, always seeing good in everyone. It made Rose feel worse about her own behaviour. Mary was also, like Mum, firm and quietly determined to see that justice was done. It was as if Mary had taken on Mum's role – of peacemaker.

'Well,' Vivienne said. 'I'm glad she's gone out. She keeps getting everything wrong. Everything I say to her is wrong!' Vivienne jumped up from the table.

Both her sisters looked at her, at her flushed, angry face. Mary put her lips together firmly as Vivienne flung down her napkin.

It was impossible to be self-absorbed with Vivienne around, Rose thought. Vivienne, selfish and wilful as she was, brought everyone down to earth with her one-sided, dramatic personality. When Vivienne acted, her audience sat up and paid attention.

'What's she done – Aunt Carrie? What has she done to you now?' Rose asked.

'She's not gone rushing out because of you anyway,' Vivienne declared. 'She's gone to a rehearsal at her precious Sunday School. The Choral Society, what's left of them, are giving a concert at the weekend. That beastly man of hers said so.'

'Has he been round again?' Rose asked. 'Cecil Rat-cliffe?'

'He's always round here in the daytime. School's on half days don't forget!'

Both Mary and Rose looked now at the outraged look on their sister's face. Vivienne, wearing Rose's scarlet jumper over her own green gymslip, looked like a furious Irish fairy. Only taller and startling in her prettiness.

'Don't laugh!' she ordered. 'I've lost some of my best things because of that man.'

'What things?' Rose asked.

'You tell her, Mary,' Vivienne said.

345

'She thinks Cecil Ratcliffe has stolen some of her dressing-up things,' Mary began with soothing patience.

Vivienne's eyes were alight now. 'It's not my dressing-up clothes, Mary,' she cut in. 'It's my French knickers and my Kestos.'

Vivienne had developed earlier than either she or Mary had. Unlike herself and Mary who were, they believed, a bit top-heavy, Vivienne had high, round breasts. She said they needed the support of a Kestos. Aunt Carrie always referred to it as a bust-bodice. In fact it was nothing so much as scraps of pink silk seamed down the middle to which were attached ribbons and long elastic button-straps. Rose had decided to buy one for herself. 'Where did you lose them?' she asked.

'I didn't lose them,' Vivienne insisted. 'I wash them every other night. You know I do. And I hang them there.'

She pointed with a theatrical gesture to the empty rails of the wooden, drying rack, high above the fireplace.

'Quite blatantly, if you ask me!' Mary said. Mary thought such things should be kept out of sight, Rose knew. Mary always professed shock at the sight of the underwear; French knickers hanging by their gusset with the brassiere dangling from its shoulder straps beside it.

'What on earth would Cecil Ratcliffe want with them?' Mary asked. 'The reformatory girls don't dress up or have concerts you know. Really. It's not as if it's a theatre or anything. Sometimes you try my patience, Vivienne.'

'He steals them for himself,' Vivienne said, her face still red and furious. 'You don't know. You really don't!'

'Don't know what?' Rose said. 'What don't we know?'

'You don't know what that man gets up to,' Vivienne said eagerly. 'Flo Gallimore said he's a . . .'

'Viv!' Rose interrupted her, sharply. 'Don't! Don't talk like Flo Gallimore. And don't listen to her.'

'No,' Mary agreed. 'And don't upset Rose. Not today.'

'Sorry.' Vivienne went to the door that led to their stairs

346

then turned what seemed to be a look of sympathetic sorrow on them. 'You are so innocent. You two.'

'Come back,' Rose said. 'Finish your story.'

Vivienne came across the room to them again. 'I've got to tell you this,' she began passionately. 'Flo Gallimore told me that he – Cecil Ratcliffe – goes to Dog Lane! To Lily Streeter's!'

They stared at Vivienne; astonished by her vehemence.

'It's a brothel!' Vivienne added unnecessarily.

'Viv!' They both chorused in alarm.

'It's true!'

Mary let out a long-drawn breath. 'She's no business saying things like that,' she said. 'He's a town councillor.'

'Aunt Carrie says he's the most respected man in Middlefield,' Rose said as calmly as she could, though she could not keep the anxious note out of her voice.

'You know they call it Streety Lil's?' Vivienne went on.

'Course we know.'

Vivienne put her shoulders back, waited a second; waited for them to appreciate fully what she was saying. 'He goes there. Dressed as a woman!'

Rose didn't know whether to laugh off Viv's nonsense or to take it seriously. 'It can't be true, Viv,' she said at last. 'Flo Gallimore's lying. Everyone would know – in a place like Middlefield – if a town councillor went about doing things like that.'

'How would they know?' Vivienne was indignant. 'If he went in disguise? Dressed as a woman?'

'Listen Viv,' Rose went on, as calmly as she could. 'Why would a man go to a . . . to Lily Streeter's dressed as a woman?'

'So that men will – instead of women – some men do it with other men!'

'I don't believe it.' It sounded quite incredible to Rose.

'That's filthy talk, Viv!' Mary said. 'Is that the kind of thing Flo Gallimore talks about?'

'And other things.'

'Like what?' Mary asked.

'Like Cecil Ratcliffe used to do wrong things to his own daughter.'

'Vivienne!' Rose was shocked. 'That is sick. Really sick talk.'

'Can't you imagine it? Can't you see him doing things like that?' Vivienne herself was almost crying now in her impatience to get them to believe her. 'Every word he says. Every move he makes! Oh, honestly!' She flung herself into the railed armchair in a paddy of exasperation.

They fell silent. They could imagine it.

'Does Aunt Carrie know?' Rose asked quietly.

'Of course she doesn't.' Vivienne had turned her face away from them, towards the wall, hiding her tears. 'Aunt Carrie's never had anything to do with men. How would she know?'

Rose got up from the table and went to her. 'Go and look for your things, love,' she said gently. 'If they are not in the bedroom then maybe they fell off the rack into the fire. You've got another Kestos haven't you? And plenty of knickers?'

'Are you going out Rose?' Vivienne asked in a small, normal voice.

'No. I'm going to bed. I want to think.'

She went back up the stairs. She was tired; tired, sick and frightened.

She undressed and got into bed.

There was nothing she could do to stop Aunt Carrie from walking right into Cecil Ratcliffe's trap. He was a wicked, evil man and Aunt Carrie had not recognized the menace in him. Now, in a way, she was relieved to find that her sisters shared her revulsion for him. It meant, without a shadow of doubt, that Cecil Ratcliffe was not her father. Aunt Carrie could never have loved – never have wanted to marry – a man like Cecil Ratcliffe. She would have seen right through him when she was young. But she would not want any advice from the three of them. And they could not give it.

Her prayers were a jumble of pleas: for Alan's safety – she knew, she just knew he couldn't be dead – and for forgiveness for her own ingratitude and unkindness to Aunt Carrie, and for Aunt Carrie to see the terrible danger she was in with Cecil Ratcliffe.

It was not to the Sunday School that Carrie had gone. She had been told by Mrs Bettley that morning that Douglas McGregor's son was missing. After tea she headed for the Swan.

She had put on her navy-blue coat and hat. They seemed appropriate things to wear though it was warm and sunny and she would normally have gone out in her light dress. She stopped, breathless, halfway up the Hundred and eight steps where Churchwall Street intersected them. Was sleeplessness going to be joined with heart-trouble or something? She had never ailed in her life before now and here she was, at only 45, panting and gasping like an old woman.

She leaned against the iron handrail to get her breath back. Perhaps it was the old feeling of panic come to torment her again. She hadn't had an attack since Jane and Danny had died. She had never been good in emergencies.

A bird was singing its little heart out above her head somewhere. Churchwall Street was quiet. Everyone who had a wireless would be listening to the news. She'd get back for the nine o'clock.

Lately, since Jane and Danny had died, she believed, she didn't get the same comfort from her things. All her lovely pictures and ornaments were packed away; crated and stacked in the cellar in case the bombs or the Germans came. And she hadn't even missed them.

She wanted to cry. She'd forgotten to take her medicine. She found herself wanting to cry unless she took it regularly. It was daft to cry over Rose's spurning of her. She could understand why she did it.

When she listened to the terrible stories Mrs Tereschenko told. And Mr Singer. Of people being dragged from their homes in the night, old Jewish men being forced to scrub the gutters. Mr Singer's daughter – they'd had no news of her and her children. Jo Tereschenko, the only son of that nice couple, taken prisoner by the Russians whom the Polish people feared more than they feared Hitler.

And now Alan McGregor. It didn't bear thinking of. She had been nasty to him. And the poor lad was dead. He was all Douglas McGregor had. And he was dead.

Hot tears were smarting her eyes. She rummaged in her bag for a handkerchief. Now everything was blurred. Carrie snatched the glasses from her eyes. She could see as well without them, near to.

It was a blackbird singing. It swam into her vision as soon as she'd wiped her eyes; perched high on a wild lilac tree that overhung the steps' wall. It gave her a strange feeling, to think that the little fellow knew nothing of men and wars and cruelty. She took a deep breath. The sweet heady scent of the blossom and the birdsong seemed to rally her. She stuffed her glasses into her silver-hinged glasses case and continued on her way.

In the old days she would never willingly have crossed the threshhold of a tavern but as she crossed the empty square and entered the public bar of the Swan she was conscious only of the need to give what comfort she could to Douglas McGregor.

She saw him speak to his assistant as she went over to the bar, then he lifted the bit of counter at one end and ushered her into his parlour.

'I'm sorry, Douglas,' she said as soon as the door was closed. 'So very sorry about your Alan.'

'Sit down, Miss Shrigley.' Douglas led her to one of the armchairs by an empty firegrate. 'Let me get you something to drink.'

'No.' She shouldn't have said that. Quickly, to cover any embarrassment she'd caused, she added, 'If you had some pop? Or orange squash?'

Douglas left her for a moment and it was as she turned her head to watch him go that she saw the photograph. It was a wedding photograph. And Patrick, standing stiff and straight, a flower in his buttonhole, best man at the other side of the bride. She could recognize Patrick even without her glasses. She and the girls had not heard from him for months. She could not ask or even let on she'd seen it. It made her want to cry again.

Douglas returned with their glasses. 'There is still hope, you know,' he said as he handed hers to her. 'Nobody saw Alan bale out but that doesn't mean that he didn't.'

She swallowed the great welling lump in her throat before she could sip the orange. 'Did you know he'd asked her – asked Rose – to marry him?'

'I did. I was delighted for them.'

'Well I wasn't. But it wasn't because I don't . . . didn't like your son, Douglas. I thought they were too young.' She put down her glass, took out her handkerchief again and blew her nose. 'I'm that sorry, now.'

'Rose is being very courageous,' Douglas said. 'I saw her at the bank.

'She doesn't believe he's dead.' Her voice didn't sound right at all and she'd wanted to give comfort to him.

'I know. Let's pray that she's right,' Douglas added. 'She has given me hope.'

'Douglas?'

'What?'

'Will you be singing . . . on Sunday . . . at St Michael's . . . with the Choral Society?' Carrie asked him. This was something she could cling to. It was beginning to mean a lot to her – singing at St Michael's. The Church of England did it best, the singing and music. Their hymns were better than anyone's. They had a great organ with pipes going almost to the top of the vaulted roof. It was lovely singing to a great organ, much better than the wheezy harmonium at the chapel.

'I will. It will be my last day in Middlefield.'

She looked up, shocked. 'Where are you going?'

'Into the services. I volunteered . . . Coastal Command . . . I served in the last war . . .'

'I know.' She didn't want to think about the last war. 'Have you seen what we're singing?'

Douglas nodded. 'I'm singing Mendelssohn – *If With All Your Hearts* – from Elijah.'

'I mean the duet.' She could ask them to change it if he didn't want to do it.

'What is it? Is it you and me?'

He didn't know, then. 'It's the Mozart. *Possenti Numi*. *Eternal Ruler of the Skies?*'

'Yes,' she said. 'Can you sing it? After all this?'

'Aye,' he said softly. He had a terrible, sad expression on his face.

Carrie felt a lump come into her throat again. There was a weight on her heart as well and nothing now to hope for.

She stood and held out her hand to him. 'Douglas?'

'Yes?'

'If he gets back – if your son comes home – we will see that they have a lovely wedding.'

She knew that Douglas was fighting back his tears. 'We will, indeed,' he said as he took her hand and held it firmly in his.

He took her to the back door and escorted her through the stable yard so she'd not need to go into the bar again. She wouldn't have minded if he had taken her through the bar. That kind of narrow-mindedness seemed out of date. It was no longer part of her persuasion.

'Thank you, Miss Shrigley.' They were out on the pavement in front of the Swan. Douglas extended his hand to her. 'Thank you for coming. It means a lot to me.'

★

St Michael's church was filling up on the Sunday afternoon when Carrie stood in front of the chancel with the Choral Society. People were coming not just to listen but to gather and to give thanks for the deliverance of the army from the enemy's clutches.

Only the strength of the new leader of the National Government, Winston Churchill with his obstinate bull-dog qualities, was pulling them all together into one nation with one aim. Carrie had memorized his last speech and it came to her now: 'You ask, what is our aim? I can answer in one word. It is Victory, however long and hard the road may be.' He had a powerful voice that stirred everyone.

Everyone she spoke to felt as she did that now, with France fallen, they were on their own. At least they knew where they stood; alone against an evil force.

There was the empire of course – the commonwealth they were calling it. What had happened to Empire Day? She used to watch the children; teams of children criss-crossing to music in the market place, making Union Jacks from colourful streamers and squares and singing *I Vow to Thee my Country*. Would they ever do it again? There was talk of the old barracks being used for Canadian soldiers.

There were a number of men in uniform in the congregation. There were a few in black. Jessie Burgess was in mourning for her Ronnie.

Carrie had come into the cool church an hour before the rest of the choir. She had never been able to see it all clearly before; only the general shape. It was as if her sight was being restored overnight, the improvement was so rapid. Each new day brought her field of vision sharper and nearer.

This afternoon, dressed in a dark-green, silk two-piece with cream hat and gloves she had gone, tip-toeing about the wood block floor, under a high hammerbeam roof that was carved with foliage and angels. She'd been reading the inscriptions over tombs. She was particularly taken with the one which read,

Here lyeth the bodie of Perkin-a-Legh
That for King Richard the death did die,
Betrayed for righteousness,
And the bones of Sir Peers, his sonne
That with King Henrie the fight did wonne in Paris.

The sexton had come up to her there and told her about the Legh family who had lost a son at Agincourt. He had taken her round the church, shown her the side chapels with priests' rooms and she'd been immensely gratified to find in a wall niche, not far from where she was standing now, the effigy of a knight who, the sexton told her, was thought to be a Shrigley man.

The oaken choir stalls, three deep, faced inwards in front of the chancel steps where she would stand for her solo and the duet. She gave a quick smile to Douglas McGregor who stood opposite and had signalled, discreetly, to tell her that he had their music. He had pointed to her eyes, as if to remind her that she wasn't wearing her glasses.

Cecil had asked her not to come. He said that once she went through the big wrought-iron gates into the churchyard she was walking on heathen ground with the idolaters. Cecil said that going in for that, the chanting and singing, dressing up, choirboys . . . He didn't like it. He said she'd be leaving the paths of righteousness, going astray. He said it was the same as worshipping idols. It was all there, he'd said, in the Old Testament. It was giving in to base and primitive desires. It was pagan.

But this wasn't idolatory. Here were the names of respected Middlefield people; the Stanleys and the Savages, the Downes of Shrigley. You couldn't help but feel proud. Here were the names of Venables, Roe, Fitton and Hesketh. She knew their descendants. There were some who knew her. Why, Mrs Venables was in charge of the billeting office. They treated one another with respect, she and Mrs Venables.

354

No. Cecil was wrong. It was not idolatory. It was history. These people were not devil-worshippers, unless paying homage to your ancestors was a sin.

She nodded to Douglas McGregor. They were singing the duet straight after the processional hymn. The organist had raised his hand. The choirleader was telling them to stand back a little so that the church choir would be able to pass them and get into their stalls. The seats were all filled. The church was packed; there was standing room only as the introduction started and the choirs and congregation sang, 'At the name of Jesus . . .'

The girls were out, at work and at school when the priest called at the Temperance Hotel. Cecil never came on Mondays. Carrie invited him upstairs into her sitting room.

'Have you come to see the girls?' she asked politely as soon as she had closed the door. A priest had never been to the house before and she was not quite sure how she should treat him. He was only a few years older than herself yet she felt him to be much older and wiser.

'No. It was yourself I wanted,' he answered.

'Sit down. Mister . . . er,' she began awkwardly.

'Father,' he said, seating himself. 'Father Church.'

'Oh. Right you are,' she said. 'Father Church.' It didn't seem so bad, saying it, even if you weren't one of them.

'Even so,' she said. 'The girls are in need of guidance. They are not behaving as they should.'

'Oh?' He smiled encouragingly and she felt emboldened to go on.

'They don't seem to be giving me the . . . the respect that's due to me.' She hadn't really meant to say that. 'What I mean is,' she began again. 'Is that they are resentful of me.'

'It has been an unhappy time for you all, Miss Shrigley. The girls losing their parents, you losing a sister.'

Carrie leaned across the octagonal table which was

355

between them, near to the empty fireplace. 'Perhaps you can have a word with them yourself,' she said. 'Tell them that I am suffering as well.'

'Would you like to send them up to the presbytery, Miss Shrigley?' he said in the gentle way he had. 'I can see them any time.' He gave her an understanding look. 'But I am sure that you – you all – are aware of the need for solace.'

She felt nervy again, excitable. She wondered if he knew everything that went on. 'You've been at St Alban's a long time, Father Church.'

'I have.' He smiled at her. 'Twenty-five years.'

'Do you remember Patrick Kennedy, Danny's brother?'

'Indeed, I do.'

Carrie felt colour flood into her face. What would he be thinking, this father who had heard all about her, heard all those old confessions? Did they remember them all? He had never heard her side of the story and she wanted, all at once, to put things right; to explain, to confess.

'I wish I knew what he'd told you,' she blurted out.

'Did you know that Rose wants to get married? To Alan McGregor,' he was saying.

'Yes,' she said. 'You know, of course, that Alan was lost over France.'

'Indeed, I do. But we cannot assume that he will not come home. In fact, Miss Shrigley, that is the very reason I am here.'

She took a deep breath and looked him in the eye. 'What do you think about marriage?'

'In which way?' he asked. He was taking it very seriously.

'Do you think marriages are made in heaven?' she said.

He was considering his reply. 'I rather think they are made on earth – with heaven's blessing,' he said at last.

'And what do you think of people who . . . who act married when they're not?'

'In which respect?'

356

She wasn't sure she was putting it well. 'Suppose a couple want to get married but they can't?' she said.

'Because one of them is underage?'

'I beg your pardon?' Carrie was taken aback for a moment. It seemed to her that they were talking slightly at cross-purposes.

'Are you asking if they should be allowed to marry if one of them is underage?'

'No. Not that. How can I put it?'

'Are you asking what God thinks about couples who love one another in the earthly sense and are not married? Is that it?' he asked.

He'd put it exactly right.

'Yes. What does the Roman Catholic church think of that?'

'I cannot speak for the Holy Father, though his views are well known, you understand?'

Maybe Father Church's views would be held by most of them, Carrie reasoned. 'What do you think? Yourself?' She waited, holding her breath, as he thought about it for a moment.

'The marriage ceremony, taking the religious vows that is, is not as old as marriage itself, Miss Shrigley,' he said, slowly and thoughtfully. 'I would think . . . I think that the young couple in a case such as you have put to me might be justified in considering themselves to be married in the eyes of God.'

She let out her breath and smiled in relief. 'Thank you. Thank you, Father Church.'

He looked directly into her eyes for a moment as if debating whether to say more. Then he went on, 'And I, myself, would think it wrong for anyone to withhold their blessing – their consent – to sanctifying such a marriage, Miss Shrigley,' he added. 'Now. Do I understand that, if the dear boy is safe, if Alan is spared, you will consent to the marriage?'

'Of course I will. I have already said so.' Carrie looked

357

at him squarely. 'Did you know that I was contemplating marriage – before the girls came to me?'

'No.'

'Yes. Cecil Ratcliffe and I were going to announce our intention.'

'And having the girls has made you postpone the wedding, is that it?'

'Something like that.' But it wasn't. It wasn't that at all. In the eyes of God, Patrick Kennedy's God, their Roman Catholic God, she was married already.

'Well. Indeed.'

Carrie stood up. 'Can I offer you a cup of tea, Father?'

He got to his feet and extended a hand towards her. 'No. No, thank you. I must be on me way.'

She went ahead of him to the front door, which she held open for him.

She took his hand. 'Goodbye,' she said.

'God bless you.'

She closed the door behind him and went to the kitchen to prepare tea. Of course. Of course, she kept telling herself. That was it. At the time of their wrongdoing she had not known he had a wife. She had considered herself to be married to him. It was he who had committed adultery. And now he'd done it again.

CHAPTER TWENTY-ONE

Rose sat, cramped in the window seat on the train to Manchester. Inside the compartment the air was thick with cigarette smoke which, since she had given cigarettes up in disgust months ago, was making her feel queasy. There was little conversation though plenty of coughing and sniffing going on. Everyone was aware of the dangers of talking to strangers. 'Careless Talk Costs Lives' the posters and papers constantly reminded everyone.

There was one on every station – a poster. They might have been funny in another time, depicting as they did the careless, talking, with Adolf Hitler hidden under tables or behind doors; even on luggage racks in trains. She glanced upwards – nothing but a few cases swaying in the rope cradles above their heads.

She returned her gaze to the window. It was mid-October and the grass and fields were brown and dry. Never had there been such a summer with such an unbroken succession of long, hot days and cloudless skies. And every day a battle, the Battle of Britain had been fought overhead. And all the time she had been glad that Alan was not up there and sick to the heart with worries about him.

She was not losing faith in his still being alive – she felt in her very core that he was – but as the days had grown to weeks and then to months she had found it harder to convince anyone else, friend or family, of her belief. Her friends, Norah, Sylvia and Pamela, seemed embarrassed when she started to talk about Alan; as if they wished she would forget him.

Pamela Tannenbaum had spent two summer weeks in Kent with relatives. She had gone in June, just as the Battle of Britain had started and had told Rose all about the air battles on her return.

Middlefield was classed officially as a reception area and Rose had seen none of it. But Middlefield people like everyone else waited for the news bulletins – the count of German fighters shot down – our own losses – and prayed.

Vivienne, machining parachutes in the factory now, spent her spare time collecting and raising money for the Spitfire fund, just as Rose and the bank did. Five thousand pounds would buy a fighter plane.

Mary had surprised them all, in July, by announcing that she was going to train as a nurse. Nothing would change her mind. Rose was reminded again of how like Mum her sister was growing. Mum had always been determined to do what she felt was right. Mary lived-in at the nurses' home near the park, visiting them at the Temperance Hotel when she had a halfday off. She seemed only to get them, the halfdays, once a fortnight and often neither she nor Vivienne was at home when Mary came.

Mary was as happy as the day is long though her tasks were of the most menial and, according to their aunt, involved hours spent scrubbing bedsteads with carbolic. When they were not on duty, yet had not been given permission to leave the hospital premises, the cadet nurses spent their time rolling bandages or visiting the patients who had no family.

Aunt Carrie, to both the girls' astonishment, began to talk about Mary's interest in such matters having been inherited from herself. It transpired that their aunt had been something of a midwife in the old days, before everyone paid their penny a week to the panel doctors and went into hospital for their confinements.

Once again children were being evacuated to Middlefield and the town was filled with strangers, for London was being bombed day and night. Along with the Cockney children and those families who had begun to 'trek' north from Coventry and Birmingham after the night pounding their cities had taken, Middlefield's streets and the WVS cafe rang with the different, exciting voices of Canadian and Dutch soldiers.

Rose looked around the compartment again, wondering if everyone was on urgent business, as she was, for it was seen as selfish to take up a place on a train unless the journey was really necessary. She returned her eyes to the passing scene, pulled her navy gaberdine coat around herself and thought back to last Wednesday.

She had fallen asleep in her cubicle at eleven o'clock in the morning, when she should have been counting the silver.

'Rose!' Pamela had entered and shaken her on the shoulder. 'What's the matter?'

She had come to at once. 'What?'

'You were asleep again.'

'Oh. Blast!' Rose gave Pam a weak smile. 'Thanks, Pam,' she said as she went to lift a bag of shillings from the floor on to her counting table. 'Pam?'

'What?'

'Would you bring me my soda-mints? They're upstairs. In my handbag.'

Pamela gave her a cross look. 'You aren't still swallowing those things are you?'

Rose grinned at her. 'No – you fool! I chew them, slowly.'

'Still got heartburn?'

'If that's what you call indigestion.'

Pamela hesitated for a second before saying, 'I'll ask Sylvia to take over for you. Come upstairs. I want to tell you something.'

Rose nodded. 'All right,' she said. 'I'll finish this bag and then come up.'

When she had done and Sylvia had arrived to relieve

her, Rose went running up the stairs to the cloakroom. Pamela was leaning, her back to the washbasins, head thrown back, in her usual challenging manner. Rose knew now that this was not, as she had first thought, an attitude of supreme confidence but Pamel's way, as she put it of 'bearding the ruddy lion in his blasted den'.

'Now what?' Rose asked, out of breath from the run up the stairs. 'What have you got me here for?'

'Shut the door.'

'All right.' Rose pushed the door to. 'Come on. Out with it.'

Pamela's face was bright red. 'I think you're pregnant, Rose Kennedy,' she announced. 'And I don't think you even suspect it.'

Rose felt herself going weak at the knees. 'What?'

'And Daddy says you are. I've told him all about it.'

Rose dropped down on to the only chair in the cloakroom; a rickety old bentwood. 'I can't be, surely?' she said.

'You're falling asleep all over the place. Daddy says you need an iron supplement,' Pamela went on insistently, keeping her voice low so that they wouldn't be heard.

'Yes . . . but . . .'

'And you're constantly chewing these things.' Pamela held out her hand, displaying the little cylinder of soda-mints.

'Oh, Pam!' It was ridiculous. She couldn't tell Pamela about her – her peculiarity. And girls who didn't have periods couldn't have babies. It was obvious. 'I'm not.'

Pamela's face was even redder. She was silent for a moment. It had probably cost her a lot, Rose knew, to speak like that. Pamela wasn't insensitive.

'Whatever did you tell your father?' Rose asked.

Pamela ignored the question. 'He said, "Has she seen a doctor?"'

'No.'

'Look, Rose,' Pamela went on quickly. 'Daddy says to

tell you – that if you want to see anyone – if you find you can't go to your own doctor – living with your aunt and all that—'

'Well?'

Pamela gave a great exhalation of breath. 'Oh hell, Rose!' she said. 'This is so awkward.' She began again. 'Look here. Come on Saturday. Come for the day. We're off this Saturday. If you want Daddy to look at you. He has a surgery for his private patients – only of course he won't charge you – on Saturday afternoons.'

Rose wanted Pamela to know that she wasn't annoyed. She felt a warm rush of affection for Pamela. 'Thanks,' she said. 'I'll come. I'll see him. Aunt Carrie isn't on a doctor's panel and I daren't go to my old one.'

She smiled reassuringly at Pam. 'There is something wrong. But I know I'm not pregnant. And I'll buy an iron tonic tonight from Cartledge's, on my way home, if that's what's making me tired.'

She had bought the tonic and certainly the tiredness seemed to be lessening but now, on her way to Pamela's, Rose felt nervous. The notion of pregnancy was crazy. But she had been feeling awful this summer. She had put it down to the way she was living. She felt that she was the only person who was steadfast in believing Alan would return and this made it impossible to talk to anyone about him.

Then there was the food. She had always minded what she ate and now, despite the uneasy truce that existed between them, despite her best efforts, she was unable to enjoy Aunt Carrie's offerings. Their meals were short on protein: there was not enough meat, few eggs and tiny portions of bacon and cheese to go round. She missed these things. She even craved them and felt guilty and selfish about her greed.

And, though she had no wish to fill herself up with them, she was forced, to appease the raging appetite she had developed, to eat a lot more bread and marge and potatoes. The starchy foods were making her bloated. For the first time in her life she had a thick middle. There was a bulge which started right under her sternum and ended below her waist. It was in quite the wrong place for a pregnancy whose increase surely would start lower down and work its way up.

Because of it, to hide the fat, she had sneaked upstairs one Sunday afternoon when Aunt Carrie was out and stolen two old pairs of her corsets from a box in the attic. She wore them all the time, putting them on when her sisters had left the bedroom. She had to breathe in as far as she could and fasten the rigid line of hooks which went from just below her armpit to the top of her leg. When the hooks were done she'd start at the top again, lacing them tight until she tied them in a knot and tucked the ends under the stiff pink canvas.

They did the trick. She looked straight-up-and-down when she'd finished corseting and flattening herself. She could get into all her clothes – as long as she left the waistband buttons undone.

But the corsets – the pressure – gave her heartburn. It was awful – a great rush of acid came to the back of her throat and gave her a hideously full and painful feeling right across her diaphragm and up into her chest. Aunt Carrie, compensating for her earlier tempers perhaps, was most solicitous. She told her to take a teaspoonful of bicarbonate of soda in warm water before going to bed. The burning went instantly. She would dash upstairs immediately she had taken it so that she could belch away in the privacy of the bedroom without comment.

Then she'd take off her tight brassiere and the corsets and have to suffer rumbling and jumping of wind in her abdomen all night long until she strapped herself into the corsets again the next morning.

The train was approaching a station. Rose looked quickly at it as they went. The nameboards had been painted over to confuse the enemy when they invaded, but she had recognized Levenshulme. They were nearly there.

There were crowds everywhere and long queues. At last she got on to the tram that would take her to Chorlton-cum-Hardy. Slowly they rattled along the centre of the Barlow Moor Road, past the cemetery. Rose looked at her watch. It was almost half-past two before she arrived at Pamela's. Pamela was waiting at the tramstop.

'I'd nearly given you up,' Pamela said.

'It's dreadful, Pam. The trains are packed.' She slipped her arm through Pamela's as they turned off the straight road into a quiet tree-lined avenue.

'I know. I use them every day,' Pamela said. 'Here we are.'

The house, hidden from the road behind a tall hedge, was imposing and Rose felt a quick shudder of fright.

'I'll take you round to the consulting room,' Pamela said as she went ahead down the gravel path at the side of the house.

Rose followed her, stopping before a brown door over which was a white china globe bearing the word 'Surgery' in black letters. On the door was a brass plate with Pam's father's name and a string of letters. All at once she wished she hadn't come.

'Go through to the waiting room,' Pamela was saying. 'Then Daddy will show you the way into the house. He has to go back to the hospital afterwards. You needn't feel embarrassed.'

'It's all right,' Rose said quickly. 'I don't mind.' She went inside. She could hear voices behind the door marked 'surgery' but was the only person in the waiting room. She tugged down the hem of her skirt under her gabardine; the navy blue skirt had shrunk and kept riding up. She dug her nails into the palms of her hands to stop them from shaking and picked up a copy of *Woman and Home*. Before she could open it she heard the outside door close and footsteps cross the surgery floor. The door opened.

'Miss Kennedy?'

Pamela's father, it must be, was shaking her hand and ushering her into a consulting room that smelt of wax polish and Dettol. He was bespectacled and tall and Rose saw that Pamela bore a strong resemblance to him.

'Come in. Sit down, Rose,' he said. 'Pamela talks a lot about you.'

He nodded to a nurse in starched apron who left them at once, disappearing behind a curtained area at the far end of the big room.

Rose felt more at ease. He was charming. He had greyish fair hair and observant grey eyes but over all he had an easy manner that made her want to confide in him.

He asked her all about her symptoms, nodding and smiling as she described them – the sickening sense she had when she got out of bed, as if she were descending in a lift – the feeling that her skin was stretching, pulling tight across her stomach, almost as if it were being pushed outwards.

He was prompting all these answers, she knew, beginning every question with a, 'Do you ever feel that . . . ?'

For some unaccountable reason she wanted to laugh at herself. She felt her mouth creasing at the corners as she answered him. He was nodding sagely at her replies.

'Have you noticed a change in your breasts?' he asked.

Rose felt herself blushing. How silly it was to blush at the mention of breasts, she'd answered his other questions without embarrassment. 'They are – seem to be – growing,' she said. 'And they prickle and go all pins-and-needly.'

He nodded. 'And movement? Have you felt any movements?'

'Oh, yes,' she said, relieved that he had asked. 'Every night; in bed. It's wind – from the bicarbonate of soda and the soda-mints.'

He smiled again. 'I'd like to examine you,' he said. 'Will you go with nurse?'

The nurse came from behind the curtains and led her into the cubicle. 'Take your things off,' she said kindly, to put her at her ease. 'And put on this gown.'

Rose felt idiotic now. She brushed aside the nurse's offer of help as she unlaced the pink corsets.

'I can do it,' she gasped, her fumbling fingers tugging at the strings to release them. There were red marks around her body from their tightness.

At the sight of the marks the nurse raised her eyebrows and said, 'They must hurt you.'

'Oh, no.' Rose said quickly. 'Not at all.' She slipped on the green gown and climbed up on to the leather couch where she lay, shaking, all desire to laugh gone. What was going to happen? What would he find? A growth?

Doctor Tannenbaum came in and washed his hands solemnly at the washbasin. Then he came towards the table and nodded to the nurse to pull down the sheet.

Then he was standing over her, looking over the top of his glasses into her face, one hand resting on the bulge that had been her waistline. He seemed to be fighting back a smile.

'There is no need for me to examine you internally,' he said.

'There's not?'

He patted her gently and allowed his amusement to show. His eyes were twinkling in his intelligent face. 'I think you must discard the corsets, my dear,' he said. 'You are in your sixth month of pregnancy and everything seems perfectly normal.'

Rose felt tears come to her eyes; they were tears of relief and illogical, incongruous happiness. The other, sensible side of herself was signalling caution, problems to be solved, arrangements to be made. But these were practicalities. She was going to have a baby. Her own – and Alan's baby.

She sat up on the couch, a great, happy smile illuminating her face as the tears streamed down it.

'Thank you,' she said. 'I'm so . . . so glad.'

'You will have to think about everything,' he was saying. 'Most carefully. I understand that your . . . that the baby's father is missing?'

'He's not dead,' Rose said firmly. 'Nobody believes me but I know.'

He was standing back now, hands behind himself, leaning against the wall as she was helped to her feet by the nurse. There was a look of pleasure on his face and Rose knew that he delighted in telling a woman what to him would always be the good news of their condition. Alan will be just like that one day, she told herself as she smiled back at him.

'He is coming back,' she said with utter conviction. 'And he will be thrilled to find he has a child.'

Then she gathered the gown around herself and moved to the screened area of the cubicle to dress.

Back at the desk, dressed, a few minutes later, Rose said. 'I can't possibly have the baby at home. I daren't tell my aunt.'

'Can you tell your church? You are a . . . ?'

'Roman Catholic,' Rose answered. 'Yes. I could see Father Church and go to their Home but I think I'd rather . . .'

'Would you like me to make arrangements for you to go to a Mother and Baby Home? There is one in Manchester. You can be admitted as soon as you like. You will be delivered there and can stay for three months afterwards.'

He was looking serious now. 'You will be able to decide what to do afterwards.'

'I hadn't thought – hadn't considered.' Rose said. 'I will have to think. When is it due? Can you tell me?'

'I can tell you exactly when it should arrive, Rose. You were quite specific about the date of conception. Your baby is due . . .'

'When?' She was all eagerness now.

'The end of January. I would say the twenty-ninth.

Though, of course, it could be a week or so either side. Babies seldom come on the appointed day, you know.'

The smile went from his face. 'Will you want to have the baby adopted?' he said. 'Or looked after – put into a Home – until you and your young man can make a home together?'

'I think . . . I think I will come here. To Manchester. I can't have the baby in Middlefield. I can't begin to work out all the details, not yet. But I have a little money. Perhaps I can look for a house . . . in Manchester. Live here with the baby until Alan gets back.'

He stood up now. 'I will make all the arrangements for you. Tell Pamela when you want to move in. And try to make it soon. I would advise you to leave it no later than the middle of December.'

He took her into the house where Pamela was waiting for her in a large, elegant drawing room, that was three times the size of any room Rose had been in before now.

'Pam,' she said. 'It's true. I am having a baby.'

She heard the door close behind her as Pamela's father went out. 'Oh, I'm so glad I'm having a baby. You will help me to keep it a secret won't you?'

'Of course,' Pamela came towards her, hands outstretched. 'I'll do everything I can to help you. In every way.'

Then she found herself sitting, laughing one moment, worried the next, listening to Pamela who, all at once seemed to know all there was to know about babies, confinements and unmarried motherhood.

And all the time, inside, she was bursting with joy. She would have to continue to conceal her state, she knew that. Aunt Carrie would not be able to hold her head up in Middlefield if any one of them knew, but more so if she, Rose, brought disgrace on to the family.

Feeling as she did now she wondered afresh at her aunt's decision to relinquish her own child – herself. Her own delight, secret and wrong though it might be, made

Aunt Carrie's actions even harder to comprehend.

She wanted to run and shout it from the rooftops, 'I am going to have a baby. And I'm glad . . . glad . . . glad!'

On the journey home she sat in the dark compartment that was only palely lit by a bluish light from the overhead bulb. The blinds were drawn and the travellers, as on the outward journey, were cramped together, uncommunicative and cold. It gave her time to think, to decide how she would get through the next few weeks. She needed to conceal her shape until the middle of December when she would leave Middlefield.

It was as if her prayers had been answered when, on the following Friday, she and Pamela were detailed to fill in at a village branch of the Regional Bank, some twenty miles from Middlefield. Experienced staff were needed since two men had been called up. There would be no possibility of their getting home for the first month but there was accommodation in the bank house next door where they would be looked after by the caretaker.

Aunt Carrie was not pleased but there was no arguing with orders from Head Office. Nobody would dream of questioning orders in wartime. Every pair of hands was needed.

CHAPTER TWENTY-TWO

It was the middle of December and Rose had been back at
the Temperance Hotel for a week. Carrie did not know
what to make of it. She, Rose, had arrived last Sunday
night, when she had just come in from church. It had been
unexpected. Only the day before there had been a letter
from her to say that she would not be back until Christmas.

Carrie had been delighted, of course, when she'd come
in and found her, sitting by the fire in the kitchen.

'What a lovely surprise,' she'd said. 'I thought you were
staying on in Derbyshire for another fortnight.'

Rose had pulled her big coat round herself and stretched
her hands towards the blaze. 'I've left,' she said. 'I'm not
going back.'

She sounded tired out yet she was rosy-cheeked and sort
of filled-out looking.

'Why?' Carrie wanted to know. 'Is anything wrong?'

'I'm not well. I've been in bed for the last week.'

'What is it?'

'I've had enteritis.'

'Have you seen a doctor?'

'No.'

'Then I'll ask mine to come and see you tomorrow.'

'Don't. Please don't. I'm sure I'll be all right, if I can
just . . . just have a week in bed.'

She stood up and walked towards the door. It seemed to
Carrie that she had put weight on, from what she could
see. The tweed coat she was wearing used to be big on her
and now it was stretched tightly across hips that had
certainly grown much wider.

Rose had always been slim yet here she was, with a behind on her like Brenda Gallimore's. Her legs too, from being long and slender were chunky-looking, heavy, as if the ankles were swollen. Enteritis generally made you lose weight. It looked more like that thing – was it dropsy? – that made your body hold water.

'You ought to see a doctor, love,' she said.

'Let me have a good night's rest, Aunt Carrie, will you?'

She was so glad to have her back that Carrie would have agreed to anything. She had missed her when she'd been away. And Vivienne was not herself, without Rose.

Anyway, she thought as Rose went out of the room, she herself was as good as a doctor at looking after her own. She'd go up to Frank Cartledge's in the morning and get one of his tonics.

And Rose hadn't been ill, not really ill. She had taken to her bed. It must have been exhaustion, for the poor girl just slept and ate for the first four days.

By Friday she was much better, but prickly and easily moved to tears, as when Carrie had suggested that she get dressed and come downstairs for an hour or two.

But Carrie didn't mind carrying trays upstairs for her, nor did she object to lighting a fire in the bedroom and trying to cosset her a little. It would have been better if Rose had been a bit more appreciative or even if she had looked pleased at all the love and care that was being lavished upon her.

Her friend Pamela, who had returned to the Middlefield office of the bank at the same time as Rose had come home, came round to visit her most evenings after work and Rose talked to her all right. Carrie could hear them, talking animatedly, upstairs in the bedroom.

Now, a week later, Carrie was at the chapel again. There were fifty children in the Sunday School hall this afternoon, the fifteenth of December.

Carrie sat, adding new names to the register, on the little raised platform. From here she could see them all and give Cecil a nod when it was time to play for the collection. She pushed back the wristband of her blue wool blouse and glanced at her watch. Half past three. She'd better tell the teachers to settle the children who were moving chairs noisily across unpolished boards.

She stood, clapped her hands and said, 'Put the chairs in rows, children. Put them how you found them. Then stand in line.'

She nodded to Cecil who went to the piano, adjusted his trousers and the piano stool and sat, looking at her. Waiting.

A lot of them had come for the first time. Every day since the terrible blitzes on Coventry, families and children had poured into the town. Carrie had divided the newcomers into groups and set them to crayonning pictures of shepherds and sheep. The poor little souls. Some of them had never seen a sheep. One little girl asked what they were. The symbolic meaning was lost on them.

They were ready now. She went to the cupboard, opened the door and took out the collection jar. It was a big glass kilner with a wide slit in the lid. She nodded to Cecil to start and raised her hand, signalling to the children to begin their song.

'HEAR THE PEN-NIES DROP-PING . . .' She wished Cecil could play it a bit faster. It only sounded right when played cheerfully. She moved along the row of children, passing the jar. Some of them looked as if they could do with a good hot dinner – and a bath. Half of them were dressed in cast-offs, many had patches of impetigo on their cheeks and hands. Some of the children didn't even have a ha'penny, never mind a penny to drop in the jar.

'LIS-TEN WHILE THEY FALL . . .' It made you wish you could do more, seeing these poor little mites. And there were hundreds more being bombed out of their homes in the cities. How much more can Britain take? We're fighting alone now. The whole of Europe's been over-run.

Cecil did it to annoy her, played slow. He'd offered to play for them after Mrs Gregson died but she knew it was just another excuse to be with her.

'EV-ERY ONE FOR JE-SUS . . .' Come on Cecil! Speed it up! He was going to drag it out since it was such a short tune. She wanted to be back before four o'clock. Vivienne had been in a bit of a state at dinner-time. She kept coming over all tempestuous lately. She'd been harder to manage since Mary had gone.

'HE SHALL HAVE THEM ALL . . .' Rose couldn't do anything with Vivienne either. But Rose didn't look well again, after her good few days. Now she was pale and tired again.

'DROP-PING – DROP-PING – DROP-PING – DROP-PING . . .' That's better. He'll not need to play it through twice. Only another row to do.

'HEAR THE PEN-NIES FA-A-ALL . . .' There was one little lad who asked if she took them up personally – the pennies – to Jesus, in that jar. She wished Cecil would leave her alone. It was becoming clearer to her every day that she would never marry him.

'EVERY ONE FOR JE-SUS. HE SHALL HAVE THEM ALL.'

She ushered the children out on to the chilly, foggy street before setting off for home. Cecil was going to lock the chapel up. He'd be going back at night, preaching. She was going to go to St Michael's. It had got that she never went to chapel when Cecil was preaching. She knew what they all thought. They thought she was going peculiar. They said that women of her age, 45, were likely to go off their heads. It made her laugh to think about it. She'd not been made to the normal pattern so she certainly wouldn't become like the rest now.

She felt unusually cheerful, walking along by herself, thinking that she wouldn't see Cecil for a few more days. She didn't think she had any right to be cheerful. There was nothing to be joyful about, not with eggs at three and six a dozen and cream banned by law. There were hardly any sweets in the shops, no biscuits, soap scarce, a paper shortage and Lord Woolton telling everyone to go carefully with the tin-opener.

But she was cheerful. That medicine of Frank Cartledge's was doing her good. She drank a bottle a week. He laughed now when he dispensed it. She'd asked him what it was and he'd smiled and said, 'The Elixir of Life' – whatever that meant. As long as she never forgot to take a dose, for the effects wore off after an hour or two, the world looked rosy and she felt herself to be distanced from it. It didn't do to think of the excitable, highly-strung state that lay beneath the surface. The medicine damped it down nicely.

Winter suited her. It was very cold this afternoon, with that smell, that pleasant evocative smell, of rank, rotting leaves as she went alongside the park. The park railings had been taken down; the iron was needed for guns. She could hear ducks beyond the trees, squawking around the ornamental pond. It was still light. They weren't going to put the clocks back this winter.

The cheerful mood persisted when she arrived home. Vivienne had got her tea ready. The table was laid and a place set for her. They must have had theirs and gone upstairs. She wouldn't disturb them. She would have hers then go upstairs to change into something smart for church. The service started half an hour before the chapel's so she'd have to hurry. But then she'd be out at least an hour earlier – especially if Cecil was preaching at chapel – and be home in time for the news.

It had been a lovely service. She liked it all now; the order, the form. It gave a feeling of continuity, saying the same prayers week after week. She loved singing the *Magnificat* at evening prayer though she was fondest of singing the *Te Deum Laudamus* at the morning service. You could really let yourself go on that one. The organist was the music master at the boys' school and when it came to the last lines – 'OH, GOD. IN THEE HAVE I TRUSTED. LET ME NEVER BE CONFOUNDED' – it made a shiver go through you.

Carrie was humming it to herself as she let herself into the front door of the Temperance Hotel.

Mr Tereschenko was standing, tall, grey, in the half-dark of the hall. 'I have something to tell you, Mees Shrigley,' he said, hardly giving her time to take her hat and coat off.

'Well?'

He didn't usually come downstairs in an evening, unless it was for good reason. He looked serious and tight-lipped. 'What is it?'

'Please. Can we talk in your sitting room? I do not wish for your beautiful girls to hear us.'

'Whatever's up, Mr Tereschenko?' Carrie demanded, her voice rising.

'Upstairs? Please?'

'Very well.' She went ahead, up the stairs and opened her door. 'Just a minute. I'll pull the blinds before you put the light on.'

When she turned to look at him in the electric light she saw that he was worried and anxious. 'What's the matter?' she asked. 'You must tell me.'

'Mr Ratcliffe, Cecil, has frightened Vivienne. He is very bad man.'

He was waiting for her reaction. Carrie felt herself grow cold. What was this? He did not look as if he had made this up. She did not understand what he meant. 'What?'

'Mr Cecil. He makes passes at her. At Vivienne. He puts his hands on her . . .'

This was silly. Horrible. There must be some mistake.

'Mr Tereschenko,' Carrie said, lowering her voice so that they would not be heard, 'Is this some kind of a joke? You are not serious?'

He didn't answer her for a moment and then he came

towards her and put out his hand as if to offer comfort to her. 'You did not know. I was sure you did not know. But Mees Shrigley, that man, these men I have seen before. They are a danger to young girls – and to yourself.'

It was as if the room was very still. There was a strange taste in her mouth and clear, cold steel in her head. Her mind was all of a sudden sharp, as it used to be. 'Just what has he done? Tell me!' she demanded.

'Vivienne – that lovely talented girl. Vivienne was screaming. I heard her. I ran downstairs. I saw him. I saw Cecil run from the house. I found Vivienne crying as if her heart would burst.'

'Stop!'

'No. I will tell you. I ask her . . . I asked her Mees Shrigley. But there was no need to ask. Her dress was torn. There was blood on her neck, on her little bare breast.'

'When? Stop! When was this?' Carrie had grabbed his arm.

'Two hours ago.'

She pushed past him to the door and ran down the stairs into the kitchen. 'Vivienne, Vivienne,' she called as she ran up the girls' stairs.

Their door was locked on the inside. She beat her hands on it. 'Open up. At once! I must know.'

There was only a muffled crying coming to her through the door.

'Tell me!' She shouted and slammed on the door. 'What has he done to you?'

'Go away. Oh, please, please go away, Aunt Carrie.' The voice was muffled. And it was Rose's.

But she was crying now; crying and shouting. 'Is it true? What has he done?'

'Vivienne isn't hurt. She's just frightened. Go away.'

Carrie ran down the stairs and back into the hall. He would be at the chapel. They would be coming out in ten minutes' time. She'd kill him. What was there to hand?

On the hallstand was a selection of walking sticks. The heaviest was made of hickory. It had a sharp-angled hand grip. It would do her very well.

She ran. Through the cold, clear and frosty streets, her feet pounding the pavements, unseeing but for the redhot haze that was swimming in front of her eyes she ran all the way. Her hair had come free and was falling wild across her face, strands flying into her mouth.

She was there. The chapel doors were open; the congregation beginning to pour out on to the dark street.

'Cecil Ratcliffe!' She heard herself screeching the words. 'Come out here!'

They stood back, mesmerized, as he came towards her. It seemed that they were turned to stone. Nobody came forward to help him.

Wild, uncontrollable rage erupted in her. She brought the stick down upon his skull and he dropped to his knees.

'You vile beast! Your worse than a beast!' She raised it again and smashed it down across his back. He fell, face-down, groaning, on to the street.

Carrie turned to the chapel members. Now they were crowding around. 'Do you know what he's done? Do you?' She was screaming and crying as she fell on him and took his head into her hands. She was going to smash it down on to the street but someone had hold of her. They were pulling her away.

'He has raped her. That sweet little girl. One of my children,' she was crying. 'Let me go. I want him to die.'

They pulled her upright. Someone had lifted him to his knees now. There was blood pouring out of a cut in his forehead but he was alive. He looked dazed.

She tore herself free and found herself standing before him. 'You will pay for this, Cecil Ratcliffe. I'll have you arrested. I am going straight to the police.'

Then she spat. Full in his face. Like some cheap little trollop. It went right into his open mouth.

'Don't think I don't mean it,' she shouted. 'I've done it before. You'll get life for this.'

She struck him then, across the side of his head, turned and ran back as fast as she could.

She would go to the police tomorrow. She would have to take Vivienne with her. She knew that much. First she'd go to the girls, cast herself at their feet. How could she have let it happen? She was sobbing as she went into the kitchen.

Rose stood there, as white as death, wrapped in a great check dressing gown she'd found in the attic.

'She's gone,' she said in a voice of ice. 'Vivienne has gone. She's run away.'

There was a pain in Carrie's chest. It was a tight band that was closing around her. She dropped into the chair, her breath lurching in her throat as she let her head fall into her hands.

'Oh, Rose.' She began to babble now. 'Go for the doctor. Tell him I think I've killed someone. Oh! The pain; the pain . . .'

Then she was being helped to her feet by Rose and Mr Tereschenko, being helped up the stairs to her room, still babbling, assuring them that Cecil Ratcliffe was alive though he didn't deserve to be, crying for Rose and Vivienne to forgive her.

They brought her tea and hot bread and milk. They gave her three tablespoonfuls of her medicine and stayed with her until she slept.

Rose filled a hot-water bottle for herself when Aunt Carrie was asleep. She was hungry. Tears dropped down her face on to the breadboard as she cut herself a wedge of bread. She felt awful. There were two patches of cracked skin at the corners of her mouth. Her tongue was sore and that too, had a split at the tip.

Vivienne had gone from the house not, as Aunt Carrie believed, simply because of Cecil Ratcliffe, though he had behaved like a maniac, tearing Vivienne's clothes off her. He had caught her packing all her dressing-up clothes and dancing costumes into Aunt Carrie's case. Vivienne was going to join a concert party. They had come for her in the afternoon; telling her that they were a dancer short and they were booked to perform at army camps all over the country.

Rose knew that she too would have to leave. She could only just fasten the corsets round herself. The baby could be born in six weeks' time. She couldn't stay here any longer, that was certain.

What if she had the baby in the bed one night? What if she woke up and found she'd had the baby? Could it happen like that? What was a labour? How long did it last? Ten minutes? A week? It was painful. She knew that much. She had seen it at the cinema: people running upstairs with kettlefuls of water, the poor father pacing the floor, shouts from the mother, her perspiring brow being dabbed.

But what happened? She knew how it got out – that was obvious. But would it be so bad, the pain, that she'd be shouting and pulling on towels tied to the bedhead? That last film she'd seen had scared her to death.

There was some of Aunt Carrie's bramble jelly in the cupboard. She went to open the cupboard door and as she did so the infant kicked her – hard. It had never kicked so hard before. She looked down, opened the dressing gown and watched, fascinated, as her swollen belly seemed to move its prominence from the left to the right under the kicking little heels she could feel beneath her ribs.

She had been amazed that nobody had guessed her condition. Pamela said she was 'carrying it all round' and that tall girls like herself could get away with it for longer. And it was winter and cold. Coal was scarce and everyone was expected to wrap up well indoors as well as out. She had learned to lean forward slightly, letting her thick jackets and coats hang loosely in front. But there were only six weeks to go now. She could not hide it any longer.

A month ago she had handed in her resignation at the bank. They were not expecting her to go to the bank again. The next hurdle would be the journey to Manchester. Pamela would wait to hear from her, that she had arrived at the Mother and Baby Home. If Aunt Carrie was recovered she would go, tomorrow.

She poured boiling water into a glass on to a spoonful of Aunt Carrie's blackcurrant jam. She'd been longing for oranges for weeks now. Quite ridiculous it had been. There were none to be had. The drink was hot and sweet and a reasonable substitute for an orange. She carried upstairs a plateful of bread and jam and the hot drink. She would be able to get her knitting out now, with Vivienne gone. She had only to do the button band on the matinee coat and the second set was finished. She would watch the baby moving for a while, as well.

She must have slept very deeply because the first thing she was aware of, the following morning, was Aunt Carrie shaking her shoulder gently.

'Here's a cup of tea, love,' she said. She looked white and grim-faced but spoke with great kindness. 'I'm going to bring a tray up for you. You looked tired out yesterday. I think you ought to stay in bed again today.'

'Oh, thanks. I'm all right.' Rose sat up, drawing the covers up to her chin. 'How about you?'

'I'll survive,' Aunt Carrie answered. Then she added in a bitter voice, 'I'm half sorry that Cecil Ratcliffe will survive, though.'

Rose took the tea and began to drink.

'Maggie Bettley said he'd left a message, first thing,' Aunt Carrie said. 'I burned it. It said, '"Called away. Friends in Cumberland want me to live with them."'' That's so I won't be able to send the police after him.'

'Will he come back?' Rose asked.

'Not if he's any sense,' Aunt Carrie said. 'He's had a lucky escape.'

'I think you have, too,' Rose said softly. She wanted Aunt Carrie to know that she was on her side. Soon she would have to deal her aunt another blow, by leaving her, and she was sorry, so sorry that their wounds had never healed.

'I wasn't going to marry him,' Aunt Carrie said. 'I had no heart for it. But I didn't know . . . I never thought he was the kind who'd do those . . . those sick . . .' She was fighting back anger and tears now, Rose could see.

'. . . those vile things to an innocent child.'

'Vivienne was going anyway,' Rose told her. It was not fair to let Aunt Carrie think that she was to blame. 'She's gone to join a concert party. They were one short. To dance for the troops.'

A little relaxation came to her aunt's face at these words and Rose was glad that she had brought some comfort to her. 'Are you sorry you won't be marrying,' she dared to ask. But Aunt Carrie's reply took her right back in her memory to the time she had asked the same question, on holiday, all those years ago.

'Marriage? Of course I'm not sorry.' The words came sharp and biting. 'Apart from Jane and Danny's I've never seen a happy marriage.'

'Mine will be.'

Aunt Carrie looked at her now with pity. 'I hope you're right,' she said. 'But the Kennedy family seem destined to make a poor job of it.'

'Why do you say that?' Rose asked, defensive now. 'Who else is there?'

'Your Uncle Patrick. He married the wrong woman once. And he's married again.'

'Uncle Patrick isn't married.'

'He is. I saw a wedding photograph.'

Aunt Carrie began to go towards the door. It was as if she wanted to end this conversation. But Rose felt, all at once, that she must defend the family honour. 'He is not!' she said hotly. 'John McGregor was married. Uncle

Patrick is being sent to Scotland. Alan told me so.'

'When did he tell you so?'

'In his letters. Before he went missing.'

Her aunt had stopped, her hand on the door. Two bright spots of colour burned now in her pale face. 'Are you sure?' she said in a voice high with agitation.

'Absolutely. I am absolutely sure. That's why we haven't heard from him for ages.' She turned proud eyes towards Aunt Carrie. 'So you have no cause to say we are a faithless lot.'

'I'm sorry, then.' Aunt Carrie stood as if shocked. It was a few seconds before she pulled herself together and then she appeared to fumble for the door handle before she could open it and go downstairs.

But Aunt Carrie seemed to be in a world of her own half the time. She swore that she could see better now she no longer wore glasses and yet she had missed all the signs of what was going on around her: the lecherous looks Cecil Ratcliffe gave to them all, the fury and scorn on Vivienne's face, the worry on Mary's and her own steadily increasing girth.

She came back twenty minutes later, carrying a tray that was beautifully set: embroidered cloth, a little china teapot with matching cup and saucer, boiled egg, warm, crisp toast and her home-made marmalade.

'Here you are,' she said breezily. 'Sit up.'

She puffed up the pillows behind Rose. 'Now. What about the doctor? Shall I call him to you. You don't look too well again.'

'Don't do that!' Rose said quickly. 'I mean,' she went on in a softer tone, 'I'm feeling a bit better again. I'll be getting up tomorrow.'

'Good,' Aunt Carrie said. She was all efficiency now. She went, quick and lightfooted, from the bedroom.

Rose sank back against the pillows in relief. Aunt Carrie was all right after her ordeal of yesterday. She seemed in good heart, as if a weight had been lifted from her. It made

Rose feel dreadful, knowing that tomorrow – there was nothing for it – she would put her aunt to a great deal more grief when she found her gone.

All her things were in the bag, under the bed. They could not be seen and it would be a simple matter to slip out of the house unobserved when Aunt Carrie was asleep tonight. There was an eleven o'clock train to Manchester and she had bought her ticket in advance. She would sit in the ladies waiting room at the Manchester station until six o'clock the next morning when a taxi would take her to the Home.

In spite of her nervousness the day passed quickly. Aunt Carrie appeared at regular intervals, bearing trays of food and hot drinks and Rose took them gratefully, hiding her body beneath the heaped up eiderdown and padded quilt.

At last they said their good nights and, half an hour later, the house was still. Rose prepared herself for the journey. She had bought and concealed a wrap-around dress which she now took from the wardrobe drawer. There was a big cardigan to wear over it and, for underneath, an outsize under-slip, knickers, stockings and garters. With the navy-blue gaberdine buttoned but left unbelted she looked large but not noticeably expectant, she thought.

She pulled the bag from its hiding place and, quiet as a mouse, left the bedroom, slipped down the stairs and out into the backyard.

The station was only yards away, across Waters Green and she was not seen as she went over the square. The station was deserted and nobody saw her, sitting in a dark corner of the platform. Her pulse was racing. She found herself straining her ears towards the tunnel, willing the train to come.

It seemed interminable, the wait, and freezing cold. Her eyes were aching from the strain of looking into the darkness of the tunnel. She felt as if she had been here for hours. She made her way to the blacked-out waiting room and went to stand under the eerie blue-shaded light and looked at her watch. Twelve-thirty. She had been there for two hours. She left the waiting room to go back to her seat outside.

'Who's there?' A railway porter was walking towards her down the platform. 'Who is it?'

Rose got to her feet. 'I was waiting for the eleven o'clock to Manchester,' she told him.

'Didn't you see the notice?'

'Which notice?'

'The one chalked up outside?'

'No.'

'It will take 'em a day or two before this station's in use. The line's been bombed south of Crewe.'

'When do you think it will be clear?'

'You'd best make for t'other station,' he said. 'This place will be out of action yet awhile.'

Rose picked up her bag and went to the exit. She was cold, hungry and faint. If she walked down the Manchester Road she could wait for a bus as soon as it was light.

She passed the Temperance Hotel, climbed the Hundred and eight steps and set her feet in the direction of Manchester. She must put a few miles between herself and Middlefield before she stopped for a rest, though there was a dragging sensation low down in her back, from the climb.

CHAPTER TWENTY-THREE

Thinking about it afterwards, Nat revised his belief that chance or coincidence were the explanations of fools. If everything had not come together as it did, then the outcome might have been tragic.

There were so many differences from the old pattern of his days, right from the start. For one thing, that week he'd started to deliver his milk in the late afternoon instead of early morning. It was pitch black in the mornings and he was training a new horse since Dobbin was old.

But that night he'd taken Dobbin because it was a Monday, Mona's free night and Dobbin was used to being left in the stable behind the Swan. He had taken Mona to the pictures.

Again, that night he'd been later than usual in leaving Mona's house. Her mother was up and they'd waited until she went to bed before he could get down to business, do what he'd been wanting to do for months, what he should have done years ago – ask Mona to marry him.

She'd said 'Yes.' It was to turn out to be the best decision he'd ever made in his life but on that night he'd not been sure she would have him. He'd wanted to ask her for weeks but she was very popular, was Mona, and he'd always felt there might be someone waiting to snatch her away from him.

Mona said she'd been hoping he'd ask her; she said she'd like to be a farmer's wife, so it was with a heart full of hope and anticipation that he'd left her. He walked back to the Swan, hitched the cart, lit the little lantern, fixed it to the front and set off for Rainow at half past one in the morning.

The cold was intense and the road fast and icy but Dobbin was well shod and heavy on his feet. Nat was eager to get home and get his head down for a couple of hours before the morning milking. He sang a little, there on the box, his muffler round his neck, woollen hat knitted by Mam pulled down over his ears, the reins loose in his gloved hands as he watched the glittering new frost he could see on the bit of road ahead of Dobbin's steadily jigging ears.

It was one of those dark nights with a high half-moon. There was a halo round it and had been for three nights on the run. It was going to be a hard winter.

All at once, about a mile after they had left the houses behind, Dobbin lifted his head, put back his ears and, within half a dozen paces, halted. Nat was almost pitched out on to the shafts.

'Giddup,' he urged when he'd righted himself. He sent a wave of pressure along the rein. 'Go on. Giddup.'

Dobbin threw back his head, rattling the harness as he whinnied in protest. Something must have startled him. Nat clambered down to have a look.

Aye, there was something. It was a body, almost tucked under the hedge. Someone lay there, an arm outstretched, clutching a bag. It was a woman.

'Good God,' Nat said as he went towards the slumped figure. 'What's to do?'

He crouched down beside her and moved aside the coat that was covering her face. It was Rose Kennedy, half frozen to death and moaning in pain. He'd have to do something and quick.

He went to the horse's head. 'Hey-oop! Hey-oop! Ease Over,' he said, drawing the shafts alongside so that he could get some light from the lantern.

Dobbin stood quietly, snorting softly, his steaming breath warming the side of Nat's face as, carefully, he rolled Rose on to her back. He'd have to watch how he lifted her. There might be something broken.

387

He unfastened her fingers from the handle of the bag. Where on earth was she going, with a bag, in the dead of night?

She was alive and her arms weren't broken for now she had grabbed at his hand with both of hers. She was turning her head this way and that; groaning.

'Help me. Please help me.' Her face was twisted with pain. 'Alan, Alan,' she was calling.

'It's not Alan, love. It's me. Nat.' He put a hand under her head and slipped the muffler behind her neck to keep it off the earth. He wanted to check her legs before he lifted her on to the trap.

'Nat! Take me to Manchester,' she was saying. 'Take me to Manchester. I have to go to . . .' Then she fell back again.

'Eeh. Rose. Yer in no state to go off ter Manchester, love,' he said, to soothe her. 'How are yer legs? Can yer move them?'

He saw her bring her feet up a little way. Good. There was nothing broken then. 'Where's the pain?'

'My back.'

'Now,' he said as he slipped an arm gently under her shoulder. 'Put yer 'ands round me neck. I'm going to lift yer.'

She tried but dropped back, catching her breath against a second spasm of pain. Nat grasped her shoulder and slipped his other arm under her knees.

She weighed more than he expected her to but he lifted her easily, taking her up in his strong arms. Her coat fell open at the same moment he realized that the heaviest part of her was in the middle. He'd expected the head and arms to balance the weight of her legs. The lass was having a baby. And by the pain she was in she'd have it before morning.

He laid her gently on the floor of the cart and reached into the box for a horse blanket to wrap around her shaking limbs. He went back for her bag and rolled it to lie under her head.

'Take me to Manchester,' she was crying. 'I have to go to the Home.'

'You'll be all right, lass.' Nat tucked the blanket around her, to keep in her warmth. She was much too cold. 'You'll not get to Manchester afore yer babby comes. I'll tek yer up to Mam. Hold tight now. All reet?'

He fastened the little door at the back of the cart and jumped up on to the driving seat. He'd get her up to Rainow safely.

'Go on!' He flicked the rein.

The old horse, old Dobbin, must have known it was her. He made the trip faster and smoother than he'd ever done, easing that old cart gently round the corner of the lane on to the frozen cobbles of the silent yard.

Nat fastened Dobbin's reins to the post before lifting Rose from the floor of the cart. She was unconscious. He carried her to the back door, opening it by placing his shoulder against the latch.

Mam had left the kitchen lamp on low and he made his way through into the living room where he laid her gently on the big deep settee that was drawn up to the last glowing embers of the fire.

The other door led to the front hall and the steep wooden staircase. He went quickly up them and into Mam's bedroom.

'Mam. Come quick!' he said, shaking her shoulder. 'Come downstairs. You're needed. She's havin' a baby.'

His mother was awake in an instant, sitting up, staring at him. 'What? What's goin' on?'

'Come down, Mam,' Nat said. 'As fast as yer can. I'll go and sit wi' her.'

He descended the stairs and found Rose conscious again, coming to, her knees drawn up in pain. He leaned over the back of the settee and spoke comfortingly to her. 'You'll be all right. Mam'll be down in a minute.'

Then Mam was there, in her dressing gown, kneeling beside her, talking to her, her capable hands easing, loosening, feeling her abdomen with expert fingers.

She turned an angry look on to him. 'Is this your doing?' she snapped. 'Are you responsible?'

'Eeh no, Mam!' Nat said. 'Of course I'm not. She's Alan McGregor's girl.'

'Well, she's in a poor way,' Mam said. 'Lift her up while I get her coat off.'

Nat went to lift her as Mam asked, 'Who is she?'

'Don't yer know? I thought you'd a' recognized her. It's Rose Kennedy.'

Mam looked from him to Rose, who was groaning again. 'Oh, Nat,' she said. 'I didn't know. I haven't seen her since she was born.' With her hand Mam brushed back the hair from Rose's face. 'Heavens, yes,' she said. 'I'd have known her anywhere.'

She stood up, brisk and capable. 'Go back to Middlefield,' she said, 'and fetch her mother.'

'Her mother's dead, Mam.'

Mam looked down quickly at Rose who appeared to be losing consciousness again. 'Carrie Shrigley's her mother,' she said in a quiet voice. 'Carry her upstairs for me, will you? We'll have to put her in your room until I make up the attic bed. Then go back as fast as you can and fetch her. Fetch Carrie Shrigley. She ought to be here.'

He lifted Rose again and carried her upstairs to his bedroom with Mam two steps behind him all the way. He put her down on his bed and looked at his mother.

'Go now,' she said. 'As quick as you can.'

He went out into the night and unfastened the horse. 'We've got to get back there, Dobbin,' he said, closing the right rein to turn the poor old beast. 'Giddup.'

There was someone hammering at the front door. Carrie came out of a deep sleep at the sound.

Her hands were shaking as she reached for her dressing gown. Who could it be? A dozen possibilities came to her as she went down the dark stairs.

'I'm coming. Stop that noise,' she called.

It stopped. She stood behind the closed door. 'Who is it?'

'Nat Cooper. Open up.'

It was a voice like his. Carrie unbolted the top and bottom bolts on the door, grasped the big brass handle and opened it a little way. It was Nat Cooper.

'What's going on?' she demanded.

He pushed the door wider, making her fall back into the hall.

'It's your Rose. She's up at Rainow. Come quick.'

'Rose?' Carrie said, puzzled and annoyed at the same time. 'She's here. In bed. What are you doing, disturbing people in the dead of night?'

Nat Cooper looked as if he hadn't the patience to explain. 'She's with Mam,' he said. 'I found her on the Manchester Road. About an hour ago. Get yer things. Come quick, Mam says.'

'Martha?'

'Aye. Come on!'

She couldn't believe it. 'Wait here,' she said. 'Shut the door.'

But he was halfway out, telling her to hurry. 'I'll be outside. I've got the cart. Hurry up.' He went down the step, pulling the door to behind him.

There must be some mistake. Carrie hurried, wide awake now, through to the kitchen and up the back stairs.

'Rose?' she said as she opened the girls' room door. 'Rose?'

She put on the light. There was nobody there. The room was empty, the beds made neatly, a few clothes over the back of a chair.

Carrie went fast, down the stairs and back up to her room, panic rising in her as she went. What was Rose

391

doing? Why was she walking to Manchester? Whatever for? Had she run away? Why?

She dressed as fast as she could, dragged her hair into a knot and pulled on a close-fitting hat. If she had to go to Rainow on that cart she'd need to wear something warm. She was going through all the practical motions, finding her heavy coat and strong shoes, and her lined gloves.

What was going on? Was Rose ill? Had she collapsed?

Carrie ran down the stairs and outside to where Nat sat, reins in his hand, impatient to go.

'Get in quick,' he ordered. 'Fasten the back and hold on tight. It's goin' to be a rough ride.'

Carrie held on to the seat with one hand and the side with the other as they went racing through the dark streets, on to the Manchester Road, then steep-turned and began to climb into the hills, the cart lurching and swinging over deep frozen ruts.

Was Rose ill? Had she become delirious in the night, gone wandering away? Carrie felt sick, from fear and the jolting motion of the ride.

They were in the yard. The movement had stopped and the only sound the horse's snorting breathing as Nat climbed down on to the cobbles.

'Go in at t'back. Mam's with her,' he said, handing the lantern to her. 'I'll stable the horse and get ready for t'milking.'

Carrie pushed open the back door and entered. 'Martha?'

She heard feet clattering down the stairs then Martha came into the dimly-lit kitchen.

'Get your coat off, Carrie. She's upstairs,' she said. Her voice sounded severe.

'What is it, Martha?'

Martha clasped her hands together and came closer. By the light of the lamp Carrie saw the stern look go from Martha's face, saw sympathy replace it. 'You don't know?' she said at last. 'She's in labour Carrie. Her waters have broken. It's going to be a long, hard one.'

'Rose? A baby? Oh, my God.' She couldn't believe it. Carrie took off her coat and put it in Martha's hands. 'Take me to her. Where is she?'

'She's upstairs.' Martha carried the coat into the living room. 'Follow me.'

Carrie followed Martha to the bedroom.

Under the covers on a high bed in the room where a fire burned in the little grate Rose lay very still and white. The poor child must have been desperate. Lonely and afraid. How could she have concealed it? What kind of a mother had she been, that her only child ran away in her hour of need? It tore at Carrie's heart, seeing her here, in a stranger's house, pale and fearful.

She went towards her, reaching out her hands to her.

'Rose, oh, Rose love,' she said in a voice full of love and regret. 'Why didn't you tell me?'

Rose turned her head to look at her. Tears began to brim, quiver and fall in the sweet face that lay frightened and ashen against the pillows. Then a hand came out and reached for Carrie's and all the love and protectiveness that she felt for this child of hers rose up in response to Rose's need of her.

She held on to Rose's hand and tried to pass all the strength that was in her to the girl who, she believed, was her only reason for living.

She leaned over and gently, she kissed her. 'You're going to be all right, Rose,' she said softly. 'I'm here.'

Then Rose's arms were around her neck and wet tears were running down both their faces as they held one another close for the first time in their lives, Carrie making soft sounds of comfort into her daughter's face and neck; tears and hands and cheeks and lips mingling as they clung together.

It felt as if they had been there for hours, not minutes, crying and murmuring to one another until at last Carrie disentangled herself, gazed at her with tenderness, picked up a towel and began to dab carefully at Rose's face.

'Now, love,' she said in a voice breaking with emotion. 'We're going to get this baby born.'

'I'm frightened.' Rose said.

'Well, you're not to be. There's me and Martha here to see you through it. I want you to do as we say.'

She lifted the coverlet to examine Rose. Martha had placed hot-water bottles, wrapped in flannel all round her to warm her and had dressed her in a long white shift which was already stained with blood.

Carrie looked up at Martha. 'How far is she, Martha?' she asked.

'The pains have stopped,' Martha said. 'That's the worry. If the afterbirth separates before the baby comes . . .'

'Yes, I know . . .'

Martha looked at Rose's face. 'We'll have to keep her warm and quiet until we can get those pains coming again,' she said.

Rose was shaking her head. 'No more,' she whispered.

Carrie went to the head of the bed. All at once she felt herself filled with a sense of purpose. This was something she could do – and do well. She had never lost a mother or a baby. And she wasn't going to start with her own flesh and blood.

'We'll have no more of this talk, Rose,' she said firmly. 'This baby is going to be born today. You'll have pain but it won't be beyond you. It won't be more than you can stand. And when they start again love, you must go with them. Don't fight them. We'll be here – helping you.'

'Don't leave me . . .' Rose began.

Carrie straightened her shoulders. 'I'll be here,' she said. 'All the time. But I want you to rest. I'll get you a hot drink. There'll be something in it to make your pains come on.'

Carrie looked at Martha. 'Have you given her anything?'

'I gave her ergometrine, and quinine,' she answered.

'Good. Then I'll make her some hot tea with plenty of

sugar in it to warm her.' She looked at Rose, willing her to respond. 'And you're to get it down you and try to sleep until your labour starts again. All right?'

There was a moment or two before Rose answered, then a look of courage came into her eyes. 'All right,' she said.

'I'll go down for the drink, Martha,' Carrie said. 'You sit with her until I get back.'

Carrie went downstairs and found Nat in the kitchen, filling a kettle.

'Can you make a cup for me and Rose, and your mother?' she said.

'Aye,' Nat said. 'Sit down. It'll tek about five minutes. Is she goin' ter be all right?'

'Yes,' Carrie answered him. 'Your Mam and I can see her safely delivered.' She went to the kitchen range and sat in the chair while she waited. 'It's a good thing you found her,' she said.

'If I hadn't she'd be dead,' Nat answered. 'It were a near do.'

'I don't know how I missed it,' Carrie said. 'How she hid it. She must have been carrying it all round.'

'I'd a'known,' Nat replied as he placed the kettle over the fire and put the teapot to warm on the trivet. 'She'd not a'fooled me.'

Carrie looked up into the big lad's red face. 'You wanted her for yourself, didn't you?' she said quietly.

He smiled at her. Not the embarrassed smile she'd seen on his face when he saw Rose at the Temperance Hotel. He looked sure of himself. 'I thought I did,' he said. 'But it were a kind of – a kind of childish fancy, that lasted a bit long.'

'And you've found someone else?' she asked.

He was smiling hugely now; a big proud smile spread over the broad, happy face. 'I've got meself a little smasher,' he told her. 'We're goin' to get married as soon as I've told me Mam.'

He poured tea as soon as it was drawn and Carrie took a cup up to Rose.

She sat up in the bed and sipped it slowly. 'It tastes good,' she said. 'I've not drunk tea for months.'

'Fancy me never noticing,' Carrie said. 'I can't get over it. You expecting. Me not seeing . . .' She was about to say that it had been the same for herself when she'd had to conceal her own pregnancy, but Rose never liked her to talk about it, so she would keep quiet.

'Have you any pain yet?' she asked when Rose handed the empty cup to her.

'I've got a kind of nagging thing, very low in my back and it's as if little fingers of pain are creeping round me,' she said. 'But I'm going to try to sleep for a bit.'

They sat with her, herself and Martha, taking turns through the rest of the night whilst Rose slept, deeply at first then fitfully.

The intervals between her pains grew shorter as the morning dawned until she no longer slept between them but held on to Carrie's hand tightly whilst they passed over her.

'I want you to go limp when they come, love,' Carrie said after a much stronger one, when Rose struggled to get to her feet.

'If you weren't bleeding you'd be better walking around but we can't risk it,' she added.

'Another one's coming . . .' Rose was gripping her hand again. Carrie looked at her watch. They were coming fast. The first part was nearly over.

'And another . . .'

Then everything happened at once as Carrie knew it would, as it had with her. 'Come on lass,' she said. 'This is where you have to work.'

'I can't. I can't.' Rose gasped as another, long and strong one came.

But she could. She was pushing well into them and Carrie was encouraging, urging, helping her.

'Put some pillows behind her, Martha,' Carrie ordered. 'Let her see what's going on. Come on, Rose, push. Push your baby out.'

'Oh, no!' Rose was shouting. A good strong shout it was, putting all her energy into it.

'Hold on to my shoulder, lass. Come on!' Carrie said. 'It's coming.'

She was leaning across her now. Rose's grip was tight on her shoulder. Carrie looked, from the little crown of the head that was coming towards her waiting hands, to Rose's face so intense and striving.

'Don't push now, love!' Carrie said quickly.

'I must!'

'Hold it,' Carrie said, but it was coming well.

'I can't!'

'It's here! Oh, love, it's here!' Carrie put her cupped hands around the infant's head as it came, easily and gently into the world, gasping for breath, yelling the piercing newborn, like no other, cry that made tears come to your eyes.

'It's a boy,' Carrie said. 'A lovely, perfect little boy.'

Then Rose was leaning forward, reaching out her arms for him, her face alive with love and welcome as Martha tied the cord and wiped his blood-streaked, crumpled little face.

Carrie wrapped him – her own grandson – in a flannel sheet and put him into his mother's arms.

Then she let Martha get on with the rest of it whilst she sat, a huge lump of happiness in her throat, an arm around both of them. Rose, with an expression of rapture on her face, gazed at the infant who, eyes screwed tight shut, was mewing like a new kitten.

Rose looked at Carrie. 'Have you ever seen such a beautiful baby?' she asked. 'Such a little marvel?'

'Never,' Carrie said emphatically. 'Never in my life.'

'Neither have I.'

'What are you going to call him?' Carrie said at last, when Martha had done and left them together.

'Alan. Just Alan, I think,' Rose said. 'Unless Alan gets back before he's christened and wants something different.'

She held the baby up and looked into his peaceful little sleeping face. 'Hello, Alan,' she whispered. 'I'm your Mummy.' Then she looked from him to Carrie and smiled; a sure, knowing smile. 'What will he call you?' she asked.

Carrie hadn't thought. It had never crossed her mind. 'What do you want him to call me?' she said.

'Mamma.' She took Carrie's hand in hers. 'Mamma. I've heard children call their grandmothers Mamma.'

Carrie couldn't speak for the overwhelming flood of feeling that was rushing through her.

'Do you want to hold him, Mamma?' Rose was saying as she put the baby into Carrie's arms.

Then it was her turn to come over all daft and silly as she liked to remember it afterwards, tears of happiness pouring down her face, holding her grandson close, hearing her daughter say Mamma for the first time in her life.

When Carrie and Martha had left her, and the baby was sleeping peacefully in a wooden cradle placed on a low table beside the bed, Rose curled up under the soft, feather eiderdown and tried to sleep.

She was warm and snug and very, very excited. She was not in the least tired. She didn't think she would ever want to sleep again. She just wanted to lie here, luxuriating in the feeling of peace and satisfaction. Suppose she went to sleep and woke to find it had all been a dream? Was it a dream?

She looked over the side of the bed and saw her son raise his tiny pink hand to his face, saw a worried frown cross his forehead and flee away. She couldn't take her eyes off him.

Aunt Carrie – no, Mamma she would be to the child and, for herself, she would call her Carrie. Carrie was going to come upstairs in an hour, when Rose was rested, and show her how to put him to the breast. They were downstairs now, Carrie and Martha. She could hear the murmur of their voices.

The baby was very like Alan she thought. There was a definite look of Alan about the nose. It was a much longer nose than she had ever seen on any other baby. And the hands too. They were long and slender. Like Alan's were. The baby had dark hair, dark and silky-straight. He was moving.

She saw the frown come and flee again, saw him turn his head. She would pick him up and hold him.

As soon as he was in her arms, held close, the worried look went from his face and she watched in fascination as his lips pursed and the little eyebrows lifted.

He opened his eyes; blue, deep and lustrous eyes. They were so clear. They were looking at his world for the first time. They seemed to be looking right into her soul. In that moment as her feelings welled up inside her, the bonds of her love for her child were fixed for ever.

It was a different love from that which she had for Alan and one which she needed, so desperately, to share with him.

She would show him to Carrie and Martha, show them that he had his eyes open. Gently she laid the infant, wrapped in a fine woollen shawl, on the pillow, whilst she stood and slipped her arms into the crocheted bed-jacket Martha had put on the chair. She picked the baby up and smiling and silent went to the stairs and down.

Two stairs before the bottom she stopped. The baby had closed his eyes again. She sat on the stair to wait until he did it again and she would go proudly into the room to show the two women whose voices were coming, clear as bells, through the door.

'She's going to call him Alan,' Carrie was saying. 'After his father, of course.'

'Has there been any word about Alan?' Martha asked.

'No,' Carrie said. 'But she thinks he's still alive. She thinks he's a prisoner of war.'

'He might well be a prisoner of war,' Martha replied. 'They never found any proof that he died.'

'I hope you're right,' Carrie said.

Martha was chuckling. 'Eeh! Alan will get a shock when he gets back – if he's a prisoner – finding out she's had a baby.'

'It seems incredible, Martha,' Carrie was saying. 'That I, I who had done the same thing myself, should have missed them – all the signs.'

'You hid yours just as she did,' Martha answered. 'Nobody guessed.'

'I know.'

'Another cup of tea?'

'Thank you,' Carrie went on. 'It brought it all back to me. It was just the same as when I had her – hiding it. I wore tight corsets, you know.'

'And both of you with no man.'

'Aye,' Carrie said. 'Both of us with men in prison.'

Rose froze. Had she heard right?

Martha was speaking now. 'So it was him – Patrick Kennedy,' she said. 'You never said.'

There was a moment's pause. 'I didn't mean to say it now, Martha,' Carrie answered in a softer voice. 'It was a slip of the tongue.'

Rose straightened up and silently, afraid of being seen, she went back to bed. She placed the baby in his cradle and got under the covers again as relief and a great surging happiness came over her.

She lay there, idly looking at the sunlit hillside she could see beyond the window at the far side of the room, all need of sleep gone, thinking.

Should she tell Alan, when he came back, about Carrie being her mother? Not yet, for he would want to find out who her father was. And her real father was Alan's own godfather. She would keep it to herself, for ever if it was necessary. She had always been a keeper of secrets. It was only important that she knew, not that she broadcast it.

400

One day Carrie would tell her the whole story – and then she would ask her permission to repeat it to Alan.

It was all so wonderful. It was such a wonderful relief to know that her real father had been Dad's brother. It was obvious really. Why hadn't she guessed? Of course. Of course that was the way it must have been. Every piece of the puzzle fitted into place now.

She could forgive Carrie completely.

Downstairs Carrie was peeling potatoes, helping Martha to prepare the midday dinner. She found she was talking more than she had ever done in her life before. All at once she felt unable to stop. She had never gone in for that kind of thing, chattering and gossip. It must be the shock and the excitement that was loosening her tongue.

'I don't know what's come over me,' she said as she dropped a potato into the pan of water that was set on the table in front of her. 'It isn't just the baby. I feel a terrible kind of agitation that's all mixed up with happiness.'

Martha, who was cutting leeks and onions into tiny pieces at the other end of the kitchen table said, 'It's understandable. We none of us know if we'll be here for long.'

'Have you heard the wireless this morning?' Carrie asked. 'I listen all the time.'

'London got it again last night.' Martha chopped furiously at the little heap of vegetables on the board in front of her. 'The Middlefield fire brigade's been in Coventry for nearly a week. There's hardly a building standing. Poor Coventry!'

'I shall have to get home.' Carrie lifted another potato out of the pail that was placed on the floor at her feet. 'I'll go back on the cart with Nat when he delivers the milk.'

'You can stop here if you want to, Carrie.'

'Thank you. But I'll have to see to everything. Go and tell Mary, get Rose's room ready for her and the baby.'

'She'll have to have her lying-in here,' Martha said

401

quickly. 'We can't have her travelling on that cart with a baby. And the baby. He's strong and healthy, but he's six weeks early Carrie. He'll need feeding every hour or so for a good while yet.'

'I know. She'll have a fortnight here. Then I'll take her home.' Carrie peeled slowly and very thinly.

'What about Middlefield? All the gossip? Will you be hurt by it?' Martha looked across at her, unsmiling. 'You didn't want it for yourself. You could leave her here.'

'Everyone's too concerned with the war now to worry about keeping up appearances,' Carrie answered. 'Anyway, I don't care a fig for 'em. I don't mind what anyone says. All at once it doesn't matter.'

When she had finished the vegetables she went to the sink and scrubbed her hands. 'I'll go up to Rose,' she said. 'I'll get her started on the feeding before I go home.'

'Will you come back tomorrow?' Martha asked. 'I can ask Nat to fetch you after he's delivered the milk. I'm going to light a fire in the spare bedroom. There's two beds in there. And get out all the baby things and air 'em.'

'Yes. I'd like that. I could come up every afternoon and go home the next day for a bit.' Carrie dried her hands thoroughly on one of Martha's spotless towels. 'I'll look out my baby things an' all. I've got a lot of stuff. I kept it all from . . .'

'Go on up, Carrie,' Martha said, smiling broadly now. 'Your daughter wants you.'

Throughout the following week Carrie felt her agitation increasing. There was a lot to do and she had no time to dwell on her own fears and fancies but they were there, intruding into her sleep; fears and fancies that had nothing to do with her daytime occupations.

Christmas would be upon them and there was little in the shops. The counters which used to be attractively set out were almost bare. Cardboard cartons, empty, filled the shop windows and women queued, impatient and worried, for the few goods that were available.

There were no oranges to be had and, infuriating to Carrie, no onions. There were brazil nuts at one and sixpence a pound and sweets, only bright wine gums and round mints, at four shillings.

Vivienne, who was dancing for the troops at the barracks in the evenings, helped her during the day. She, Vivienne, when told of the birth said that she had guessed, months ago and had assumed that they were all trying to keep it from her.

They were making mincemeat in the kitchen. Vivienne was mixing the ingredients as Carrie put them through the mincer.

'Will Mary be home for Christmas?' Vivienne asked. 'I want her to come to the Christmas Eve concert. There's going to be a party afterwards for the soldiers. We need some more girls.'

'Yes. She's got Christmas Eve off. She wants to work on Christmas Day. They have a "right good do" she says,' Carrie answered. 'Martha Cooper wants us to go up to Rainow for Christmas dinner. Nat will bring us back in the afternoon if we can get up there ourselves.'

Vivienne looked eager. 'I can get us a lift there and back in an army car,' she said. 'If Mrs Cooper will invite a couple of Canadian sergeants.'

Vivienne was quite advanced, for her years, Carrie thought. It was not a bad thing in these times, especially in the kind of life she had chosen, to have your head screwed on right. Though Carrie was alarmed by the sight of her niece, not yet sixteen and looking twenty years old. 'I can ask her,' she said. 'I don't expect she'll say no.'

The town was full of foreigners. The mayor himself was a Canadian. He'd promised a wedding present to any Middlefield girl who married one of his boys.

'I think that Mr and Mrs Tereschenko are going to have some Czechs and Poles in for dinner,' Carrie went on.

'She's been making all sorts of funny things for weeks.'

'Are the Singers still here?' Vivienne asked.

'Yes. Didn't I tell you? Their daughter and her children have been found. They were here all along. Interred in a camp down south. They are coming to Middlefield as soon as Mrs Singer has found a house for them.'

Carrie stopped turning the mincer for a minute, remembering the old couple's joy on receiving the telegram. 'I wish you could have seen her face,' she said. 'When Mr Singer read it out.'

'Will you get it all done?' Vivienne interrupted her little reverie. 'The mincepies and everything? It's Saturday now. Christmas Day's Tuesday you know.'

'Yes. Come on,' Carrie said. 'Get that mixture into the jar and I'll start on the pastry.' She went to the cupboard for flour and into the cold pantry for her lard. When she brought them back to the table Vivienne was putting on her coat.

'Are you going to stay in those lodgings, Vivienne,' she found herself blurting out. It had come over her again. A kind of fear, an urgent feeling that something was going to happen. She saw a perplexed look cross Vivienne's face which was swiftly followed by one of irritation. 'I could do with a bit of company,' she explained lamely.

'I have to stay there, Aunt Carrie.' Vivienne spoke firmly. 'I belong to the company. We are all together. We have to be.'

'Of course you do.' Carrie was annoyed with herself for giving in to them – the feelings. It was the same for everyone. Everyone felt the need for love and comfort when the world seemed to be crashing around your ears.

When Vivienne had gone, Carrie was overcome with a sudden urge to make everywhere safe. It was as if a voice was telling her to do so, to go through the routines she had been careless about of late.

She went upstairs and put all her jars and bottles in paper bags at the bottom of her wardrobe. Something was going to happen. She knew it. She went down and tidied the kitchen, taking the jars of mincemeat and the pies and placing them on the floor of the larder with cloths on top. Then she dashed upstairs, shaking now with fear and told the Tereschenkos and the Singers to come downstairs and prepare for a night in the cellar.

They were all there, dressed in their warmest clothes, when the sirens went. Then they heard, droning overhead, hundreds of bombers heading for Manchester.

They could hear the guns from their hiding place in the deep cellar where they kept a few candles burning throughout the night.

It was too much for her, cowering in the depths of the earth. There was a smell of damp that clutched at her throat and turned her sick. At half past two Carrie drew her overcoat around herself and told them all that she was going upstairs.

She went to the attic. If a bomb fell on the Temperance Hotel she would rather be killed instantly than buried and suffocated in the cellar. She pulled back the curtain and looked towards Manchester. She could hear the crumping sound of bombs and the puttering of our guns. Fire glowed on the horizon and spread across the night sky. They went overhead continuously; German bombers in formation flying lower and slower than she had imagined them and she cried with fury against the Germans and with fear for the people who were the enemy's target.

Rainow was much nearer to Manchester. Rose, Martha and Nat had been awakened by the grunting noise of bombers overhead. They dressed and went down to the kitchen, bringing the baby in his cradle and placing him under the dining table. The infant slept soundly as they debated whether to remain in the house or find shelter in one of the barns.

'There's been incendiaries dropped afore,' Nat said. 'There were three dropped at Wildboarclough. They set fire to a haystack. We'll be safer 'ere.'

Martha opened the back door. 'My God!' she said. 'Look!'

They stood with her on the paved yard watching them go overhead. They were in lines, never-ending lines it seemed to Rose, heading for the burning city they could see a few miles away.

Rose could smell the fire and the smoke from where she stood. Flashes high over the inferno were the bursting shells from our guns. Searchlights were swinging, criss-crossing columns of light that probed the sky from the hell of explosions and fire that was Manchester.

They did not go to bed that night but snatched an hour of sleep each the next day, taking turns at watching into the red, blazing distance.

The fires from the night before were still smouldering under a pall of smoke when on the following night the blitz came again to Manchester. There would be a pitiful stream of bombed-out families arriving in Middlefield and the villages between on the following day.

Nat had been down with his milk and reported back that Middlefield had not been hit and that Carrie would not be coming to Rainow until Christmas Day when Vivienne, Mary and two Canadian sergeants would join them. Martha was only too happy to have them. She said it would be a great pleasure to give something back for all they were doing for us.

There was no attack on Christmas Eve and they decorated a little fir tree that Nat brought in from the copse. In the afternoon Rose left the baby with Martha, who was going to feed him with a bottle for the first time, and went with Nat into Middlefield. She had not wanted to lie-in for two weeks, she told Martha. She had never felt better in her life and she wanted to buy presents for them all if there was anything to be had in town. She also wanted to attend the mass at St Alban's and to pray for Alan's safe return.

Christmas Day dawned clear, cold and sunny. Rose was up early. She fed the baby, dressed herself in her best skirt and jumper and went down to the kitchen at six o'clock.

'I 'ope yer brought a lot of winter clothes,' Nat said when she entered the shining, lamplit kitchen. 'I reckon as we'll 'ave snow tomorrer.'

Martha cut him short. 'Happy Christmas,' she said. 'He's always right, like his father was. But it isn't snowing now and we've a day to enjoy ourselves.'

Martha had a stuffed turkey ready to go in the oven, sausages and ham, potatoes and celery from the garden. She had made trifles and almond tarts, a rich plum pudding and a big fruit cake. There were jars of honey and lemon cheese, jams and pickles in the storecupboard and in an outside coldstore salted hams and flitches of cured bacon.

Rationing seemed not to have troubled them here at the farm though Martha said they had to go carefully with tea.

'Do you really think it will snow?' Rose asked Nat. 'Will we be cut off from the town?'

'Aye. We generally gets cut off for a day or so,' Nat said. 'But I have a feeling this lot's going to last a bit longer than a few days. Sit yerself down, lass. Get yer breakfast.'

There was an enormous spread laid out on the kitchen table; enough to last a week Rose would have thought. 'Thanks,' she said. 'What do you do – about the milk – if you're cut off?'

'You'll see,' Nat laughed. 'Mam will 'ave yer mekking cheese and butter till yer won't ever want to see another.'

'I'd like to learn,' Rose looked eagerly towards Martha. 'Will you show me?'

Martha smiled at her whilst Nat continued to recite his catalogue.

'And we'll feed it to the calves, and the pigs, mix it with the hen meal. The cats'll have bellies like little pumpkins.' He broke off, laughing heartily. 'You'll never see a drop wasted anyroad,' he said. 'Not with Mam around.'

'I'm looking forward to meeting this girl, Mona,' Martha said, getting a little fun at Nat's expense. 'If she's half as good as he says she is my days of toiling are nearly over.'

Rose ate a good breakfast and then went upstairs for her presents. She had bought presents for everyone: a pound of botany wool in a lovely shade of apple green for Martha, a knitted pullover for Nat, scent and talcum for Vivienne, three pairs of black wool stockings for Mary and a tin of Quality Street for Mona and her mother. She had positively made a coquette of herself to charm the sweets out of old Mr Potts. For Carrie she had bought, weeks before, a cashmere scarf and a dresslength of cream silk shantung. These she had persuaded from Mrs Singer. Mr Singer's factory was making silk maps – it was all secret work – and his wife had kept a few lengths of the fine silk they used to print.

She handed Martha and Nat their presents and took the others to the parlour, a room that was only opened on special occasions. She placed them under the tree in the pretty room where a fire was laid ready for lighting, little wax candles were clipped to the tree and all was ready for the celebration.

It was going to be a wonderful day for them all. But where was Alan? Tears prickled the back of her eyes as she looked around. Would she be able to get through it without breaking down? Sometimes she felt herself ready to go down into a sea of black depression. It had been so hard to go on believing when all around her people were losing hope.

Surely she would know if he were dead? Surely the little flame in her heart would have been extinguished if he were not going to return.

'Alan, Alan,' she whispered, 'come home soon. I can't bear to live without you.'

CHAPTER TWENTY-FOUR

Every night for a week they had come down to the dunes at Canet-Plage, twenty of them. Alan was one of five RAF pilots who, night after night, had to return, disappointed. Their despair was increasing with each disappointment. They were near to exhaustion with eyes red-rimmed from scrutinizing the flat, empty sea in the early January darkness, haggard from lack of sleep.

Every night they expected to see the rescue boat. Every night the resistance leader went ahead, over the dunes, to flash a signal across the water and every time there was no answering light. They had been forced to give up before dawn and return to the cramped conditions of their hiding place, a tiny cottage which was crowded to bursting, hot and fetid inside.

Alan's nerves were as strung out as everyone else's. His leg was playing up. He was filthy, though fitter than some of his companions who had arrived at this place, near to the Spanish border, without ever having had a night's shelter. He had been sheltered, fed and hidden throughout the long months.

Tonight, in shadow, his back to the sandhills, he kept his eyes on the move, scanning the dunes for a sight of the man who was leading them, looking out over the sea to change his eyes' focus. There was only the regular crushing sound of waves hitting sand a few yards in front of him. The nineteen men who were hiding in the shadows were silent.

Then it seemed to appear from nowhere – a black mass, coming towards the shore, a creaking of oarlocks, a splashing and a shadow looming up in front of him. The resistance leader appeared from behind, slipped past him and went towards the rowing boat.

'*Où sont les fraises?*'

It was the password.

'*Dans le jus.*'

The password was complete and now they came, silent and eager, from their hiding places along the beach. Tiredness was forgotten as the electrifying nearness of liberty seemed transferred from one to the other of the men wading out to the boat.

Four days later, rested, fed and buoyant with expectation, they sailed from Gibraltar for Southampton in a boat that ran dark and swift through enemy-infested waters.

Alan leaned over the rail, watching the bow wave breaking. A storm was blowing up and soon he would go down to the lower deck. He stayed a little longer, relishing the icy wind against his ears that was blotting out sound, as his mind went back over the months of his escape.

He remembered the nerve-wracking start when he had been discovered, hiding in the farmhouse barn. He remembered the French family's bravery in sheltering him, calling medical aid and hiding him for the four months that the burns and the fracture of the distal end of the fibula had taken to heal.

They had contacted a priest who was arranging passages south for the feeble-minded young Frenchmen in the care of the church. He, Père Dupont, had moved Alan, then latterly many other men from monasteries to convents and safe houses on their slow but well-planned journey to Marseilles. His own companion had been Antoine, a young man of extremely limited intelligence.

Here, from the relative safety of the boat, he cast his mind back to the nightmare of the train journeys, especially the crossing of Paris. He remembered his first encounters with the enemy at railway stations and ticket barriers. The part of imbecile had proved easy to play, he remembered with a wry smile, but always he had expected at any moment that the Germans would challenge him, that they would see through it, for he would find himself watching them with a keenness that would be foreign to Antoine and his like.

His reverie was interrupted when he turned his head and saw that a sailor had joined him on the deck.

'You all right, sir?' the rating said.

It was, oddly, good to hear someone speak respectfully to him, though he had never taken any pleasure in pulling rank.

'Fine,' he answered. The good feeling must have come, he thought as counterweight to the months of being regarded as an imbecile and the strain of having to pretend.

'You'd be better below, sir,' the sailor cautioned him. 'There's going to be a hell of a storm.'

He turned angrily, surprising himself. He wanted to tell the fellow to go to hell. If he chose to stand here, alone and watching, then he would do so. He had become edgy with strangers.

There was nothing to be gained by being arrogant. He looked at the sailor and shouted into the wind. 'What are the chances of getting there in one piece?'

The sailor grinned before answering cheerfully, 'A bloody sight better in this weather, sir, than in fair. U-boats won't be hunting in this.'

The wind was tearing at his greatcoat now, making his eyes sting. He looked out to sea for a few more minutes, towards the north, towards home, and Rose. A feeling of anticipation spread through him. At last – at last he would see her. Maybe within forty-eight hours she would be in his arms.

He left the rail and, sliding and slipping, made his way down into the darkened ship.

They reached Southampton three days after leaving

Gibraltar and Alan was given a rail docket to London. Before he left the docks for headquarters, medical checks and debriefing, he found a telephone and dialled his home. There was a chance that his father was on leave.

Nan Tansley answered. She was shocked into unaccustomed hesitancy.

'Alan?' he heard her voice, thin and faint. 'Is it really you?'

'Yes.'

'Where are you ringing from?' This after a few moments hesitation.

'I'm in Southampton.' He had given her a fright. 'Are you all right?' he asked.

'Is it really you?'

'Yes. I'm alive. I'm well and I'm coming home. Where's Dad?'

'He's in Edinburgh.' Her voice was sounding more normal now. 'He's all right. He comes home for his leaves.'

'Thanks, Nan,' he said. 'I'll try to speak to him now, if I can get through.'

'Will you be home soon?'

'Yes. As soon as I can get through all the formalities.'

'Goodbye.' He heard her put the phone down and smiled to himself.

He had the number of Coastal Command, Edinburgh. He dialled the operator and was speedily put through.

Dad was at sea. They would give him the message.

Next, he rang the Regional Bank in Middlefield.

'May I speak to Rose Kennedy, please?' he said. His heart was going fast with excitement.

'I'm afraid she no longer works here.' It was an old man's voice. He didn't recognize it. The excitement left him.

'Where is she?' he asked impatiently.

'I'm afraid I don't know.'

Damn! Damn! he muttered to himself. What on earth

was that other girl's name? That's right. He remembered.

'Is Miss Tannenbaum there?' he asked.

'Yes.' There was a pause then the man asked, 'Do you want to speak to her?'

'Of course I damn well want to speak to her,' he snapped. He found it incredible that, with a war on, these people could be so easy going, so stupid. 'Bring her to the phone. Please.'

He heard Pamela's voice coming clear and confident. 'Hello?'

'Alan McGregor here.'

There was a pause. Then she spoke again. 'You're safe! How wonderful.'

'Where's Rose?'

'I don't know.'

'You must know. What has happened?' His anger was going. He was beginning to feel the first stirrings of fear.

'Alan. You'd better get up here. Go to see her aunt. She'll tell you. And, Alan?'

'Yes?'

'Thank God you're back.'

The line went dead.

He caught the next train to London. From the windows of the overcrowded compartment he saw the devastation the blitz had wreaked. Towns and cities, shrouded and mantled in snow, looked as he would expect a lunar landscape to appear. Bomb craters in the landscape resembled the moon craters he had seen through a telescope. Here and there a church spire pointed to a sky that was as white as the surrounding country.

It took them three days to examine, question and release him before they gave him a first-class ticket to the camp. The journey that used to take two hours, with detours and delays, now took twelve.

The train went at a snail's pace and he found himself being provoked into rudeness towards everyone whom he imagined was impeding him. Station staff, Red Cross

413

volunteers who stood on the freezing stations serving steaming tea, all must have found him, at the least, uncivil. He determined to pull himself together.

News of his return had reached the camp ahead of him. There were new faces at the fighter station including a new flight lieutenant. Jeffreys had 'bought it' at the Battle of Britain a few weeks after he had come down.

'Martin Forsyth?' Alan asked.

'He's a squadron leader. He had a couple of prangs but he was a lucky blighter,' they told him. 'They'll be in in half an hour.'

Alan stood in front of the hangars watching the squadron coming in to land. He had no sense now that he wanted to be part of it again. Perhaps he was preparing himself for the possibility that they might not let him fly. He had seen the medical men. They had told him that, though skin grafts might be suggested in six months' time, there was some other trouble. Apparently his lungs had suffered smoke damage in the fire. His lung capacity was reduced to below the flying standard.

He would have more tests done. In the meantime he was on leave for a month and ordered to rest. He smiled to himself, at the thought that there was nothing like marriage, a bride, to aid his recovery. Then he began to worry again as to her whereabouts. Had her aunt proved impossible to live with? Where could she have gone? Middlefield was one of the safe areas.

Martin was the last to land. He came haring across the grass as soon as he spotted Alan.

'Alan!' Martin slapped his shoulder.

'Watch it!' Alan laughed. 'I'm only here to ask if I can borrow the Riley.'

'I'll be glad to see it being used,' Martin said. 'I've not used my petrol coupons for three or four months. There's enough for about six hundred miles.'

'Sure you won't need them?' Alan asked as they went across the grass to the mess. 'I want to get the wedding

414

fixed up. You could come up for it and drive the Riley back if it all works out.'

'I'll get there if I have to fly up,' Martin said. 'Anyway, you take her. I think the main roads are clear of snow. Have a couple of pints first?'

'Right-o.'

He left the camp as darkness fell. The countryside was white and shining. It was perfect weather for bombers. They would have no trouble finding their targets. But there were no raids as he journeyed north through the night.

He put his foot down and the Riley went, splashing and crunching over the sand-and-cinder-laden melting snow of the towns and over icy new-frozen tracks of the country roads as he trundled anxiously northwards to Cheshire and Rose.

He reached Middlefield at nine o'clock and went straight to Waters Green where the snow had been cleared. It was heaped right up to the railway bridge and filled the Hundred and eight steps to the handrails. The Wallgate had been too treacherous to attempt and Alan had to drive to the Temperance Hotel from the direction of the Manchester Road.

He banged on the front door. Carrie Shringley answered it herself. He saw her face go white.

'Is it you?' she asked. 'Is it Alan?'

He grinned at her, relieved at last to be here. 'In person,' he said.

She looked bewildered. She was not wearing her glasses and he assumed that she was not sure it was he who stood there.

'Oh, my!' she said. 'You'd best come in.'

He stayed where he was. 'Is Rose here?'

'No. No, she's not here. Come in won't you?'

'Where is she?' He did not want to go inside if Rose wasn't there. He wanted Rose, not a conversation with her aunt, and his unease and plain bad-temper, as he thought of it, was growing by the minute.

'She's up at the Coopers'.' She was smiling at him now.

'Nat Cooper's?' he demanded.

'Yes.' She hesitated then said. 'I should tell you . . . No I shouldn't.'

'What's going on?' He spoke sharply. He had no time for this prevarication. 'Why is she at the Coopers'?'

Carrie Shrigley was agitated, yet she had seemed genuinely pleased to see him. Alan did not know what to make of it. She kept transferring a sheaf of notes or bills, or whatever it was she was holding, from her right hand to her left and back again.

'I . . . I can't tell you,' she said.

Alan turned away. 'I'll go there,' he said.

'You'll never get there,' she was calling after him over the distance of the pavement. 'The snow. Nat Cooper's not been down with the milk since Boxing Day – and it's the tenth of January.'

The woman was off her head. Did she think he didn't know what day it was? 'I'll get there,' he assured her as he reached the car.

'They're snowed in in the hills. Cut off,' she was calling.

'Then I'll have to dig her out, won't I?' Alan started the engine and let in the clutch.

He had put chains around the Riley's wheels. He headed out towards the Buxton Road from where he would turn again, towards Manchester and the easier, trodden route to Rainow. And all the time he was questioning everything.

Why was Rose at Nat's? Surely Nat hadn't enticed her away from him? He knew he would have been posted 'Missing, presumed killed', but she would have known he'd return. Wouldn't she? What were they all hiding from him? The staff at the Regional Bank, Pamela Tannenbaum, Carrie Shrigley.

He had turned off the Manchester Road now. He put his foot on the accelerator, double de-clutched and the

416

Riley slid easily into second gear for the climb up to Rainow.

Rose fed the baby and went down to the kitchen. It was eight-thirty in the morning the tenth of January. She was going to help Martha in the dairy.

The cows were milking well. Sixty gallons a day had to be dealt with. Nat had not been able to cut a way through to the road yet. The land-girls, the evacuees from the cottage, she and Martha had been working non-stop to use up the milk that was left after the animals had been fed to capacity.

There were cheeses in the five iron presses and a dozen more in makeshift containers – cans with tops and bottoms removed – wrapped in muslin and weighted down under planks of wood and half-hundredweight blocks of iron, bricks and sacks of stones.

There was a barrel of salted butter and four pillowcases half-full of cottage cheese – a mistake, the cottage cheese, in Martha's opinion. Today they were going to make another, a big Cheshire cheese, and scald and clot a gallon of cream.

Rose put on a white apron over the slacks and jumper she had taken to wearing. She left the kitchen and went outside to gaze for a moment over the meadow. The sun was dazzling off the crisp whiteness of the field which sloped gently down to a stream. It was still running, a black gash that ran along the dip before the land rose up again towards the road.

She could see Nat. He had cut a path, almost as far as the road. Martha came to stand beside her. 'He's not got far to go now,' she remarked.

'Will he be able to get the milk out this afternoon,' Rose asked.

'If it doesn't snow again.'

Rose looked up at the glaring blue of the cloudless sky. 'It looks clear enough.'

417

'He's going to lead Dobbin down there, pulling the sledge. Then he'll carry the churns to the road and the horse will pull them down the hill to the smithy. The smith's got a cart. We'll borrow that until we can get ours out of the yard and down the lane.' Martha had been tying on her clean apron, on top of her floral one as she spoke. Now it was done. 'Are you ready?' she said.

'Yes. The baby's asleep. I can hear him from the dairy if he cries.'

They went into the whitewashed dairy where the cheeses and butter were made. The floor was of scrubbed stone, the walls white as snow and all around the room slate shelves held the flat dishes of cream and slabs of butter they had prepared.

Rose loved it all. She liked fleeting the cream with a flat skimmer and churning it until it 'came'. She enjoyed working and squodging it until all the buttermilk was out and it could be salted and shaped with flat, wooden patters into shining, yellow slabs. But most of all she liked to make cheese. She was becoming quite expert she thought as she scrubbed her hands and went to inspect the vat.

Martha had stirred in the starter an hour before breakfast and now the curd was perfect, like a pale, yellow jelly that filled the deep vat. It looked solid but she knew that when the knives went in, sliding around and under, and she had cut the curd gently and carefully into little cubes, the whey would run.

She cut it. The little pieces were floating now. She slipped her hands into the warm liquid, felt the slithering softness of the curd, spread her fingers and began to move it gently. In another ten minutes she would drain it and hang the curd in the large square of boiled muslin she had prepared.

'Who's that?' Martha said.

Rose turned her head to see Martha peering through the window at the meadow. 'It's Nat,' she answered.

'Who's with him?'

Rose stopped stirring and went to stand beside Martha, hands dripping wet with whey.

Nat was talking to a man. Now he was pointing in their direction, waving, shouting something.

Rose felt her heartbeat increase. The man was tall. He had a long, loping stride. He was coming across the snow-deep meadow, hands in the pockets of a leather jacket. It was a leather flying-jacket. She'd seen them before.

She ran outside, her heart racing, hands clapped to her mouth to stop herself from crying out if it wasn't him. If it wasn't . . . it was . . . it was him.

'Alan!' she screamed.

He stopped and put out his arms to her. 'Rose!'

Then they were running towards one another, stumbling and falling through the snow, crying and laughing at the same time until they were in each other's arms and his mouth was on hers and her hands were fastened at the back of his neck, holding him so that she would never ever again lose the feel of his face against her own.

At last he held her and looked into her eyes. 'Oh, Rose. Oh, Rose. You don't know how much I've missed you,' he said.

'And I you,' she answered. She had tears of joy running down her flushed cheeks. She brushed them away with her hands then took his hands in her own.

'Come. Come into the house,' she said, tugging him after her as she went, fast and eager towards the farm.

He followed her into the kitchen.

'Here,' she said. 'Give me your coat.' She unfastened the clasp and helped him out of the jacket, then eagerly, not saying a word more, began to pull him towards the stairs.

Outside the bedroom door she stopped and turned to look at him. He was one step below her and their faces were level.

'Can you bear a surprise?' she asked in a whisper.

'Yes.' He grinned at her. 'What?'

She opened the bedroom door and led him inside.

Then, so as not to miss a single second, she never took her eyes off his face as he looked from her to the cradle.

He went white, then red. His eyes first registered surprise, then amazement and, lastly, he let go of her hand and went towards the cradle.

'Ours?' he said.

'Yes.'

'When?' He looked at her tenderly. 'Oh, Rose! When did . . . ?'

'The seventeenth of December. His name's going to be Alan, if you agree.'

Alan knelt by the cradle and gently lifted his child into his arms. 'Oh, God,' he whispered as tears poured unchecked down his thin, strained face. 'I never . . . never in my wildest dreams, expected anything like this.'

She went to him. She put her arms around his waist and pressed her warm cheek against his wet face. 'You are home, my darling,' she said. 'You will never know just how much I love you.'

She could feel in his body, see by the set of him that he needed her love and her strength. He would recover from his ordeal with her at his side.

'I think we'd better get married now, don't you?' she said.

They sat for an hour in the bedroom, watching their son and talking, holding hands and embracing, as if afraid to let an unfilled second pass. They wanted to lie together in love but knew that this was not the place nor the time for it and that they would have to contain themselves.

But he could not stop himself from holding her, from taking her into his arms and, feeling her full warm body responding to his every movement, having to fight back the desire that threatened to overtake him. He pulled himself up and looked down at his beautiful wife to be who lay, flushed and aroused, on the bed beside him.

'I want us to be married,' he said, 'before we make love again. What about you?'

'If every time we do, we start another baby, I think it would be more . . . more seemly,' Rose answered before she pulled his head down and kissed him full and passionately on the mouth. 'But I can't wait too long, my darling. I'm quite shameless.'

The ill-humoured person that had been his alter-ego for so long was evaporating in her nearness. He laughed softly at her. 'Get up, then, you hussy!' he said. 'Fasten your clothing. Go downstairs and help Martha with her cheeses. I'll watch our son for half an hour, then I'll help Nat.'

He lay there, after she had gone downstairs, looking at his son, remembering Rose's sweetness and knowing that from this moment on he needed nothing so much as he needed this little family he had created. He wanted to feast his eyes on them, wanted to watch their every movement, hear their every sound. Then he slept, a deep contented sleep, until Rose woke him at three o'clock in the afternoon.

'Do you want something to eat, darling?' she asked. 'I've made something for you.'

He was wide awake in seconds. The months of hiding had made him wary. Then he saw her face and again relief and love washed over him. He stood up and took her in his arms.

'I'll be down in a minute,' he said. 'Give me some food and I'll deliver the milk in Middlefield for Nat.'

'Shall I come too?'

'No,' he said firmly. 'You must stay here, with the baby. I shall be back later, when I've seen Father Church and your aunt. I want to get this wedding arranged.'

He went downstairs and ate the meal she had prepared for him. She sat watching him, waiting for his murmurs of approval at every mouthful. It delighted him to see her eagerness to please.

When he put down his knife and fork he took her in his arms again before asking her to bring his outdoor clothes.

Then he went outside and carried the churns through

the field with Nat. They wedged them into the Riley and he returned, the hood down, in the bitter cold, to Middlefield.

After the milk was delivered to the bottling plant and the empty churns were in place in the little car he set off for the presbytery where Father Church told him that, if they could get a special licence, he would marry them in nine days' time, on Saturday the nineteenth of January.

Alan thanked him and went immediately to the Temperance Hotel. He was shown into the kitchen by Vivienne and Mary who were visiting. They talked non-stop to him until their aunt came downstairs.

He was astonished at the change in Carrie Shrigley. She was eager now for them to marry. She chatted to him in a slightly frenzied way as if she were nervous. Perhaps she wanted to make amends. He had never seen her like this before.

'Sit down, Alan,' she fussed as soon as he had followed her upstairs and been shown into her sitting room. 'I'll get Mrs Bettley to send some tea up.'

He sat and gazed around the room until she returned. It was a peculiar room. Rose had told him about it and now he saw for himself the furniture that looked as if it should be in a king's palace; ornate, gilded and glazed. There were lighter patches on the walls where pictures once hung and china cabinets, empty of all but her less valuable ornaments.

'Here we are,' she said brightly as she followed the woman into the room. 'Help yourself.'

'Thank you,' he said.

As soon as the door had closed behind the woman who brought the tray he came straight to the point.

'I have arranged the wedding for Saturday the nineteenth,' he told her. 'You will have to sign consent forms.'

'With pleasure,' she answered. 'Now, then. We'll have the wedding breakfast here. I'll have the dresses made. For Rose and her sisters . . .'

'You have no objections, then?' He frowned and looked at her closely. He had been prepared for contest of wills.

'None,' she said. 'I'm pleased. For both of you. You have a lovely son.'

He would have thought she was on the brink of a nervous collapse had he not known that she was not the kind of woman who collapsed under strain. And she looked so well. She looked years younger without those thick glasses. Her hair was rich in colour and shining with health and her pale complexion was glowing.

'Now, where are they?' she asked. 'I'll sign them and take them up myself, at once. I'll get some dried fruit at the same time. I'll start on the cake tonight.'

He stood up to leave.

'Will you fly again?' she asked as she took him to the door.

'I don't know,' he replied. 'I may be invalided out.'

'Shall you be sorry?' She had taken hold of his arm as if he needed help to negotiate the stairs.

'If I am, then I will go back to my studies,' he said. 'We – Rose, the baby and I – will live in Edinburgh until I am qualified.'

'You'll leave Middlefield?'

She seemed to be taking it quite well, he thought. He had expected an outburst of temper at the news that she could be parted from Rose.

'Until I'm a doctor. Then I'll come back and try to get into obstetrics.'

They were at the front door now. 'What's that?' she asked. 'Obstetrics?'

'Delivering babies, that kind of thing,' he answered with a smile.

'Oh, that?' she said with what he could have sworn was a rather superior air. 'You don't need to be a doctor to do that, you know.'

He left her and returned to the farm where they all sat around the fire and talked until supper. It was good to be here, amongst his friends. He felt himself warming, relaxing in their presence.

After supper they went up to the bedroom. It was cosy and warm up there. Rose had made a fire in the little iron fireplace and, in its flickering light, he felt a great contentment and peace come over him as he watched her. The baby sucked contentedly at her breast and she smiled over the infant's head whilst he related the afternoon's events to her.

'She seems eager now,' Alan said after speaking of her aunt's co-operation. 'She is going to make all the arrangements for the reception. She's making the cake tonight, she said.'

'She has been wonderful about everything,' Rose answered.

'She says she is going to have your dress made. She knows your size. And she wants Vivienne and Mary as bridesmaids.'

'The baby has made a big difference to her,' Rose said. 'And yet she's lost us all now. Mary and Vivienne have left home. Did you know?'

'Yes. I saw Mary and Vivienne. They were at your aunt's. Mary will get the day off for the wedding. And Vivienne will be there. She's dancing in Middlefield until February.'

Rose lifted the baby and put him to the other breast. When he was settled comfortably she looked at Alan again. 'Have you been able to speak to your father yet?' she asked.

'No. Tomorrow. Dad should be docking in Leith tomorrow night.'

'I wish I could be with you when you speak to him.'

'Well, sorry, love. You and the baby must stay here. I won't have you going to town with him yet. There's going to be more snow, Nat says.'

'What will we do with the baby on the wedding day?' Rose asked. 'Take him to the church?'

'No. We'll take him to Middlefield. Your aunt's lodgers are going to watch him whilst we're at church.'

The baby had fallen asleep at her breast. Rose placed him against her shoulder whilst she fastened the front of her woolly nightdress. 'What time's the service?' she asked.

'Twelve midday. We'll be back here at four.'

'Am I to walk down the aisle. All that?' she said.

Alan had thought of that too. 'I'm going to ask Dad to give you away,' he said. 'You can't come down on your aunt's arm. It would look silly.'

'That will be lovely. If he can get here.' Rose put the sleeping baby into the cradle and turned to him. 'You are in my bed,' she said. 'Shove up.'

They slept soundly, wrapped round one another in the narrow bed that was piled almost to the height of the sloping ceiling with goose-down quilts and a deep feather mattress. The child must have been contented too, Alan thought, when he opened his eyes at six and found that Rose was feeding him the first feed of the day.

He dressed and went outside to help Nat for most of the day. They cleared a path through the drifts that had blocked the yard and the lane. Now Nat could take the milk down to Middlefield on the cart and Alan could put the hood up and drive to the town in comfort.

As soon as he had spoken to Carrie Shrigley about the arrangements he went to invite Rose's friends – Sylvia, Pamela and Norah – to the wedding. Then, that done, he made his way up to his home in Lincoln Drive to see Nan Tansley and to ring his father.

Nan Tansley was her old self, fussing and making much of him. He let her indulge herself for half an hour, sitting back, basking in her admiration and attention. Then he went to the telephone.

This time there was a delay in getting through to Edinburgh and the line itself was bad, crackling and whistling in his ear.

'Is Second Engineer Douglas McGregor there?' he shouted into the instrument.

'Speaking.' It was the voice he knew.

'Dad! Is that you?'

'Alan!'

'Yes.'

'Oh, wonderful to hear you, son! I knew you'd made it home, of course. They sent a message to the ship.'

Alan grinned into the silly mouthpiece. 'Did you celebrate?' he asked.

'Aye. We had an extra ration that night.' His father was chuckling.

'Then get your crew together for another one tonight.'

'All right. What is it? When's the wedding?'

'A week on Saturday – the nineteenth. And, Dad . . .'

'Yes?'

He held his breath before speaking, quickly and eagerly. 'You are a grandfather. I've got a son.'

There was a silence. He could picture Dad's face. Then the familiar, rich voice came clearly across the miles. 'Oh, son. Congratulations. I'm lost for words.'

'Will you be able to get leave, for the wedding?' Alan asked. 'I am dying to see you. To show the baby to you.'

'I'm coming home on the Friday – the eighteenth. I'll come by train.'

'Where's the car?' Alan thought Dad would have driven up there.

'In the garage at home. You could have been using it. And Alan?'

'Yes?' he answered.

'You'll never guess who's here – in Scotland.'

He had no idea who it could be. He didn't know any of Dad's colleagues. 'Who?' he asked.

'Patrick Kennedy.'

'Good heavens. He got the job of correspondent then?'

'He's covering the activities of the Canadian troops. For

a syndicate of American and Canadian newspapers.'

It would be like old times for Dad, having his old naval friend with him. 'Have you seen him?'

'He's coming to Edinburgh tonight,' Dad answered. 'By the way, who's giving Rose away?'

'I thought – you,' Alan said.

'Delighted. But, wouldn't it be nice if Patrick Kennedy could do it? He is her father's brother, her only male relative.'

Alan thought for a moment. 'What about the feud? Between him and Rose's aunt,' he said.

His father's voice went stern. 'It's time it was ended,' he said. 'It's time they buried the hatchet. It has gone on far too long. And it's Rose's big day.'

'I agree,' Alan said. 'Will you ask him then?'

'Yes. You'd better not say anything to Rose – in case he can't. Or won't.'

'All right. I'll see you a week on Friday. I'll spend the night with you at Lincoln Drive.' He laughed now as he added, 'Anyway, it's traditional not to see the bride on the eve of the wedding. We'll have a stag night.'

CHAPTER TWENTY-FIVE

Patrick Kennedy alighted from the staff car into the market square with a feeling of trepidation. He told himself that it was ridiculous to feel this way.

In the capital cities of Canada, America and the British Isles he was recognized. He counted as friends politicians, broadcasters and news editors. So why should this little town of Middlefield make him feel like a recalcitrant schoolboy whose past misdeeds had caught up with him?

He grinned to himself as he realized that perhaps that, though a simplification, was the truth behind the feeling that had come over him the moment he had stepped on to the cobbled square.

He had not travelled down to Middlefield with Douglas who had caught an early morning train to Manchester. Douglas would be here already. Patrick had set off the previous day and had been driven to Cheshire in an army staff car, part of a convoy, by a young woman of the WAAC. A Canadian Army major and a British Army lieutenant of a guards regiment had been his travelling companions.

The journey had taken them eighteen hours; there had been long delays in the Borders though high Shap Fell on the Carlisle to Kendal route had been cleared of snow.

However, they had reached Middlefield before the afternoon light went and, tired of sitting, he had asked the girl to drop him off in the marketplace.

All the buildings and the sidewalks, as he now called them, were layered with snow. It had been cleared from the cobble-stones and piled, packed snow and ice like a low wall, along the margins of the narrow streets. Nothing much had changed he noticed as he made his way up Churchgate and along the Chester Road; except the faces. For he did not recognize a soul.

He stuck his hands into the pockets of his greatcoat and started to walk to Lincoln Drive. He made a wry face as he went. Had it been a foolish thing to do – to come here? Would his presence upset the family? He would not hurt them for the world – but, again, the prospect of at last setting eyes on his daughter was driving him on. Rose would never know how much she meant to him but, his heart quickened, he would not want to upset Carrie.

The icy little breeze was stinging his face as he walked, faster now, towards Douglas's house.

Perhaps it was all arranged. Alan would have let Rose know that he was at her disposal. He told himself that if Douglas's proposal that he give the bride away came to naught he would not waste his time here. He would cover the story of Canadian troops in the town.

Either way, he had to be back in Scotland before Tuesday. The empty staff car was to pick him up early on Sunday morning for his return to Edinburgh.

Alan met him at the door of the house in Lincoln Drive and shook his hand warmly. 'Come in, Patrick,' he said. 'It's good to see you. Dad's at the Swan. He'll be home in half an hour.' He held open the door for him and Patrick went ahead into the drawing room where a fire blazed and a tray of drinks was set on the low, wheeled table.

'Help yourself to a drink. We'll have something to eat later, when we get back.' Alan pointed to the decanters. 'I'll take your bag up.'

Patrick poured himself a Scotch and walked over to the window. He could see, beyond the garden, the row of houses that he and Danny had built.

Alan had come into the room. 'How does it feel, to be back? And looking at your own handiwork?' he asked.

Patrick turned. 'I see Danny's house is empty.'

'Yes,' Alan said, coming to stand beside him. 'Rose's aunt has refused to re-let it. But I think she'll have to do so before long. They are requisitioning empty houses now for the homeless people from the cities.'

Patrick raised his eyebrows. 'Isn't she going to live there herself?'

'No. Whatever made you think that?'

'She's going to marry isn't she? I'd have thought it an ideal house for them.'

'Marry? Oh, you mean the . . . the arrangement with Ratcliffe?' Alan smiled now. 'No. I'm afraid old Cecil got more than he bargained for. Miss Shrigley almost killed him when she found out . . .'

Alan put his own glass down on the windowsill and turned towards the door. 'Here's Dad,' he said. 'I'll tell you both all the scandal about Rose's aunt on our way up to Rainow.'

'Rainow?'

'Yes. We'll drive up there, to see Rose and show off my son.' Alan went from the room to open the front door to Douglas as a smile of welcome and anticipation lit up the strong, rugged features of Patrick Kennedy.

Rose was in the kitchen, washing the little woollen matinee jackets and the baby's bonnets when they arrived. She looked out, at the familiar sound of Alan's car winding its slow way up the lane towards the farm. She heard him pull up in the yard and had just folded the tiny garments inside a towel, to remove the water, when three tall figures passed the kitchen window.

The door opened and Alan came in, smiling the smile of pride in possession that came so readily to him now. He was followed by his father who looked younger and very imposing in the navy-blue uniform of Coastal Command. Alan's father was followed by a man tall, broad, tanned and – oh! – Patrick Kennedy. She recognized him in an instant. He was just like the photographs and had the very

430

same expression her own Dad used to have.

All this registered on her in the few seconds it took for them to enter the kitchen and close the back door behind them. They filled the low-ceilinged kitchen. It seemed full of enormous, hearty masculinity. Then they were all talking at once and she was quite flustered, not knowing which one to shake hands with, which to kiss on the cheek, until, laughing at the confusion, Alan put an arm around her shoulder and they ushered the two men, Douglas and Patrick, into the warm, cosy living room to greet Martha and Nat.

Martha was evidently delighted to see them. 'Eeh, Douglas! And this must be Patrick Kennedy.' She clapped her little hands together. 'Put the kettle on, Rose, love. I'll soon have a nice bit of supper on the table.'

Then they were all talking, admiring the baby, asking and answering questions until the supper was eaten and they could sit at the fireside and make the arrangements for the following day.

He was nice. Rose had been stealing glances at him all through the supper but found herself unable to confront the fact that he was her real father. It made her feel shaky, self-conscious and nervous to imagine it were true. She had asked herself, in the last weeks, if Patrick Kennedy even knew that he had a daughter. Could Carrie and her Mum and Dad have deceived him? But she had sensed, the moment their eyes had met, that he knew she was his. She knew that he had wanted to see her for, politely and without overt sign, he had been feasting his eyes on her all the evening.

He was looking at her now.

'Do you think I might ask you to show me around, Rose?' Patrick asked. 'Will you put your coat on and walk up the hill with me?'

She nodded, left the room and went into the hall. There she took down her tweed coat, reached up to the shelf for the woollen fair-isle beret and gloves she had knitted, wound a knitted scarf around her neck and pushed her feet into the high, zippered suede boots that Alan had given to her.

He was waiting in the living room, dressed in a greatcoat of khaki serge. She followed him out into the white, cold stillness of the January night and they walked, side by side in silence, to the top of the hill from where they could see in the distance the city of Manchester. It would have been an ideal night for a raid, as light and clear as daylight under the high full moon. But tonight all was quiet.

They stood at the summit and looked on the panorama of mountains and valleys and it was as if he were uncertain of how to begin.

'Rose,' he said at last. 'I am very glad to be here.'

She reached for his hand and held it, without looking at him.

'Do you think I should give you away tomorrow? Stand in for my brother?' he asked, sounding unsure and diffident.

She hadn't known that it had even been suggested and all at once she knew that this would make everything perfect and right. Tears came to her eyes.

'Please,' she whispered. 'Please do.'

'Rose?'

'Yes.'

'Let me look at you.'

He had a lovely voice and there was such a deep-sounding sorrow in it that, as she turned her head towards him, tears began to fall slowly down her cheeks.

'I know,' she said softly, trying to whisper, trying to choke back her sorrow. 'I know who you are.'

She saw tears, like her own, leap to his eyes as he put out his arms and she went into them, burying her face against his chest, as she cried.

Then the great dam of feeling she had been suppressing since Mum and Dad were killed burst in her heart and she found that tears were pouring down her face and from her

432

throat came a terrible, grief-stricken cry. 'Forgive me. Forgive me. I can't help it.'

He held her there until her sobs lessened, rocking her and making soothing sounds.

'Who told you, my child?' he asked gently, holding her close against him. 'Was it . . . was it your mother? Have I made you unhappy?'

Her shoulders were shaking but she lifted her tearful face to him and found that she was smiling and weeping at the same moment. 'No. Oh, no. I can't tell you how wrong you are. I am so . . . so very happy.'

He held her back from himself and now she saw too, the light of pleasure on his face as she said, 'I am crying for you. For you and Carrie.'

'For me? And Carrie? But why?'

'Why were you – why were you both – so unforgiving?' she said.

There was a silence as he considered her words but his eyes were full of regret when at length he replied. 'I loved her, Rose. I have never stopped loving her.'

Then she was crying again. 'Then tell her. Tell her that you love her. Carrie, my poor, darling Carrie. She has never had anyone . . . nobody has ever . . . loved her.'

His arms were tightening around her and she heard the break in his own voice. 'If only . . . If only she would listen. If only she would go through those gates.' Then he laid his cheek against the top of her head and they stood, still and silent for a long time.

At last he released her. 'Come, child,' he said. 'We can't know what might have been. Tomorrow is your morning. It belongs to you and Alan. You start a new day, a new life.'

He held her hand as they went back to the farm, every so often looking at her. 'My little Rose,' he kept saying, making her smile at the look on his face; the proud way he said it.

Before they reached the house she told him, 'Alan

doesn't know yet that you are my father. Or that I am Carrie's daughter.'

'Will you tell him? Do you want to?' Patrick asked.

'When I am ready. I will tell him when we have left Middlefield. My sisters would be upset.'

'You are a good girl,' he said at last. 'I know that you will do what is right.'

'And you?' she asked. 'Will you do what is right?'

He laughed now. 'And what might that be?' he said.

She stopped in her tracks and looked at him sternly. 'You must do the honourable thing! You must marry my mother.'

The day of the wedding dawned bright and bitterly cold. There would be snow later. Vivienne and Mary had stayed overnight at the Temperance Hotel and were downstairs in the kitchen, laying the breakfast table.

Upstairs in her room, Carrie looked out over the yard, over the backs of the houses of Churchwall Street. She had been awake for hours, gripped by a strong feeling of growing excitement. Four times in the night she had put on her bedside light, looked at the little travelling alarm clock and seen her wedding outfit hanging over the door of her wardrobe.

Outside, the sky was cloudless though more snow had come in the night, coating roofs and the tops of walls. Inside, the air in the room seemed stuffy, though she had hung fresh lavender bags in her wardrobe. The sharp, sweet scent of the flowers she normally found invigorating began to irritate her.

She pushed up the window and the cold air seared her throat. She slammed the sash down quickly. The snow would hold off she thought.

Her watch said nine o'clock. The wedding was at twelve.

When she went down to the kitchen, where a fire blazed in the high fireplace, she found Mary and Vivienne sitting at the table.

'Well, are you two getting excited?' she asked.

'Yes. What time will Rose be here?' Mary wanted to know.

Carrie felt her own excitement growing again. 'They are arriving at half past eleven,' she said. 'Rose and the baby, Nat and Martha Cooper.' It would be a close thing. What if their taxi was late? What if there had been a lot more snow and they couldn't get through? She tried to give an impression of composure. It wouldn't do to get the girls into a state.

'Pour the tea, Vivienne,' she said. 'And you, Mary, get the plates out of the warming oven.'

Mary got up from the table, went to the fireplace for the pot-holder that was hanging on the bar of polished steel above the ovens. She brought three plates to the table. 'Then what happens?' she asked.

Carrie took a dish of scrambled eggs from the hotplate over the fire and brought it to the table. 'Martha gave me a dozen eggs,' she explained. 'So eat up.'

She began to dish them out before answering Mary. 'I go off in the taxi that brought them here. I go to the church with Nat and Martha,' she explained. 'And you two and Rose wait here for Douglas McGregor. He's taking you in his car.'

'Our dresses are lovely,' Mary said. 'Thank you. They fit us perfectly.'

Mrs Singer had made them presents of silk dress lengths, two in sky-blue crepe de chine for the girls and a silvery grey moire silk for Rose. They had come back from the dressmaker's only yesterday. Mary and Vivienne's dresses had tucking in a lattice effect on the bodices and the same at the wrists of the long sleeves. The shoulders were wide and lightly padded and the sleeve heads had little scalloped caps to them. They had tried them on last night with the matching pill-box hats that were festooned with tiny, spotted veils.

Carrie hoped the church was warm for it was to be a

long service with a nuptial mass. It would be quite a spectacle, even though it was not a grand, white wedding. The Roman Catholics knew how to make the most of an impressive occasion. She hoped Father Church would be wearing his robes and not the long black soutane he wore every day.

'I think Rose will like her dress,' Vivienne said. 'And the flowers. They are all in the hall. Did you see them?'

'No. I'll look after breakfast,' Carrie answered. Rose's dress was long with a skirt that trumpeted out around the ankles. It was plain, cut on the cross and decorated, from the right shoulder to the left of the lower hem with a swirl of artificial flowers that came from France, the dressmaker said. The flowers were exquisite, made from velvet in shiny grey, violet and blue. The stalks and leaves were of green satin.

Carrie felt butterflies jumping in her stomach but was brought down to earth when Vivienne said, 'It's a pity Rose and Alan won't be going to watch the concert and go to the dance tonight.'

'Is that what you two are doing?' Carrie asked.

'Yes,' Vivienne went on, unconcerned by Carrie's startled question. 'After the reception Mary is going to watch my show.'

It had become 'my' show, Carrie noticed, since only last week when she had been declaring herself to be one of the troupe.

'Then we're going to the Stanley Hall. Dancing,' she said importantly.

'You'll be tired out,' Carrie protested. She didn't know what else to say. She had once been to the Stanley Hall when a dance was in progress. She had gone to deliver some leaflets about war bonds to Mrs Venables at the Conservative Club in their room adjacent to the main hall.

It had been mayhem in there at the dancing: hundreds of feet pounding, thick smoke, a solid wall of music – jazz.

The Canadian lads had a band like the American ones you saw at the pictures. To her horror she had seen three couples, Flo Gallimore and a soldier lad being one, jitterbugging in the corner nearest the door.

It was dreadful. It had been a respectable hall before the war. Now she was afraid for Mary and Vivienne.

'You don't know what you'll pick up in a place like that,' she said.

They started to giggle and she shot them a severe look. 'Fleas, nits, germs,' she added. 'All those people . . . You don't know where they've been.'

'Oh! Aunt Carrie!' They had finished their breakfast and Vivienne was gathering the plates into a pile. 'You are so old-fashioned.'

Mary began to help her. 'Have you heard Rae Parker's band playing *In the Mood* Viv?' She looked at Carrie. 'You should see Viv dancing to that one,' she said.

'I hope you girls aren't doing anything daft,' Carrie cautioned.

Vivienne stopped clearing the table and looked straight into her eye. 'If you mean that we might go the same way as Rose – then the answer's no,' she said. Then as if she felt she had been unfair to Rose she added. 'I'm not saying that Rose did wrong . . .'

'But we won't, will we, Viv?' Mary finished.

'No.' Vivienne had straightened up. She had that obstinate look about her. 'As soon as I'm famous,' she said, 'Mary is going to be my . . . my . . . my . . .' she looked at Mary. 'What do you call it Mary? When a film star has someone to do everything for her. What's she called, the girl who does everything?'

'Your sister!' Mary said, laughing.

Carrie knew she would never be able to stop Vivienne from doing what she wanted to do. 'I'm going upstairs,' she said, 'To have a wash and get ready.'

She went to her bedroom and saw again the dress, hanging there. The dressmaker had made it from the cream silk Rose had given to her for Christmas. Her hands were shaking again. So much so that she nearly knocked the dress off its hanger. Why, oh why, was she feeling so jittery? There, she was even thinking in the girls' slang.

The dress, with its draped and looped skirt had asymmetrical yokes, embroidered in the same cream, at the bodice and the hips. The waistline flattered her. It was fastened up the side seam with tiny, looped buttons. It had long sleeves with the same embroidery at the wrists. It had a deep vee neckline that was much lower than anything she had worn before. She had bought a hat – Vivienne had found it in Manchester – that resembled nothing so much as a curl – an apostrophe – of cream stiff velour that was attached to a skull-cap. It was a long sweep of cream that sloped forwards over one eye. It was trimmed with three strips of deeper cream velvet that ended, at the sweeping creation's narrowest point, in an elaborate tassel that settled along the length of her neck. She would have to pin her hair high.

The butterflies were starting again as she looked at the dress. She hoped to goodness that she would not look like mutton dressed as lamb. She was 46 after all and most women of her age wore black or navy.

She filled her bowl with water, hot and cold, and dropped an oatmeal bag into it, to soften it. Whilst it was soaking, she looked into the mirror to see if there were dark rings under her eyes from nerves and lack of sleep. No. They were fine. She had never seen them look so big and clear. But then she saw everything better now.

As she soaped herself, the night's thoughts and fears came back to her. She had lain there for hours, heart beating like crazy, wondering what was going to become of her.

The darkness of the room had only made it worse – the feeling of something about to happen. Over and over the questions had gone in her head. What have I got left? I have lost everything. But then I always have. Everything that meant anything to me has always gone from my life. My mother, my father, my sister and my daughter.

And now, she believed, even her faith. For she had not been back to chapel – not since Cecil Ratcliffe had gone away. It had come to her afterwards – they, the gossips, might imagine that she'd done what she did because Cecil Ratcliffe had raped Rose. She couldn't bear it, couldn't bear to talk about it, wouldn't explain, wanted to forget it all.

Everything that had happened since had made her nervousness increase, made her more sure that something was going to happen. The baby. Surviving the bombings. Alan coming back.

She should be grateful. She should go down on her knees and thank God for her blessings yet here she was, trembling like a fool, her hands hardly able to hold the soap whilst she sponged herself clean, dried her body on the soft, white towels and reached for her scented lotions.

When she was dressed she went into the dining room to check that all was ready.

Maggie Bettley and the bedroom girl were busy putting out all her best china. It was going to be a proper wedding breakfast. Chickens and ham, a present from Martha and Nat, had been cooked overnight. These were going to be served after the tomato soup. There would be roast potatoes, apple sauce and three vegetables to go with the meat.

There were four crystal dishes on the sideboard; trifles and bottled fruits with cream. Cheeses – another present from Martha stood alongside with water biscuits and petits fours.

The wedding cake looked splendid. Douglas McGregor had been round, bringing a case of champagne and three bottles of raisin cordial.

Everything was well under way. So why was her heart banging away? She brought her mind back to the arrangements. After the meal and the speeches she and Douglas were going to sing a duet. Mr Tereschenko was going to play the piano. It was all ready. Nothing to get worked-up about. So why was she in such a state?

'Thank you,' she said to Maggie and the bedroom girl. 'Everything looks grand. Will you manage all right? The serving out?'

'Yes. Stop frettin',' Maggie Bettley said. 'Get yerself down them stairs. They'll be here in a few minutes.'

She went downstairs, carrying her coat – dark green with a deep collar of fox fur.

'Ooh! Viv! Look at Aunt Carrie,' Mary cried as she reached the hall.

'Whewoo!' Vivienne whistled. She stood stock still. 'You look like . . . like . . .'

'Myrna Loy,' Mary suggested.

'Greer Garson!' Vivienne declared. 'I've never seen you look so beautiful.'

'Now then!' Carrie chided them. 'None of that talk. I'm plain. Always have been. Are you two ready?'

'Don't we look as if we are?'

'Of course. You look a picture. Both of you.'

There was the sound of a car drawing up outside. Mary ran to the front door and opened it.

'They're here,' she shouted. 'Ooh, look at Rose.'

Then they were all 'milling about' as Carrie called it, in the hall and the kitchen, Rose, wearing her best coat, a hat box in one hand, a bag in the other.

Behind her came Martha carrying the baby who wore a little lace cap and looked like something out of an old-fashioned picture book. He was wrapped in a long lace shawl that was draped over Martha's arm and reached to the floor.

Nat came last, carrying the cradle. He was dark suited, with a boiled white shirt and stiff collar shining under his cheeks that were as red as rosy apples.

'It's goin' ter snow tonight,' he said, smiling happily at everyone as he shook their hands. 'I reckon we'll be lucky to get back afore it comes.'

Martha placed the baby into Mrs Tereschenko's out-stretched hands.

Carrie felt her heart going like billy-o. Then, before she could take it all in, it was time to get into the waiting taxi, with Nat and Martha behind, chatting breezily about anything and everything.

They had tied white ribbons to the bonnet of the car and people were standing at the pavement's edge here and there as they progressed slowly so as not to skid on the white road. Along Sunderland Street they went, up Rivergate – people were waving and Carrie couldn't make out their faces so she waved back, discreetly – through the market square and down Churchgate.

There were more people here, waving. Up Chester Road they went, drawing up outside St Alban's. There was a big crowd outside the church. The priest was waiting at the door to shake her hand. He looked magnificent in his robes. Then one of the ushers; a relative of Douglas McGregor's no doubt, uniformed in navy, escorted her through the packed church.

There were so many people. She didn't know so many would turn up. Fur coats, morning suits, air force uniforms as well as naval ones. The church was warm and incense was heavy in the air. She went, nodding and smiling blindly – there were tears shimmering in her eyes – she was so touched by it all. The organist was playing Bach.

They took her to the front pew at the left of the aisle and asked her to leave a space on her right. Perhaps Douglas McGregor was going to stand beside her when he'd brought Rose down the aisle. She kept blinking, to focus properly.

She looked across the aisle. There was Alan, in uniform. He looked very smart and handsome. His best man, uniformed too, was beside him. He gave her a brave little smile. She looked back a little. Who was that on the row behind Alan? She blinked again. It was Douglas McGregor. Surely he shouldn't be here.

441

Her heart was going twenty to the dozen now. Perhaps Douglas would go to the back of the church when they arrived, Rose and the girls.

Oh, God, she prayed. What is going on? Why is my heart hammering in my chest like this?

She heard the door opening wider. She didn't dare to look. She might cry.

The organist was looking beyond her, now he was starting to play *Here Comes the Bride*. And here they were, alongside her, whilst her heart was leaping and banging louder than the music. It was Rose and . . . She'd sensed his presence before they passed her.

Rose was on her father's arm. It was Patrick.

The organ music ended. The priest came forward.

'Dearly beloved,' he intoned. 'We are gathered here . . .'

Carrie had a great knot in her throat, her eyes were misty, her hands shook, she could feel herself trembling as she pressed her hands tightly over the missal.

Alan was standing at Rose's side now.

'Who giveth this woman?'

The rich, warm voice. 'I do.' Patrick Kennedy placed Rose's hand into the priest's then he stepped back as the bride and groom went forward to the altar rail.

He came to stand in the place beside her. She glanced at him. He was just the same; tall, broad, greying. More of an air of maturity about him. A man of the world now, she supposed. And as she glanced, he looked into her eyes and held them. Then, it was like a miracle, in the instant that their eyes met her nervousness left her and a great feeling of calm came over her.

'Those whom God hath joined together, let no man put asunder,' the priest was saying.

Tears sprang again to Carrie's eyes as she watched her daughter, radiant, beside her husband as the mass was said.

Then it was over. The doors were thrown back and the

new man and wife, hand in hand, came towards her. Carrie fell into place behind them and he was at her side. Patrick – holding her hand in a warm, firm grip.

A great feeling of well-being went through her as they arranged themselves into groups for the photographers and were driven back to the Temperance Hotel. He sat behind her in the car with Martha Cooper and Nat. And she was aware of his closeness, felt she was drowning in the warm voice that was just as she had remembered it, melodic and Irish-lilting.

He made a speech at the table; clever and amusing it was. Referring to Rose as his niece . . . Alan as his godson . . . his many years of absence . . . his intention not to let them out of his sight again . . . a lovely young couple . . . their lives ahead of them . . . Raise your glasses.

Oh, it was wonderful. It was like a dream.

Maggie Bettley and the girl came in then, cleared the tables and brought in the big wedding cake. The photographer who had been there throughout the meal set up his camera again and posed Alan and Rose in front of the cake, as if they were about to cut it whilst he took another picture. When he had done and put away the camera they, Alan and Rose, amidst much jollity and teasing, cut up the cake and served it to the guests with coffee and tea and, for the men, brandy.

'And now,' Douglas announced. 'It is time for the singing.'

The tables were cleared, the piano was brought into the middle of the room and she and Douglas McGregor had never sounded so good before. They sang to requests, accompanied by Mr Tereschenko.

They sang sacred songs as duets and parlour tunes with everyone joining in and, at last, when they imagined they had run out of songs, Patrick got to his feet.

'Do you know *Morning has Broken*,' he asked.

It was a strange request, but a lovely song and Rose and

443

Alan seemed eager to hear them sing it, clapping and applauding like mad as she and Douglas stood again.

'MORNING HAS BROKEN, LIKE THE FIRST MORNING . . .'

Why did he ask for this one?

'BLACKBIRD HAS SPOKEN, LIKE THE FIRST BIRD . . .'

There had been a blackbird singing to her the last time she had sung with Douglas McGregor.

'PRAISE FOR THE SINGING . . .'

Had somebody put champagne in her glass with the lemonade and raisin cordial? She felt dizzy.

'PRAISE FOR THE MORNING . . .'

That was it! He wanted to remind her of the things he used to talk about – her being unable to open the gates.

'PRAISE FOR THEM SPRINGING FRESH FROM THE WORD.'

He was smiling at her, the same devil-may-care smile of his youth. What an extraordinary man he was.

Caroline Aurora Shrigley rose from the bed of her husband and went to stand at a window of the Temperance Hotel in Middlefield's Waters Green.

High above, the heavens were a pale turquoise, suffused with rose towards the east where the sun was breaking in a crescent of burning gold under crimson streaks that glowed across the morning sky.

Her bag was packed. In an hour's time they would leave; she and her husband-in-the-eyes-of-God. She smiled to herself to think that she cared not a jot for the scandal that would spread at her going.

She turned and looked with tenderness and desire towards the man who lay, naked and careless in sleep, upon her soft, scented bed.

Before she shook him awake she would sit for a moment and dwell on it, all that had happened yesterday; the wedding and Patrick's giving his daughter away, the

444

reception with the speeches and the singing, the gathering of all the guests in the hall to see Alan and Rose off, departing in Douglas McGregor's red Lanchester. They were only going to Rainow but they didn't mind postponing a honeymoon until later, when they would travel to Scotland.

It had been five o'clock before her final guest left – Douglas McGregor, who was going to catch his train to Scotland. Vivienne and Mary had gone an hour ago, to get Vivienne ready for her concert. Martha, Nat and the baby had been taken back by taxi ten minutes before and in a moment, when she closed the door, Carrie knew, it would all be over.

She stood, waving goodbye to Douglas on the step and turned to go back inside. She had seen everyone off. Everyone except Patrick. Where was he? Had he gone before the others?

It didn't matter. It had been a lovely day. She would never forget it.

The house seemed very quiet, though she could hear the sounds of dishes clattering and the murmur of voices coming from the kitchen where Maggie Bettley and the bedroom girl were clearing up.

She went up the stairs and into her bedroom to take off her beautiful clothes. She pushed the door to and walked towards the dressing table. In the mirror she saw that she still had the hat on.

It was fastened at the back with two crossed hatpins. She raised her arms to unpin them but as she did so she was aware, all at once, that everything was sharper – all her senses. She could smell the lilac-scented soap on her washstand. It was all mixed up with the almond oil hand lotion and, growing stronger, the coal-tar and leather scent of the man whose face now appeared in the mirror behind her own.

She felt his strong arms slip around her waist, felt his hands sliding upwards towards her breast. His body was pressed close to hers, his face was burying itself into the bare nape of her neck and now he was turning her around to face him and she was hard up against him.

And, as if the intervening years had never been, she was responding to his kisses, to his mouth on hers, her pulses racing. She felt the familiar feeling that everything in her was straining towards him, the deep, sweet madness of desire drawing him into her embrace.

He held her by the shoulders, when she was shaking with need of him; the male smell of him, the taste of his mouth in her own. He looked into her face, laughing, questioning, brown eyes holding hers as he spoke in the musical Irish voice.

'You still love me, don't you, Caroline Aurora?' he said, laughing softly.

'In a way,' she whispered.

'In the only way that matters my darling? Do you love me?'

'Kiss me,' she answered, pulling him in towards herself.

'Not until you tell me.' He held her back.

'Tell you what?' she asked. But she knew.

'That when morning comes, you will not leave me.' His eyes were not laughing now. They were demanding – demanding that she said the words he wanted to hear.

'I give you my word,' she said. 'I will never let you go again.'

Now, the sun was up over the horizon. She would wake him and tell him that she was ready. She was ready to go through the Gates of Morning.

THE END